MAKE READY

JONATHAN OATES MBE

DISCLAIMER

This is a work of fiction. Names, characters,
businesses, places, events, locales, and incidents are
either the products of the author's imagination or
used in a fictitious manner. Any resemblance to
actual persons, living or dead, or actual events is
purely coincidental.

Honestly, I wrote this book for myself. But I couldn't have done it without the support and inspiration of some amazing people; my family, my friends, and my former comrades. A special mention must go to my incredible wife Laura, and my dear friend Jamie, who've been along with me for the whole ride.

'Those Brits are a strange old race. They show affection by abusing each other, will think nothing of casually stopping in the middle of a fire fight for their *brew up*, and eat food that I wouldn't give to a dying dog! But fuck me. I would rather have one British squaddie on side than an entire battalion of Spetznaz! Why? Because the British are the only people in the world who when the chips are down and there seems like no hope left, instead of getting sentimental or hysterical, will strap on their pack, charge their rifle, light up a smoke, and calmly and wryly grin, well are we going then you wanker?'

Unknown American Soldier, Iraq 2005

PROLOGUE

The ghostly figures emerged from a cloud of dust. Fine particles hung in the air, whilst larger debris pitter-pattered down all around. Only one of the shells had detonated in the daisy chain. The other two remained dormant in the hard-packed earth. It was a minor miracle that no one had been seriously injured. Much like the other minor miracles that seemed to occur on an almost daily basis. Near-misses from poorly aimed shots, a wayward rocket here, a dud-RPG there; the list was extensive. The search team had managed to successfully identify the device. But as they crouched in the putrid drainage ditch, running parallel to the path where the IED had been buried, they were unaware of the nervous pair of eyes watching them.

Ninety nine times out of a hundred the device would have been pressure-plate activated. On this occasion, it had been initiated by a command wire. As soon as the team leader had approached to make an assessment, the excitable young man, sat at the other end of forty metres of decaying electrical cable, had connected the power source. Only the first of the three reclaimed artillery shells had initiated. The interconnecting wiring work had been botched. Archie immediately pressed the transmitter on his radio.

'Dude One, IED activated in the vicinity of Green Twelve. Any chance you can conduct a sweep of the area to identify anyone attempting to egress. How copy?'

'Dude, looking now,' calmly replied the American pilot. He was peering into a small screen that displayed the thermal feed from the surveillance pod, which hung underneath his F15. It was no surprise at all that they had encountered something. This area, south of Sangin District Centre, was riddled with booby traps. They had already disposed of two during this patrol alone. Archie was grateful that the disposal team had been supplied by the US Marine Corps and not the Brits. A cursory search, followed by an enthusiastic call of *fire in the hole* was by far preferable to the meticulous approach employed by his fellow countrymen. Their method would have resulted in a two hour wait, spent sweating his balls off in the scorching heat.

'Nothing seen yet. I'll keep you posted.' The noise of the circling jet overhead was a comforting sound. Archie couldn't blame the pilot. Attempting to glimpse through the dense tree canopy at this time of year, was always going to be challenging. Undoubtedly, the triggerman had planned his escape route carefully, fully cognisant of the fact that he would be pursued in three dimensions.

'Boss, F fifteen can't get eyes on anything at the moment. I'll let you know if he spots something,' Archie quickly relayed the information to the captain kneeling next to him.

'Cheers Archie, good stuff.' The young officer was studying his map, and didn't look up. The medic had come forward to conduct a triage. He was snatching various medical items out of his daysack. Thankfully, it didn't look like anything more serious than a first field dressing, and a handful of antiseptic wipes were required. At first, when an event like this occurred, there had been an enormous commotion; everyone trying to

2

get in on the action, trying to make themselves useful. Now, it was a much more routine affair. Sometimes people didn't even look. Just adopted a comfortable fire position, swigged some water, and lit up a dodgy local cigarette.

Archie was one of the lucky ones. At least he was connected to a world beyond the rather myopic one that most of his colleagues inhabited. His headphones almost continuously relayed the robotic voices of pilots from various nations, keeping him abreast of what was happening around them. It elevated him beyond the immediate drudgery of existence on the ground. Sometimes, he even felt like he knew what was going on. This was going to take a while to unravel. Archie looked for a spot to settle where he could monitor the radio. A wall ran alongside the path that they had been patrolling. He awkwardly lowered himself into a squatting, and then sitting position, removed his heavily-laden pack, and rested his back against the solid structure, made from compacted dirt. It felt amazing to relieve his shoulders of the weight. Rolling them forwards and backwards under his damp body armour, significantly improved the circulation to his arms.

'Widow Five Five, I may have a possible on a moped travelling north from your location. He's high-tailing it outta there. You want me to track?' The pilot's distinctive New York accent crackled through the earpiece.

'Affirm. Track and report Dude. Many thanks.' It was almost certainly pointless. Unless the suspected perpetrator was about to stop and wave a weapon at someone, or bury another IED, which they wouldn't, the rules of engagement weren't going to allow the jet to do anything useful other than burn through aviation fuel. Daz, one of the sniper lads, came ambling down the path towards Archie.

'Got a bine mate?' he enquired innocently. He was always on the scrounge, but Archie liked him nonetheless. They shared the same accommodation, which could often be too close for comfort given Daz's appalling behaviour and poor personal hygiene. In all honesty, everybody had no idea how the man was still walking given the grotty habits he regularly indulged in. However, whilst he would often cause mischief around the Forward Operating Base, Daz was a consummate professional out in the field.

'Yep, here you go chum.' Archie expertly knocked the packet so that a single cigarette protruded, and offered it up. Daz hungrily grabbed it, immediately stuffing it into the side of his mouth.

'You got a light?' *How predictable* Archie thought. He sparked up the lighter and held it aloft whilst Daz leant down towards him. Puffing away, the air was filled with acrid tobacco smoke.

'Lucky bastards. At least we get a break. It's fucking redders,' Daz observed.

'Absolutely, I was hanging out earlier. Probably the sight of you banging one out this morning that put me off my stride.'

'Well, better out than in they say.'

'It was utterly foul. Please don't do it in front of me again.'

'No promises.' Daz's cheeky grin accentuated the roundness of his face. 'Mind if I grab a seat?'

4

'Mi casa, su casa.' Archie waved to a patch of space a couple of metres further down the wall.

'Sweet. Cheers dude.' Daz carefully placed his L115 sniper rifle against the wall, and braced to slide into a sitting position, before slowly lowering himself downwards.

The moment Daz's rear end made contact with the floor, Archie was caught by a blast of super-heated air, completely saturated with sharp grains of dirt. His vision was consumed by incandescent white light. The world went silent. Instinctively, he placed out a hand to prevent himself from falling onto the ground. He could feel the chalky brown sand between his fingers. Choking dust overwhelmed his respiratory system, mixed with the distinct taste and smell of cordite, and acquiring sufficient oxygen suddenly became a serious challenge. They often layered IEDs. In Northern Ireland they were called secondary devices. Here, it was difficult to differentiate between primary, secondary, tertiary, and beyond; they all simply blended together into one relentless nightmare. Archie scrunched his eyes up, and blinked a few times. Amoebic shapes danced around his vision. He couldn't clear them no matter how many times he blinked his eyelids. Reaching for his water bottle, he unscrewed the lid, and washed his face with the tepid contents. He could feel the coat of filth dropping away, before his focus began to return. Everywhere, he could see people scurrying about frantically, just like they had done earlier in the tour. He turned his head to the right to survey the scene.

Through the artificial fog, Archie could see a small crater, about thirty centimetres in diameter, was smouldering at the base of the wall. Scraps of camouflaged material lay strewn around a canvas webbing belt, which had sprung open up at the waist, and Daz's charred daysack, peppered with little black holes, lay on its side. Glancing upwards, a clearly visible brown-red stain ran up the height of the wall. Viscera clung to the rough surface in several places. Some of it made wet slapping noises, as it laboriously flopped its way towards the ground. Two faint bloody grooves had formed in the path where Daz's legs had passed through the dirt. The limbs now sat next to each other, comically hanging by the edge of the drainage ditch like they were about to dip a toe in to gauge the temperature. The L115 had fallen on its side. Just beyond it, laid a dismembered arm, which was still holding a lit cigarette between its fingers.

Archie swallowed hard. Inhaling through his nose, he let the air escape slowly from his mouth in an attempt to control his breathing. He raised the water bottle to his mouth with a shaking hand, before gulping down what remained.

'Archie. Archie! You all right mucker?' The captain stood above him barely audible.

'I think so,' he replied meekly.

'Can you get up? We need to move away from here.'

'I'll try.' Archie placed his hand on the floor, and pushed himself up into a kneeling position. Grabbing his rifle, he used it as a crutch to get to his feet, whilst the captain took him by the arm and led through a section of path that had already been cleared. As he walked along, Archie checked himself over for injuries working methodically from his head down to his toes.

Other than a handful of minor perforations, he couldn't identify anything too sinister. At least he was mobile; another minor miracle to add to the ever-growing list. No miracle today for Daz though. Looking back, he took in the gruesome sight in all its glory. Further along the path, the medic was still tending to the injuries that had been incurred during the earlier incident. Various people were talking on radios, attempting to relay information back to the Forward Operating Base. Then Archie noticed something out of place. Drawn by an invisible force, he drifted towards one of the willow trees that lined the ditch's bank.

'Oi, where are you going? That hasn't been cleared!' an alarmed voice called out to him.

Archie ignored the warning, and continued stumbling towards the tree. As he closed the distance, he could see the object, nestled amongst the tangled cradle where the branches met at the top of the trunk. Through the clamour of background noise, he could make out the sound of debris still plopping into the foetid water. The smell of burnt flesh, mixed with fragrant leaves, filled his nostrils. And there, right in front of his eyes, was Daz's decapitated head, staring lifelessly back at him.

CHAPTER 1

Wrapped in a clammy sleeping bag, Archie reflected on life, whilst swilling the remnants of a supermarket own-brand bottle of cognac. His unsavoury surroundings weren't exactly the height of luxury, but nor were they the worst he had endured. His mind drifted to what he might have for supper that evening. He still called it *supper* after all these years. Reduced price sausage roll, or out-of- date sandwich? Neither a terrible option. Just enough calories to get him through to his next fix. He needed to catch Todge, his regular dealer, before it started getting dark. Fishing with filthy, cracked hands, Archie gathered the few remaining coins in his pockets to make an assessment. £13.55 including the skanky £10 note he had tucked away for a rainy day. A day very much like this one. Sadly, not quite enough for a wrap *and* a sausage roll.

He had found a comfortable spot out of the elements, and would have liked nothing more than to stay put, but duty called. Staying mobile was a good way to keep the cold from setting in. Systematically checking through his meagre belongings, he ensured that he had not inadvertently dropped anything. It was a method he utilised prior to every move, knowing exactly what should be contained in each compartment of his rucksack. Shuffling out of the underpass, he surveyed his surroundings. The sky was grey and foreboding. A strong north easterly wind was blowing directly through the graffiti strewn underpass. It would inevitably bring with it rain from the North Sea. One of Archie's great talents was reading the weather. He knew, with some certainty, he was going to get wet.

'Fucking awesome,' he muttered under his breath, so quietly it was barely audible.

He knew of a place with decent shelter where he

could get high, before bedding down for the night; an abandoned furniture showroom not too far away from his current location. But it came with risks. There were plenty of others who might be thinking the same on a night like this. His other option was a doorway on the high street, where he was less likely to be mugged, but more likely to be moved on by the police, or worse still, ogled at by some passer-by. The supermarket would be his first stop. Making a quick time estimate, he assessed it would take approximately thirty minutes to tab there, which would mean arriving around 18:00. This should ensure that some of the choicest cuts were still available before the other scavengers descended. It should also allow sufficient time to track down Todge. Just in case, he thought he would drop him a text. His pay-as- you-go phone was running precariously low on funds.

WINE BAR, 1 HOUR, 2 X WRAPS, OK?

He hated missing out on the premium sandwiches. Crayfish and avocado were his favourite. Unfortunately, the best his local supermarket could manage was prawn mayo. If he was lucky a few of their *Extra Special* southern fried chicken wraps would be available. He knew Colchester well, having lived in the Roman market town for almost a decade, on and off. He determined that the best route would be to hand rail Castle Park, before utilising the pedestrian bridge to cross the railway lines, gaining access to the retail park where the supermarket was situated.

Head down, swinging his arms rhythmically across his body, Archie strode down a back street that ran parallel to the dilapidated bus station, making a conscious effort not to engage with anyone. The shop fronts were tarnished and grimy. In the flat light, they looked utterly uninviting. As he crossed the high street,

9

he was suddenly accosted by a middle-aged woman carrying too many discount store grocery bags.

'Excuse me mate. Scuse me! Any chance you have the time?'

Who on earth doesn't have the time available this day and age? Archie pondered internally. The rotund lady clearly couldn't be bothered to put down her high-cholesterol snacks and check for herself.

'It's seventeen thirty six,' he replied.

'Oh shit, I'm late for school collection. Oldest is in detention again.'

'Sorry to hear that,' was all Archie could think of saying in response to the banal statement.

'Hey, I'm sure I recognise you from somewhere. Weren't you mates with Big Lee?'

'No, I think you're mistaken.'

'Nah, definitely. I remember now, I met you at that summer function last year after the parade. You're that posh bloke aren't ya? How ya doin?' She was throwing out his timings, risking the chances of any supper at all.

'Absolutely smashing thanks,' Archie retorted, before quickly side-stepping the women, and speeding off without looking back. Still time to make it.

He had been mates with Big Lee and remembered the day well. Nice weather, free booze, and a decent barbeque knocked up by the chefs. Somehow, the event had ended in a mass brawl. It was never clear who started it, but Archie had ended up requiring six stitches, and footing the blame. With Castle Park in the rear-view mirror, he motored on through the leisure centre, and across the railway line. 17:52, bags of time. It had begun spitting. The impending downpour would certainly catch him as he returned to the bar for the meet.

He determined that it would be best to get a waterproof jacket on as soon as possible, having left it far too late, far too many times before. Taking a knee, he quickly identified the bag containing the jacket. As he pulled out the contents, he was hit by a familiar musty smell, accumulated over years of use. It was strangely comforting for such a *distinct* aroma. The supermarket was in view now. A large, featureless, box shrouded in neon green. It was 17:58.

Rounding the corner, Archie took in the familiar sight of the waste disposal area. A young lad with a bum-fluff beard, and wannabe hipster haircut, leant against a wall. He was puffing on a vape. Archie recognised the flavour as Mother's Milk from the days when one of his colleagues would constantly smoke the sickly-sweet liquid whilst they were deployed on exercise. Just beyond the vaper, another employee had begun to empty the sandwich trays into one of the large wheelie bins. Archie couldn't see any competition lurking around. The good fortune meant that he could be discerning in his selection. Making a bee-line for the sandwich bin, he produced a Tupperware lunchbox, which would help preserve the food.

'Back again Archie?' the girl enquired. 'It's been a while. I hope you're staying out of trouble'. She was confident for her age, and rather pretty. He couldn't remember her name. It said Lily on her badge.

'Yep, not too bad thank you Lily. Just stocking up for the evening. Anything good up for grabs?'

'I'm afraid not, mainly tuna sweetcorn, and egg mayo. I think there's a ham salad in there as well if you fancy it?' she asked with genuine concern.

'Hmm, not ideal but better than nothing I suppose. I'll grab the ham salad if it's going, and a tuna and sweetcorn. Plenty of protein and niacin in the tuna.'

'You always surprise me. How can you possibly know what's in tuna?'

'I used to work as a fisherman when I was living in South East Asia,' he replied casually. 'Just needed some pocket money. It actually paid quite well. Terrible smell though, and I'm not particularly good out at sea.'

'Wow, that sounds interesting. I'd love to go.'

'Do it then. There's clearly nothing keeping you here.' Archie could never understand why people proclaimed that they would *love* to do something. He had always taken the approach of just doing what he wanted, when he wanted.

'What do you mean *clearly* nothing stopping me?'

'Well for a start, you work in a supermarket. And I can see you're not married due to the absence of a ring. Although, I suppose that you may still have a kid, what with being from round here. So perhaps you do have a reason for taking such a dull job after all.'

'What did you say? I'm not going to be lectured by a homeless bloke. People in glass houses Archie,' she snapped abruptly, although he thought he could detect jest in her voice. He briefly considered explaining that if she just reflected on her life a little, she might realise how ludicrous she sounded. That there's a big wide world to explore. That it's easy to make excuses. But then remembered she was the gatekeeper to free sandwiches, and thought better of it, opting to keep his mouth shut.

'I'm terribly sorry, I didn't mean to offend. You must make the time to visit. I can highly recommend Kota Kinabalu. The diving there is magnificent.'

'Kota where? I'll take your word for it. Doubt it'll ever happen, but you never know.' She seemed satisfied enough with his slightly hollow apology. 'Anyway, what was it? One ham and one tuna?'

'Correctamundo.' Archie felt his phone buzz in his pocket.

SEE YOU AT SIX THIRTY. DON'T BE LATE.
BRING CASH. NO FREEBIES.

'Shit,' he blurted out. 'Must dash I'm afraid. Pressing appointment.'

'All right, here you go. Maybe see you again soon?' She wouldn't. Archie quickly stuffed half a sandwich into his mouth, devouring it as fast as possible. He stored the remainder in the box, before setting off.

As he departed, other members of the extensive homeless community began arriving for their free feed at the trough. *It pays to be a winner*, he thought triumphantly. The bar was about half an hour away. It would be tight, but he could make it. Todge was nothing if not punctual. He wouldn't wait if it was costing him business elsewhere, and unfortunately was Archie's only option; none of the pubs or clubs would permit Archie entry, having achieved the distinction of a town-wide ban from all establishments serving alcohol, thanks to a string of unpleasant incidents.

The rain had really started to fall. Archie's messy auburn hair kept dropping in front of his eyes. He fished a fraying Lowe Alpine Gore-Tex hat from one of the map pockets of his trousers, and pulled it onto his head. He and that hat had been through some adventures together, and it showed. The once fleecy lining had all but disintegrated, and the popper on the little visor was no longer functioning. However, it kept the rain off, and his head warm.

Fifteen minutes in, and he was making reasonable progress, although the spray from passing cars had soaked him through. At least his trousers were getting a bit of a wash; Christ knows they needed one. Archie had never worried too much about laundry, even when it was readily available to him. He had always viewed cleanliness as a functional, rather than social necessity. Hitting the bottom of North Hill, he leant in for the final leg. By now he was breathless, and sweating underneath the numerous layers he wore.

Archie remained in reasonably good shape, despite the toll that drink, drugs, cheap cigarettes, and a terrible diet had taken. Honestly, he had never been much to look at. But back in the day, he had been a machine. His physical prowess was coupled with the type of mental fortitude that only good breeding and the right type of upbringing can develop. Perhaps most impressively, he was blessed with a gift possessed by only a chosen few; the ability to consume his own body weight in alcohol during a night out, and still being able to function perfectly well the following morning. In his prime, he truly was a force to be reckoned with. Pounding up the last few metres of an alley that he was intimately familiar with, he caught sight of Todge, waiting as promised.

'You're lucky you made it in time. I was about to disappear to another bar.' Todge was not like most other dealers in the area, or indeed the country. Well groomed, eloquent, and thoroughly organised, he took his profession very seriously. He was exactly the type of man Archie was keen to continue doing business with.

'Terribly sorry, I was waylaid finding something to eat. All sorted now though.'

'Whatever, you weirdo. What can I do for you?' Todge demanded.

'As agreed, two of your finest wraps, if you please.' Archie was eager to get this transaction completed as soon as possible.

'Not a problem. That'll be the usual price, twenty quid.'

'Ah, there may be a slight technical issue with that I'm afraid. I've only got thirteen, almost fourteen pounds, on me. If you could find it in your heart to give me a loan until, let's say next Wednesday, I guarantee you will receive payment in full then,' Archie grinned in hope. It wasn't the first time he had attempted this trick.

'You must be joking. There is absolutely no way I am loaning you a fucking thing. You're lucky I do business with you at all after all the shit you've tried to pull,' he replied, looking genuinely riled by Archie's audacity. Collecting himself, Todge ran a hand through his dark, slicked-back hair, for dramatic effect.

'One wrap, ten quid. Take it or leave it.'
It didn't take Archie long to decide.

'I'll take it, and would be most grateful if you could throw in a couple of Rizlas,' he chanced.

'Done. Now please piss off and stop wasting my time. And make sure that next time I see you, you have the cash.'

'Absolutely.' Archie took the gnarled £10 note from his pocket and handed it over, delicately placing it into Todge's manicured hand.

'Where have you been stashing this? Up your arse?' Todge visibly flinched as he reluctantly took the money.

'In a sock actually. I find it to be much more comfortable.' Archie had learnt the hard way the necessity to secrete his money.

'That's a relief. Looking at the state of you, I'm going to have a tetanus jab just in case. Enjoy your evening. I'm sure I'll be hearing from you soon pal.' With that, Todge walked away.

Archie was keen to get on with the night's entertainment. Although heroin was a fairly new addition to his repertoire, he was already becoming quite adept at making a little go a long way. Smoking, rather than injecting, he had discovered, was the way ahead. Although the hit was not as intense, it certainly did the job. When mixed with some weed, one wrap could last him up to three days. Of course, he was not averse to sampling other products if he could obtain them. He was particularly keen to get his hands on some fentanyl, which he had only heard good things about. In the past, a decent single malt, or robust Pinotage, would have sufficed, but with so much on his hands, more powerful intoxicants were required. The abandoned showroom was located in the east of the town. The rows of terraced houses in the surrounding area reminded him of his brief time at university in the north of the UK. Although not a resident there for long, he had made quite an impact in the student union. He still retained the record for the most shots downed off the bar in one sitting. Unfortunately, his academic prowess had not been quite as impressive as his drinking skills. He had only managed to attend a handful of tutorials required, and failed to submit a single essay. A disagreement with the faculty head for Politics and International Studies had ensued, which did not end well for either participant; one escorted off the campus, the other left with a bloodied nose.

Pushing on through the murk, he left the main road, before scaling a rusting chain link fence marking the boundary to the showroom's plot. From previous visits, he knew that the site was occasionally patrolled by a local security contractor, but their inspections were sufficiently infrequent and indifferent enough that they wouldn't notice his presence if he maintained good light discipline. The staff entrance was his preferred method of entry. It was a security door that could be easily prized open using a leftover piece of scaffolding. He always left it jarred very slightly open in order to facilitate a hasty exit if required.

Before barging in though, Archie considered that a quick reconnaissance of the site would be prudent. *Time spent in recce is time seldom wasted* had always been one of his favourite mantras. Skirting down the narrow, overgrown gap, running alongside the showroom, he manoeuvred his way past the detritus of a failed suburban retail park. Plastic rubbish bags, empty drinks cans, and Styrofoam fast food containers, lay strewn everywhere. The majority a by-product of the food stall that used to operate out of the car park. He hoisted himself up to look through a dingy window, which overlooked the main sales area. Carefully rubbing away the veneer of filth, Archie peered through. Nothing obvious had changed since his previous visit. There was no indication that anyone else was squatting in the premises. He listened carefully for a couple more minutes, to confirm that he was not walking into anything unexpected. Although he was confident he could handle a couple of junkies, they could be unpredictable creatures, and if caught at the wrong moment, things could go badly wrong. More importantly, he wanted to ensure that there was no sign of anyone more threatening, be it security guards, local kids, or gang members on the prowl. Once satisfied that the coast was clear, Archie returned to the entrance point and slipped through.

The odour inside the showroom was surprisingly pleasant for such a forlorn place. The scent from numerous diffusers, which had been used to create an inviting ambience for customers, had permeated everything, creating a bizarre tribute to the venue's former glory. As well as the cavernous sales area, there was a sizeable storeroom, a couple of mezzanine offices, and a staff area in the corner of the premises. The latter was Archie's favourite spot, due to its secluded position, and because in their haste to empty the store of its contents on a tight timeline, the removals company had neglected to remove the soft furnishings. Old health and safety notices, and a diversity and inclusivity poster, were pinned up close to the entrance; a depressing reflection of society's steady decline, in Archie's opinion.

Dumping his rucksack on the table, and removing his jacket, Archie went through the ritual of assembling the paraphernalia that he would require for the evening. First and foremost, a head torch with red filter. The light was already limited and fading fast. Soon, it would be pitch black in the small room, which was only illuminated by a narrow window that ran across the top of the external wall. Next, a heavily scratched Camelbak water bottle. A rubbish bag followed. He was always careful to ensure that he didn't leave any sign of his presence following visits, so that others would not be able to identify his places of refuge. Finally, a battered silver cigarette box, sealed with black duct tape. It had his initials, ARM, stamped on the side, and an intricate family crest engraved on the lid. He had carried it with him for as long as he could remember, having received it as a gift from his father.

Carefully peeling away the tape, Archie removed the items he would require. The upturned lid created a small tray, where he could assemble everything. It didn't take long to roll an acceptable joint. Once satisfied with his craftsmanship, he reclined onto the sofa, and removed his hoodie and boots. His nose was instantly assaulted by a pungent waft emanating from his hiking socks. He had always been careful to look after his feet, and always carried a bag of talc with him, as well as a spare set of dry socks, which were one of the few items he would wash regularly. Placing the joint to his chapped lips, he lit it, and inhaled. Thick smoke filled his lungs. Almost instantly, a feeling of warm contentment washed through his body. Holding the caustic fumes in for as long as he could bear, he slowly exhaled, filling the room with a heavy haze that hung suspended in place. He took another long draw. His limbs began relaxing, and his eyelids began to droop. Determined to obtain the full benefit of his investment, he forced a further deep inhalation, before sliding back onto the sofa. As Archie drifted into semi-consciousness, his hand fell open, and the smouldering joint dropped onto the cold concrete floor.

CHAPTER 2

A bright light was being shone directly into Archie's face.

'Prokydaysya,' a stern voice commanded.

'Prokyn'sya, suka,' the man repeated. Someone was urging him to wake up. He rubbed his eyes, spluttered, and held up a hand to obstruct the glare. 'Shcho ty khochesh?' he replied.

'What you say?' a gravelly voice, which had seen the business end of too many poor quality cigarettes, replied.

'Ya skazav, shcho ty khochesh?' Archie repeated.

'How you speak Ukrainian?' quizzed the surprised man. How had they found him? The showroom was either a regular spot on their rounds, or they had followed him into the premises. More likely the former given the precautions he always took.

'Oh, I spent some time living in Kiev when I was younger. The Pechersky Lipki district, you might know it?' It was one of the more upmarket and prestigious neighbourhoods in the city. Tree-lined avenues and modern apartment blocks, interspersed with medieval churches, and imposing government buildings. It was almost certainly not the kind of place that the man originated from.

'I not have been Kiev.'

'Ah, your loss I'm afraid.' Archie slowly sat up. 'It's lovely this time of year.'

'What you do here?' a second voice demanded. Not quite as gruff as the first, but menacing nonetheless.

'As you can see, I am between jobs at the moment, and just needed a quiet place to partake in my raging drug habit.' Archie jested, hoping it would be a satisfactory answer. However, he suspected that the pair had other plans.

'You give us money now,' Voice One commanded.

Archie's response was nonchalant, 'Well I'm afraid you're barking up the wrong tree. I can assure you, I have nothing to give you, and even if I did, I certainly wouldn't be handing it over.'

'You give us money or we hurt you,' Voice Two chipped in.

'It's simply not an option my friends. Perhaps you would be better off shaking down a more well-to-do victim? I can suggest some good spots if you'd be interested?'

'We don't want look somewhere else. Give us now,' Voice Two repeated, more insistently.

Against his better judgement, Archie was unwilling to back down.

'I'm not giving you a penny. Now do fuck off before someone gets hurt.' His head was aching. His mouth was dry as a bone. Rather than labouring the conversation any further, he rose up adopting a more defensive position, from which he could improve his options. Strike out first, move behind the sofa to create some space, or make a dash for the door.

Unfortunately, he didn't get the opportunity to take any of them. As soon as he placed his feet onto the floor, a firm blow caught his sternum, knocking him back down again. Winded and disorientated, he attempted to roll away, hoping to place the dining table between himself and his assailants. Most muggers would expect someone to acquiesce after the first use of physical violence. Archie hoped to have had the element of surprise on his side. But these guys were from a place where hesitation was not an option, and the use of violence an almost daily occurrence. Another stinging strike to his right ear left him dazed, and sprawling on the floor. At this point, he knew there was little he could do to deter the attackers. He simply needed to protect his vital organs, whilst looking for an opportunity to either somehow incapacitate them, or escape.

Archie quickly tucked in his arms, and positioned himself to get onto his knees. Having received some self-defence training, he knew which posture to adopt given the circumstances, and hoped he could at least grapple one of the men to the ground. However, unlike his instructors had suggested, there was very little chance of him achieving his aim. His two adversaries had an unassailable advantage. Although a decent fighter, Archie knew he was no Jackie Chan. A foot caught him in the ribs. Only a glancing blow, but enough to topple him out of position. It gave the other aggressor an opportunity to strike down on the back of Archie's neck, delivering the knockout blow. Archie dropped onto his stomach, and accepted his fate, whilst the two men began ruthlessly laying into him. He had been concussed before. More than once. On this occasion, he knew full well the consequences of slipping into unconsciousness. Narrowing vision, a high pitch ringing in his ears, the taste of iron on his palette. It was too much. He succumbed to the relentless bludgeoning, and blacked out.

It only took a few minutes to come around. The room was deathly quiet, and impenetrably dark. He gingerly reached out, trying to locate the head torch that had been flung from his head, to no avail. Acute stabbing pains in his chest, coupled with laboured breathing, provided a sure indication that he'd cracked a rib or two. His nose, which was already skewwhiff, had been broken yet again, and his right eye had closed up underneath a significant swelling. Only a huge dose of willpower enabled him to hoist himself up onto the couch. From this vantage point, he could attempt to locate the rucksack that was sitting on the table. Fumbling awkwardly into thin air, he could feel nothing.

Not even the table, which he concluded must have been knocked elsewhere during the course of the attack. Archie closed his eyes, and attempted to gather himself. *It's not that bad. You know where you are. Get a grip.*

All of a sudden, an overwhelming sense of helplessness overcame him. It was an emotion that he had only experienced very rarely during his life. Anger, sure. Loneliness, occasionally. Desperation, now and again. But helplessness felt exotic and unfamiliar. He was unsure how to react. Sobbing was not in his DNA. Neither was hyperventilating, whimpering, or any other such nonsense. So he simply froze, trying to consider his options, playing them through in his head. *Stay put, wait until daylight, reassess, and react accordingly. Find a light, assess extent of damage, and attempt to obtain help. Crawl around room, find drugs, numb the pain, and pass out.* They all had their merits. Archie had never been one for inaction, so after a brief moment of contemplation, choice number two won out. There were only four light sources available that he knew of. The head torch, his lighter, the light on his phone, or a Cyalume glow-stick he kept in his rucksack. He quickly concluded that a concentric search of the room would be the most efficient method for locating one of the items.

Sliding painfully off of the sofa, he adopted a kneeling position, and crawled his way to one of the corners that was being gently illuminated by the ambient light shining in from the narrow window. It provided a starting point to work from. From there, he moved his way clockwise around the room, feeling out with his arms. Nothing. Nothing. Then, the corner of the foosball table. He wormed past and continued working his way along the wall. Conducting the knee equivalent of a side step inwards, he repeated the process. Nothing. Nothing. Foosball table again, this time head on. He returned to the starting point. Another side step. This time, he almost immediately came into contact with the rucksack. The Ukrainians had flung it unceremoniously across the room after having rifled through its contents. Most of the items had been discarded, and laid strewn across the floor. Archie quickly identified the side pouch where his emergency provisions were kept, including the Cyalume. The pouch was mostly empty, but a handful of articles remained. Fishing around, his hand came into contact with the cylindrical foil wrapper, which was possibly too close a match to a surgically-sealed syringe set to appeal to the robbers. Thankfully, they had chosen to leave it behind.

He cracked the stick and shook the contents, waiting for the magical chemical reaction to occur. An eerie blue glow duly appeared. Chemoluminescent salvation. It was sufficiently bright to bring the larger items in the room into focus. Archie held the stick aloft, waving it left to right, in the vain hope of identifying a more reliable light source. He couldn't see a thing. Dipping the glow stick into the main compartment of the rucksack, he peered in with his one functioning eye to see what could be salvaged. They had left his waterproof jacket, and some spare trousers, but everything else had either been stolen or scattered. Searching through the side pouches, he managed to locate a few odds and ends, but nothing that would be of immediate use. Finally, he looked through the top pouch of the rucksack, but only found some spare batteries and a spoon. The search needed to be extended.

Archie began crawling again. His crumpled sleeping bag lay by one of the dining table chairs, which in the dim light looked like unnervingly similar to a body in the foetal position. Beside it, he could also make out a pile of clothing near to the centre of the room. Flattening out onto his stomach, he used the Cyalume to examine underneath the sofa, and, to his enormous relief, caught glimpse of his head torch. It had been dislodged during the struggle. Tentatively, Archie reached out with one hand, whilst grasping the sorer side of his rib cage with the other. For such a simple movement, it was excruciatingly painful. As is always the way with items lost underneath a piece of furniture, the torch was just out of reach. Close enough for his fingertips to brush it. But not close enough to grasp the item. Every attempt simply nudged it a little further away. A change of tack was required.

Archie manoeuvred himself so that his legs could be used to push the sofa aside. It was clearly one of the shop's cheaper brands, and had no real substance to it. With just a little effort, the sofa slid away, exposing the torch. Archie snatched it up, and flicked the light on. The small room was suddenly bathed in pale white light, exposing the extent of the devastation. It was a mildly disappointing sight, given that Archie's entire life had been emptied out onto the floor. Beginning with the sleeping bag, he jammed all the items he could see into the main compartment of his rucksack, occasionally catching the back of his hands against the abrasive material. It left small white striations where his tarnished skin was scratched away. Having gathered everything that was immediately obvious, Archie turned his attention to the nooks and crannies of the room. Around the dining table, beside and beneath the recliners, underneath the foosball table, and amongst the chairs. He found nothing else.

The feeling of helplessness returned like a punch to the gut. Archie took his head in his hands. Rubbing his swollen eye, he attempted to shift some of the fluid in order to reduce the pressure. It didn't work. Combined with the broken nose, his face felt like it had inflated like some grotesque Halloween mask.

'Well. I'm fucked,' Archie couldn't help blurting out in a rather timid voice. Limping over to one of the dining chairs, he sat down with the rucksack between his legs, and took stock of what remained:

A sleeping bag.
A pair of trousers.
A hoodie.
Two t-shirts.
A plastic bag containing two pairs of socks, and a bag of foot powder.
A small wash kit.
A handful of assorted boiled sweets.
A battered section of roll mat.
Some batteries.
A spoon.

Everything of real value had gone. It's not that the assailants needed, or necessarily even wanted, the items. They were just vindictive arseholes. Nausea was beginning to set in. For the first time he noticed how cold he was. Retrieving the hoodie from the rucksack, he carefully pulled it over his head, trying to avoid catching anything too fragile. As it passed over his ears, he noticed that the left one had been slightly torn away. He extricated it from the fabric in an attempt to avoid further damage. The wound had begun to clot, but the disturbance caused the wound to begin trickling again, and blood seeped into the collar of his t-shirt.

Pushing through the pain, he eventually managed to get the hoodie on, before wrapping both arms around himself for further insulation. Although he was sorely tempted to lie on the sofa in an attempt to recover some strength, Archie realised that inactivity was not an option. His injuries were significant enough to warrant medical attention. The possibility of internal bleeding, or swelling to the brain, was of particular concern. He had witnessed first-hand the consequences of ignoring the symptoms. Colchester Hospital was at least a forty five minute trek away. In his debilitated condition, probably longer. There was a walk-in surgery near the Castle Gardens, but the chances of it being open at this hour were nil. Other than that, he would have to hope a concerned citizen might assist him. Very little chance of that either. The hospital, he concluded, was his only choice.

Next, he needed to decide whether to take his belongings with him, or to leave them in situ, hoping by some miracle that they would still be there when he had an opportunity to return. It wasn't as if anything that remained was of critical importance. He could replace most of it at one of the refuges dotted around town, although he despised visiting the miserable places. He determined that his best option would be to see what the load was like, before committing either way.

Archie leant down and placed an arm through one of the shoulder straps of the rucksack, grabbed the bag with both hands, and braced to take the weight. As he rose, a terrible pain shot through his side, forcing him to place the load down immediately. At least it made the decision to leave his belongings where they were an easy one. Secreting the rucksack behind the sofa, Archie hoped it would be sufficiently well-hidden to ensure that anyone passing by the doorway wouldn't be able to spot it. With any luck, he might be able to return to collect his belongings following his hospital visit. Before departing, he fished the waterproof jacket, and the wash kit out of the main container. Contorting this way and that, he tentatively managed to don the jacket, before tucking the wash kit into one of the ample pockets. As prepared as he was ever going to be, Archie headed out of the door.

Stepping onto the mezzanine walkway overlooking the main floor, Archie peered over the railing. The arc of light from the head torch shone out across the enormous room, creating the illusion that he was standing above an endless carpet- tiled precipice. Reaching the top of the stairs, he steadied himself using the banister, before sliding one foot at a time down the steep industrial steps. The metal clanging echoed noisily around the empty space. It made Archie wonder how he hadn't heard the Ukrainians enter the building, concluding that it was probably a mixture of fatigue, and the effect of the powerful opiates coursing around his system. Once he eventually reached the bottom of the stairs, it wasn't too far to the exit. Using a wall for support, and shuffling along like a geriatric, Archie managed to reach the barred staff entrance. He placed a hand on the bar mechanism, and leant into the misshapen steel security door. Slowly, it juddered open, grating along the arced groove that had been cut into the asphalt surface outside.

The rain had subsided, and a light mist hung in the air, which loitered underneath the street lights surrounding the site perimeter. Droplets of water clung to the chain link fence, which chinked back and forth in the breeze. A half-lungful of the cold air was sufficient for Archie to splutter involuntarily. The motion made him wince, as the brutal stabbing pain from his broken ribs shot back into sharp focus. He had a reasonable idea of the general direction of travel required. As long as he headed back towards the centre of town, he could retrace his previous route to the supermarket. Colchester hospital lay further north, near to the rugby club where he used to play. He had no idea what time it was. Somewhere between very late, and very early, given the lack of activity on the streets. The next major challenge he faced was escaping the confines of the site, which involved tackling the perimeter fence. Ordinarily, he would have bounded over it with little concern. Now, a more sophisticated approach was required. Getting to the top of the fence wasn't too concerning. He could utilise some of the waste items that were piled up in one portion of the courtyard to create an improvised platform. It was the drop the other side that would hurt. Going under the fence would involve prying up the bottom of it, before squeezing through; another suboptimal option that would, at best, result in some serious discomfort. The other choice may be to return to the store front to smash one of the large display windows, enabling direct access to the street, but the cacophony would almost certainly draw attention, and run the risk of adding further criminal charges to his already substantive rap sheet.

After weighing up the options, Archie determined that going under the fence would minimise the chances of further serious injury. Scouting around the yard, he quickly identified an old scaffolding pole that would be perfect for the job. Manhandling it clumsily to a section of fencing that had begun curling slightly at the bottom, he slid the cumbersome metal tube through the gap. Then, placing a shoulder underneath the makeshift lever, he began pumping his legs up and down in an effort to enlarge the gap. The effort required was agonizing. He drove on, until a suitably sized gap had appeared. Allowing the bar clatter to the floor, he followed suit, pressing himself into the wet gravel surface, trying to make his profile as slender as possible.

Slowly, painfully, he slithered through the tight opening by rocking back and forth on his elbows and knees. In his debilitated state, it took a dishearteningly long time to worm his way through. Eventually, dripping with perspiration, and fighting for oxygen, Archie emerged the other side. He clambered to his feet, and steadied himself against the fence for a moment. Once he had adequately regained his composure, he paused a moment to get his bearings, before hobbling off towards the main road. The soft orange glow of the street lights marked his route back into the town centre. A half-eaten kebab lay spilt out across the pavement, leaving slices of iceberg lettuce, chilli mayo sauce, and dark brown donner meat, in its wake. Nearby, an accompanying can of Carling had rolled off into the gutter. The refuse provided an indication that he was returning to civilisation, or at least something that approximated to it.

A kilometre into his journey, Archie reached the outskirts of the town centre. He could hear the noise of traffic slushing along the damp roads. Their lights reflected off the glass shopfronts creating a kaleidoscope of colours. The most direct route would be to continue along the main road. Alternatively, he could take the more convoluted route through the back streets. Opting for the first option, because it would be the quickest, Archie continued plodding along the pavement towards the station. Caught up in his own world, and simply trying to manage the discomfort, he was suddenly startled by a muffled voice coming from over his left shoulder.

'You all right boss?'

Archie swivelled his head around and could see that a Toyota Prius had pulled up on the other side of the road. The driver's window was open. A dark face with high cheek bones, and deep set eyes, peered out.

'You don't look so good. Big night out?' the man enquired. Archie was somewhat at a loss. His first inclination was to put his head down and motor on, but inherent good manners demanded a response.

'Fine, thank you. I just had a little accident. I'll be okay,' he lied.

'Are you sure? Where are you headed to my friend?' the driver asked in a firm, but affable way.

'I'm on my way to the hospital. I've picked up a couple of knocks that probably ought to be looked at.'

'Let me take you. I haven't got any customers, and I need to go to the station anyway. Come on, get in, get in. No charge.' Archie could often be impulsive, but was naturally suspicious of people, and hated relying on assistance; normally for good reason. Was this a genuine offer of help, or a trap to exploit his vulnerability? He had heard stories of abductions occurring, even of young men. The depravity and savagery of mankind never failed to amaze him. However, this chap seemed pretty genuine. After the ordeal he had experienced that evening, he needed to chalk up at least one point in the plus column.

'That would be most kind. Thanks,' he replied sincerely. Moving as swiftly as he could manage, Archie made his way across the road to the passenger side door. He almost collapsed into the seat. It had a cover made from little wooden balls, which offered no comfort whatsoever, but protected the soft fabric below. Prayer beads hung from the rear view mirror. A packet of tissues sat carefully aligned on the rear parcel shelf. Getting a good look of his benefactor for the first time, the middle-aged man was unmistakably Somalian. He was also a man who clearly took great pride in maintaining a high standard of cleanliness in his place of work. The air freshener attached to one of the heater vents filled the car with a pleasant vanilla aroma.

'My goodness, you are not in a good way at all,' the driver exclaimed. 'We must hurry. My name is Abdi. What is yours?'

'Archie. Nice to meet you,' he extended his right hand. 'It's not as bad as it looks.'

'Well, let's get going. I think it will only take ten minutes at this time of day.' Looking at the clock on the dashboard Archie noticed it was 03:27.

'It's very late. Why were you driving around here?' The car accelerated away down the road with a quiet hum.

'I have just dropped off a passenger, and I am returning to the station. I believe they say *Thursday is the new Friday*. People coming back from London you know?' Archie had no idea what day of the week it was, but nodded politely.

'Fair one. It's been a long time since I've been down to the city. Am I correct in saying you are from Somalia, Abdi?'

'That is correct. I have been in the UK for almost five years now. A great country. Horrible weather. Luckily I love the rain!'

'Well, I don't know about that, but Somalia certainly has some beautiful parts.' They hit a roundabout, and took the exit heading down the hill towards the station. Archie clutched his side, struggling to make conversation. His shallow breaths were barely providing sufficient oxygen. He was beginning to feel seriously lightheaded. However, it would be poor form to pass out, and he persevered with the conversation.

'You know Somalia?' Abdi exclaimed excitedly. 'I have only had one previous customer who has been there. Where did you stay?'

'Just outside of Mogadishu, along the coast. The Liido beach is a lovely spot. I remember they did a great latte in one of the cafes there. Where are you from?'

'I am from the north. A town called Hargeisa near to the Djibouti border. I have visited Mogadishu many times, but not to go to the beach,' he chuckled. 'What were you doing there?' They crossed a junction on the final stretch to the station. The hospital was a couple of miles beyond.

'I was in an advisory role for the peace keeping force. It was fascinating working with so many different countries.' For the first time Archie noticed the ache in his jaw. One of his incisors had been knocked loose. Yet another item to add to the repair bill.

'Very interesting, although I fear there is much to do. My country is in a very bad way. Corruption is a curse that will not be easily eliminated, and the extremists are preventing development. One day things might be better insha'Allah,' Abdi proclaimed, kissing the back of one of his hands. 'We are almost there. I will drop you outside the A and E.'

'That would be amazing. I don't know how to thank you.' Abdi's upbeat demeanour was born out of knowing genuine strife. Archie deeply admired the man's kind nature. He wished he could carry himself with the same dignity.

'It's not a problem my friend. It is good to help people, and you needed help. One day, maybe someone will do the same for me,' Abdi replied with a grin.

'Well, hopefully it will be me who gets the chance. Although I hope it never comes to that.'

The car pulled up outside the brightly-lit entrance to the accident and emergency department. The fluorescent lights flickered in stark contrast to the dreary grey-brown pebble dash surroundings. The building truly was a monstrosity. Only a small handful of people loitered around, due to the time of day. The usual crowd; drunks, druggies, concerned parents, and geriatrics. It was probably the only place where such a bizarre gathering would occur with such regular frequency. Archie reached up and grabbed the handle above his door, which he had never known the official name for, but at that moment, was extremely grateful that it was available to him. Slowly hoisting himself out of the seat, he tried not to twist his body too much, using his legs to facilitate most of the lifting. As he rose, he let out an involuntary groan. A concerned Abdi started beeping the horn, attempting to gain attention; a terribly un-British manoeuvre. Archie could picture the staff muttering about the commotion. However, it had the desired effect, and a porter soon emerged with a wheel chair.

'Abdi, you really have been a life saver. If I ever get the chance to repay you I shall. Scout's honour.' Archie weakly held up three fingers in a salute. He genuinely meant it, always having done his best to live by an old-school chivalric code.

'It's nothing boss. They will look after you now. I hope your stay is not too long, and you feel better soon,' Abdi said, maintaining his gummy perma-smile. He put the Prius into drive, and whirred off to finish his shift.

As soon as Archie had settled into the wheelchair, the porter unceremoniously spun it around, and headed through the automatic doors.

'What's your name fella?' he demanded. The man was in his thirties, and clearly hated his job. His hair was gelled into little spikes. He had a small cubic zirconia stud in one ear, and wore a chunky silver necklace. His cheap cologne was far too powerful for the workplace. The man reminded Archie of the guy who pimped out comatose patients in the film Kill Bill.

'Archie,' Archie replied.

'You've been in the wars aven't ya?' the porter enquired in a patronising tone. He was the kind of guy who would gob-off down the local Wetherspoons about the scum bags coming into hospital, and the nurses he had supposedly bedded. Archie immediately concluded that he was a detestable prick.

'I don't know how quickly they'll see ya. Looks like it could be self-inflicted to me,' *Dr Porter* commented smugly. He wheeled the chair over to the reception desk, where an equally disinterested middle-aged nurse sat. She was matter-of-fact, but surprisingly engaging. Archie really didn't envy her job dealing with irritable, self-entitled, members of the public all day and night.

'What's your name, my love?' she asked.

'Archie,' he responded.

'Archie, can you please fill in this form for me, my darling?' She had that slightly unusual habit of adding a term of endearment to the end of every sentence for no apparent reason.

'Of course. Do you know how long it will take to be seen?'

'Well, that depends on what's wrong with you. I can see you're in a pretty bad way. It shouldn't be too long. In the meantime, if you could just fill in the form for me that would be super-duper.' She turned to face the porter. 'Gary, can you please park Archie over there whilst he fills it in, love?' *Of course he's called Gary.*

Archie turned his attention to the cluttered piece of paper. The usual information was required:

Date
Name
Date of birth
Address
Next of kin
NHS number
Known allergies
Existing medical conditions
Blah, blah, blah

He knew half of it would remain blank.

'Do you have a pen I could borrow please?' he asked Gary.

'There you go.' The porter reluctantly grabbed a small disposable biro from a pot on the reception desk, before cautiously handing it over in an attempt to avoid being infected, by what he obviously considered to be, the piece of filth sitting in front of him. He then dumped Archie in the spot the nurse had pointed out.

'I'm going out for a smoke. Don't go anywhere,' he said winking. It was obviously not the first time he had used this *joke*.

Archie ignored him, and re-focused. As he went to put pen to paper, he noticed the flickering of the lights had grown more intense. Swallowing hard, he shook his head slightly, attempting to clear the cobwebs. What had been a barely noticeable high-pitch whine in his ears, suddenly increased in volume, and the room began to spin. Archie tried crying out, but nothing would pass his lips. Panicked, he attempted to get out of the chair, but the effort was too great, and he tumbled forwards, first into darkness, and then headlong onto the highly polished laminate floor.

CHAPTER 3

'Mr Maine. Can you hear me?' a distant, distorted, voice called out.

'Mr Maine, if you can hear me, try blinking your eyes.' Archie strained to open his eyelids. They felt like they had been stitched together. 'Mr Maine, my name is Dr Singh. You are in Colchester hospital. If you can hear me, please try to open your eyes,' the voice demanded. Archie concentrated, and managed to will his left eye to open slightly, forming a narrow slit. Sterile light shone through. The right eyelid wouldn't budge. He could just about distinguish a handful of blurry silhouettes.

'Mr Maine, I'm glad to see you're awake. You are recovering from surgery. You took quite a knock to your head, and we had to operate to relieve the pressure. Everything is okay. There is nothing to worry about. Can you please tell me your full name?' The doctor wasn't messing about. He probably had several similar cases to manage.

'Archie,' he managed to whisper hoarsely.

'No, your full name please. We need to make sure your brain is functioning properly.'

'Archibald Ranulph Maine. Can I have some water please?' His throat was as rough as sandpaper, and his tongue felt like a slug that had had salt poured over it.

'Of course. Here you are.' Dr Singh gently pressed a plastic cup of water against Archie's lips. He eagerly took several short sips of the invigorating cool liquid. Forcing his left eyelid to open, further shapes came into focus. The doctor was a greying Indian man, sporting a neat goatee beard, and lightweight, rimless, glasses. He had a stain on his grey shirt, probably from rushing through a sandwich in the canteen at lunch. The blemish tarnished his otherwise immaculate appearance.

'How long have I been out for?' Archie asked feebly.

'Oh, not too long. Only five or six hours. After you passed out, we quickly had you into theatre. The operation was very straightforward. Now, can you tell me what the date is?' the doctor had a routine to follow. He wasn't going to break from it to indulge in small talk.

'I'm afraid I haven't a clue. I didn't before I blacked out either. I can tell you it's February 2019.'

'Okay, what about your address?'

'How do I put this? I don't currently have a fixed abode. If you need proof that my short term memory remains intact, I can tell you that there are two emergency exits in the A&E room, one to the rear left as you go through the entrance, and one just behind reception. The shift manager's name was Claire, and the porter's name was Gary. There were three vending machines at the back of the room, one selling chocolates, one cold drinks, and one hot beverages.' Archie thought he would save them both a bit of time.

'Very good Mr Maine. Not the usual response, but it will suffice. Now, can you tell me if you are feeling any significant pain anywhere?' The hurried doctor briefly appeared mildly impressed by Archie's power of recollection, before quickly returning to the script. Archie considered the question for a moment. He hadn't had time to notice. Nothing immediate sprung to mind, although now he had been reminded of it, the dull ache from his broken ribs rematerialized with a vengeance. His puffy right eye still wouldn't open.

'Nope, nothing I can't cope with.'

'Excellent, we have you hooked up to an IV to help manage your blood pressure, and you've been given some painkillers and antibiotics, reducing the chances of infection. I had to perform a ventriculostomy, which is essentially making a tiny hole in your skull to extract some of the fluid that was causing the swelling. Nothing to worry about. It should all heal up nicely in no time. As for the other injuries, they were all relatively minor. You have three cracked ribs, a broken nose, and a broken finger, but they should all heal up in no time as long as you take it easy, and continue the course of medication I will prescribe. I won't ask about how you sustained the injuries, but the police and social worker will, once you have had some time to recover. Do you have any questions for me?' Everything the doctor relayed was as he had expected. Archie was simply glad that no permanent damage had been caused.

'No I don't think so. How long will I be in here for?' he asked, swallowing hard. His voice was becoming clearer, but it still felt uncomfortable to talk.

'It's difficult to give an exact timescale, but I would imagine you will need at least a week's recovery time under observation, so that we can monitor the head injury. I wouldn't rush to get out if I were you. Is there anyone you would like us to contact?' Archie considered the question very briefly, before firmly replying

'No. Thank you.' He was keen to escape the hospital as soon as possible, and would do everything in his power to minimise his stay. He hated the places; the constant attention and fuss, the strange assortment of characters, the perpetual noise, the lack of recreational drugs and booze. Hell on earth.

'All right, if you don't have any other questions, I'll leave you in the capable hands of the nursing staff. They'll take good care of you. I'll be back to check your progress later this evening.' Dr Singh turned to one of the junior doctors who was shadowing him, whispered something inaudible, and continued onto the next stop of his unfeasibly long rounds.

Before Archie could lay his head back into the pillow, he was interrupted by a nurse.

'Hello Archibald, my name is Sandy. I'm one of the ward nurses who'll be looking after you. There's a jug of water on your bedside table. If you need any urgent assistance, you can pull on this red cord. I'm afraid you won't be able to eat until dinner now because you've just missed lunch. I'll bring the menu around later for you to have a look. If you need the toilet, it's over in the corner, but you must remember to wheel your IV over with you. There's a personal TV on the arm just by your side. You need to make sure you wear the headphones. I'm afraid it's only crappy Freeview channels. Is there anything else you need at the moment?'

Archie looked the nurse up and down. He must have been at least six three, and heavily built. A tribal tatt peeked out from under one of his sleeves. He was wearing a chunky Garmin watch. Despite his imposing size, his voice was rather mellifluous, never rising above the level of a forceful whisper. It reminded Archie of a concerned funeral director. *I'm very sorry for your loss. Taken before their time. How will you be paying, cash or card?*

'It's Archie, not Archibald please.' This was the first time he had used his full name used in years. It's not that he didn't like it. It simply had the effect of causing people to make too many presumptions. It had been altogether easier sticking with something a little more palatable.

'Oh, no problem. You look like more of an Archie anyway. I've got to ask, did you serve?' Sandy's kind face leered down at him. Archie was taken aback. How did he know? He was sure he hadn't mentioned it. Nothing amongst his possessions would have provided any real indication.

'Why do you ask?'

'Well, I noticed the bullet wound to your shoulder, and you've got your dagger and wings up. I was Sixteen

Med Reg. Got out a couple of years ago. How about you?' A bit sharper than he looked, old Sandy. Archie really didn't like to talk about the subject, but felt compelled given Sandy's gentle curiosity. Also, he was in control of the painkiller dosage.

'I got out about a year ago. I was a JTAC. Decided it was time for a change after fourteen years.'

'That's mega. We might have been on the same ops together at some point. I won't disturb you now, but it would be great to chat about it once you feel better,' Sandy suggested. He was obviously quite keen to reminisce.

'That sounds great,' Archie fibbed. 'I am feeling a bit weary now. Could probably do with a rest.'

'Sure thing mate, just get your head down, and I'll come back later with the menu. Got to admit, the food's pretty shit, but better than a rat pack! Small world, eh? See ya later.' Sandy gave him a big grin, before bounding towards the desk situated just outside the ward entrance.

'Great,' Archie sighed under his breath.
He had no desire to talk about the *good old days*, and set his mind to how he could escape the bright-white prison as quickly as possible.

Surveying his surroundings, he could see his was one of eight beds on the ward. All but one were occupied. To his right was an elderly man. His leg was elevated. A row of grotesque heavy-grade metal stiches ran almost the entire length of it. The skin around them had an orangey tint, and looked like it had been pulled too taut, like an overloaded plastic bag. To his left, was a young man with both his arms in casts. He lay perfectly still with his eyes closed. Archie struggled to make out the other occupants with his one, semi-functioning, eye. As promised, a jug of water was resting on the small table beside his bed. Next to it was a plastic cup. He reached across to pour himself a glass, and almost yelped out loud, as he unthinkingly rolled onto his damage rib cage. The painkillers weren't so great after all. He opted for a more cautious approach, and shifted himself onto his side, before slowly extending his right arm. Firmly grasping the handle of the jug, he carefully poured half a glass. Even such a simple task required significant effort. When he finally managed to take a large gulp of water, Archie could taste chemicals and blood. It made him want to gag. However, he managed to force down the rest of the cool liquid.

What to do? He needed to regain strength. Allow time for his injuries to mend. There had to be a way of accelerating the process. In the meantime, he concluded that he should keep a low-profile, whilst trying to avoid people as much as possible. Be the grey man. Propping himself up into a sitting position, he closed his eye, and concentrated on the sound of his breathing. How had he been so careless at the showroom? Normally, he would have taken further precautions; bar the external door, set up a rudimentary alarm, barricade the staff room. Animalistic craving had gotten the better of him. He'd paid the price for his weakness. On reflection, he wasn't really sure why he was in such a rush to depart the comfort of the hospital. Three square meals, a soft bed, prescription painkillers. It could be a lot worse. However, the oppressive routine, and false niceties, would undoubtedly get to him sooner or later. And anyway, he needed to track down the Ukrainians if he ever wished to recover his possessions.

Reopening his eye, the rest of the room began coming into focus. He could make out the man opposite, who didn't immediately seem to have anything wrong with him. He was chortling at something on TV. To his left, in the bed nearest the entrance, was another elderly guy, who was asleep. Archie wasn't sure if there was an order of precedence in the ward for the most high-risk patients being placed closer to the door for ease of access. More likely, it was simply a case finding the first opening, and shoving any poor bastard in, knowing the NHS. The room smelt overwhelmingly of antiseptic, canteen food, and stale farts. The unusual aroma somehow filtered directly into Archie's sinuses, through his mouth, circumnavigating his bandaged nose. There was a bit of commotion coming from the far end of the room, where an overweight middle-aged fellow had visitors. The adults were discussing an upcoming birthday party too loudly, whilst the children sat glued to an iPad.

'We need to sort out a card for Kiara. You got any idea how old she is?' the woman demanded in a whiny voice.

'Nah, no idea babe. You're normally the one who knows that sort of stuff.' By the look of him, Archie had no doubt he was telling the truth. He looked like an overgrown, bald child. A prominent Watford FC tattoo sat nestled amongst several other crap tatts, which had likely been completed sometime in the 90s over the course of numerous visits to cheap Spanish beach resorts. *He probably couldn't even spell his own name in a card, even if they managed to find one,* Archie concluded.

He couldn't make out the occupant in the far bed on his side of the room, without uncomfortably craning his neck around, and was content to leave that one a mystery for the time being. For the first time, he noticed that his hands were looking much cleaner than normal. They must have given him a scrub prior to surgery. A plastic cast covered his left ring finger. It forced the digit to point straight out and made it surprisingly uncomfortable to bend his other fingers. He wriggled them slightly in an attempt to keep the blood flowing. They had removed his watch, a cheap black Casio that he had bought many years previously. At the first opportunity, he would ask for it to be returned. The staff had dressed him in a standard turquoise hospital gown. None of the clothes he had been wearing when he arrived were in view; given the state they were in, they had probably been incinerated. Very quickly, Archie began growing restless. His attention span had always been limited. A born nomad, constant movement was in his DNA. It probably had something to do with his unorthodox upbringing. He briefly considered watching something on TV, but the likelihood of something decent being on was very slim.

Surveying the room again, he noticed a clock above ticking away above the entrance. It was 09:42, confirming his suspicion that there would definitely not be anything worth viewing. *A quick trip to the toilet wouldn't do any harm.* Leaning forward, and bracing himself, Archie cautiously unravelled his left leg from the crisp hospital sheets, before swinging it over the side of the bed. The IV bag hung from a polished metal trolley. Roughly a third full of the clear liquid remained. He took hold of it with his left hand and placed his feet on the floor, which was surprisingly warm given its sterile appearance. Rising up was more straightforward than he had anticipated. Taking a moment to steady himself, he began shuffling over to the cubicle in the corner of the room.

'You're up are you?' asked a voice from beside him. It was the old man with Frankenstein's leg.
No, I'm obviously fast-a-sleep. Too sarcastic Archie reflected.

'Yep. Looks like it.'

'That's good. I need help every time I need the loo. You're lucky.' *I sure am,* Archie thought to himself.

'That's not ideal. If you'll excuse me, I'm rather

desperate.'

'Oh, of course. I'm sorry to interrupt. We can chat once you're done.'

Returning his attention to nature's call, Archie increased his shuffling speed, and hurriedly pulled open the white wooden door. The cubicle was reasonably spacious. It was decked out with a throne-like disabled toilet complete with red safety cord, an unfeasibly small sink with a long lever tap, and a sit-down shower. The smell of drain and own-brand shower gel hung in the damp air. He thought he'd treat himself to a sit down wee.

Gathering the ungainly gown out of the way, he noticed that he had been supplied him with some NHS pants. They were probably better than the ones he came in with. Letting them drop to his ankles, he sat down and felt the pressure in his bladder release. His urine was unnaturally dark and pungent, like treacle. Archie determined that he would polish off the whole jug of water once he had returned to his bed.

As he rose to wash his hands, he caught his reflection in the mirror. His right eye remained closed. It was turning a yellowy-purple colour. With some luck, it would reopen in a day or so. His nose was covered with gauze, held in place with surgical tape. Peeling it back slightly, he could see some fairly severe bruising, and dried spots of blood around the nostrils. His left eye had dark spots around it, but other than that looked relatively intact. A stitched ear, angry red graze on his neck, and dry split lips, completed the list of visible injuries to his head. A large bandage protected the ventriculostomy wound from infection. Instinctively, he reached up to touch the place where he thought the hole might be, but thought better of it. Surveying the rest of his body, the only other overt signs of damage were the splinted finger, and purple-red rib cage, which he admired by pulling the gown to one side. *Could be worse* he reflected.

Opening the door, he was grateful that one of the nurses had come to check on the geriatric. He could probably slip past unnoticed. Making a beeline straight for the far side of the mattress, he attempted moving as stealthily as possible. However, he failed to avoid detection.

'That was quick!' the man commented cheerfully.

'I hope you weren't timing me.'

'Of course not. Don't be ridiculous. Hope it wasn't too much of a struggle. Mine often are these days,' he replied with melancholy in his voice. The man evidently craved conversation. Archie clambered back into bed as efficiently as he could, nestling his head in the rubbery pillows. They softly exhaled air, as he leant back into them. The nurse was finishing up some paperwork.

'All looking fine Mr Thompson. Now, you must take it easy, you hear me?' the nurse instructed. She sounded pretty serious.

'Of course, of course. Please stop fussing!' the old man replied curtly. This clearly wasn't the first time he had been chastised.

'Okay, well, I'll leave you to it. Stay out of trouble.' She placed the clipboard on a hook at the end of the bed, before sauntering out of the room. The old man rolled his eyes, shook his head slightly, and then turned towards Archie, fixing him with a piercing gaze.

'My name is Gerard. What's yours, young man?'

'Archie.' he responded, feeling like he was stuck on repeat. In fairness, he hadn't talked to this many people for some time.

'Well, wonderful to meet you Archie. You're not looking too good if I might say. Hope it's nothing too serious?'

'Nothing I can't cope with. You're not looking too

hot yourself.'

'Oh this. It was my own silly fault. Tripped down some stairs a couple of weeks ago, and broke the damn thing. Never broken a bone before in my life. Now look at me! They had to insert some metal plates to pin it all together. I should begin my physiotherapy soon enough, once the stiches have come out,' he yawned loudly. 'Can't wait to get out of this bloody place. Hate being cooped up you know?' He spoke with a firm clipped voice, full of confidence. Judging by the accent, he wasn't local, probably originating from somewhere in the south west. He maintained constant eye contact, with eyes that were still full of life for someone of his age. Perhaps he wasn't as much of a bore as Archie had feared.

'Well, I'll agree with you there. I'm not planning on hanging around here too long either.'

'I certainly hope not, a fit young chap like you. You've got better things to be doing than lying around in this godforsaken place. Do you have anyone coming to visit?' Gerard reminded Archie of his father. Opinionated.

'Not that I know of. I like my own company.'

'Well that won't do. It's good to have something to plan for, even if it is your ungrateful daughter, and useless son-in-law coming to feign concern. I have that pleasure this afternoon. At least I get to wind them up by asking them to bring me obscure farming magazines. Don't even read the bloody things!' he chortled, whilst nodding towards a pristine stack of Farmers Weekly sitting on the table next to him. Archie instantly began warming to Gerard. Anyone who enjoyed a windup so much couldn't be all that bad.

For the first time, he noticed the size of the man. It was unusual to see someone still so bulky for his age. At a guess he still weighed at least a hundred kilos. And it wasn't like he was fat. Just, solid. His hair line had seen better days, and the dappled skin on his face, intersected by a web of faint red capillaries, suggested that he must be at least in his seventies. Otherwise, there were very few indicators of his advanced years. Gerard's power-lifting Father Christmas look was topped off by a short white beard.

'Did I hear you saying you were a military man whilst you were chatting to Sandy?' *Oh no, here we go,* Archie thought disappointedly. Here comes a boring dit about along the lines of, *In my day, National Service was a great thing. They should bring it back I say. Blah, blah, blah.*

'I was, but I left about a year ago. I needed a change of pace.'

'Yes, well I can understand that. Very demanding profession. Never time for family and all that. Best days of my life though.' Standard answer. *I bet they were.* Dressing up, and running about in some fields playing at soldiers, whilst fighting against a make-believe enemy. He had probably spent most of his time eating and drinking his way across Germany.

'Yes, well I suspect things have changed quite a bit since then.'

'Oh undoubtedly. The technology's amazing now, and the media interfering all the time doesn't help. No privacy anymore. But I think you'll find that life for the chaps on the ground is not all that different. I assume you've been to a few interesting places given how much has been occurring in the world lately?' Gerard commented, seeming very assured of himself.

'Yes a few. I'm not sure I would use the term interesting though. Shit perhaps.'

'Ha, well, they certainly are that,' Gerard grinned. 'I can think of one or two myself!'

'I'm not sure Germany counts.' A low blow, but it

might put him off his stride.

'Well I was thinking more Korea, or perhaps Malaya actually. Never did get to Germany, more's the pity. I hear the whore houses were fantastic. Certainly better than traipsing around in the trees.' Gerard was full of surprises. 'Which outfit were you with?'

'Originally down in Plymouth with the Commando Gunners, and then transferred just up the road to the airborne unit. I did fourteen years in all. Managed to get out to the Balkans, Iraq, Somalia and Afghanistan three times. Never a dull moment.'

'Absolutely. A stinking Gunner, eh? I was with the Sappers during Korea in Nine Squadron, and then got selected for the Regiment when I returned. Went all over the place with them, Aden, Suez, Oman, Malaya. Great times. We were nowhere near as constrained as you boys. The military imperative took precedence, not some namby pamby human rights agenda. And we got decent medical care. I took some shrapnel from a North Korean grenade in fifty two, and was whisked straight back to a military hospital. We didn't rely on NHS waiting lists and charities for goodness sake.' Gerard was becoming visibly agitated by the recollection.

'Well it's not that bad. I was looked after really well in Birmingham after being shot in Afghanistan. I think they've eventually managed to develop a decent set up.'

'Yes, maybe because some politician was backed into a corner to find some funding and the public were feeling generous at the time. But it's simply not sustainable. I think it's a travesty that our servicemen and women don't have their own dedicated healthcare system.' He had propped himself up slightly for dramatic effect.

'Maybe. I can't say it was the easiest ride returning home, but I know plenty of people who had it worse.'

'Couldn't agree more. To comrades past!' Gerard

lifted his plastic glass of water in the air, and finished off the remnants. 'I suspect being shot wasn't all too pleasant? What are they using there? Seven six two I'd imagine. Got to sting a bit?'

'Well it wasn't great, I must admit. Relatively clean wound through the shoulder. It healed up pretty well, not too much tissue damage. When it happened, I thought someone had tried to knock me over with a sledgehammer because of the impact. I didn't realise I was bleeding until a mate pointed it out. It was better than standing on an IED though, for sure. That gets messy.'

'It certainly does. Ghastly weapons used by cowards. Of course, it was mainly land mines in my day. Same end result though. I remember one poor fellow stepping on one in Malaya, and having his foot blown off. He point-blank refused to leave it rotting in the jungle, insisting that someone could sew it back on once he was back at the RAP, so he stuffed it into one of his webbing pouches for safe keeping. Sadly, we couldn't extract him in time. He caught a rather nasty infection, and died about a month later,' Gerard simply relayed the information as a matter of fact. Archie couldn't detect any emotion whatsoever.

'That's not ideal. Unfortunately, I witnessed a couple of similar episodes.'

'I can well imagine you did. Ugly business over there. Shame to see that not too much was learnt from my day. Basically the same sort of chaps up to mischief. Can't say I blamed them honestly, most were just poor desperate men caught in the middle of things. Doesn't make a blind bit of difference when they're trying to kill you though. It always boils down to us and them in the end.' Archie could almost see the recollections running through the old man's mind. Gerard broke his gaze briefly, and looked towards the floor. 'This is all getting a bit morose isn't it? I should leave you to rest.'

'I think that might be a good idea. Nice to meet you Gerard.' Archie was experiencing the effects of the operation. A thudding pain was developing in his skull around the area where the incision had been made.

'And you too Archie. I'm sure we'll talk some more. I'm certainly not going anywhere for the time being!' Gerard beamed a big yellow-stained smile.

Archie rolled back onto his bed closing his eyes. He reflected on the conversation. It had been a significant period since he had spoken to anyone about his time in the forces, and now it was twice in one day. It wasn't that he was overtly trying to avoid it. It was easier just to draw a line under the past, and move on. Overall, it had been a hugely positive experience; challenging, exciting, varied, occasionally exotic. The aspect that he had enjoyed the most, though, was the sense that he belonged to something bigger than himself.

Unfortunately, everything had been tarnished by other destructive emotions, which had grown increasingly strong over the years; apprehension, isolation, guilt, fear, regret, and above all, resentment. In the end, the negatives had slowly eroded the positives, resulting in his behaviour becoming increasingly reflexive and erratic. His unruly conduct finally reached the point where it had exceeded his employer's tolerance. The final nail in the coffin came after he viciously assaulted a Sergeant Major, following a dispute regarding a bacon sandwich of all things. What an anti-climax.

The worst thing was that he couldn't directly link his decline to a single tipping point or incident. God knows there were plenty to choose from. It had been more like death from a thousand cuts. Things had simply accumulated to a point where he couldn't control his actions. He hadn't exactly been the most straitlaced person in the first place. Serious boozing had undoubtedly compounded things. However, in spite of the haze, some moments had shone brighter than others. It's not like he relived them every day. Or that he endured vivid flashbacks, like some awful Hollywood action movie. But now and again, some elusive catalyst, a sound, a smell, a phrase, would trigger a memory that would, for the briefest moment, catch Archie's attention, often making him feel melancholy and utterly insignificant. Talking to Gerard had been one of those triggers. As he drifted off to sleep, he couldn't prevent the same sense of helplessness returning that he had felt in the showroom.

CHAPTER 4

Despite a long uninterrupted sleep, Archie still felt
exhausted. The IV bag had successfully delivered its
serum, blanketing him from the toing and froing of the
world. It was dark outside the window, but the stark
ward lights were still on, indicating that it was probably
early evening. Sandy was in the middle of his rounds.
His trolley carried several plates of that evening's
dinner. He was currently parked up at the fat bald man's
bed. His family had thankfully disappeared. A familiar
smell of mass produced food, wafted around the room,
but it couldn't penetrate though Archie's nose bandage.
Gerard was watching TV. The headphones looked
laughably small on his bulbous head.

'Hello, you hungry?' Sandy asked. He had finished
serving fatty, and swivelled around to face Archie's bed.
He must have noticed the movement when Archie
stretched his limbs.

'Absolutely starving. What's on offer?'

'Well, you missed the choices when the menu came
round earlier, so I put aside a cottage pie, and some ice
cream for dessert. Is that all right?'

'Smashing. Any chance you have some Tabasco?'
Archie liked to douse most of his food in the popular hot
sauce.

'I'll see what I can do. Ready for it now?' Sandy
had closed the distance and was now stood next to the
bed, obscuring Gerard from view.

'Why not? Let me just get comfortable.' Archie
wriggled into a sitting position, and pushed away the
sheet, freeing his torso. Sandy pulled a table across

Archie's lap, before plonking a dubious looking plate of food onto the centre of it. Next, a bowl of half-melted, bubble-gum pink, ice cream. Finally, a thick plastic glass of weak orange squash. It was the type that Archie's grandma used to buy, and tasted more of preservatives than orange.

'Looks fantastic. I don't suppose there's any lobster thermidor, and a large glass of Chablis going begging?'

'Fraid not mate. This isn't too bad actually. Trust me, it could be a lot worse. Did you manage to get some rest?' Sandy had been on the receiving end of plenty of complaints about the quality of the food, and batted off the slight without flinching. He deftly placed down a set of cutlery that was somehow marginally too small for the plate that it accompanied.

'Well it's better than nothing. The last thing I had to eat was an out-of-date sandwich.' Archie shoved the first forkful of cottage pie into his mouth. It wasn't great. There was also some stewed broccoli and cabbage dumped to the side of the pie. They were leaching greenish fluid into the mashed potato topping. He stabbed at the unappetising vegetables with his fork. Their addition didn't make the mouthful taste any better. In fact, it probably made it worse. Whilst he chewed on the budget meat and vegetable mix, Sandy disappeared from the room. He returned a few moments later, when Archie was on his third mouthful of gruel, carrying a little red bottle.

'Thank you so much, you're a life saver. On reflection, this is absolutely gopping!' Archie exclaimed between mouthfuls. He grabbed the bottle, and liberally doused the food with piquant orange droplets.

'No problem. Hope it's an improvement,' Sandy replied, brimming with sincerity.

'For sure. Tabasco improves everything.'

'Dr Singh will be back in about half an hour. Do you need anything before then?'

'Nope. I don't believe I do,' Archie blurted without thinking, before immediately correcting himself.

'Actually, do you have anything to read?' He had always enjoyed reading, but hadn't recently been in a position to indulge. Ultimately, a toss-up between reading or smoking hard drugs had always been a very one-sided competition.

'Yep, we've got loads of books. People donate them or leave them behind all the time. Anything in particular you're after?' Sandy asked, sounding slightly surprised by the request.

'Anything non-fiction would be great. Maybe a travel book or a political biography. Or something by a Russian author. Failing that, any decent thriller.'

'Well, most of the stuff is like Harry Potter, or Jilly Cooper, or that. But there's probably something. I'll bring it round after Dr G has been in.' Reading rarely featured on Sandy's agenda either, it would appear.

'That would be great. Also, anywhere I can grab a brew?'

'If you ever fancy one there's a vending machine just down the hall. Other than that, you need to wait for meal times. I can grab you one when I come back with the book if you want?'

'Wow, room service and everything. It's like the Dorchester in here!' Archie proclaimed.

'I wouldn't know mate. I guess that's a hotel is it?'

'It sure is. A very decent one.'

'Sounds nice. Right, I best get on with the rest of dinner. I'll see you in about an hour or so.' Sandy shifted a couple of items about on the trolley, and then headed to the other side of the room. Archie wolfed down the rest of the meal despite its poor quality. *Food is fuel*, he reminded himself. The ice cream was no better than the main. Processed, artificially-coloured, milk powder, but it felt good on his tongue. Ordinarily, he would have lit up at this point, probably with several brandy or gin chasers, but sadly, no such luxury was available. He wondered whether it would be possible to get his hands on some methadone. Probably not. He didn't consider himself an addict. He just really liked all the things that other people considered vices. More importantly, they held reality at a comfortable arm's reach, so that he could get on with living his life. Without them, things became too focused. Too unsettling. Best to keep everything slightly blurred.

Hospital was too comfortable, too sanitised, and too sober, to prevent his mind from wandering. He needed a distraction. Reaching out for the TV, he pulled the small screen across his lap, and pushed the power button. It sprang to life, erupting with light and noise. The sound made several other occupants look up. Archie felt a jolt of pain through his side, as he scrambled to find the headphones, before plugging them into the jack. A BBC talk show featuring minor celebrity guests was on. The presenters looked like grinning, spray tanned, mannequins. The guests simply looked bored. Archie couldn't name a single one.

Allowing the images and noises to wash over him, he

reconsidered what had brought him to this appalling place in the first place. After having been kicked out of the Army, he had sought employment at first. It seemed the sensible thing to do. But the more rejections he received, the more disillusioned he became. His options were narrowing to the point where he was going to have to either accept something truly menial, or live without an income. The latter was more palatable. He began roaming the streets soon after. In the Army he had kudos. He had been a leader. And what's more, he was good at his job. There was no way he was going to be someone's skivvy. For him, living homeless meant living free. No expectations to live up to, no schedule to adhere to, no one relying on him.

But it also lacked purpose. This, above all the hardships, had been the bitterest pill to swallow. Without a framework to operate within, and a goal to work towards, he was liable to drift, which was exactly what had happened. So often throughout his life he had been told he wasn't living up to his potential. Whether it was the Housemaster of Mustians, during his time at Eton, the aborted attempt at university, or his Commanding Officer urging him to apply for a commission. They had all seen a spark. Something worth investing in. But, the flame would eventually be extinguished, given sufficient space and time.

The simple fact was Archie considered himself his own man. He wanted to live in the here and now, rather than hypothecate about the future. He was also a little bit lazy. Commitment to long-term endeavours simply bored the shit out of him. After a few minutes, Dr Singh appeared at the end of his bed and said something inaudible. He had noticed the stain on his shirt, and made an attempt to clean it up. Archie removed the headphones.

'I beg your pardon doctor?'

'I asked how you are feeling Mr Maine?'

'Oh, very well actually. I think some food has done me a world of good, and I managed to get a bit of shut-eye earlier. Probably about ready to leave, I reckon.' Archie did his best to seem convivial, hoping to receive a shorter sentence for good behaviour.

'Well that's excellent news, but I'm afraid you're not ready to go anywhere yet. Just be patient and allow the healing process to occur,' Dr Singh said smiling. His eyes were heavy, and bloodshot.

'I'll do my best doctor.'

Dr Singh pulled the privacy curtain around Archie's bed. 'I'm just going to conduct a few checks if you don't mind?'

'Fill your boots.'

'Great. Blood pressure first, then respiration, then a few other bits and bobs. Please roll up your sleeve.'

Archie pulled up the loose fabric of his gown, and presented his arm to the doctor, who applied the Velcro cuff. It inflated, tightening around his arm. Archie could feel the blood pulsating, and tried to relax. The bag wheezed noisily as it deflated.

'That's all fine. Now please sit forward for me, and pull up the back of your gown.' Archie did as commanded, although the pressure on his ribs was uncomfortable. 'Deep breaths in and out please.' The ensuing breaths weren't exactly deep, but they seemed to do the trick. 'Super. You can relax. I'm just going to check your dressings.' Dr Singh probed around Archie's head. Peeling back various areas of bandage, and looking beneath them; he was presumably checking for infection or anything else untoward. 'Excellent, no issues. Everything is healing as expected. I'm going to have to take a blood sample as well. It's normal protocol following the type of operation you've undergone. It will also show up any other nasties that might be lurking about.' *He means HIV* Archie mused. The doctor assembled the various blood test items on a small tray, covered by a paper cloth. The cannula protruding from his arm made it a straightforward affair. Dr Singh wiped everything with a sterilising fluid, before placing the vial into a clear plastic bag, and writing some details on it. 'There. All done. I'll leave you to your TV. I'm not on shift tomorrow, so another doctor will come to check up on you in the morning. Happy?'

'Delighted. Thank you doctor. Have a good evening.'

'You too Mr Maine.' Dr Singh pulled back the curtains, and moved on to tend to the young man in the bed to Archie's left. Archie considered watching TV again, but before he could, he heard a familiar voice from his right.

'Archie. How are you feeling my boy?' Gerard had removed his headset, and pushed aside the screen.

'I'm well thank you. Everything seems to be working as it should be.'

'Capital. I'm just about clinging onto life too it seems. Food wasn't up to much was it?'

'Not really. I've had worse though. As I'm sure you

59

have?'

'You're right there. I remember having to survive on a pack of biscuits for three days in the desert.' His bushy eyebrows rose slightly at the memory.

'Sounds pretty brutal. I never had it that bad. Is the food always the same quality?'

'You mean is it garbage? Pretty much. Now and again something decent crops up, but generally the grub is god awful.'

'Well, I can't say I'm that surprised. Sandy should be bringing me a book later on, which should help to pass the time. You never know, they might have something decent.'

'That's good. It's very easy for your brain to turn to mush in here. I've got a spare sci-fi novel if you'd like. Not really my thing.' Gerard held up the paperback for Archie to see. It looked pretty battered, and must have come from the hospital library.

'Not really for me either thanks. I'll wait and see what Sandy comes back with.'

'Suit yourself. Now if you'll excuse me, I'm going to call for some assistance. Can't even go for a piss on my own. My strong advice is don't get old!' Gerard pushed the call button for a nurse, before shifting his bulk to the side, in anticipation of the complicated ordeal required to relieve himself.

Archie still felt terribly drowsy. His enflamed right eye was slowly improving. He prodded it gently to see what the inflammation was like. Not great, but certainly better than it was. He attempted forcing the eyelid open to assess whether his eyeball was injured as well. It was an awkward and slightly painful manoeuvre, but a slither of light shone through confirming that at least there didn't appear to be any serious damage. Next, a nudge of the nose. Archie couldn't help but probe injuries. He had always done it, even as a child, despite receiving constant tellings-off. His impatience meant he simply couldn't abide nature's laborious healing process. Scabs never survived their full term. The nose was fine. No worse than any of the previous breaks he had endured; at this juncture there was very little cartilage left to spoil. Just as he was finishing up his personally administered MOT, Sandy returned. He was carrying a tray containing a small silver pot of tea, a miniature jug of milk, a cup with an implausibly small handle, and an assortment of books.

'As promised. I'm not sure if you take milk or sugar so I brought both. Hopefully the books are to your liking. I was surprised by the request. Most ex-squaddies would prefer a copy of Razzle.' Sandy placed the tray down on the bedside table, and cleared away the leftover dinner items.

'I'm partial to a Razzle as well if you've got it. Thanks very much for making the effort. It really is most appreciated.' He attempted to help Sandy load the last couple of pieces onto the dinner tray, but probably got in the way more than he assisted.

'No dramas. Have a look. If none are any good, I can look again.'

Archie rifled through. A couple of thrillers, *A Journey* Tony Blair's autobiography, a Dostoyevsky that he had already read, and a well-thumbed hardback about the Israeli-Palestinian conflict. Against his better judgement he took *A Journey*. At least he might gain an insight as to why he had ended up in so many shit holes during the best years of his life.

'This will do. Can't believe I've stooped so low. The bloke's a prick!' Archie grimaced as he placed the book beside him on the bed.

'You can grab another if you want. People get through them pretty quickly round here.'

'Smashing. I think I shall.' He picked up one of the thrillers, placing it on top of the autobiography.

'Just let me know if you want to swap out any more. Like I said, there's loads knocking about. The last time I read a book was on tour in Afghanistan in two thousand and ten. Were you there too?' Sandy was eager to get back to reminiscing.

'Yes I was. Based in Nad-e-Ali for most of it, near to Shawqat. Not a great tour really, certainly not as good as HERRICK Five or Eight.' He thought he would indulge Sandy for a while, returning the favour for the books.

'No way man. I was just over the river, in Lash med centre. I spent most of the time treating Afghan soldiers and locals. Where were you for Eight?'

'I bounced around quite a bit. Sangin, Kajaki, FOB Rob. Did the turbine Op. Actually, that tour was pretty punchy. I dropped a decent amount of ordnance.' Archie wasn't lying. At the time, he had the highest tally of airstrike controls conducted across the whole of Afghanistan. 'Nothing could beat HERRICK Five though. That was the shizzle. Proper soldiering, without all the bullshit. I spent quite a bit of time attached to the BRF, which was hoofing.'

'Well we weren't on Five, and I was in Bastion for

Eight. It was crazy busy though. Managed to get out on the MERT a few times. Saw plenty of messed up shit. Too much actually.' For the first time since Archie had met him, Sandy appeared sombre. He knew what the after effects of injuries looked, and felt like, and he had only encountered a generous handful of them at most. Sandy was confronting that horror on a daily basis.

'I hear you. Can't say I envied your job. It must have been pretty cheeky seeing all that crap. The worst thing is that it was all a complete waste of time. All the while we were running about in the green zone like idiots, the Afghan senior officers and politicians were pocketing all the aid being sent in, whilst colluding with the Taliban. I swear there was this one Colonel we were supporting who would siphon off all the fuel coming in for his Kandak, and sell it on to the local insurgents almost immediately. We just had to watch as they filled up their pick-ups, and hand over the cash. What an absolute joke!' Archie recounted. He was becoming genuinely agitated, which is why he avoided the topic if at all possible.

'Well, I guess so. But I think we did some good as well. There are a few parts of the country that are doing pretty well from what I know. And it was all right when we managed to inoculate the kids and help out the old folks. I probably had a different perspective though. What did you do once you got back? Being honest, I found it difficult to adjust.'

Archie wasn't sure how to answer. There's no doubt that he preferred the excitement of being on tour to the drudgery of life in barracks. His steady fall from grace had to be attributable to something. But equally, he didn't feel like there was a direct correlation between the two. It's not like he had been diagnosed with PTSD or any of that nonsense.

'It was okay. Just got back into the usual boring readiness cycle. Oh, and went on the piss as much as possible. If I'm honest, I actually got discharged for knocking out a Sergeant Major when I was rat arsed. He wasn't a bad bloke really. I'd just had enough of being treated like a moron.' Sandy was the first person he'd discussed the incident with since leaving. It felt vaguely cathartic to share, yet still rankled for some reason.

'And what have you been up to since leaving? The transition can be pretty tough.' Sandy looked intently at Archie. He was definitely building to something. Archie wasn't sure how to answer. It was fairly obvious he hadn't exactly thrived, but in his own way he had found what he was after; autonomy.

'This and that. I couldn't really be doing with a nine to five, so took work where I could find it and kept moving about. I've rather enjoyed it!' he said honestly. Although his lifestyle was unconventional, it suited him. He wasn't planning on doing it for the rest of his life. Like a gambling addict, he was of the opinion he could simply stop when he felt like it. Mortgages, insurance premiums, dinner parties, and school runs. Fuck that! He'd seen enough of it as a child to put him off for life.

'Well, I don't want to interfere because I know that everyone has a different journey, but I noticed you must've been living rough. Your clothes were in shit state, and I could smell the drugs on them. I'm not judging, I promise.' Archie could tell he clearly was. *Probably going to follow up with some bible bashing nonsense*. Archie didn't want to take the chance.

'Look mate, I don't want to be rude, but I couldn't care less if you were. There's a reason I don't normally talk to people about this stuff, so please don't give me the whole *you're wasting your life away* speech. My life, is *my* life. I've heard it enough times,' Archie replied firmly enough to ensure that Sandy got the message.

'I get it. If you don't want to talk about it I understand. I've met plenty of blokes in the same position. For what it's worth I spent some time in the same position. I left on a medical discharge due to mental health issues. For ages I felt ashamed and guilty. No one else on civvy street understood what we'd been through, and I didn't want to give them the privilege of asking stupid questions. I spent most of the time walking around resenting everyone I came across, like they were some lower form of life. I even started treating my family that way. My missus dumped me eventually,' he explained sorrowfully. Archie started drifting off. 'Anyway, it wasn't until I talked to someone about it that things started to improve. There's an amazing network of veterans out there who are happy to help. I got in touch with an old mate who sorted me out with a rehab programme. Don't jump to conclusions. It was awesome. Really got my head sorted out. I wouldn't be working here if I hadn't taken the leap.' Archie could feel himself becoming tense. He must have been trying to clench his fists, because the broken finger really began aching.

'All right, all right, I get it. Thanks for the sermon but I'm not interested. With all due respect, working somewhere like this isn't exactly my idea of heaven. I'm glad you're happy, but it's not for me.' Surely he would get the message. Sandy grinned back at him.

'Cool, no problem. I just wanted to make sure you're okay, which you clearly are. I won't bring it up again if you don't want me to. I'm not as much of a dickhead as you probably think I am. Anyway, I sort your meals out, and change your dressings so you better not be too much of an arsehole to me.' His face beamed even brighter.

'It's all right mate. I've just heard it all before. I'm happy doing what I'm doing,' Archie said, trying to sound as genuine as he could. Sandy seemed like he could take no for an answer.

'All right. I'll leave you to do some reading. If you need anything, you know where I am.' He picked up the dinner tray, and headed off.

This wasn't the first time Archie had been propositioned with offers of redemption. There were all sorts of people who thought that they knew what was best for him. He had even considered taking them up on their charitable offers during the more challenging moments of living rough. But, it had become almost a personal challenge to stick by his convictions. Archie felt it was a victory that he had managed to survive, and occasionally thrive, this long. He wasn't about to start selling his soul, because yet another Samaritan had joined the queue. His thoughts returned to what he might do after his release. The hours, and days, passed slowly. He finished *A Journey*, the thriller, and five other books, in quick succession. He continued chatting with Gerard on a regular basis, and through necessity, with Sandy as well. Two of the original co-inhabitants of the room moved on. He had made no real effort to get to know any of them, beyond paying the minimum basic courtesies, in the hope they would leave him alone, which they had. Gerard's stories were more than enough to occupy him in any case.

He had lived an extraordinary life full of adventure, excitement, and intrigue. Whether fighting off cobras during his time managing a sugar palm plantation in Burma, or gambling, and losing, whilst playing backgammon against Bedouin tribesman in the desert. Archie's favourite tale was from an episode when Gerard had been visiting his nephew in London. He needed to withdraw some money from a cash point. As he was removing the notes from the machine, a young man had accosted him, demanding that he hand over the money and any other valuables. The old man had warned him to back off, but the deluded youngster attempted to prize the money from his hand. Gerard ended up snapping the lad's arm, and then holding him in position until the police arrived. He still had it after all these years.

Archie admired and respected Gerard immensely. He had lived the type of life that he aspired to. And he'd achieved it without having to compromise to other people's whims. However, after five days of sharing tales of derring-do, Gerard surprised him. The conversation left Archie feeling totally dejected. Gerard had spoken to Sandy regarding the suggestion of the veterans rehabilitation centre, and he had agreed to discuss it with Archie.

'Look Archie, the simple fact is it can't do any harm to try. You're clearly a very bright and capable chap.

You can achieve a great deal more with your life than living on the streets, drinking, and taking drugs, if you apply yourself. People only want to help you succeed. To fulfil your obvious potential.' There it was again, the *P* word. He had truly believed that Gerard was a kindred spirit, but apparently not.

'Gerard, I appreciate the sentiment, but I can't stomach it. A bunch of self-indulgent losers, bleating about their so-called struggles. Half of them haven't even been near a proper fight, but still they jump on the bandwagon, expecting sympathy whilst pretending they're heroes. It's a complete fucking joke. I'd rather live anonymously with some self-respect still intact.' For once his gaze had become even more penetrating than the old man's.

'Listen my boy. You need to get over yourself. I know it feels like weakness to accept help, and you think the world can't possibly understand you. But let me assure you, it's even worse than that. The rest of the world simply doesn't care about you one iota, or what you've experienced, as long as it makes *them* feel better. If they can wave their flags, whilst pretending they've done their bit for queen and country, all without risking a single tangible thing, that's good enough. Even better if they can do it all from within the confines of a little, protective, bubble,' his voice began to rise in volume. 'It's not about conceding defeat to them. It's about using them. Exploiting their desperation to bring some excitement into their own miserable lives, whilst extracting what you can from it. Let me tell you, when I returned from Malaya I was in a bad way. We did some things over there that I'm not proud of. The communists played dirty, so we thought we needed to out-dirty them. And we did. Heads left on posts, villages starved to death, homes burnt to the ground.' His agitation made his thick neck flush rouge. 'It was gruesome stuff. When I got back to Blighty, I felt just like you do. Unappreciated, misunderstood, and all that other rubbish. I can promise you, people cared much less about good old Tommy than they do now. I wish we had half the psychological support you have available; it's much easier to mend a body than a mind. So, if they're offering you any kind of assistance, you should bloody well take it. And if it just means using them the way they are using you, everyone's a winner.' Gerard had comfortably reassumed the title of most intense man in the room.

Archie hadn't really considered it in those terms before. Yes, he found it humiliating to accept help. And he couldn't stand the type of people that circulated around those centres. But suddenly it hit him. Perhaps there was another angle to this situation that he could use. For once, he'd been giving some thought to his immediate future, and had developed the kernels of a plan. What those centres did possess, was an abundance of a resource that he would require to put his plan into action. Hordes of vulnerable, impressionable, veterans with nothing left to lose.

CHAPTER 5

Stepping out into the fresh morning air, Archie took a deep breath, and admired the view. This place really hit the mark. The scent of the freshly brewed coffee, emanating from his travel mug, complemented the country aromas surprisingly well. He wandered into the single storey building, and screamed.

'Wakey, wakey, eggs and bakey! Get up you filthy animals!' This was the best part of his day. A couple stirred. The rest tried to ignore the clamour. More drastic measures were required. He lit a cigarette and held it up to the smoke alarm. The shrieking siren activated, making it unbearable to remain in the room. Most of them grumbled, but the occupants eventually prized themselves from their cots to begin the morning routine. Archie simply stood and watched, as each man set about preparing themselves for the day's activities. Two months earlier, even this simple procedure would have been impossible. Collectively, they had come a very long way.

'Once you've finished ablutions, scoff's on in the cook house. Then we're hitting the hills. You've got thirty minutes to get yourselves sorted.' Archie left them to it. He walked over to the small wooden hut that served as the group's dining hall. It was sparsely furnished with cheap salvaged items, but it served its purpose well, and felt homely enough. A large pot of porridge was bubbling on a four ring gas stove. A couple of loaves of bread waited in anticipation by the toaster, accompanied by a tray of condiments, ready to add some variety to the otherwise basic menu. Of course, Tabasco featured amongst them. Archie would wait for the others before he began eating. Mealtimes had become something of a ritual. They were important for maintaining team dynamics. More importantly, he had a challenging day prepared for them, and needed to ensure that everyone had breakfast.

His life had changed dramatically since having been discharged from hospital just over six months previously. The discussion with Gerard, all that time ago, had planted an idea in his mind that he simply couldn't shake. Against the odds, he had seen through his plan, and was now living in the Welsh countryside, en route to achieving his ambition. It had never really felt entirely feasible, but as Archie pursued each milestone, everything just seemed to fall into place. Most of the time, progress had felt almost beyond his control. Once other people became interested, and began offering assistance, the momentum simply carried them along. Gerard had been absolutely right; they just couldn't help themselves. And now, unwittingly, they had placed him on the cusp of fulfilling his intent.

The landscape was rugged, unforgiving, and remote enough to be miles from the nearest civilisation, and therefore any alcohol or drugs. It offered precisely the right conditions for breaking people down. Archie had visited the surrounding areas many times before, during his time in the military, as had they all. He knew it was the ideal location for their endeavour. The dark skies were dissected by rays of bright sunlight that bounced off craggy rocks, and mossy knolls. Gusting winds funnelled down broad valleys, carried with them moisture picked up from the Irish Sea, which was dumped in great swathes onto the lush green hillsides. Here and there, patches of densely packed conifers offered some respite from the onslaught, but were so impenetrable and foreboding, that they appeared a worse prospect than facing the elements out in the open. Perfection.

It was pure chance that he had secured the permit to operate in the area, no small thanks to the generosity of the land owner, who had been struck by both Archie's enthusiasm, and the scope of the initiative he had proposed. It had also helped that the man was a fellow ex-squaddie.

The first of the recruits began filtering into the dining room, helping themselves to great bowls of porridge, and stacks of toast. Steaming cups of tea and coffee littered the tables. Archie had managed to obtain some fresh fruit from the local supermarket a couple of days previously, which was beginning to run low. A large, bald, head appeared from the doorway to the small kitchenette that adjoined the dining area.

'You fuckers better not use all my peanut butter!' the man shouted. His voice was comically high-pitched, and raspy. It really didn't suit the sizeable frame that it emerged from. Pure hate was etched on his face.

'Calm down Uncle Fester. There's loads left,' a small, swarthy guy piped up. He clearly took great pleasure in goading his larger colleague.

'I've told you. Don't fucking call me that, or I'll knock you out.' Unfeasibly quickly, his head had begun turning an incandescent red, whilst he shook a large fist in rage.

'You'll have to catch me first, you fat bastard!' The

small man rose to his feet and began shuffling left and right, bouncing on his toes.

'Come here I'm going to batter ya, you little prick.' His awkward lurch did little to trouble the spritely younger man, who deftly side stepped, putting a table between himself and the attacker. The little guy was in hysterics. Several other members of the group had begun laughing too, only incensing the big fellow further. 'You lot can fuck off and all!' he yelled. It emerged an octave higher than intended. The laughing intensified.

'All right enough,' Archie interjected. 'You don't want to waste your energy on this bollocks, I can assure you. Even if Frank does sound ridiculous,' he smirked.

'Do one Archie. You sound ridiculous, you posh twat.' Frank looked like a bull about to rampage.

'Maybe. But you'll still need your energy. I don't know how else you're going to get that yoghurt body up those hills.' He couldn't help himself. It was just too much fun. Frank stepped towards him, and raised an arm in the air. Archie flinched. The reaction was sufficient to quell Frank's blood lust. A faint smile emerged, and the redness began ebbing away. People turned their attention back to their breakfasts, and a soft hubbub resumed. Archie poured a bowl of porridge, before sitting down on one of the benches next to the small man.

'Abu, you really need to stopping winding him up. It's not good for his blood pressure, and when he does catch you, he'll flatten you.'

'He's not going to catch me. And if he does I'll choke him out.' Abu genuinely believed it. He was the personification of someone with small dog syndrome. It was difficult to identify exactly why, maybe it was his constantly flitting eyes, and jerky movements, but he was a man who gave the impression of always being active, even when stationary. He had earned his nickname from Aladdin's monkey companion, because of the way he constantly sprang around causing mischief.

'You know he can shift when he needs to, and there's no way you're getting your arms round that neck. Anyway, are you prepped to lead the route today?'

'Yeah, all good. I've marked out each checkpoint, and have a couple of cheeky surprises thrown in for good measure.' His wide grin told Archie all he needed to know.

'Cool, but we don't want to melt anyone. It needs to be testing, not impossible,' Archie suggested, unintentionally adopting the tone one might use to talk to a child.

'Don't worry, it's all good bruv.' Abu held out his fist, and waited for a bump in return. Archie reluctantly obliged.

This type of behaviour was pretty common place. It was essential for maintaining a form of equilibrium in the group, and distracted them from the hardships they were collectively enduring. Archie had designed a Spartan regime in the truest sense. Nothing was taken for granted, every privilege earned. Every individual had to contribute or they were gone. It's not like they weren't aware of what they were stepping into; he had been explicit from the outset. Five had already fallen by the wayside, unable to adapt to the harsh environment, or simply too committed to their wayward lifestyles to be redeemable. Archie wasn't fussed. He would rather have nine lions, than a thousand sheep.

'You've got ten minutes. Finish up, and get over to the briefing room.' It was a grand name for yet another featureless room in a rudimentary wooden hut. There was no muttering or complaint, like there had been a few weeks before. Acceptance, possibly even pride, had set in. They knew moaning would do no good anyway. The credos that Archie had instilled was something to be marvelled at really.

Every one of his companions had, until recently, been at their lowest ebb in one way or another. Broken, aimless, dishevelled husks. What he had given them was, by far, more valuable than anything else they had possessed for a long time; a sense of purpose. To a man, and they were all men by design, they had struggled to find their path after leaving the military. Archie had reinvigorated, and re-inspired them. It was this vision that had drawn so much support in the first instance.

After departing hospital he had wasted no time in establishing contact with the rehabilitation group that Sandy had mentioned. They were as expected. Sympathetic, supportive, and completely uninspiring. They had delivered the necessary provisions to survive, whilst failing to satisfy some of the attendees' most basic human needs. After spending a month or so attending classes, he began nurturing his scheme. The concept was simple. Replace what these men had lost, using exactly the sort of regime that had helped to develop their best qualities in the first place. After all, the vast majority of young people joining the military weren't exactly from the most stable backgrounds.

By depriving them of their cravings, and removing all other forms of distraction, he would rekindle their values, based upon a common ethos. It was like rehab on steroids. In other words, recreate the environment that they felt they were escaping from in the first place. Most didn't realise it, but they were completely dependent upon structure. The concept was the easy part. The real challenge was substantiating it. *He* was clear what the outcome was meant to be, but he couldn't market his true intentions and expect to get very far. He had to disguise the scheme as something more palatable. Eventually, he had been able to develop sufficient buy-in so that it became something of a self-fulfilling prophecy. Quietly at first. Then, all of a sudden, his network began to grow, reaching a point where his concept began receiving regional, and then national attention. The coverage unlocked the requisite resources, enabling him to begin turning the vision into a reality.

His original group, if they survived the training, would establish the nucleus of the organisation. They would subsequently recruit and develop further volunteers. Once trained, the pool of manpower would receive ongoing support through the establishment of communal garrisons, where they would be housed and fed, as well as having access to other useful amenities. The majority of the infrastructure would be self-managed, creating further jobs. Once stable, the ultimate aim was that the members of the organisation would be guaranteed employment through partnerships developed with companies such as security, logistics, and events firms in order to sustain the endeavor in the long-term.

It was a holistic approach that would satisfy both their physical and existential requirements. He had registered the charity under the name *Make Ready*; a title that he felt would appeal to the participants, whilst speaking to its purported aim. Although there had been many dozens of applicants for the first rotation, Archie had been discerning with whom he had selected. Men, ideally under the age of forty, without dependents, who were living rough. This had not been possible in some cases, but of the nine that had made the cut, only two had dependents that he knew of, and they very rarely, if ever, saw them. The final selection criterion was that they had to be ever so slightly, bat shit crazy. All nine qualified comfortably. Interviewing them had been quite an experience. After having spent several weeks together, Archie knew he had made the right choices.

'All right gents, today we are going for a walk up and down some big fuck-off hills. You'll be familiar with most of them, but some of them are new territory so make sure you continue to check your nav. You'll also need to bring some paper and a pen. All will become clear at the checkpoints. If anyone has any injuries declare it now, or else you're coming along for the ride.' Abu paced back and forth constantly, occasionally smacking a fist into an open palm for emphasis. 'If you look at the map you can see the route, which totals approximately thirty miles. I expect it to take us no longer than eight hours. Make sure that you bring plenty of water, and your emergency equipment. Any questions?' Abu concluded his brief, before looking towards Archie for acknowledgement.

'It's your show mate. Crack on,' was Archie's abrupt

response. He was keen to emphasise the importance of ownership and responsibility, and so tried to interfere as little as possible with their plans at this juncture in the training.

'Okay, everyone grab your gear. I'll see you at the start point in ten minutes.' Abu grinned, whilst the others rose to their feet and dispersed to grab their kit.

'What do you reckon?' Abu asked, once the others had vacated the room.

'Pretty decent. It was definitely an improvement on last time. Just make sure that you get acknowledgement back from them so that you know they have understood, and consider not moving about too much. I know it's not in your nature, but it can be a bit distracting.' Archie always tried to conclude the briefs with some feedback so that they could continuously improve their performance.

'Fair one. Next time eh? Peace.' Abu held up a V sign and headed out of the room. It was going to be a long day, but Archie was looking forward to being out in the fresh air. He felt most comfortable outside, particularly in the country. Being cooped up in an office all day was his idea of hell. As he stepped out the door, he watched his colleagues busying themselves preparing their equipment. They looked comfortable. This was familiar territory, and the routine brought out the best in them. Bomber was packing the final items into his daysack, ensuring that the straps were adjusted correctly.

He was a heavily built man. Stocky, not very tall, and most definitely not very bright. His skinhead hair cut revealed tattoos etched onto this skull. They blended almost seamlessly into the ones on his neck, which, in turn, blended into the full suit, covering the vast majority of his body. He had acquired them during annual sojourns to Thailand. In fact, he had been married to a Thai woman for a while, but she had left him when she learnt that he previously hadn't been too discerning when it came to the gender of his sexual partners when visiting the country. Or indeed how many he would keep on-the-go at any one time. Hailing from East London, he spoke with a strong cockney accent, which he had not lost despite having spent many years living in Germany. He had been part of a Neo-Nazi group whilst based there, but they had thrown him out. Partly, for not being able to speak German, but mainly for being a complete liability. The Army had been unaware of his involvement with the extremists. As soon as his membership was discovered, it provided the perfect excuse to discharge him, avoiding difficult questions about his many other professional shortcomings. 'You sorted Bomber?'

'Yeah, I fink so. Just need to fill up me water bottles, and I'll be good to go.' He almost always, had an inane grin etched onto his face. The friendly visage had proved misleading for several unlucky individuals, who had subsequently ended up on the receiving end of his hooliganism.

'Good, we need to get going on time, or it's going to be pitch black by the time we return. I'll see you over at the start point.' Archie had been unsure whether he should permit Bomber to join the group. Of all the unhinged men he had selected, Bomber was the least predictable, and didn't necessarily offer a lot in the way of talent, or intellect, in return. However, he was loyal to a fault. And, when it came to the crunch, he could always be relied upon to do the things that others might hesitate to do. Sometimes, only a blunt instrument would do the job, and he was nothing if not blunt. Archie headed to the accommodation to grab his own pack that he had prepared the previous evening.

'I see you've even managed to civilise Bomber. Bravo,' announced a voice full of false platitudes. Marv had a way of making even genuine compliments sound insulting.

'Well, I guess miracles can happen now and again. I'm still working on you.' Archie replied. Marv was a complicated character. Not unlike himself. Highly intelligent, a razor wit, genuine leadership qualities. Unfortunately, he simply could not bring himself to conform, and took enormous pleasure in riling individuals in positions of authority. Invariably, he would outsmart them, belittle them, and then do something or other to actively undermine them, just to expose their weaknesses. What was baffling is that he never did it to further his own fortunes. In his mind, he felt that if someone was going to be filling a position of responsibility, they ought to at least be doing their job properly. And he made damn sure that they knew it.

'I fear that you may be working for some time to come. You'll certainly be the first.' Marv's wry smile was absolutely fitting. He looked a lot like a Bond villain; narrow face, prominent eyebrows, wild eyes. In his day, he had been rather promiscuous, luring women in with his silver tongue, before doing unspeakable things to them. Unsurprisingly, he had never settled down. However, now in his forties, his appetite had somewhat diminished.

'Well, I enjoy the challenge either way. How's the old man bod holding up?'

'Just about clinging on. This had better be worth it!'

'It will be. It's actually not too long to go now before we'll be welcoming the next batch.'

'Bring it on. I'm much happier directing than participating.' Marv shouldered his kit and began wandering over to join the others. Archie located his rucksack in the accommodation, and did likewise. The small gathering looked like a bizarre sociology experiment. Men of all ages, shapes, and ethnicities, had gathered together in a random field in rural Wales. It was quite an accomplishment. Abu called them to order, and they set off apace, along the picturesque valley.

CHAPTER 6

'Come on, we're on the home straight naw boys!' Donald's booming Scottish accent felt entirely appropriate in the rugged environment. As he shouted, a sweaty, groaning mass of trainees, drove the stretcher forwards with renewed purpose. The cumbersome burden, designed to replicate the challenge of extracting a casualty, was a great mechanism for testing their stamina and teamwork. Despite the pain in his lungs, Archie managed a brief smile, as he surveyed the determined faces around him. They were almost ready.

'Dig deep! Let's get this wee bastard back!' Donald struggled to get the words out, but his temporary position of authority as leader for the day, provided him with the extra oxygen required. There were only a couple of days left before the programme would conclude, at which point Archie could brief them on the next steps. Until then, they would focus upon the job at hand.

'Simmo, get up here. I need a change!' A muscular figure appeared at Marv's side, sliding in behind him to take the weight of the handle. Marv moved out of the way. The load visibly accelerated once the replacement had taken up his position. Simmo was the youngest of the group, and by far the fittest. Of Sierra Leonean heritage, he had joined the Army as a Commonwealth soldier during a recruiting surge in the mid-2000s. Softly spoken, and extremely polite, he had quickly endeared himself to everyone. It had been a real surprise to Archie when he learnt that Simmo been kicked out of the military for taking drugs, leaving him stuck in limbo.

Without the funds to return home, he had no alternative but to live homeless. The crime simply did not match the character. However, once Archie learnt of the man's childhood, it made the things that he had personally experienced on operations seem like child's play. Like him, Simmo was probably just looking for an escape. During their conversations, Simmo had described an occasion when some rebel forces had come into his town. He witnessed them publically cutting off both of his best friend's arms, having accused her of stealing from them. She had not survived the ordeal. It was just a drop in the ocean compared to the full range of barbarity he had endured.

'Great work Simmo,' Archie cried out through gritted teeth. Simmo hadn't even broken a sweat.

'It's a gift mate,' came the jovial response. Their camp appeared just around the corner. The sight served as a catalyst, kicking the pace up a notch once again.

'Thar... It is... Keep goin!' Donald was really suffering now, but he attacked the stretcher with the same attitude that he had attacked everything else in life. Glasgow had been an uncompromising place to grow up, and moulded him accordingly. Soon, the metres were eaten up. As they arrived over the line, the group carefully placed the heavy burden down, before dispersing to find some open space to recover. Some bent double with their hands on their knees. Some looked to the sky for salvation with their hands placed behind their head. Most just sprawled on the floor gasping for breath. Marv was dry retching, in between noisy burps.

'Well in chaps. Great effort!' Archie was genuinely

impressed by the performance he had just witnessed, delivered by a rabble of ex-homeless, ex-addict, misfits.

'That was… howling,' Marv spluttered, in between belches. Strings of thick saliva clung to his face and t-shirt.

'All right men. Make sure ya have a drink naw, ya hear me?' Donald commanded. His thick Glaswegian accent intensified by a parched throat. Still, he definitely looked the part. It was like he had been born to roam those hills. A sort of Neanderthal throwback. Barrel chest, thick red-brown beard, burly arms, and messy thinning hair, which was just about clinging on for dear life. Through it, you could make out the scar from the head injury that had nearly cost him his life. It ran almost the full length of the left-hand side of his cranium, carving a long white arc. He had been caught by a piece of shrapnel from a road-side bomb, whilst commanding an armoured personnel carrier in Iraq. His helmet had borne the brunt of the blast, but a slither of metal had penetrated. If it were not for his head being so enormous, the fragment would have almost certainly dissected half-way through his skull.

As it was, he was left with only minor brain trauma, and a diminished ability to process words as a result of his left temporal lobe being damaged. Fortunately, his vocabulary wasn't that extensive in the first instance, so no one really noticed any difference. Once they had all recovered sufficiently, Donald briefed the plan for the remainder of the day.

'Okay. Next up, we're gonnay have a couple o lessons about teachin techniques, and such like. They'll start at eleven hundred, so none o ya hadda better be late.

You'll need ya notebooks and pens, and after lunch your'll be needin ya sparrin gear.' As he briefed, Donald stood with his hands on his hips, and his legs disturbingly wide apart. In political circles, it would have been described as a *power stance*. For him, it was just how you spoke to people if you wanted them to listen.

'Thanks Donald. I'll be delivering the instructional techniques lessons, and Mike will run the sparring as per usual. Has anyone got any injuries from this morning?' Archie questioned.

'Nah bruv, except some serious ring sting.' Abu's helpful contribution received a ripple of laughter.

'I'll look at it later for you mate,' Frank responded quickly. He was the only gay member of the group. The sniggering continued. Frank had been notorious in his day as being the scourge of the accommodation blocks. He had joined at a time when homosexuality was forbidden in the military, prior to 2000. It had not stopped him from either joining, or fully exploiting, the rich vein of opportunity placed in front of him. After the rules regarding sexuality changed, he became increasingly brazen, regularly targeting any of the younger men who might be slightly curious about having a gay experience. Once he had them in his grasp, he did not let them go easily. For once, Abu looked a little sheepish.

'Cool, if that's the only ailment we have, then let's get ourselves sorted out and I'll see you in thirty minutes.' Archie rolled his eyes, before heading for the accommodation block. He had been keen to develop a varied curriculum. Their physical condition was easily improved. In only the first few weeks, most had begun to attain the previous high standards that they were once capable of. A much greater challenge, was rekindling their sense of responsibility and wellbeing, whilst teaching them some new tricks along the way. Mindless thugs were no good to him. Nor were wimpy intellectuals.

If he could reanimate them as motivated group of professionals, focusing their efforts in support of his cause, it would open up a world of opportunities for all of them. The timing for revealing his true intentions would be everything. Too soon, and they would almost certainly walk away. Too late, and it might blow the whole endeavour, or worse still, incentivise them to turn on him. His sales pitch had been written, revised countless times, and rehearsed over and over again. If even a solitary individual didn't buy into the concept, it could lead to a domino effect of dissent, ending in mutiny. That's why he had been careful to trickle snippets of the plan into the lessons. Shaping their minds in preparation for the right moment. He had also identified those individuals who he assessed a being more susceptible to the concept. In quiet moments alone, he had begun shaping them to act as his champions. It was dishonest, conniving, and absolutely necessary for success, as far as Archie was concerned.

He showered and changed, before gathering the relevant items required for the instructional techniques class. Much of it, he had revamped from lessons he had received himself, but had also conducted online research to bring the content up-to-date, making it more exciting and relevant. The group seemed to enjoy them, many having been instructors themselves, once upon a time. Each had had the opportunity to put the methods into practice during the course of the programme. Some were nervous, some were brash, some were downright bonkers, but all had improved. At any rate, the aim of the lessons was really to develop their self-confidence, rather than to transform them into university lecturers. To that end, they had undoubtedly been a success, even if Bomber still couldn't really string a coherent sentence together.

After lunch, they gathered in the barn that served as a makeshift gym and dojo. A Rage Against the Machine song was playing in the background. It provided the perfect soundtrack for their training, and was one of the few choices that they could all agree upon. Archie had been fortunate to find Mike. He was a highly talented MMA fighter, who had represented the Armed Forces at several international Brazilian Jiu Jitsu competitions . He had been on the verge of going professional before injury had forced him into early retirement. One had only to glance at him, to tell he was a man not be trifled with. He was remarkably handsome given the number of fights he'd been in; a true testament to the moniker that the *pretty fighters are the best*. Only a slightly crooked nosed gave away his favourite pastime. For a fighter, he was unusually quiet and thoughtful. In fact, sometimes he went for whole days without ever really uttering a word. But he would always somehow be present, and fully involved in every activity. It meant that when he did say something, people tended to listen.

'When you have them in an arm lock, make sure to continue applying pressure so that they can't reach round and counter,' Mike instructed, firmly but calmly, whilst he levered Jones 59 around so that the class could see.

'Fuckin ell boyo. Be careful. You're going to snap me arm!' 59 grimaced, as Mike deftly manoeuvred him into the position he wanted. He wasn't exactly a delicate flower himself, and had done a fair amount of boxing in his day, but it was nothing compared to the extensive pool of expertise and experience that Mike possessed.

'Now lean your weight into their side, forcing them to the floor.' Mike didn't discernibly move, but a gentle shift of his foot was sufficient to collapse 59 onto the mat.

'Enough, enough!' 59 yelped.

'And now you've got them exposed, it's just a matter of deciding how to incapacitate them.' Mike feigned a kick to 59's groin. The look of panic on the Welshman's face was priceless. 'Partner up, and try it a couple of times each. Once I'm happy you've mastered it, we'll do some striking practice.' He appeared utterly serene. But Archie knew Mike had not always been so mellow.

His favourite example of Mike's infamous Jekyll and Hyde personality emerged during an incident that occurred before he had joined the Army. Mike had once been a bus driver in Swindon. On this particular day, someone had cut him up, before gesticulating at him through the window, and shouting a series of insults; *F this, F that, you blind C, etc.* Ordinarily, he would have let it slide, but that morning he had received some bad news about his father's health, and was in no mood to be messed with. So, with a bus full of passengers on the commuter run, he followed the car for twenty minutes before it parked up in a residential area. He then proceeded to get out, approached the car, and grabbed the unsuspecting driver. Without uttering a word, Mike dragged him onto the pavement, and battered the hell out of him. Luckily for Mike, the incident occurred at a time before the proliferation of smart phones. Most of the passengers sat aghast, whilst others actually applauded his bravery for confronting the little gob shite. The best aspect of the tale was that he calmly remounted the bus, and finished the route, albeit somewhat behind schedule. For his behaviour, he had received fifty hours community service, a hefty fine, and lost his job. Fortunately though, he had not accrued a sufficient tally of criminal offences to prevent him from joining the Armed Forces. Archie was hoping that Mike would become one of his key lieutenants when the time came. If he could manage his emotions, the quiet man absolutely had the wherewithal and presence to thrive.

Jones 59 was a very different prospect. A *Valleys Boy* through and through, he had endured a harsh upbringing. His view of the world had not changed much in thirty years. He still considered most things in uncompromising black and white terms. Either something was wrong, or right. Good, or bad. Someone a good bloke, or a prick. And once his mind was made up, he was not for changing. His father, grandfather and great grandfather, had all worked in the mines, which was no longer an option for him by the time he reached adulthood. The Army seemed like a suitably testing alternative, and he duly joined the Welsh Guards, with whom he enjoyed an unremarkable career, before being injured in an IED strike in 2007. Having been moved into a role working in the stores, his already relaxed approach towards life reached new levels. Eventually, he lost his comfortable job during a round of redundancies, when the Armed Forces were forced to shrink following the conclusion of their two largest campaigns.

Somewhat bewildered, he had struggled to find work back home. His family life had suffered significantly. 59 was the only member of the group who technically remained married, although he and his wife had been long separated. Or to be more accurate, she had left him after he had languished on the dole for too long. The offer of a fresh start with this group was just the opportunity he needed. Archie had certainly not recruited him for his brains or ability. It was his lost soul that made 59 an interesting prospect.

'Simmo good. Abu, make sure you get your feet in the right position. Donald, control your breathing.' Mike circulated around the room checking each pair's technique.

'I'm tryin' te control ma breathing. Believe ma!' Donald gasped. He was panting heavily, due to the exertions of having his body contorted into unfamiliar positions.

'Just relax a bit. You'll get used to the discomfort, and learn what your real limits are.'

'I donnay want to get used to it, and I know ma limits just fine!'

Archie looked on, glad to see them all participating. Some were genuinely excelling. More often than not, he would be paired off with Mike, already having some experience under his belt. He was more than happy to learn from such an accomplished fighter. Equally, it allowed him to apply some direct influence in preparation for Mike's future role.

'They're actually all right. I've definitely seen worse.' Mike nodded his head gently, sneering in approval.

'I was just thinking the same. Certainly a big leap from a few weeks ago. You're obviously doing a good job teaching them mate.' Archie wanted to bring Mike out of his shell. The more he could reinforce success, the better.

'Maybe. It definitely helps that we're fitter now.'

'I think you're being modest. They clearly respect you. Whether you realise it or not, many of them look up to you as a role model.' Archie was laying it on thick.

'Give it a rest. No way man!' Mike retorted, with a wry chuckle.

'Well I'm telling you, you're a great instructor. And you've been excellent with contributing to the other activities.' It was true. In characteristic fashion, Mike would always offer his assistance to anyone who wanted, or for that matter, needed it, without hesitation. From running events, to washing the dishes, he had been utterly dependable. All often achieved without uttering a word.

'Kind of you to say, but I'm just enjoying the experience, and the opportunity to get on with my life. Fingers crossed it leads to something good.'

'I guarantee it will,' Archie replied, patting Mike on the shoulder.

'I hope so. I seriously don't want to end up inside again.' Mike's unpredictable rage had spelt the end of his military career. He had received a custodial sentence following a bar fight that he had been drawn into. For once, it wasn't actually him who had instigated it, but he accepted the punishment as karma for the many others that he had started. Prison had been surprisingly challenging. Not necessarily due to the conditions, or the company. But because of the seemingly endless time to reflect and assess his life, which he had quickly surmised, had not gone as well as it might have. Archie was slightly surprised by Mike's melancholy tone. For the first time, he had seen some vulnerability in the man. It made him feel all the worse for potentially exposing him to a life back behind bars.

CHAPTER 7

They had all gathered in the dining room. A gentle murmur of conversation penetrated the thin walls, although Archie couldn't make out the content. He had imagined this moment for a long time, rehearsing what he would say over and over again. Uncharacteristically, he was nervous and his palms had become clammy. There was a very good chance that all he had worked towards could crumble during the next few minutes. He would be back to square one. Or possibly worse. The sun was setting over the undulating landscape, casting long lines of warm orange stripes. It provided a fittingly dramatic setting for what was to follow. He took a deep breath, opened the door, and entered the cramped space.

'Okay chaps. Thank you for all gathering in good time. I'll try not to be too long, but what I am about to discuss with you is very important so please indulge me. I would appreciate it if you would leave any questions you have until I have finished. I know there are going to be plenty.' Archie examined the faces assembled in front of him. Some were stern, some confused. Bomber was grinning. Occupying a commanding position at the front of the room, he began.

'We have been here for eight weeks now, and I have been tremendously impressed with the progress that each and every one of you has made. Reflecting upon where we started, I think it's fair to say, that many of you are back to your best. Some are possibly even better,' he spoke with a light tone, upon which he could build the drama. 'You came here because I promised you a fresh start. A renewed purpose in life. Although, I suspect most of you signed up to this scheme based upon the assurance of a roof over your heads, and three square meals a day. Those promises remain very much in place. As does the guarantee of employment, on completion of the selection phase; a core element of the *Make Ready* mission. Throughout our training, I have sought to push you out of your comfort zone, and really tried to get you to consider what you ultimately want to achieve. I know that everyone here has had a different journey, but I selected you personally, because I could see that you each have something to offer. Collectively we will achieve great things. I know for a fact, that none of you aspired to end up where you did after leaving the forces. And, I also know, having witnessed what you are capable of, that none of you deserved it.' He still had their attention. So far, so good.

'Unfortunately, society doesn't see that. Any praise or acclaim you received was temporary, and shallow. It was simply a trend to *support our brave lads*. In reality, it only ran skin deep. To be blunt, society sees you, and I, as victims. Helpless souls to be pitied and lamented. It doesn't recognise or appreciate the many talents that you possess, now that you are no longer directly working for their benefit. They don't recognise you as the unique individuals that you are. Simply as a *former* soldier. When you were serving, you were barely recompensed for your sacrifices. When your time came to an end, the organisation that you gave so much to simply moved on, leaving you to fend for yourselves.' Some heads were nodding, others looked increasingly puzzled.

'And when others attempted to assist, they could never really empathise with what you'd experienced. Or what you've achieved. You were simply another statistic to add to their roster. To hold up as an example of their generosity, all whilst exploiting your misfortune. Whether you realise it or not, you are a charity case. A problem to be solved,' he stated with a concerned tone. The atmosphere had grown palpably more intense. 'There was once upon a time when you would have rather fucking died than be considered in that way. None of us ever wanted gratitude, or worse still, sympathy. But we could always hold our heads high. Safe in the knowledge that we had faced, and survived, what the rest of society was simply too scared, or too idle, to confront. It defined us. Shaped us into the warriors that I see sat in front of me now. All of us have lost our way at some point. But every single man here still has that sense of pride burning within them. That's why we're here, and that's what will give us the strength to overcome the challenges that will follow.' Archie paused and surveyed the room again. He knew he had laid it on thick, but hopefully the message would resonate with a sufficient number of them to get them thinking along the right lines. Make them more pliable for what was about to come.

'What are those challenges? Well, when I conceived of this scheme I realised that there is a great untapped resource in this country that should be, no, must be, utilised. Namely, you. Whether you realise it or not, you have a singular skillset that is almost impossible to replicate beyond the type of scenarios you have encountered. I want to harness those skills. To channel them into something for which you will be suitably recompensed and recognised. You've suffered hardships, endured privations, and experienced triumph and failure, in a way that the average person on the street couldn't begin to comprehend. And yet ultimately, you ended up side-lined, marginalised, and redundant. A few months ago, like the majority of you, I was living rough. Actually, truth be told, I was rather content. Booze, smokes, drugs. Nobody telling me what to do. It took me a long time, and a hospital visit, to realise that every minute, of every day, I was being exploited by people far less capable, and far less deserving than I. Drug dealers, wannabe gangsters, thieves, all out to squeeze me for every penny they could. What really got to me in the end was the way they looked at me. Like I was prey to be toyed with and eaten up. And to my deepest shame, I simply accepted it, going along with their game,' he relayed with melancholy in his voice.

'Then I remembered that I once looked at people the same way. Knowing that they were vulnerable, and I was in control. I wanted that feeling again. You know it too. That elevated sense of pride you felt every single day. When you could walk the street knowing that in some small way, you were better than everyone you encountered. That's what I want to offer you. I want to give you back control. The opportunity to, once again, become the predator instead of the prey.' A couple of smiles had broken out. But for the most part, they sat listening stony faced.

'How can I deliver that to you? Well, the first step was to rekindle your spirit, which I believe we have achieved. The next is to offer a suitable opportunity. When you volunteered to be here, I'm sure that many of you were motivated by the chance to help rehabilitate some of your fellow comrades. That remains the case. However, what I'm proposing is a different method to achieve it. One that is higher risk, but much more rewarding in every sense. I want you to help grow an army. One built upon all the skills, talents and values that you possess; discipline, loyalty, courage, selflessness. But instead of others profiting from your sacrifices, it will be an army that will exploit the undeserving scum who once abused you,' he began building towards a crescendo.

'The official figures say there are roughly six thousand homeless veterans in the UK. But that's nonsense. If you simply look at the estimates of how many are suffering with mental health issues, at least fifty thousand, and those in the prison system or probation, another ten thousand, the figure is almost certainly higher. That means that there are almost as many potential recruits out there as are currently serving in the actual Army! I want us to go out and find them, re-train them, and re-channel their energy into something more mutually beneficial.' Suddenly, a voice piped up from the rear of the room.

'Yeah, yeah, yeah. All very nice words, but you still haven't told us what your plan actually is. I've sat and listened to you talking about purpose, and focus, but you've been skirting around the issue the whole time. Just hurry up and spit it out will ya?' Bazza was the last member of the group that Archie had recruited. An eternal pessimist, Bazza had always been something of an oddity in the Army. With a Northern Irish father, and Chinese mother, his heritage was complicated, which was reflected in his general demeanour. A former corporal in the Parachute Regiment, he had been a nightmare for his chain of command. He constantly challenged every decision, whilst actively inciting mutiny amongst his peers whenever the opportunity presented itself. But, he had been a superb field soldier. In fact, had passed Special Forces selection, and was on his way to begin continuation training before deployment on a Squadron. However, before he could join his unit, he was arrested for aggravated assault, whilst celebrating a bit too enthusiastically back in his home town. The ensuing prison sentence had resulted in him being dismissed from service. Archie had expected an interjection. In fact, he was surprised someone had not spoken sooner. He also fully expected that Bazza would be the one to challenge him.

'That is a very fair question Bazza. I was just about to address that very point. If you look at the skills we all possess, honed over years of service, they have some common themes; patience, attention to detail, meticulous planning, the application of controlled aggression. And they all lend themselves perfectly to a profession where I am convinced we could very quickly outperform the current protagonists. Namely, organised crime.' Disappointingly, Bomber was the first to pipe up.

'Fuck yeah! That's what I'm talking about!' he blurted out, unable to contain his glee. Most of the others looked doubtful at best.

'I will elaborate further for those who are understandably dubious. As I previously mentioned, I lost count of the number of times I was exploited by moronic thugs and chancers during my time living rough. Every time I was being assaulted and robbed, I felt myself critiquing their actions, thinking to myself *I could do a better job of this*. There is a rich vein of opportunity out there just waiting for someone more accomplished, and better coordinated, to tap into it. An opportunity to target the countless gangs that are preying upon vulnerable members of society. That, gentlemen, is where we will focus our efforts. Take from them, and reinvest the profit into getting more of our brethren off the streets. Hopefully some of them will join us along the way.'

Marv started laughing. 'You have to be joking mate! What you're proposing is ridiculous. I guarantee that we'd all be arrested or killed within a week.'

'Aye, ya cannie be serious Archie. What are ya thanking?' Donald added to the dissent.

'Before you come to any firm conclusions, consider this. Most of the people in this room have spent some time inside for one reason or another, or at the very least, time in a police station. Invariably, whilst you were there you looked around at your fellow inmates and thought *I don't belong amongst these animals*. And you were right. You were better than them in every way, but you still got caught and ended up in there with them. Why? Because you were careless, enraged, impulsive, or all three at the same time. And normally, I can bet, it was because you were off your tits. They were caught because they are fundamentally inept. If things were different, there's no way you would have made the same errors, and ended up getting nicked. If you had carefully planned what to do, had a team supporting you, rehearsed and executed your plan with precision, and established a suitable exit strategy, I can guarantee you things would have turned out very different. It's the application of those elements that will elevate us above the amateurs who are out there at the moment.'

'But those were pub brawls. You're talking about ripping off some dangerous people. Who perhaps aren't as inept as you suggest,' Marv spoke measuredly, as always. 'This is a huge step to take. The risks are enormous.'

'Yes it is. But once we take it, I guarantee you'll be surprised by how far ahead of the competition we can be. Trust me, I've already looked into it in a lot of detail, and lined up some options. I know that all of you will have fantasized about how you would execute a bank robbery, or something similar. This is the opportunity to make it a reality, whilst hurting those who deserve to be hurt, and helping those who require our assistance.'

'But that was just talk. A problem solving exercise to be worked through. This involves real consequences.'

'Indeed it does, but anything has to be better than continuing the way we were. Helpless victims. We already have most of the things we require in place; premises, transport, communications. More importantly we have things that our competition most certainly does not; knowledge and a highly skilled work force. Don't get me wrong. It will take time and patience to become established. But as our ranks swell, and we gain experience, the risks will invariably reduce.'

'And how on earth do you propose keeping this scheme a secret? The more people that are brought on board, the more leaks that can spring, and the risk of being caught shoots right back up again.' It was good that Marv was thinking it through. It demonstrated that he hadn't completely dismissed the idea out of hand quite yet.

'That's the beauty of it. We don't have to hide. The charity can continue to run as proposed, rehabilitating veterans, and providing employment in a safe haven. Links to firms can still be established, which will deliver the added bonus of providing intelligence gathering opportunities. For example, think about assisting with event security. How easy would it be to quickly identify who was dealing drugs, their distribution methods, where they operated from, who their networks were? And from there, utilising a delivery, or logistics, connection to conduct surveillance, placing us in position without arousing suspicion. The possibilities are extensive.' Archie noticed that some of their expressions were beginning to change. There was a chance this might actually work. Then, Bazza really surprised him.

'Do you know what? I like it,' he said, nodding and pouting his lips. 'Sure, there are loads of issues to work through, and we'll probably get caught or killed like Marv said, but there's some logic to it, so there is. I, for one, am bored of feeling so feckin helpless. At least this way, we take back some control, and maybe help some people on the way.'

'I can't believe what I'm hearing. This is mental.' Marv was becoming slightly irate. 'What you're proposing is criminal, and extremely dangerous. It was one thing taking calculated risks whilst we were in. But now we're on our own. There's no support. No cavalry coming over the horizon. If anything, and I mean anything, goes wrong we're screwed. Surely you agree?!' A hush consumed the cramped, chilly room. Marv looked around in the hope someone would vocalise their concerns. Most of them looked sheepishly at the floor, others to the ceiling, for inspiration. The ticking of the cheap plastic wall clock suddenly became deafening.

'Well, I think we ought to at least look at the possibilities.' Archie was delighted that Mike was the first to speak. Abu quickly added his approval.

'I agree mate. This could be awesome if it works. It's not like we've got much to lose either way.'

'This is mega! I've always thought it would be awesome to fill in some of those scumbags. Fucking bunch of little pussies. They all deserve a good hiding.' Bomber was typically enthusiastic, if not somewhat misguided with his comments.

'Gents, I can assure you that whatever path we take, it will be a carefully calculated one that minimises risk as far as possible. I really don't want to end up locked away or back in hospital. But I also refuse to be a victim again. Together, we can reclaim our dignity. What do the rest of you think?'

'I'm still not convinced. I get the concept, so I do, but it's the details that matter. Where on earth would we start? There aren't too many rich pickings around here, I can tell you,' 59 commented. He made a fair point.

'Yeah. Where are we going to live? What are on earth are we going to tell people we're doing?' Simmo exclaimed, adding to the concerns.

'Fear not. I already have our accommodation and credentials arranged. Everything will be managed through the charity. I can assure you, we won't be based here. However, I'm not going to reveal any further details until we have a consensus. And certainly not before anyone who wants out has left. I need to know that you are committed, and that you won't jeopardise the endeavour. Which brings me onto the covenant.' This was it. The point of no return.

'Covenant. What are you on about?' Frank asked, looking perplexed. Deep furrows had appeared across his wide brow.

'Well, like any organisation, we require a set of rules and regulations if we are going to be successful. This will also apply to the charitable front to make it appear legitimate. The covenant made between you, and the other members of the organisation, will form the basis of these rules. And I must emphasise that this agreement is between you and your colleagues, not with me or some ethereal entity. The consequences are real. Should you adversely impact the safety or security of the group there will be a price to pay. The covenant is very simple really:

My brother before me.
No outsider knows.
Once in, never out.
Do good, always.
Better every time.

All very cryptic I know, but I will elaborate further, once you've decided whether you want to commit.'
Frank began chuckling.

'Archie mate, with all due respect, that's a load of bollocks. *Better every time*, *Do good*. It sounds like a

Save the Children advert, or some shit.' Most of the others sniggered.

'I get it. A bit soft and nondescript, but once I've explained further you will see there is some substance behind them. Also, this is only the first version. If something better emerges they can always be altered.' Even though there were obvious, very understandable, doubts, Archie could sense that genuine intrigue was beginning to develop.

'Look, to be completely honest I'm not convinced, and unless I hear something more reassuring I'll be out of here in the next ten minutes.' Marv remained defiant, folding his arms, and sitting up slightly. 'This is all about the details. Unless you provide some, how are we expected to commit blindly to this crazy proposal? I get that you want to be cautious, but I for one am not risking what little I have left, even if it's just my freedom, based upon what you've described.'

'I'm not going to compromise the security of this endeavour by revealing any further details, I'm afraid,' Archie retorted. 'I know that it's a lot to ask. You're absolutely welcome to leave and continue along your own path. What I would ask, is that you consider this. During all your time since leaving the service, have you ever felt as connected or comfortable with a group of people as you do with the other men sitting in this room? Have you had a single day where you feel you have really accomplished something worthy? Over a short space of time we have forged a bond between us that I think equates to something akin to the trust that you once felt with your former colleagues. And, because of that, I hope you would trust me when I say that I have researched this carefully, prepared meticulously, and would not want to engage in anything that was likely to compromise any person sat here.' Archie did his best to sound earnest. No one spoke for a painfully long time.

'I believe him.' Bazza came to his rescue. 'Think about what he had to do to pull all this together in the first place. I couldn't even have booked the train tickets to get here, the state I was in. Archie's managed to pull off a miracle getting us all to this point, and I trust that he has a plan going forward. The guy's a posh twat after all. And posh twats always have a plan.'

'I have to agree,' Mike added, before falling silent again. 'He is a posh twat.' The quip broke the tension. 'Seriously though, what we've achieved over the last couple of months has been the most I've managed for years, and it's all thanks to Archie. Perhaps we owe him our loyalty for the time being. I think this could be an amazing opportunity if we do it right,' he added in a typically hushed tone.

A few of the men began muttering to each other. The mumbling drone reverberated around the room, quickly rising in volume. Archie remained silent, watching as people became increasingly animated. He had said all he could.

'Gentlemen,' he raised his voice to be heard over the clamour. 'Gentlemen! It's excellent that you all have a view, and I want to give you the opportunity to discuss the proposal with each other. I think it would be best if I stepped out for a while to give you some space. You must consider what I've said carefully. Make up your own mind whether you wish to commit. This is not an all or nothing situation. To reiterate, if anyone wants out, they are very much entitled to depart. However, if you decide to commit, there's no going back. I'll wait outside. I would be grateful if someone could come to let me know once your discussions have reached a conclusion.' He looked around the room, hoping to catch each man's eye, before heading for the door, and stepping outside into the cold, blustery wind.

CHAPTER 8

'There's not much movement after zero one hundred. A couple of them popped out to grab some snacks from the local petrol station, but nothing other than that. The main entrance is definitely covered by CCTV, and there's an approach from the rear garden that doesn't look like it's under surveillance,' Simmo delivered his brief with confidence, making sure to tick off all the boxes on his reconnaissance report. The other men listened intently, whilst occasionally scribbling in their notebooks. They would all be destroyed well in advance of the job, and were only being used for the purpose of committing the details to memory.

'What are the neighbouring buildings used for?' 59 queried, peering over the top of his reading glasses.

'One's a building merchant that closes around eighteen hundred every day,' Mike responded, using a laser pointer to indicate the location on the small model that had been constructed for the briefing. 'The other, is a storage unit of some sort. We haven't seen anyone go in or out for days. I've checked for possible CCTV. There are cameras covering the main and rear entrances to the builder's place, but they're easily avoided.' Abu had the next question for Simmo. Archie was delighted to see them so engaged.

'Any other CCTV on the approach to the site?'

'Yes, along the main road, about six hundred metres to the west. There are other approaches we can use to avoid it, although it does provide the quickest access and egress if we need it. Also, some of the shops along that road have their own cameras, but they're all focused on their own entrances, so they shouldn't be an issue.' The briefing room was spacious and comfortable. A far cry from the rickety shed, which they had crammed into only a few weeks previously. Archie had found the perfect venue for their garrison. A former bank, situated at the edge of Colchester town centre that had been converted into a mix of commercial and residential properties replete with office spaces, briefing rooms, a series of self-contained apartments, and as a bonus, included a couple of seriously heavy-duty safe rooms. The whole refurbishment project had been financed through the charity, which now provided a perfect front-of-house. Casting his mind back to that critical evening when it had all hung in the balance, he reflected on how everything had come close to falling apart.

He had expected dissent and concern, of course, but his colleagues had been much more cautious than he had calculated. During several hours of heated discussion, he had ambled around the training site wrapped up tight in his thick parka jacket, chain smoking cigarettes. Throughout the long night, he tried to keep within earshot of the briefing room, hoping to overhear some of the exchanges. But the breeze had been too strong, carrying away with it the muffled conversations. Eventually, just as the pre-dawn chill had begun to set in, Mike had emerged from the doorway and beckoned him in. They had decided against putting the decision to a vote given what was at stake. In the end, each man had to state his case for and against the proposition before they individually decided whether they were in or out. They had also vowed that if they decided to leave, they would make no mention of the plan to anyone else, out of loyalty to their comrades.

By some miracle they had all committed. It was almost certainly Bazza's influence that had brought them around. Given his ordinarily pessimistic outlook, the passion that he felt for this opportunity had helped to girder the spirit of the more reluctant members of the group. Most dissenters felt that if even he could see the positive aspects to Archie's proposal, it was probably an opportunity that was worth backing. Ultimately, it was their fear of slipping back into depression, discomfort, and isolation, which had proved the most compelling motivator though.

'Any other questions?' Simmo's voice brought Archie back to reality. No one spoke.

'Excellent work Simmo. As you can see the recce team have done a great job, and I'm confident in saying that we have an accurate pattern of life for the target. Next up, Frank will talk us through the insertion.' Archie had instinctively risen to his feet.

'Cheers Archie.' Frank's comically high voice never ceased to be a source of amusement. 'Right, I've sourced some motors with fake plates, and serviced them all personally to make sure they're in good running order.' Frank had been a motor transport specialist in the Army, and was entirely comfortable in his new role. 'I don't want you fuckers ragging them about though, coz it took me bloomin ages to prep them.'

'Any chance you're going to get on with the insertion bit soon bruv?' Abu queried.

'I'm just getting to that, you twat,' Frank snapped back. Good fortune had resulted in the composition of the team being extremely well balanced. It was an aspect that Archie hadn't considered when selecting recruits. In fact, his was probably the only position where his prior experience was not directly relatable to his current one. As a result, they had naturally adopted roles where their expertise complemented each stage of the planning and execution of an operation. Simmo and Mike had served in reconnaissance and surveillance roles. Frank managed vehicles. Marv was a communications guru. Abu had been an engineer with a great technical head on him. Bazza and Bomber were the muscle, and knew how to enter and clear a building. 59 had extensive experience as a medic and storeman. Donald had spent the majority of his career as a logistician. Although they supported each other where required, a natural equilibrium had emerged. It kept things simple.

'As I was saying, we'll be using two saloons and a van to conduct the insertion, with another saloon as a command and support vehicle, held at a stand-off point. We'll depart this location at midnight, utilising the main road until this junction.' Like Simmo, Frank used the laser pointer to indicate the position on a map, which was projected onto one of the walls of the room. It provided a broader overview than the model. 'I reckon it should take roughly thirty two minutes to reach this point with light traffic, having driven the route a few times. It'll be known as Red Spot One. I'll give you all a marked up map to study. Make sure that you don't put any of the waypoints into the satnav just in case the vehicles get lifted.'

From the outset, Archie had continuously emphasised the requirement for caution throughout the entirety of the process. In the military it would be known as OPSEC. Now they described it as *employing some simple common-sense to make sure you don't get fucking caught.* If they did get arrested, their diligence would ensure that there was as little evidence as possible with which the police could assemble a case. Everyone had played the game so far. Frank concluded his brief with a reminder to *first parade* the vehicles; military parlance for ensuring that they were in perfect working order, and wouldn't cause any last minute issues. Bazza stood up to deliver the next portion of the orders, covering the entry and clearance process. He was surprisingly engaging. His Northern Irish accent gave a sense of gravitas to proceedings, which helped to maintain everyone's attention.

'We're going to split into two groups. We'll make simultaneous entries through the side and rear entrances. The first group will be me, Mike, and Archie. The second group will be Bomber, Simmo and 59. Abu and Frank will be on standby as the Quick Reaction Force, waiting in the van in case of any unexpected issues arising. Marv will manage comms from the command vehicle. He'll provide early eyes-on, should anyone move into the area, based at a stand-off position here. Donald will stay with the two saloons, ready to bring up any items we require.' He paused, before going on to describe the building clearance in further detail.

'Once inside, Team One will be responsible for shutting down any security they have in the main warehouse area. Team Two will take the offices and storage rooms. We don't believe that there is a mezzanine floor in the building, but the QRF will be called in to clear that if required, so it will. Make sure that you visually clear all your corners, like we practiced, and look for any concealed areas. Once you've put your targets down, plasticuff and hood them, and then move them to this point.' Bazza pointed to a room on the building schematic, which they had obtained from an old floorplan Abu had discovered on an estate agent's website. They had rehearsed the clearance in an abandoned industrial building, under the guise of conducting team building exercises. Tape had been placed down to delineate the rooms. Mike had run incapacitation drills ad nauseam, so that each man was entirely comfortable with executing them no matter the circumstance. Final rehearsals would occur prior to them departing for the operation, which would help cement every detail in their minds, and ensure that they could perform their roles in complete silence.

'After anyone in the building has been collated in the holding area, Team Two will take on responsibility for locking them down. If the QRF have been called in, they'll move back out to cover the entrances. Concurrently, Team One will begin their sweep for target items.'

Archie had been quite careful to manage expectations. They would only be looking for cash, drugs and weapons; items that should be light enough to extract quickly, could be easily offloaded, and could potentially be utilised during subsequent operations. He didn't expect huge quantities of any of them to be present. This was only their first outing as a team. He had selected the target, a storage facility for a small local outfit, more to focus upon testing their procedures, than with a view to acquiring an enormous haul of bounty. He had become aware of its presence during his time living on the streets, when some of his fellow down-and-outs had visited to score drugs. Bazza continued.

'We believe that the most likely location for target items will be one of the offices to the rear, but we haven't been able to pinpoint a location. So the sweep needs to be methodical. Prioritise lock-up boxes, sealed containers and any safes. Anything that looks like it's going to require specialist equipment to get into, either bypass it if it's too heavy to shift, or move it to this point for extraction.' He systematically covered the rest of the clearance, a few *action-on drills* for dealing with unexpected developments, and asked if anyone had any questions. There were none.

Archie ensured that each man had the opportunity to brief and take the lead for a portion of the plan. He felt that the more personally invested they were, the more enthused and committed they would be to achieving a successful outcome. One by one they stood, moving to the front of the room to address the others. Bomber covered the extraction. It wasn't the most eloquent oratory ever delivered, but it covered all the necessary details in between expletives.

Marv took them through the communications plan. Each man would carry a primary device, which would be an encrypted TETRA radio with covert earpiece. They would also carry a burner mobile as a back-up. Marv's secondary role would be to monitor police channels, providing the teams with early warning in case any response calls were raised. He finished his brief by imploring them not to bring any personal devices, insisting that they hand them into him whilst collecting their radios for the operation.

Abu was responsible for technical details, including the use of an improvised wireless CCTV system, which would be used to cover two blind spots on the site. The cameras would be positioned during the insertion, and monitored by Marv in the command vehicle. He then reminded them of the importance of disabling any internal CCTV they discovered as quickly as possible, before suggesting that they collect any laptops discovered, which might provide valuable intelligence for subsequent jobs. His final contribution was as their resident safe cracker and locksmith, albeit a very amateur and completely self-taught one. He took them through his requirements should they encounter anything too challenging to kick down, or pry open.

59 had developed a fairly robust medical plan given the resources available. Each man would carry a small, but well considered first aid kit, with a more fulsome version held in each vehicle, and a trauma pack in the van. It also included the establishment of a makeshift aid post in their headquarters, complete with saline drips, a range of pain killers, antibiotics, and the necessary implements to conduct very minor surgical procedures. Anything more serious than they could handle in-house would be outsourced to a local private clinic. 59 had made arrangements so that the clinic would employ a suitable level of discretion, whilst providing a more immediate service than the local NHS option. Donald was the last one up. He covered the logistics plan.

'All right lads. I canna see us needin too much scoff for this one, even fat bastards like me should be able to survive for a couple of hours without eating! So I'll sort out a meal for before we leave. Each team will carry the following goodies on top of what ma esteemed colleagues have already covered. Team One, you'll take a sledge, a crowbar, a set of bolt cutters, a head torch, and Surefire torch per man, four sets of detention kit, an extraction bag per man, and an extendable baton each. Dress will be black out from ya head to ya wee toesies, and obviously make sure you're wearin' ya gloves. We don't want any of ya fingers leaving prints naw do we? Check each other before we step-off ta make sure that we're sanitised for any personal material.' His brief continued covering, in detail, the inventory for each team and vehicle. He concluded with the resupply procedure for anything that they required to be brought forward.

Archie was thrilled with the presentation of the plan, and particularly the attention to detail they had all applied. His role was drawing everything together. Covering the post operational activity would be crucial to making the whole endeavour a success. There was an enormous amount at stake. Many, many, things could go wrong. They had focused impressively on the job at hand, but without longer-term goals, their unity would quickly fragment.

'Thank you everyone for your hard work thus far, and your excellent briefs. We have a very solid plan here, which I am confident we can execute as intended. However, I don't need to remind you that no plan survives contact with the enemy, so we must all be prepared to deal with unexpected circumstances. Remember the contingencies that we have discussed.

Just like picking where your next piece of cover would be when out on patrol, you need to continuously anticipate what might appear around the corner.' He didn't need to labour the point. They were all in the zone, and ready to operate. 'This is just the first of many jobs we will be conducting together, so security must remain the absolute priority for every man. We can't afford any injuries. Watching each other's sixes will be key to avoiding any nasty surprises. That goes for both the teams inside, and outside the building. We want to keep unnecessary chatter to an absolute minimum. A silent execution is what we are aiming for, but if you spot something threatening, call it out straight away and deal with it ASAFP.' They had done their homework, and were well aware of what some of the more developed crews were capable of, including sophisticated surveillance techniques, firearms, and even the use of IEDs.

'Once we've extracted, each vehicle will move off to their predesignated location, before converging back here. I already have a buyer lined up for any gear we discover. Donald will be responsible for handling anything else of interest. Cash will be laundered through the charity, and reinvested, helping to fund our future running costs.' From the outset, they had all agreed that this enterprise should not be focused upon personal gain. Each man had signed up to a monthly stipend, proportionate to the success of their operations, which they would only receive after the vast majority of any profit had been re-invested into growing *Make Ready*. All their living expenses were already accounted for, so anything on top was a bonus.

'My final comment is this. Whatever happens I'm enormously proud of what we've achieved thus far. Each and every one of you has really stepped up to the mark.'

'Boring!' Abu instinctively blurted out. They all cracked up.

'Cheers mate, you're welcome,' Archie responded, through a forced smile.

'Remember the covenant: My brother before me; look after each other. No outsider knows; operational security needs to be watertight. Once in never out; you've committed, now we need to see this through as a team. Do good, always; remember this is about the redistribution of wealth from the undeserving to the deserving. Better every time; this is but the first stepping stone on our path to success, there'll be plenty more work to follow and we need to learn from it. Get some head down, and we'll meet back here for final preparations.'

CHAPTER 9

'Standby, standby.' Marv's steady voice rang through their earpieces. Each man steadied himself, mentally preparing in his own way. Bazza and Bomber would be the first ones in. Incredibly, all had gone according to plan thus far. Apart from some trouble getting reception from one of the temporary cameras, nothing unexpected had disrupted the plan.

'Breach now.' The sledgehammers made contact with the composite doors, sending them crashing inwards, before the entry teams silently filtered through, just as they had rehearsed. Archie was the last man in for Team One. They passed through the small hallway, and into the main warehouse. Pallets of boxes lay everywhere, interspersed with discarded packaging. A distinct smell of marijuana hung in the air. The glare from a television flickered through a light haze, emanating from a secluded area to the rear of the cavernous space. They suddenly heard a clattering noise erupt from the same direction.

'What the fuck is going on? Tel, is that you? What have you broken now you prick?' The accent was distinctly midlands. Not a local lad. It confirmed that there were at least two potential adversaries in the building.

Bazza and Mike swiftly closed the gap to the slightly built, middle-aged man. They incapacitated him with a carefully choreographed assault, combining a knee stomp with an expertly administered choke hold. Archie applied the cuffs, gag, and hood. The man didn't even struggle. He stank of weed and beer, and was clearly well on the wrong side of half-cut. As soon as he was subdued, Archie held him in place whilst Bazza and Mike continued clearing the warehouse. Glancing up, it didn't appear that anyone else was in the room, but they needed to be systematic. They had all seen enough movies to know it's always the guy quietly sat on the toilet that eventually catches you out. The two men worked together, visually checking every space as they moved through. Archie couldn't identify any cameras from his position. Within sixty seconds their sweep had been conducted. They returned to Archie, and signalled the all clear.

'One clear.' Archie reported over the radio. A single click of Marv's pressel switch acknowledged that the message had been received. Archie dragged the captive to the pre-determined collection point where any detainees could be easily monitored. He didn't weigh much, and didn't resist, opting to simply accept his fate. Bazza moved to cover the entrance, whilst Mike repositioned in order to link up with Team Two. This felt like the most anxious moment of the operation. Until confirmation to the contrary was received from Team Two, Archie had to assume there were still threats present in the building. Undoubtedly, the other team faced a more complex challenge due to the number of separate areas that required sweeping.

'Two clear,' 59 soon reported, his accent unmistakeable. Archie exhaled. He and Bazza remained in position, waiting to see what Team Two had discovered. The skinny man's friend Tel had been accosted. He was a younger man, judging by his clothes and sleeve tatts. To their surprise, a third person was also present. A woman. Her legs were flailing everywhere as she viciously kicked out, hoping to land a blow. She was putting up enough of a fight for all three of them. Bomber struggled to maintain control of her despite his brute strength.

'Cut it out bitch, or I'll fucking put you down for good,' he snarled with venom. Archie held his finger up to his lips. He wasn't surprised that Bomber couldn't control his emotions. The woman continued writhing. Mike stepped in to assist, locking her free arm in place, and applying sufficient pressure to ensure compliance.

They forced both individuals onto the floor, sitting them next to the skinny man. 59 produced another plasticuff, and proceeded to lock them together back to back, before cuffing their feet. Mike had anticipated that the woman would require restraining during the process, so lay his weight on top of her knees. Each of them was frisked from head to toe, ensuring that they weren't in possession of anything dangerous. Young Tel had a small pocket knife on him, which was confiscated. A couple of disposable lighters were also collected, but nothing else of concern was discovered. Their wallets and cash were thrown into one of the canvas bags, whilst their mobile phones were smashed, after their sim cards had been removed. Once he was content that the immediate threat was neutralised, Archie gave the signal to begin searching.

'Building secure. Commencing search,' Archie reported. He received another single click of acknowledgement in reply. Just as they had rehearsed, Team Two repositioned to cover the entrance, whilst monitoring the detainees. Archie and the other members of Team One dispersed to search their allocated areas. The layout of the building was as they had expected. However, there was significantly more clutter than anticipated. It was as if the inhabitants had simply left items to accrue wherever they could find space, with no discernible storage system in place. Mike was responsible for the warehouse. Archie and Bazza would examine the offices and storage rooms. As they moved to the rear of the building, he was surprised with how well-lit it was. Unfortunately, the clutter continued unabated. It would take an age to sift through everything with such limited numbers. It was time to call in the reserves.

'QRF move in to assist search.' Within thirty seconds, the extra manpower arrived in the warehouse. Simmo pointed them towards the offices, where Abu joined Bazza, and Frank began working alongside Archie. Entering the first room, a small office area roughly fifteen metres square, Archie carefully observed the contents. He indicated to Frank to take the right-hand-side. He would cover the left. Beginning with a small wooden desk, which had an outdated laptop sat on top of it, he tested all the drawers to see if any were locked. None were. He systematically sorted through all the contents, uncovering a small quantity of cash, amounting to roughly £20, and a couple of USB sticks. There was nothing else of significant value. He placed everything into his holdall, and moved on. A filing cabinet in the far corner was his next target. The metal drawers were locked this time. He mentally noted it, and moved on. They would return with the necessary tools during the next sweep. The remaining object was a tall bookcase. It was clear there was not much of interest resting on its dusty shelves. Archie gave it a cursory once over, before deciding his efforts would be better invested elsewhere. Turning around, he could see that Frank was also concluding his initial search. He waited for the big man to finish checking the contents of a cardboard box, before moving on together.

The dimensions of the next room were almost identical to the first one. This time, the space was being used for storage. From floor to ceiling, random boxes had been stacked precariously atop one another. From the eclectic mix of containers, it appeared that most of the items were stolen goods that the gang hadn't been able to shift. Shoe boxes with Nike logos, an assortment of electronic goods, even boxes of Lego, were scattered everywhere. It would take an age to work through them all. Surveying the scarce empty spaces that remained, Archie determined that there were unlikely to be any valuables stashed away. He made the decision to bypass the jumble, indicating to Frank that they should head directly to their final search area.

Re-entering the corridor linking the offices, he noticed the faint purple glow of UV lights emanating from a doorway. It boded well. The final room they had to search was much larger than the previous ones. At least double the size. It had been divided by a series of freestanding shelving units, stocked with an assortment of items for cultivating indoor crops. Bags of fertiliser, compost, watering cans, trowels, forks, and a variety of packets containing seeds. Of greater interest though, were the numerous transparent, vacuum-packed, bags of cannabis leaves resting on the shelves. Archie was sorely tempted to make directly for the prize, but managed to maintain focus. Once again, he methodically worked his way from the left, whilst Frank mirrored him to the right. He discovered only a single cabinet, which was a double-doored metal locker, reminding him of the type that he had regularly encountered in military storerooms. It was padlocked shut. Like the filing cabinet in the first room, Archie took a mental note to return with the tools. Working along the shelves, it was soon clear that almost all the carrying capacity available to them would be required just to transport the bags of cannabis, which would need to be packed away out of sight.

'Q, bring up three more bags,' Archie requested. Donald acknowledged the message, and collected the holdalls from one of the cars, prior to making his way through the entrance. Rather than encumbering himself immediately, Archie decided that they should collectively gather the drugs once they had returned with the tools required to open the locked cabinets. It would be simpler to remove everything at the same time. Frank had already concluded his search, and was waiting by the doorway. Together, they returned to the warehouse to await the others pairs. The three detainees remained sitting in the same position. Thankfully, they had remained compliant. Even the irate woman had calmed down.

Mike had completed his sweep of the warehouse, and had carefully arranged their tools for collection. The extra bags had been deposited by Donald, and were lined up next to the tools. Bazza and Abu were the only ones still absent. The group stood in silence, contemplating their next steps. Waiting was a skill they were well particularly well equipped for, courtesy of their time serving in Her Majesty's Armed Forces. Within a couple of minutes, Bazza and Abu arrived in the warehouse. As they had rehearsed, crow bars, bolt cutters, sledge hammers, and drills were scooped up ready to go to work.

Mike was first to guide their efforts. Silently, he led them to a shipping container in the corner of the warehouse that had been padlocked shut. Frank clamped the jaws of his industrial-grade bolt cutter to the shackle of the padlock, and applied pressure. His bulk was sufficient to chop through the tough steel with very little effort. The lock fell to the floor with a thud. Archie grabbed the lever of the barring mechanism, and pulled it open. As the door creaked, Mike turned on his Surefire torch, and pointed it into the pitch black space. Carefully stored under a layer of protective plastic sheeting, was a pair of Ducati 1098s, finished in superleggera corsa red. Beautiful machines, which Archie would have dearly loved to have taken ownership of. Unfortunately, they were far too cumbersome. Abu entered the container with his head torch to ensure that there was nothing else secreted inside, and quickly confirmed that the motorbikes were the sole contents. Mike shook his head, indicating there was nothing else to collect. It was disappointing outcome given that this was the main storage area. As it transpired, the majority of items were auto parts, associated with the gang's side-line venture in chopping cars.

Archie and Frank were the next to direct the group's efforts. They headed to the first office. Archie pointed out the locked filing cabinet he had discovered. Again, Frank applied the bolt cutters. The cheap lock fell away easily, before Mike stepped in to examine the contents. The only item of interest was a locked cash box. Rather than open it then and there, Mike threw it into his holdall. The coins it contained chinked as they made contact with the metal case. They turned to look at Frank. He shook his head. As there was nothing else to take, they made directly for the cannabis farm.

On entering, Archie pointed out the metal cabinet. It too opened without much resistance. Inside were a further four bags of vacuum-packed cannabis, and two ice-cream tub sized boxes of pills. Bazza held his holdall open, allowing Abu to sweep them in. The combined size of the packages almost entirely filled the large canvas bag. Archie shook his head, indicating that he had not discovered anything else that required the use of tools. Frank led them to an almost identical cabinet the other side of the room. Mike had taken over bolt cutter duty. The doors immediately sprang open once the lock had been removed. Unfortunately, nothing valuable was hidden inside. Frank shook his head, before Archie pointed out the cannabis laden shelving units. They would collect it all on the return leg from Bazza's and Abu's rooms.

A further two items required breaking into; a locked desk drawer, which contained nothing but stationary, and a small but weighty safe about the size of a microwave. Like the cash box, they determined that it would be more efficient to remove the entire safe rather than attempt to crack it open in situ. Frank stepped forward and attempted to lift it off the floor, but after letting out an involuntary grunt, quickly realised that it was deceptively heavy, and immediately placed it down again. Seeing his colleague struggling, Mike stepped in to assist. Between the two of them, they managed to hoist the safe into a comfortable position, and waddled towards the door. It was at this juncture that Archie realised they had underestimated the challenge of transporting all the material. However, he decided to stick with their original plan, avoiding the inevitable confusion that would be caused by calling in further manpower.

As Frank and Mike struggled with the safe, the remaining three men entered the UV- lit room where the crops were being cultivated. Four rows of benches supported long troughs, containing plants that ranged from seedlings, to fully grown specimens. As tempting as it was to begin harvesting the leaves, the task would be far too time consuming, and far too messy. Instead, they focused upon filling the remaining holdalls with the cannabis bags from the shelving units. Just as they were finalising the load, Frank and Mike returned carrying extra holdalls. Within two minutes the shelves had been cleared.

The group shouldered the haul, carrying at least two of the cumbersome bags per man, whilst also grappling with the tools they had brought. It wasn't elegant, but they managed to collect all the items in a single load, some pinned inelegantly under armpits, others precariously cradled across chests. Shuffling along in single file they returned to the warehouse, before unceremoniously dumping their burdens. Fortunately, an access road led down one side of the building, and

Simmo had possessed the foresight to park the van there, backing it in just outside the entrance. It would significantly reduce the distance they would need to carry the items. Forming a chain, they began transferring the load. Holdalls first, followed by the safe, and finally the tools. Everything fitted comfortably into the spacious body of the long wheel base Transit van.

'Load complete. Extracting now,' Archie transmitted. One at a time, they began filtering out of the door, ensuring that someone maintained oversight of the captives. Leaving the three tethered figures hunched in eerie silence, Archie was the last man out reporting, 'Extraction complete. Moving to vehicles.'

The headlights of the vehicles cast long shadows as Abu collected in the wireless cameras. Three of them jumped into the van, whilst the remaining men made their way to the saloons. Donald was waiting in the driver's seat of one of the vehicles with the engine running. He had also ensured that the other car was prepared to make an immediate departure. Once they were all aboard, Archie signalled for them to move.

On receipt of the command, the vehicles rolled off in unison and made for the dispersal point, where they would split. They had concluded during planning that heading to different locations would reduce the risk of being compromised. In the rear seat of one of the saloons, Archie pulled the balaclava from his head, and wiped perspiration from his brow. Outwardly, he did his best to remain stoic. Inside he was buzzing. Someone had connected their phone to the car's Bluetooth and were playing Metallica's *Master of Puppets* at full volume. He had to shout for his final transmission to be heard over the blare.

'Fucking yes boys! Great work. See you back at base.' The entire operation had taken less than fifteen minutes.

CHAPTER 10

Their significant haul was laid out in one of the large windowless rooms of the bank. It had been categorised, and divided into sections. Thirty four tightly packed bags of cannabis, three large tubs of unidentified pills, two laptops neither of great intrinsic value, roughly £350 in cash, and at the end of the long line, the money box and safe. Simmo couldn't suppress a toothy grin.

'Not bad at all lads.'

'Yes. I must say this is pretty decent,' added the ordinarily sceptical Marv, who couldn't help but admire their achievement.

'I can't wait to get that safe open. Let's get Storage Hunters up in this bitch!' exclaimed Abu, poised with his safe cracking tools that he carried in a small workman's bag.

'Calm yerselves ladies. I just need to make an inventory so we don't lose track o this stuff. I'm almost done.' Donald had a pair of reading glasses perched on the end of his nose. He was tapping details into a tablet. Archie sat in a corner observing. Their excitement was palpable. He knew this would be one of the most dangerous periods. Overconfidence and carelessness could very easily set in. He would need to maintain close control of their behaviour to avoid any mistakes. For the time being though, he was happy to let them revel in their victory.

'Hurry up you big Jock twat. I want to get this lot shifted so we can make some moolah, and get on the lash,' Bomber urged, rubbing his fingers together signifying the international sign for money. Donald held up a single middle finger in reply without looking up from the tablet.

'Patience ma simian friend. Patience.'

'Before we do anything else, we'll be conducting a debrief and reset,' Archie interrupted. He didn't want to stifle them, but neither was he going to allow ill-discipline to compromise their success.

'Obviously after that shit's done. But I'm up for a big one. Don't know about the rest of you but I'm getting twatted!' The subtlety of Archie's stern tone hadn't even registered with Bomber.

'Alreet, I'm done. Have at it Abu.' Donald removed his glasses, before delicately tucking one of the arms down the front of his t-shirt. Picking up the bag of tools, Abu rushed to the safe, and went to work. At the same time, Mike grabbed the cash box. Using a screwdriver and hammer, he forced the lock after a couple of attempts. Most of the contents scattered across the floor as it flew open. Inside was a meaty stack of notes, and several coins. Mike scooped everything into a pile, amounting to £2,218, give or take a few pennies.

Archie knew it would take a few days to shift the weed. He also knew that selling such a large quantity would undoubtedly draw attention, placing a large target on their back. However, he had been in contact with his old dealer Todge, and was confident that as crooked as he was, Todge was nothing if not discreet and professional. He could be relied upon to keep their arrangement on the down low. Archie had a rough idea of the value of their take, but until money exchanged hands it meant nothing.

'This nut's a bit tricky,' said Abu, as he continued

grappling with the safe. His tongue was sticking slightly out from one side of his mouth, as he concentrated upon accessing the safe's locking mechanism. He had used an electric drill to create a small opening, through which he could manipulate the pins. As a newcomer to the world of lock-picking, his first project was proving to be a serious challenge.

'Take your time mate. No rush. It's a good opportunity to practise.' Despite trying to sound reassuring, Archie was just as keen as the others to see what was inside.

'Why don't we just smash it with a hammer?'

'Because it wouldn't work you fucking dunce,' Abu retorted, giving Bomber a withering glance, before shaking his head in bewilderment.

'Well hurry up monkey boy. I'm gasping for a pint.'

'Give it a rest and let the man work, will ya?' Bazza had been looking at his phone. 'Anyone fancy a brew?'

The minutes dragged by. Archie had forbidden anyone from leaving the building until they had fully closed down the operation. Mugs of tea and coffee were drained by the bucketful. Several of them lay on the floor trying to get some rest. There had been a couple of false alarms along the way, but Abu hadn't managed to breach the lock by the time the sun had begun rising. After such a long period of inactivity, it came as a shock when he suddenly cried out in triumph.

'Booyah! Finally!' Abu flung his arms into the air. Frank sat up with a start at the exclamation. The others stirred more slowly. The safe's heavy door swung open with a low groan. Gathering round, everyone attempted to gain a vantage point from which they could see inside.

Abu shone his torch into the space, and began extracting the contents, laying them out on the floor behind him. A handful of documents, a small velvet bag, and a meagre bundle of notes, accounted for all the items that emerged. It was a somewhat deflating sight following the prolonged build up.

'Is that it?' queried Marv.

'Fraid so dude,' replied a crestfallen Abu.

'Open up the bag,' Mike urged.

Abu pulled the draw strings open. A faint smile began appearing. As he upended the bag, a cascade of clear stones tumbled into his palm.

'All right. That's more like it!'

'Don't get too excited Abu, man. They could be anything. I'm not sure we'll be able ta shift them, even if they are what you think they are. I don't know about you, but I'm not mates with any jewellers. Particularly not one we can trust,' Donald stated, in an attempt to bring them back to earth.

'Why would they lock them up if they're not worth nothing bruv? I reckon they're the genu-wine article. We'll definitely be able to find someone to check em out.'

'Let's not worry about it for the time being,' Archie interrupted. As lucrative as the discovery may be, Archie didn't welcome the distraction. 'Donald, get them added to the inventory with everything else. We'll store them for now, whilst I try to identify someone who can help us out. Nowadays I'm pretty sure precious stones will be traceable, so let's be cautious. There's plenty to be getting on with for the time being.'

'Fair enough. Let's call it a little rainy day fund.'

Abu returned the stones to the bag and handed it to Donald, who had already made an entry on his tablet.

'Good work with the safe mate. Next time try not to take all night though.'

'Whatever Marv. Next time you do it, rather than sitting about wanking over your radios, whilst the rest of us are out grafting.' The two of them had formed an antagonistic, yet good-humoured, relationship, from which neither could possibly back down.

'Yeah, it's lucky I had a picture of your mum to keep me company.'

'Bravo chaps. Good stuff. As amusing as this all is, let's get the debrief done shall we?' Archie gestured towards the door inviting them to move to the briefing room. Over the course of the following few hours, they conducted a thorough after action review, systematically discussing what had occurred. They occasionally paused to reflect upon what had gone well, and what needed to be improved for their next outing. Some were willing to contribute more than others, just as Archie had expected. He was keen for them all to voice their opinion, encouraging openness and honesty, telling them,

'Leave any judgements at the door. Someone may have messed up this time, but it could just as easily be you next time. Let's learn from our experiences, and move on.' There weren't too many points to pick up on. Those identified, were generally not too serious. The positioning of the vehicles could have been better. The preparation for extracting the items was not as good as it should have been. Certain individuals had critiqued their own micro-transgressions, many of which had not even been noticed. Archie was disappointed that

Bomber had not highlighted his error when handling the woman. He raised it himself. Bomber actually looked quite hurt. They all agreed that the neutralisation of the occupants had been extremely well executed, and that the reconnaissance phase had been thorough, setting them up for success. These were things that they would maintain going forward.

'Thank you for your candidness gentlemen. I hope you feel that was worthwhile at the end of a long night. You know what needs to be done now in terms of storing and reconditioning the kit. After that I suggest we all get some kip. I've taken the liberty of booking us a private table at a decent restaurant for some scoff and drinks this evening. I know I don't have to remind you about the need to remain low key. Yes, I'm looking at you Bomber. If you want to get turned inside out you can do it here behind closed doors.'

'I'm fucking planning to mate.'

'Of course you are. I might even join you.' Looking at the rest of the room, he continued.

'Once your assigned responsibilities are sorted, give me a shout, and we'll help each other out to get everything finished as quickly as possible. Just so you're aware, I'll give my contact a call now about shifting the weed. Once he's confirmed the details, we'll work out the plan for the exchange.' They all looked absolutely knackered. 'Awesome work tonight. I think it's fair to say we're off to a good start. We'll begin hunting down the next opportunity ASAP.' With that, they dispersed. Archie took out his burner phone and sent a message to Todge.

CAN YOU TALK? CATCH IS IN

He then returned to the room where the items had been laid out, to assist with their storage. As he entered, Donald and 59 were already busily scurrying back and forth.

'What do you want done with the broken safe?' enquired 59.

'Good question. We don't want to leave it out for the council to collect! We'll probably need to dump it in a river once it's been wiped down.'

'No problem Archie mate. Leave it with me and I'll get it sorted.' Archie knew that the understated Welshman could be relied upon. 59 had come on leaps and bounds from the drifting, hopeless, character that he'd first met.

'Don't worry about it until tomorrow though. It's not doing any harm at the moment.' Donald was scooping up three or four bags of cannabis under each freckled arm, and ferrying them to the safe room. He had erected storage shelves to help categorise the items, which were already filling up rapidly with the bulky cargo.

'You want a hand Don?'

'Aye absolutely.'

It didn't take them long to get everything stored away. Donald had even installed cubicles for smaller loose items like the cash and the jewels. He clearly took great pride in his role. Archie always wondered what motivated people to fulfil positions that he had always considered pretty dull. But seeing the Scotsman in action, made him realise just how crucial they were to success.

'Squared. Let's check on the others to see if anyone needs a hand.' The majority had completed their individual tasks. On top of their own kit, each man had been assigned responsibility for collective items. Marv had collected the radios, and placed the batteries into their charging cradles. Abu had disassembled the camera kits, and collected in the laptops. Between them, Bomber and Bazza had packed away all the tools. Simmo and Mike were reconstituting the detention kits. Only Frank was still working on the vehicles. The phone began buzzing in Archie's pocket.

'All right mate? What have you got for me?' Beneath his smooth tone, Archie could discern an edge of excitement in Todge's voice.

'A sizeable load of weed, and about three kilos of pills that I'm yet to identify. I think we'll need to discuss terms in person. There's quite a bit to shift.'

'What's sizeable?'

'I'd estimate sixty to seventy kilos.'

'Holy shit. That is sizeable.' An unnervingly long pause followed. 'Okay, I agree we should meet. I'm going to need some time to get the money together. How about Tuesday morning?' It was early Sunday morning. They had decided to conduct the raid on a Saturday evening, when it was most likely that their targets would be out enjoying themselves.

'Sounds perfect. I'm looking to move it as quickly as possible. Quietly, like we discussed. Can you still manage it?'

'Definitely. I don't want any attention either. Trust me. Mum's the word. I'll send you the details of when and where to meet tomorrow.'

'All right, cheers. Speak soon.' Archie hung up, and returned the phone to his pocket.

CHAPTER 11

'It's great seeing the set-up in the flesh. It's remarkable what you've achieved in such a short space of time.'

'Thank you very much. Honestly the experience has been a real pleasure. We have a great team in place who've been extremely enthusiastic. They've been absolutely instrumental in developing the foundations of the organisation.'

'Well I think you're being too modest. It was your energy that got *Make Ready* off the ground in the first instance.'

'I couldn't agree more. It looks like you're well set for development going in to the future. Are you able to talk us through your proposal for the next steps of the project?'

'Absolutely. I'm excited to announce that the next training camp will be running from the beginning of next month. We have a further batch of ten personnel attending. They will become the core of trainers, delivering subsequent courses. Concurrently, we will be identifying a further site for development, with a view to converting it into a garrison similar to this one. It will most probably be located somewhere in the north of England. Meanwhile, the existing team will continue focusing upon marketing and recruitment efforts.'

'How about links with businesses for subsequent employment?'

'We have four contracts in place, and are in discussions with another two prospective companies. So far, two logistics firms, one security firm, and a facilities management agency, have signed up. I'm confident that this number will swell once we have increased our pool of manpower.' Archie was perched on the edge of his swivel chair, wearing an inexpensive, but well fitted, dark grey wool suit. Despite a change in circumstances, he hadn't forgotten how to dress well when the occasion demanded. One of his elbows rested on the edge of the conference table. A hand propped up his chin, as he carefully surveyed the board or trustees assembled in front of him.

Marcus Talbot-Smith was the chairman. A retired lieutenant-general, he was surprisingly affable, and nowhere near as pompous as many of his station could be. Archie was in fact, very fond of him. Marcus had been his former commanding officer. They had grown close during an operation in the Balkans early in Archie's career, where he had been appointed as Marcus's driver. Marcus had immediately recognised Archie's talents, but like so many others, had failed to successfully channel them. They had remained in touch on and off ever since. The secretary was a very different proposition.

Billy Crowther was a career civil servant. He had spent the majority of his miserable life working in the Home Office. The man revelled in his minor position of power. Archie disliked him from the instant they were introduced. A limp hand shake, and terrible shoes, told Archie all he needed to know. The man was an absolute handbrake. But Marcus had insisted that he was brought on board. Unfortunately, Billy was a necessary evil, and in fairness, was effective in dealing with the significant, and extremely dull, administrative burden.

The three remaining trustees were Helen Duke, a

surprisingly cheerful accountant who was married to a naval officer. She fulfilled the role of treasurer. Farouk Malik, a successful local businessman and councillor. And Sarah Schofield, a teacher and mother, whose son had committed suicide as a result of PTSD, as well as an assortment of other mental health issues.

'I may have another suggestion for you. I'll set up a meeting so that you can deliver your brief to them at some point in the next month or so.' Farouk was very well connected, although often unreliable. Archie feigned interest, doodling in his notebook. His suspicion was that the offer was only being made for the sake of appearances. He smiled politely.

'That's great, thank you.'

'I must say I was very impressed with the boys who showed us around. They were very confident, and obviously committed. I wish Luke had had the opportunity to join you. Things may have turned out differently for him,' Sarah managed in a broken voice. Her eyes had begun to tear up. Thankfully, the mousey woman managed to compose herself. She was always going on about her precious deceased son, who by all accounts was a bit of a waster. Quite frankly, Archie was sick of hearing about him.

'I'm sure he would have been a great addition Sarah. I'm glad you liked the chaps. They've all been working really hard to make this a success.' In truth Archie had been very selective about whom he had introduced them to, and of course where and what they had been shown. He had finally begun to understand why, when his former units had received visitors, he had always been kept somewhere hidden out of sight, on the off chance that he said something a little too honest.

'Perhaps we'll get a chance to see the training camp at some point? It seems a little inefficient to keep several premises on-the-go at once. Couldn't you relocate everything here?' Billy questioned.

'Absolutely, you must take a trip down. Hopefully you'll get an appreciation as to why you can't conduct our programme in a town centre. Maybe we could even take you for a brisk walk over the hills.' They chuckled. Archie wished he could strap thirty kilos to Billy's back, and absolutely beast him. It would quickly wipe the smile off his smug face.

'Well, just let us know a convenient day, and I'll make the necessary arrangements.' Billy stopped laughing almost immediately. There was no humour in his eyes.

'I'll do that Bill,' Archie responded, knowing how much he despised being addressed by the nickname.

'I think that concludes our business for today. Billy, if you can just recount the action points so that we are all clear, it would be most appreciated.' The chairman mercifully drew things to a close. Billy ponderously read through the comprehensive list of points he had taken. Archie subconsciously let out a sigh of relief. This was a major milestone that they had overcome. It bought them some breathing space for the future. Certainly until the next quarterly gathering. Billy eventually concluded.

'Archie, thank you again for hosting us today. It has been an absolute pleasure, and on a personal note I'd like to say how proud I am of what has been accomplished. Let's get the next date in the diary. I think a neutral venue would be preferential.' They all stood, and after a brief period of small talk, began filtering towards the exit. Once the others had departed, and just before he himself headed out the door, Marcus caught Archie's attention.

'Archie, I need a word please,' Marcus demanded, his ordinarily light tone suddenly becoming more serious.

'Of course. What is it?'

'Your father has been in touch with me. He was after an update about how you're doing. He said you haven't been in touch for years. He's concerned.' Marcus's penetrating gaze bore right through him.

'No he isn't,' Archie replied curtly. 'He's prying. If he were that interested in my wellbeing he would have contacted me a long time ago.'

'I think he caught wind of what you're doing from your brother. I can assure you, he's simply keen to catch up. Trust me; I speak from experience when I say it's not easy being a parent in our line of work.' His expression had changed ever so subtly. Could Archie detect a hint of regret? Very uncharacteristic of the assertive man.

'Excuse me, but bollocks. We all chose our paths, and it doesn't excuse his disinterest when things weren't quite so rosy. I don't blame him. No one ever enjoyed success without making sacrifices along the way, but it's been like this ever since Eton. Oh, and he's always resented me joining up as a Tom. I've never lived up to his expectations. That's the simple truth. If he wants to talk, he can come and see me in person. He knows where to find me.' His tone remained flat, unemotional.

'Well, that's very disappointing, but not entirely unexpected. I'll let him know. You've always been a stubborn little bastard! Anyway, let's try and get together before the next meeting. Perhaps we could grab a drink in town at some point?' Archie knew the old man wouldn't judge him. He had always been much better at making the effort to support his children, particularly during his numerous prolonged absences.

'That sounds smashing. I'll let you chose a date. My schedule's probably more flexible.'

'No, no. I'm retired now remember.' The heavy set, yet elegant man, nodded his head, before striding purposefully out the door.

Once he was out of earshot, Archie gasped thinking *Thank fuck that's over with*. What a difference a week had made. It was crucial to uphold pretences. These board meetings needed to remain one hundred percent credible for the cover to succeed. Undoubtedly, maintaining the balancing act was going to be a challenge. As their ranks swelled, the charitable front would become increasingly self-sufficient; a plausible, sustainable, venture.

On the other hand, the chances of their criminal activity being discovered increased exponentially. Archie had been grappling with the issue ever since they began planning the first job. Thus far, he hadn't been able to identify a solution to the problem.

Thankfully, the deal with Todge had worked out reasonably well. In the end, they had been able to shift all the cannabis. Albeit, at a slightly deflated price from what Archie had hoped for. He realised that they were never going to receive a street price for such a large quantity, but the final figure of £5 a gram was roughly fifty percent of what he would have paid as a buyer. Todge had been very open, candidly talking him through the figures and logistics involved. In fairness, it had all made sense. Yes, the smooth talking drug dealer would make a healthy profit for himself. He had not attempted to mask the fact. The simple truth was that selling in bulk at a reduced price to a single, reasonably trustworthy, source, was undoubtedly worth the convenience and improved level of security, when compared to potentially more profitable, yet significantly higher risk, piecemeal arrangements. Besides, Archie didn't really know of any other suitable options.

Unfortunately, the pills would require further research before they would be able to settle on a price. Despite Bomber's offer to sample them, he thought it would be better to leave it to Todge to conduct some more scientific research. For the time being, they remained secured in the safe.

All up, the cannabis had netted a profit of £340,000. Depending upon what the pills turned out to be, they might fetch up to £25 a gram wholesale price if they proved to be MDMA, which was the most likely candidate. Between them, the boxes contained roughly 3 Kg; a further £75,000. When combined with the cash that they had obtained during the raid, in the region of £3,500, it would mean a potential total haul of £418,500. That didn't include the gem stones, which they would get valued once a suitable buyer had been identified. Archie had already put Marv on the case to solve this conundrum.

Every penny would be channelled back into the charity, once they had extracted a small quantity to cover their living expenses. *Not too shabby at all*, Archie reflected. He knew there was plenty more out there for the taking.

CHAPTER 12

The ten new recruits were an utterly miserable sight.
Assembled in the driving rain, they turned their heads
away from the wind, tucking their chins into their chests
in an attempt to avoid the chill as best they could. They
looked like a flock of dishevelled penguins.

'Alreet ya bunch o reptiles. Get yer swedes up and
start sparkin. This isn't day one!' Donald's booming
voice cut through the howling torrents that swirled
around them. He had adopted his power stance. His
tight fitting maroon t-shirt clung to his body
accentuating his paunch. Honestly, he looked ridiculous,
but he couldn't care less. 'Y'all volunteered to be here,
so stop ya drippin and get after Simmo!'

The athletic man had already begun making his way
up the steep slope situated beside them. Reluctantly,
they began trudging up the slippery pathway, struggling
to close the gap. Archie watched on with interest from
the warmth of the safety vehicle. He had his head
phones in and was relaxing to a Portishead track.
Listening to music had always helped him think.

The latest batch had been subjected to the same
process as the initial volunteers, slightly tweaked based
on the feedback received from the first course. He had
been just as careful to filter them suitably. Ever since
the charity had officially launched, following an
extensive and quite costly marketing campaign,
applications had skyrocketed. As a result, the whole
administrative and vetting process had been a nightmare.
It had become abundantly clear that the ten *originals*
would not be equipped to manage the volume of work,

whilst concurrently delivering the training, supplying manpower to businesses, and, of course, conducting their clandestine activities. They would weather the storm for this iteration, but the future division of labour would need to be considered carefully.

'Keep going. Don't make me come up there and burst yer heeds!' Donald shouted, cupping his hands around his mouth helping to project the threat. He needn't have bothered. There was no way they could hear him over the racket of the howling gale.

Archie's thoughts returned to more pressing matters. They had identified their next target. Preparation had begun already. They would fully commit once the course had been completed in a couple of weeks' time. Splitting manpower was not ideal, but necessary. He, Donald, Simmo, Bomber and Mike, had relocated to Wales to deliver the course. The remainder had remained in Colchester.

The latest opportunity had emerged almost by accident. In the course of sourcing a suitable buyer for the jewels, Marv had established a strong relationship with a man named Benji Sheftel, a jeweller based in North London. During one of their meetings, he had overheard a conversation regarding the establishment of a new supply-line, transiting blood diamonds from Liberia through Antwerp, and onto the Port of Tyne in Newcastle. The processed diamonds were being used to fund a variety of criminal ventures in the north east of the UK, ranging from the distribution of drugs, to people and arms trafficking. Nonchalantly, Marv had asked Benji what he thought of the situation. As it transpired, the dealer was disgusted by the inflow of new product.

Not because of the activities they were funding, or indeed their unsavoury source, but because they were deflating his prices. After probing a little further, the flamboyant Sheftel had divulged that the enterprise was predominantly being managed by a Polish group. They had emerged as the dominant force in the area during the previous few years, having overwhelmed the local outfits through sheer numbers, whilst exploiting their extensive continental connections. The London dealers were becoming increasingly reliant upon their goods to remain competitive.

The stones that the group had obtained during the first operation had come through this channel. In total, they were holding 16.5 carats of cushion cut diamonds. Sheftel offered them £1,500 per carat, which they had accepted. Another £24,750 to add to the coffers. More importantly, he had divulged, in detail, the name and location of his northern supplier, complaining that the flood of cheap goods appeared to be increasing. Archie immediately dispatched Abu and Mike to conduct a reconnaissance in order to confirm the details. It didn't take them long to pin point Benji' source, easily tracing him to the Pole's main distribution centre. He had made no attempt whatsoever to cover his movements.

What they had reported back was mouth-watering. Despite his supposed aversion to the gems, when offered the possibility of purchasing more, Sheftel was very quick to leap upon the opportunity.

So it was, Archie sat pondering possible courses of action in the passenger seat of a battered Land Rover Discovery, half-mesmerised by the sound of the wipers squeaking across the windscreen. There were no easy options. Unlike their first operation, this would require a temporary relocation to make it viable. Donald and Frank had been given the task of developing a sound logistics solution, including options for establishing a suitable base of operations. Meanwhile, Bomber and Bazza had begun investigating methods for conducting the raid. Neither group had managed to achieve a great deal prior to the commencement the course.

The hiatus had left them enduring an uncomfortable, but necessary, period of purgatory, awaiting the opportunity to refocus their attentions. Only Archie had really had any freedom to look ahead. The others were far too embroiled in their day-to-day roles. The prospect was a significant step up from their first endeavour for a variety of reasons. Not least amongst them, was that the Poles appeared to be an altogether more professional bunch. Better organised, better equipped, more of them. However, they were bound to have a weak point. Between them, Archie was confident that his team would find it.

'Come on. Watch your footing!' Simmo yelled, cruising down the hill. The others were strung out behind him, struggling to keep pace. This latest group contained a few very interesting characters, who Archie would almost certainly bring into the fold at a suitable juncture. For the time being, he had determined that they should predominantly be utilised to manage future courses, and run the front-of-house charitable activities. But before any of that, they needed to survive the selection process.

Later that evening, he delivered a brief to the newbies. They would subsequently utilise the content to plan and brief their own fictional operations, whilst being cross-examined by the instructors. A type of roleplaying termed *planning exercises*. They were a great vessel for testing an individual's attention to detail, and mental agility under pressure. Most struggled, never having previously endured the experience, crumbling under the withering deluge of questions. A couple, however, stood out. They had remained calm and precise throughout the ordeal, providing the panel with thoughtful responses. Archie and the others were genuinely impressed. Theirs were names to note for the future.

Similar to the first intake, this group came from a wide assortment of backgrounds. Most had been living rough, some were addicts. Almost all of them suffered from mental health issues. Notably, one amongst their ranks was a woman. She was one of the pair that had performed exceptionally well during the planning exercises. Archie was keen to ensure that individuals were selected on merit alone, and she had unquestionably made the grade. As much as it would be good to diversify, the simple fact was that there had not been many female applicants. The demographic simply was not readily available in comparison to their abundant male counterparts.

As the recruits went about their evening routine in preparation for the following day's challenges, Archie gathered his instructors together for a discussion.

'Whilst we have the opportunity, I thought it would be useful to update you with regards to our next operation.' It had been a while since they had considered their alternative life. Mention of it had resulted in their immediate, and undivided, attention. 'As you know, we haven't been able to dedicate much attention to preparation up until now, but with the conclusion of this course looming large, and things quietening down back up at Collie, I think we can begin to pivot. I've been in touch with the others, and asked Abu, Frank and Marv to focus upon surveillance and logistics in greater detail. They'll begin their research at the end of this week.'

'Shouldn't we at least get this course out of the way before getting distracted elsewhere? Those guys are going to have plenty to do closing down the course, and sorting out the admin for this lot,' Simmo suggested, whilst pointing a thumb towards the recruits' accommodation.

'You're absolutely right. That was my concern too, but they've assured me that everything is in place. 59 and Bazza can sort it between them. Unlike the previous job, we're working under a little more time pressure on this one,' Archie relayed. 'The shipments are reasonably regular, and we need to be set to move well prior to the next one coming in. The longer we're away, the more suspicion will grow, so all the prep work needs to be wrapped up as soon as possible, although I don't want to compromise the surveillance or rehearsals. I'm going to convince the trustees that we need to identify the site for the new garrison, whilst expanding our marketing up north. They should buy it without too many questions, giving us the window to temporarily relocate.'

'Any idea when we're going to get it done? I can't wait to go and give them dirty Slavs a good slapping.' The others looked at Bomber in disdain. It was difficult tolerating his opinions. Despite being chastised numerous times, the message simply wouldn't penetrate his thick skull. Archie ignored the slight and continued.

'Not precisely, no. We certainly aren't doing anything until we have a decent plan, and rehearsed it thoroughly. However, from what Marv has uncovered, the shipments generally arrive around every four months or so. He should be able to get an insight through surveillance of Sheftel's supplier, who happens to be his cousin. His visits to the site tend to ramp up significantly prior to a consignment arriving. That will be the trigger for us to move.'

'It all sounds a wee bit ropey ta me. What if ya man is increasing his visits fer some other reason?'

'Yeah. That, and we have to trust that fucking jeweller.'

'Give it a rest Bomber,' Archie snapped abruptly, whilst Simmo simply shook his head. 'A very fair point Don. Luckily, we can utilise the manifest to get an idea of when shipments are arriving from Antwerp. At this stage, we're not exactly sure which vessel they use, or if there is any consistency to the transit, but hopefully we can begin to narrow down options. I'll be the first to admit, this is nowhere near as straightforward a prospect as our first junket, but the rewards could be very significant. Based on Sheftel's estimates, they move around three to five million's worth of stones through there, per delivery. Not to mention anything else they may have lying around.' The figure certainly had them interested. A huge amount could be done to grow their cause with that sort of money, comfortably covering their running costs for the rest of the year.

'When you say this is a step up you're not kidding though,' Mike added, deciding this was the right time to interject. 'I've seen the place and it's no gift. Not even close. These guys look well-coordinated, and we're pretty sure that at least a couple of them are carrying.'

'You're absolutely right. We will need to continue being careful. Develop suitable contingencies. Safety and security remain firmly at the top of our list of priorities. However, if we do it right, I'm absolutely convinced that this is achievable.' He knew that they would come on board. He could see it in their eyes. The lure of adventure was too great for them to resist. That aspect of their personality could not be extinguished, even if they were now a little older, and allegedly a little wiser, than they used to be.

They continued discussing the plan for a further couple of hours, fuelled by strong coffee, and the prospect of solving the conundrum. Once satisfied they had covered as many angles as they could, based upon the information that they had to hand, Archie thought it would be a good idea to get some sleep. They had another long day ahead of them. It wouldn't be fair to the recruits if they didn't receive the level of investment that they deserved.

'All right chaps. Let's knock it on the head for tonight. I think we've already managed to come up with some decent ideas despite the lack of information available. Hopefully, we'll have plenty more to work with once we've established some consistent eyes-on. Anyway, I'm heading for my pit. See you bright and breezy.'

CHAPTER 13

Over the course of the following two weeks, the recruits continued developing impressively. They were challenged in ways that they had not been for several years. The process reinvigorated their sense of self-worth, preparing them to become fully-fledged members of *Make Ready*. One recruit had been a borderline case, but he managed to perform sufficiently well during the final exercise to convince the instructors that he was worth a shot. Now, the majority of them had relocated back to Colchester. A skeleton crew, comprised of three of the new members, remained in Wales to manage the site, preparing for the next batch.

In many ways, the injection of personnel was welcome. They were immediately put to work, helping to run the administrative functions of the charity. This gave the original group significantly more breathing space, which allowed them to focus on their next operation. The additional bodies did however, put a strain on the infrastructure. The sooner an additional site could be identified the better.

The vanguard had already deployed. Individuals retained the same responsibilities that they had undertaken during the first job. Mike and Simmo had initiated a thorough surveillance plan, building up a pattern of life for both the target location and the dealer. In order to make the process more efficient, Abu had installed a covert camera over-watching his premises. Donald and Frank had worked on locating a suitable temporary base location. After an initial struggle, neither of them being familiar with the area, they had managed to locate an old garage and workshop situated on a secluded site at the edge of the sprawling Kielder Forest. Unfortunately, it had a number of drawbacks: the distance from the Port of Tyne was far from ideal, there were very few creature comforts, and the real estate was limited. However, the landlord had been happy to agree a short-term lease without asking too many questions, and it was not overlooked by any other premises. These two factors alone more than made up for the shortcomings.

Concurrently, Archie and 59 had been visiting potential sites for the new barracks. The investment of resources helped to keep up appearances if nothing else. They had initiated their search around Leeds because of Archie's vague familiarity with the city. 59 had also been posted to Catterick Garrison for a few years, so he also possessed a reasonable knowledge of the area. Between them, they could at least begin narrowing down options based upon accessibility, suitability, and affordability. So far, they had found three decent possibilities. One was in the city centre, the other two were slightly further afield. At this stage, Archie was content to continue browsing. He certainly didn't wish to commit until their next operation had been conducted. It wasn't until a further three weeks had passed, that they were in a position to fully commit their attention northwards.

Collectively, they had worked hard to make the garage as comfortable and practical as possible. It would be their home for the next month or so. Frank had ample parking space for the small fleet of vehicles, which now included a couple of SUVs, an upgrade from the saloons. A functional briefing room, a well-stocked store room, dining area, dormitory, and ablutions were quickly established. CCTV had been installed to provide early warning of anyone approaching along the gravelled road that led to the premises. Rehearsal space was available in the main garage hangars, but they would need to utilise some of the adjacent woodland for more extensive practice.

Maintaining a constant over watch of the two locations of interest was an intensive, but necessary, pursuit. Archie estimated that they would require roughly two weeks to establish a thorough pattern of life, and a further two weeks to plan and rehearse, before conducting the job. Having their schedule determined by the arrival of the precious stones was sub-optimal, but he had factored in some extra time as a buffer, should anything unexpected arise. Working as two man teams, they conducted eight hour shifts watching the targets, whilst Donald and Frank managed the barracks, and conducted essential maintenance work.

As exhausting as the effort was, they managed to establish a semblance of routine, and acclimatised relatively quickly. They had been sure to identify a number of different positions and methods for conducting the surveillance, whilst also rotating vehicles in an attempt to minimise suspicion. So far, it had proved successful, although there was a scary moment for one of the teams watching the distribution site when a jittery man had knocked on the car window in the early hours of the morning. Emerging from the gloom, he had approached from the rear of the vehicle. Bazza and Marv had no chance of spotting him. As it transpired the man was simply an enthusiastic dogger with a poor sense of direction. The car park he was after was a couple of miles down the road.

Archie had paired up with Bomber. He hoped to obtain a better insight as to how the man's mind worked. If it worked. He also wanted to keep an eye on him to make sure he didn't cause any trouble.

'I am so fucking bored of looking at this building,' Bomber moaned.

'I know mate, me too. But it's a necessary evil if we want this to be a success.'

'Yeah, I know you're right. Still, I wish something interesting would happen.'

'Like what?'

'I dunno. A punch up, someone getting a blowie, a car crash. Anything.'

'Maybe.' Archie indulged him. Their time together hadn't actually been as painful as he had expected.

'There's only so many times you can watch the same vans and trucks come and go without going mental,' Bomber continued complaining, whilst he fidgeted in his seat.

'It's all important intelligence though. I think we've absorbed a lot of information. Almost enough to move on with the planning.'

'I fucking hope so. I really do. I'm pretty sure that the Stasi gathered fewer details than we have.' For such a dimwit, Bomber possessed a surprisingly comprehensive knowledge of random facts, particularly regarding military history. It was something of a passion for him. He was also an enthusiastic conspiracy theorist. Over the course of the days they had spent together, he had regaled Archie with endless tall tales plucked from somewhere in the deepest recesses of his mind. The topics ranged from the sublime to the ridiculous. Some had a modicum of merit to them. The vast majority were absolute nonsense. At least it helped to pass the time. More interestingly, Archie had learnt a great deal about the man's past. It was no wonder that he had developed into such a disturbed individual.

Bomber had been fostered at an early age and grew up in one of the less affluent suburbs of Woolwich in East London. One of seven children, his early life had been one long competition; a competition that he had rarely won. It was a mystery as to why his foster parents had elected to take on a role for which they were so singularly ill equipped. They constantly resented the responsibility, and possessed neither the means, nor the patience, to successfully raise one child, let alone seven. The monthly stipend that the council paid them was the main, possibly only, allure. Meal times were a particularly sad affair.

In one story, Bomber recounted how the children were required to share the milk for their cereal. As the youngest, he had always been the last to receive the dregs. Washing was a similar story. In order to save money on heating bills they were only permitted a bath a once week, again sharing the grimy water. It was always tepid by the time it came to his turn. More disturbingly, they had been confined to their solitary bedroom, locked in there for hours on end, so that the parents could avoid entertaining them, instead choosing to while away their time at the local social club. More often than not, they returned pissed-up and belligerent. It was during this period that Bomber had really begun to acquire his xenophobic views. Archie had listened with fascination.

Like most young men, as Bomber became a juvenile, he sought some form of community. A local group of skinheads had taken a shine to him, and took him under their wing. Bomber junior had loved it. He trained with them in the gym, drank at their club, and at weekends, made the fortnightly pilgrimage to Bermondsey to watch his beloved Millwall FC play. After the match they would routinely beat the shit out of any away fans they managed to corner. He was fourteen. Following several years of non-productivity, he had finally been persuaded to join the army by one of the old codgers down at the club, who had informed him,

'I loved my time in the forces. Plenty of booze, plenty of fighting, and plenty of fanny. You're a big lad. I reckon you'd do well.' That was all Bomber needed to hear. The following day, almost on a whim, he had walked into the local recruiting office and signed up. Only the infantry or pioneers would have him based on his mental aptitude scores. He chose the infantry because of the higher likelihood that he would get to bayonet someone.

Back in the car he was spinning yet another farfetched yarn.

'Anyway, did you know that Bin Laden isn't actually dead?'

'You surprise me. Let me guess. Is he in fact, in disguise, masquerading as Donald Trump.'

'Nah, mate that's a bit unrealistic. The Americans actually had him working as a consultant for years in order to fuel anti-Islamic rhetoric. Even the Iranian president Ahmadinejad said he's got evidence proving it. Fucking worked too didn't it? He's actually living under protection in Pakistan in case they need to whip up some trouble again,' he stated matter-of-factly.

'If you say so,' Archie sighed in response. The sun had begun setting. Visibility wasn't great. He pulled the night vision scope out of its bag and flicked it on, bathing the foot well in dim green light. Only another two hours until their shift was over. 'Fancy some coffee?'

'Yeah. I'm absolutely gasping.' Archie took out the thermos flask and poured each of them a cup. Bomber seized it enthusiastically, before unexpectedly surprising Archie.

'Listen mate. How the hell did you end up doing this? I mean, you're bright, you're confident, I reckon your family's got some money judging how bloody posh you talk. I asked one of the other fellas, and they said your dad's a diplomat or summin. What's the crack?' This was the first time Bomber, or indeed any of them, had thought to ask Archie any questions about his childhood. So far, they had simply taken him at face value and gone with the flow. He had been caught completely off guard.

'Well, we've all had our struggles. I'm no exception. After I left the army I didn't have that many options. Honestly, I wanted a break from all the bullshit. Plus, I absolutely adored taking drugs. I started up *Make Ready* because I'd had enough of feeling like a victim. It's just like I told you all whilst we were in Wales.'

'Yeah I get all that, but what about before the army. I know you've travelled a bit, from some of the places you talk about, and there's no way you visited them all whilst you were serving. You wouldn't be able to afford it. And I've heard you went to an expensive boarding school. From my experience, only people with no other choice join up. You could've done loads of other jobs.' This felt very uncomfortable. Archie hated the idea of his past dictating how people regarded him. He had worked hard to cast off the image of an entitled little rich boy.

'Maybe that's true, but I always had a calling to serve in the military. I thought it seemed like a place where you could work in the fresh air, and make a difference. Oh, and because you get to blow shit up.'

'Why didn't you join as an Officer?'

'Honestly? I didn't want the responsibility. Most of them sit behind a desk and chase a career. I wasn't interested in either. I wanted to have the authentic experience.'

'Fair enough. That doesn't explain the travelling and school though.' Archie wasn't entirely sure why he was so averse to opening up. Habit perhaps? It seemed very odd that he would be having this type of conversation with a man like Bomber. Perhaps it was time to expose a small chink in his armour. After all, this entire enterprise was built on trust.

'Well, to cut a long story short my father was, actually still is, an ambassador.'

'No shit.'

'Yes shit. I spent my childhood being dragged around various countries across the world. Some were great. I loved my time in Indonesia for example. Others, not so good. Venezuela springs to mind.' He took a sip of coffee, before looking down at the floor, collecting his thoughts. The car smelt utterly rotten. Two adult male humans couldn't be confined in such a small space, for such a long period of time, without leaving their mark.

'Once I was old enough, I was packed off to boarding school to join my two older brothers. It wasn't really my scene. Most of the other kids were complete twats. Entitled little scrotebags who were only there because their parents could afford it, not because they had a single active brain cell in their skulls. They rode on a wave of snobbery, which the school worked hard to reinforce. *We would be future leaders*, they kept telling us over and over again. I couldn't stand the elitism. There were people all over the world with real problems that I had witnessed first-hand. These pricks were living in a bubble.' The recollections were making him genuinely irate. He took a deep breath before continuing, not once looking Bomber in the eye.

'I started looking for ways to escape the mundane existence, and began drinking and smoking dope. In fact, I established a pretty decent little business, selling small quantities of weed to the other kids. It wasn't long though, before one of them grassed me up. The school didn't hesitate in expelling me. My father was furious. It was particularly bad because my two brothers were excelling. I had let the family name down, and was promptly moved onto another, less prestigious school. Not the most harrowing back story really in the greater scheme of things. From what you've told me about your childhood it was an absolute gift!' He raised his head to see Bomber's reaction. There wasn't really one. His piggy eyes remained as vacant as ever.

'Yeah, it don't sound too bad at all really. Probably a bit of a wasted opportunity, if you ask me.'

'Yes. Yes, it probably was,' Archie replied morosely.

'Do you fancy some scoff? I made up a couple of ham and pickle sandwiches.'

'That sounds like a fine idea. I'll put on some tunes. What do you fancy, Architects or Trivium?'

'Architects mate. Let's keep it British shall we?' Their taste in music was one of the few interests that the two men shared in common. It had helped to develop something of a bond between them. Bomber reached behind his seat, and rifled about in a bag, before producing two foil parcels. He handed one to Archie, and tore open the other. They sat in silence for some time, munching and watching. Archie occasionally lifted the night scope to his eye when it looked like something of interest might be occurring. They logged any pertinent information on a tablet for subsequent reference. If something really significant presented itself, they would take a photo using their Nikon camera, which was fitted with a high power lens.

'This is still fucking boring innit?'

'It sure is. Only an hour to push.'

CHAPTER 14

The black SUV skidded to a halt in a cloud of dust. They debussed, and ran over to the van. Its rear doors were already propped open. Mike grabbed one set of the stretcher's handles, Frank the other, whilst Donald held aloft a saline bag. Lying on the stretcher, Simmo's shallow gasps sounded painfully labored. One of his lungs had probably been punctured. His eyes were closed, but a grimace of anguish was plastered across his face. He clutched his arms around his chest, hugging himself for comfort. The ordinarily chirpy man was undoubtedly suffering. Marv opened one of the garage doors, and they rushed Simmo into the makeshift surgery. Within seconds, he had been transferred onto the elevated cot bed that served as an operating table. Donald flicked on a powerful LED lamp, and cut away the patient's clothes, enabling better access for an assessment. A thorough inspection revealed only a single puncture wound. Painful, but not life-threatening if treated immediately. A narrow slit, about two centimetres long, was situated just at the bottom of his ribcage oozed with blood. 59 donned a set of surgical gloves. Then, taking a sterile wipe, he cleaned the area. As soon as the blood cleared a fresh surge replaced it.

'Pass me that tray,' he commanded Abu, firmly but calmly, who had stepped in to act as his assistant. Although a reasonably competent medic, 59 was acutely aware of the limitations to his knowledge and skills. He desperately hoped that this case was not too complicated.

'There you go bruv.' Abu handed over the plastic

tray that carried an assortment of medical instruments and dressings. Taking another wipe, 59 cleaned away the blood. This time he managed to intercept the ensuing pulse with a thick piece of gauze.

'Hold that in place and apply pressure.' Abu obliged. The Welshman gently pressed around the wound, checking that nothing had broken off inside. Thankfully, it was clear. Once content, he picked up a clamp from the tray.

'All right. On the count of three remove the gauze. One. Two. Three.' Abu removed the gauze. Blood began to ooze again, but 59 used the clamp to stem the flow. 'Okay. Reapply the gauze.' They had managed to assemble a pretty comprehensive inventory of medical equipment. Effective anaesthetic, however, was not one of the items they had been able to procure. 59 leaned over Simmo's face.

'All right mate. I'm going to stitch you up. It's going to sting a bit but you're a big strong lad, and I know you'll be able to handle it.' Simmo briefly squinted his eyes in acknowledgement, before returning to a grimace. 59 assembled the necessary items on the tray.

'Again, on three. One. Two. Three.' He washed the area with an alcohol solution, before wiping it down again with an anaesthetic wipe. Then, he removed the clamp, and began stitching. Simmo's automatic response was to recoil, shifting uncomfortably on the bed. However, after taking a deep breath to compose himself, he managed to remain still enough for 59 to finish the job.

'Abu, grab me one of those dressings, some surgical

tape, and a medium roll of compression bandage will you?'

'Sure thing.' Within a couple of minutes, 59 had applied a neat dressing. They covered Simmo with a blanket, and moved him to the dormitory to recover. Archie relaxed slightly. For the first time since arriving back at base he had the opportunity to reflect. *What a fucking mess.*

It had all been going so smoothly until they missed the solitary bloke smoking out back. Sloppy. Very sloppy. They all knew that this job was going to be a tough ask. However, the weeks of preparation and planning had made them confident that it could be achieved successfully. Each man had contributed in the same fashion that they had during the first operation, adding their own expertise to the process. As always, it was the cumulative effect of small details that had resulted in a larger error. Each stage had been choreographed and rehearsed with precision, but of course not every eventuality could be accounted for. And as well practised as they were in dealing with the unexpected, things could always come and bite them in the arse. Unfortunately, on this occasion, they had been bitten harder than anticipated.

'Let's leave Simmo to rest. Everyone grab a brew and get yourselves into the briefing room. I'll see you in fifteen minutes.' The adrenaline was wearing off. Archie felt utterly drained, but he knew they needed to analyse what had occurred whilst the events were fresh in their memory. The main thing was that the mission had been achieved. They had obtained what they had sought. At least they believed they had. Until a full inventory check had been completed, they couldn't be sure.

Archie made his way directly to the draughty garage, taking a seat at the head of a wooden trestle table. The frigid space felt as if it sucked in and trapped the cold. He donned a down jacket to ward off the chill. Whilst scribbling a few notes he was unexpectedly disturbed by Mike.

'Do want a tea mate?'

'That would be smashing. Julie Andrews please,' Archie requested, using a slang term for tea, white, none.

'No problem. I'll bring it through in five. Don't beat yourself up. It was a good plan. These things just happen.' Mike gave a slight shrug, before hurrying back out the door. Archie didn't have time to respond. Maybe he was right. But one of his team had been injured. It was not something he could easily brush off. *Better every time.* Not this time though. Soon, they had all congregated in the cold, dim space. Some remained visibly wired. Others had completely emptied their tanks, making even simple movements looked painfully laborious. Each found a suitable perch, and then they collectively began to reflect.

'Okay. From the outset I want to say thank you to all of you for the way you conducted yourselves tonight. Things went awry, but you responded admirably. Although Simmo got hurt, I believe that he'll make a full recovery. We can be thankful it wasn't worse.' No one really wanted to be in that room, at that moment, but they all knew the process would be beneficial in the long-term.

'Let's take it from the start. Phase one, the insertion.'

They followed their tried and tested review process. It was systematic in order to ensure that each stage of the operation could be fully analysed, minimising the likelihood of missing any important details. The methodology was necessarily deliberate so that it would work even when they were fatigued. As it transpired, the insertion portion of the operation had been very successful. All teams had made it into position without a hitch, just as they had rehearsed. This time the vehicles were kept closer. The teams had been reshuffled slightly because Frank had picked up an injury. Donald had stepped into the QRF to cover the gap, whilst Frank managed the resupply. Otherwise they had maintained the same composition.

The site of the target building was a vast industrial complex not far from the port. A sizeable multi-storey brick property of Victorian construction positioned at the edge of a small collection of almost identical buildings. The dated structures sat nestled within an ocean of more modern warehouses and workshops. It made the classic architecture look all the more impressive. One of the key concerns had been that the multiple site users would interrupt their entry and exit. Thankfully, most of them were involved in artisan trades, and as a result, they operated solely during daylight hours.

'Standby, standby.' In exactly the same manner as the first job they had stacked up, awaiting the command from Marv. It was 01:30. The QRF had established a favourable position overlooking the main entrance. Surveillance had identified that the gang was utilising only the top two floors of the building. The other floors were let to other tenants. Rather than using a ground floor entrance, which would mean traversing through the other levels, and potentially triggering individual alarm systems, it made more sense to break directly into the target from above. This meant getting access to the roof. It also meant lugging all the requisite equipment up there. Given the portable nature of the target items, they had assessed that the compromise would be suitably beneficial. Mercifully, a set of fire escape stairs had been attached to the exterior of the old building in order to comply with modern regulations. It made the ascent very straightforward. A solitary CCTV camera had to be disabled en route, which was easily dispatched using a can of spray paint. Once onto the roof, a fire escape door could be pried open, enabling access to one of the internal stair wells.

'Breach now.' They knew that the floors were occupied. The lights were on. It was estimated that there would be four to six individuals inside based on the pattern of life they had developed.

'Breaching.' With a loud crack, the door gave way under the force of a crowbar. The teams filtered in, and made for their target rooms. A building of this size was a big ask for only six individuals, particularly with two floors to cover. However, with sufficient speed and aggression, they were confident that any threat could be neutralised. Working through the top floor first, they encountered two individuals who were playing Call of Duty on a games console. One looked up at the last moment.

'Kim jesteś?' he demanded with anger in his eyes. Before the man could move, Bomber was on top of him. Simmo incapacitated his companion. They looked like twins. Perhaps they were. Both were stocky, sporting the same tightly cropped hair and beard combo that seemed to be ubiquitous amongst young men at the time. Rather than take any chances, they employed their extendable batons. As Simmo connected with the first man's neck, Twin Two let out an angry yelp as Bomber struck him. Both dropped to the floor, making it easy to apply effective arm locks. 59 cuffed and hooded both of them. The Twins writhed furiously, in a desperate attempt to break free, to no avail.

Simultaneously, Team One cleared the floor below. It was predominantly being utilised as a recreational space, judging by the contents. The floor contained living and sleeping areas, a makeshift gym, and even a well-stocked bar. They encountered a solitary individual, snoozing on a plush fabric sofa. Empty takeaway cartons were strewn across the coffee table positioned in front of him. Judging by his size, he had polished them all off single-handedly. He had Bose noise-cancelling headphones on, which were connected to a tablet lying by his side. The sound of a muffled hip hop song was faintly emanating from them. Mike pounced on him, flipped him over onto his front with a little difficulty, and forced his face into the cushion. He had no chance.

Once content that all the occupants had been debilitated, they assembled them in the spacious room where the Twins had been located. Each was comprehensively searched, revealing that each both the Twins were carrying an identical flick knife. The most offensive thing the big man was carrying was a pack of Skittles. The teams were more than a little surprised that they had only encountered three individuals in situ. But the clearance had been sufficiently thorough that they were content to continue with the search. The Twins desperately continued attempting to break free. Tirades of muffled expletives were being masked by their gags.

'At that point I decided we were good to move onto Phase Four. Bazza, can you talk us through it from your perspective?'

'Our team split up as per the plan and proceeded to our designated rooms. All of the doors were open, less for the boss man's office so it was a pretty quick process. We didn't find much of interest in any of the side rooms, so Five Nine kicked through the locked office door, so he did.' Once they had entered the room, it became immediately obvious that it was where the stones were regularly sorted. A desk topped with a soft black neoprene material was strewn with an array of diamonds. The table lamp next to them emitted a crisp white light, which was the only source of illumination in the room. Next to the gems lay the paraphernalia required for inspecting their quality. The Poles had almost made it too easy.

'We didn't hang about. I gathered up all the stones I could find. At the same time, Simmo went through the desk and other cabinets. We grabbed the laptop, a Pelicase that looked interesting, a small safe, and a ledger that might give us some ideas for future targets.'

'When was it the fourth bloke appeared?' asked Marv. He had not been inside the building, and was keen to get the details.

'It wasn't until we left the office and were heading back to the consolidation point that he came out of

171

hiding. Simmo was the last man out the room. He was moving a little slower because he was carrying the holdall containing the loot.'

'Where was he hiding?'

'I'm not sure. We thought it may have been in the adjacent room, but it wasn't really obvious. What we know now, is that he had come up the rear stairwell after having finished having a smoke in the alleyway.' They had known it was a blind-spot, but couldn't do much to address the issue. There had been no way of positioning either a camera, or a person, to observe the area without running a significant risk of being observed.

'He must have noticed something was wrong, and stayed out of sight until one of us was isolated.' Abu interjected.

'At least he didn't notice something was wrong until he was inside. If he had more sense he could have notified someone.'

'Perhaps he did, but we had already exfilled before they arrived,' Marv responded. There were a number of eventualities that could have occurred. Any number of things could have gone desperately wrong from that critical juncture. As it transpired, he had not informed anyone else. He simply saw red after realising that they had intruders.

'Let's stick to what we do know.' Archie didn't really want to indulge in speculation. They needed to stay on track.

'Well, the next thing we heard was Simmo shouting, and the noise of the two of them crashing against the wall. It was only a partition. They almost went right through it. Five Nine and I immediately turned around, and headed back down the corridor to assist Simmo. We took out our batons, and went for the bloke. Simmo had slumped to the floor. We could see that your man was carrying a knife, so I swung and connected with his arm. He dropped the knife. Then Five Nine came in, and cracked him one on the side of his head.'

'He dropped straight away. I reckon I put a decent dent in his skull,' 59 added. Unbeknownst to them, the young lad he had struck was in a coma. It was one that he would not emerge from.

'Because we didn't know what we were dealing with at that stage, I decided to call in the QRF.'

'I think it was probably the right call. Anyone disagree?' Archie surveyed the room. No one had a counterview.

'In the meantime, we searched and secured the fella. He didn't move. We recovered the knife, but no other weapons. Then I dragged him into the room with the others, whilst Five Nine did what he could for Simmo.'

'There wasn't much I could do at that stage, like. I checked him over, and applied a dressing and pressure to the wound. As you know, he was conscious throughout. At least he could move under his own steam, so I helped him to the consolidation point.'

'QRF. How did you respond?' Abu answered Archie's next question.

'As soon as we got the call, me and Donald made straight for the entrance. I took out the CCTV whilst he smashed through the door. As soon as we stepped through, the alarm went off. At that point, we realised it was all about speed, and didn't bother trying to be too careful about cameras or anything. We legged it up the main stairwell for the top floor. You were there to meet us at the entrance.' Archie had pre-empted that they would need to gain access, opening the locked entrance door on their behalf. 'After you gave us a quick sitrep, we moved to cover the entrances to make sure no one else could get inside whilst you guys started collecting everything for the exfil.'

After each man had described what had transpired from their own perspective, the debrief moved onto cover Phase Five, the extraction. Because the operation had turned noisy, they had already made the decision to exit through the main entrance. There was a higher risk of leaving evidence behind taking this approach, but it would be a much quicker option for vacating the building, rather than scrabbling over the roof tops where further injuries may have been incurred. The building alarm was already blaring. It was only a matter of time before a security contractor, or the police, arrived to have a look.

Thankfully, Marv had not picked up anything on the scanners. The decision to park the vehicles nearby had been enormously helpful. It didn't take long to board them once they were clear of the building. Simmo was loaded into the van first. By this stage he was really suffering. He could barely walk. Having learned from Donald's example, Frank had already started the engines of all three vehicles. After Simmo was comfortable, the tools and holdalls were stowed, quickly followed by the teams. Driving carefully within the speed limit, they made their way to the dispersal point. Unfortunately, Simmo's injury had forced an alteration to the plan. The van made directly for the temporary base rather than following the pre-planned circuit, whilst the other vehicles continued on their designated route, checking to ensure that they were not being followed. Archie placed his hands on his knees and leant forward in his seat.

'Right. I think that's enough for one day.' They had covered sufficient ground to identify several important lessons. He stood up slowly, drawing the after action review to a close. 'I know it's really late, and we've had a very long day, but you know what still needs to be done.'

'Of course we do, don't we lads?' Donald responded cheerily. He could always be relied upon as a bastion when things were getting tough.

'Yep, let's get this shizzle sorted. Someone get Simmo, the lazy bastard. Now I know why he got himself stabbed up!'

'Nice one, mate,' Bomber chuckled. Within a minute, they had dispersed to begin packing away all the equipment in preparation for their departure. Archie was adamant that they needed to be out of the location as soon as humanly possible, even if it meant forgoing any time to rest. They would review their plunder back in Colchester. There was nothing they could do to alter it anyway. Each man knew their responsibility.

Without further discussion, they loaded up the vehicles. The final job was to clean the site, before a final sweep to ensure it was sanitised of any potential evidence. The whole process took under an hour. Simmo was the last item to be loaded. Rather than unceremoniously dumping him in the rear of the van, which was already filled to the brim, they had saved a row of back seats in one of the SUVs. Carefully, he was transferred from the stretcher into the vehicle. The broad Sierra Leonean barely fit in the cramped space, but it was the best they could do under the circumstances. He was covered with a sleeping bag, and 59 travelled with him in the front passenger seat, just in case of any complications.

Once they arrived back at base, one of the key points on the to-do list was find an off-the-books doctor that could give the injury a proper examination, given that the chance of infection was extremely high. Frank locked up the premises and mounted his vehicle. He would return the keys a month later. Sufficient time should have passed by then to avoid suspicion. It was a bitterly cold morning. The sun had begun to rise, burning bright red in the clear sky. Beams of light penetrated through the treeline behind the garage, stretching out over the countryside and bringing the frosty fields to life. Gravel crackled under the tyres of the heavily laden vehicles as they pulled away. Exhaust vapour hung in the air for a moment, before quickly dissipating, taking with it the final trace that they had ever been there.

CHAPTER 15

'Okay. Let's see what we've got shall we?' It was three days after the operation had concluded. They had been forced to wait for an opportune moment when their new companions would not disturb them. Everything they had secured was laid out in front of the group, just like it had been following their first job. Only this time less space was required. Much less space.

'It's probably best to start with the stones, me thinks,' Marv stated, as he poured the contents of the velvet bag out onto a large tray, being careful not to spill anything.

'Jesus. That's dead on, so it is,' commented a grinning Bazza, admiring the sight. Marv casually fingered the pile of stones pushing them around the tray.

'I don't even know where to start.'

'Maybe try and separate them by size or something? Or maybe cut and uncut?' Abu suggested.

'I'm not sure there's even any point. Why not let Sheftel do it?' Marv replied, before Mike voiced his support.

'I agree. We're not really sure what we're dealing with. Let the expert sort them out.'

'Nah. No way mate. I think we at least need to know how many we got,' Bomber interjected. As much as it pained Archie, he was inclined to agree with him. Possessing even a vague idea of their value would put them in a much stronger position to negotiate. In the end, a compromise was struck. The stones would be counted and weighed. Marv would conduct some initial research to ascertain an outline price, before contacting Sheftel for a more in-depth valuation.

'Donald. Get them secured, and let's work through the rest of the stuff.'

'Nae dramas pal.' He closed the lid on the tray and took it to the safe. The shelves had been looking particularly bare since the cannabis had been sold.

'How about the safe next?' Abu asked. He was clutching the small metal box with his tools at the ready. Disappointingly, there had been a much larger safe located in the boss's office. But there was no way they could have transported it with them, and it would have taken an unacceptably long time to crack on site.

'Sure. Why don't we try getting into the Pelicase at the same time?'

'I'll give it a go,' Simmo offered. He had made a pretty decent recovery all things considered. At least he was walking around. He hated the idea of being a burden. They had not yet identified a suitable doctor, but 59 was on the case.

'Cheers Simmo. Try not to rip any stitches though.' Whilst Abu began examining the safe, Simmo considered the most effective method for gaining entry to the thick plastic case. It had two inbuilt combination locks, each comprising of three numbers. There were no obvious weak points. Simmo was reluctant to force any part too violently for fear of damaging the contents. He pulled out his phone, and trawled through a number of internet forums to see if there was any advice on how to proceed. Eventually, he settled on the most tedious, but probably most impactful, solution.

0,0,0 0,0,0

0,0,1 0,0,1

It was going to take a while. The safe was a different

proposition. The electronic code was six digits long. It would take an age to work through all the combinations. Instead, Abu focused upon cutting out the mechanism. It was a much simpler proposition than the larger safe they had recovered during the first job. It only took him fifteen minutes to get in. He had been practising in his spare time.

'Let's see what we've got here boys.' The safe contained a watch, a passport, three chunky rings, a reasonable stack of Polish złoty, and a pack of fifty 9mm bullets. Clearly the safe had been intended for personal use. Abu opened the passport. 'Jesus. Look at the state of this creature. He looks like Kurtan from *This Country*. Lukas Symanski, thirty six, from Warsaw.' The man in the faded black and white picture looked scrawny. Emaciated even. His centre parting accentuated the length of his narrow face.

'Let's have a look.' Bomber snatched the passport out of Abu's hand and scoffed.

'You're right. Look at this skinny cunt. He even makes you look massive.' Archie couldn't help but snigger. Despite the man's many failings, Bomber had definitely been growing on him.

'Please pass it here,' Archie requested. Bomber obliged. Archie flicked through the pages. Lukas was a pretty well-travelled man. The US, UAE, Canada, Colombia. The list of countries went on. Nothing out of the ordinary though. Unbeknownst to them, Mr Symanski was a very well connected individual. His father had been one of the head men in the Pruszkow gang, an extremely powerful and violent group, who had enjoyed significant success in Poland during the 1990s.

They had diminished significantly after a massive police operation, but their tendrils had spread elsewhere; a much more feasible option after Poland's admission to the European Union in 2004. Hence why Mr Symanski Jnr had established his operation on an industrial estate in the north of England. 'I reckon we should burn this. No reason to keep it around. It's only evidence tying us to the job.' A few nodded in agreement.

'What about tha other stuff? The watch and rings might be worth a bit. Not sure what we're going ta do with tha bullets.' Donald carefully examined the weighty yet elegant timepiece, a Franck Muller Vanguard, which was worth a very decent sum of money. The rings were all solid gold, albeit horribly tasteless. The sort of thing a darts player would don for only their most important matches.

'Honestly, I don't think we should risk trying to sell them. I'm pretty sure that the watch could be tracked, and the rings are too distinctive to go unnoticed. Let's keep hold of the bullets for the time being.'

Simmo continued working through combinations. He had sat in a comfortable seat in an attempt to reduce the pressure on his wound. Now and again, he would raise a hand to his side and flinch.

'What else have we got?'

'Not too much really.' Frank held each item aloft.

'Three laptops, their wallets, this accounting book thingy, and a bit of cash.' He quickly thumbed through it. 'Five hundred and thirty quid to be precise.' The wallets contained a further £360.

'I'll chuck it all in the safe.' Frank passed the notes to Donald who transferred them into the cash box. After many frustrating hours, they had been unable to access one of the laptops from the previous job. The other one was not password-protected. Having trawled through hundreds of useless documents associated with the auto parts business, they were extremely hopeful that the latest additions may prove more valuable. Abu and Marv would commence the unenviable task the following day. At least the ledger could be examined without the requirement for some obscure password. However, the thick tome might as well have been encrypted. The scrawling inside was indecipherable. Thousands of figures and letters filled the rows and columns on each page. Their untrained eyes were unable to comprehend any of it. Marv thought he was onto something for a while, by applying a simple cipher, but it turned out to be way off the mark.

'That's your lot. What are we going to do with the stones?' Donald returned from the safe, having finalised the inventory, less for the contents of the Pelicase.

'Marv's set up a meeting with Benji on Thursday. I'm going to go with him to help negotiate terms. In the meantime, we need to return our attention to *Make Ready*. In particular, we need to begin finalising where the second site is going to be located.'

'I'm happy to travel back up with someone. At least I know the properties we've already viewed, and I've a decent idea of what might work in terms of location, so I do.'

'Thanks Five Nine. That would be massively helpful. Any volunteers to go with?' No one was particularly keen for another long car journey, and more time away from their creature comforts. Eventually Bazza piped up.

'Fine. Screw the lotta ya. I'll go up too. You'll owe me one though.'

'Super. We'll divvy up the remaining manpower tomorrow. There's quite a bit to do: assist the newbies with running the charity, start narrowing down the next batch of recruits, update the trustees. Not to mention someone needs to hook up with Todge to exchange the pills.' As suspected, they had turned out to be MDMA. Archie had already been in discussion with the dealer and they had agreed on a sum of £70,000 for the lot.

'I'll do that.'

'I'll come with you as a bit of back up mate.'

'All right, Frank and Bomber it is. He's agreed to have the money ready before the weekend. I'll let you know when it's on.' Suddenly, Simmo shouted out from the other side of the room.

'I'm in. Check this out guys!' He held up the case to reveal a pair of pristine Beretta 92FS. 'I got bored and put in the combination 1,2,3,4,5,6. It opened straight away.'

'Blimey, a couple of shooters. Look in decent nick too.' Bomber couldn't contain his joy.

'Could come in useful. And, we have a use for the ammo now,' Frank observed.

'Let's not get too excited gents,' Archie warned. 'This puts us in a very different ballpark. If we get caught with those it's an automatic minimum five year sentence. The batons are enough of a risk as it is.' It was important to minimise their level of exposure as far as possible. Archie knew that they needed the means to protect themselves. The incident with Simmo had taught them that much. After all, they weren't out there trying to make any friends. However, he realised that if firearms became involved the stakes would skyrocket, and his ability to control a situation would effectively evaporate. 'Donald.'

'Aye.'

'Please get them added to the inventory and locked away securely in the safe. Make sure they're separated from the ammo. We can keep them in there for the time being and reassess what to do with them at a later date.'

'Will do.' The last job was to give the room a once over to ensure that they hadn't left any tell-tale signs behind. It would be very easy for one of their new co-lodgers to stumble onto something.

'Okay. I think we're done. Is everyone clear what needs doing?' They all acknowledged. 'Cool. In that case, who fancies a pint?'

CHAPTER 16

Archie woke with a start. He was dripping with sweat. Half the duvet was hanging off the bed. Closing his eyes, he concentrated on controlling his breathing.

'Shit,' he sighed. His heart was thumping hard. Too hard. Why was this happening now? He thought he had it under control. When he was living on the streets he could understand it. The uncertainty, the fear, the discomfort. Even then, the last time he could recollect having similar episodes, they had only occurred once or twice when he had been forced to bed down in some particularly dodgy areas. But now? In a safe haven, surrounded by comfort. It made no sense. For whatever reason, the episodes were becoming increasingly frequent. Almost every night. He reached out to grab a glass of water from the bedside table. Groping around in the dark, he inadvertently knocked it over, spilling the contents. He could hear the water dripping off the back of the table's surface, landing on the carpet with noisy plops.

'Shit.' He turned on the bedside lamp. It took a few seconds for his eyes to adjust. The water was everywhere. Archie quickly rescued his phone, which seemed to be intact, but the paperback he was three-quarters of the way through, was sodden. Collecting the book, he butterflied it open, and perched it on top of the radiator to dry out. His mouth was absolutely parched. His breath rancid. Desperate for a drink, he picked the glass up off the floor, and lumbered to the bathroom. There was sufficient light shining in from the bedside lamp for him to fill the glass to the brim. He downed the contents, refilled, and downed them again, before remembering that he had put his towels into the wash.

'Shit.' Returning to the bedroom, he picked up an old t-shirt, and used it to dab up the water as best he could. Fortunately it hadn't landed on any electrical sockets. Looking at the alarm clock he could see it was 03:24. He felt absolutely drained. The dreams were never exactly the same. Often the theme or the characters would recur, but the scenario would alter almost every time. The one thing they all had in common was that he would awaken feeling the deepest sense of shame. Sometimes shame because he had done something. Sometimes shame because he hadn't. But the intense feeling was always there. Before, he could have excused it. Perhaps it had been related to the drink or drugs he was funnelling into his body. Now he wasn't really touching either.

Initially, having the charity to focus on had done wonders. The dreams had all but disappeared. But they had returned with a vengeance for reasons he could not fully comprehend. Clambering back into bed, he switched off the light. For him the darkness was a sanctuary. He had spent many nights awake whilst others were tucked up in their beds asleep. It gave him a sense of superiority and control that he couldn't enjoy with the world scurrying around him. The precise details of the dreams never lasted long in his mind, but the feelings that they invoked lingered like a disease. He knew that in the morning he would be irritable.

Closing his eyes again, all he could feel was an unnerving churning in his stomach, like the feeling one might experience following a car accident. It was going to be a long night.

He had never discussed the episodes with anyone else. Not because he wasn't aware it could be useful for his wellbeing; sufficient so called mental health experts had told him as much. Or because he felt embarrassed about them. It was because he wanted to keep them for himself. They were his cross to bear. His connection to experiences that he, and he alone had endured. To share them would be to weaken the memory. To taint it somehow. The same was true for all of his colleagues. He knew that. No one vocalised the specifics, but all of them suffered in their own way.

Waking in the night. Lapses in concentration. Angry outbursts. All the tell-tale signs were there. He wasn't running a therapy group though. If they wanted to bottle things up, good for them. If they wanted to pour their hearts out, good for them too. So far, no one had wanted to open up. He wasn't surprised. As long as they got the job done what did it matter? One thing was for certain. The downtime between jobs intensified the tension. They needed another operation as soon as possible. After the Newcastle mission, nothing suitable had presented itself, despite a significant amount of time invested into research. Perhaps they had enjoyed catastrophic success too early.

He and Marv had visited Benji Sheftel as planned. They had opted for neutral ground, meeting in the plush lobby of the Andaz hotel, just next to Liverpool Street Station. After ordering some outrageously priced coffees, they provided the jeweller with an overview of their haul, which included a digital image and weight for each stone. At this stage, they didn't place sufficient trust in the man to bring the goods directly to him. He was undoubtedly impressed. In principle, he was happy to purchase the lot, assuming that the descriptions matched reality.

'I must say you have done very well here my friends. But as you know it's not going to be easy to move them quietly. I'm inheriting a lot of risk. A lot of risk. That will affect the price. I'm sure you understand.' He always spoke with a light bouncy voice, whilst somehow maintaining a distinctly earnest undertone. It meant that every conversation with the man felt contradictory; entirely innocent, yet deeply important.

Sheftel was exactly as Marv had described. Although he was meeting him for the first time, Archie picked him out of the throng of people with no difficulty at all. He wore a dark suit smattered with faint stains. It was long overdue a dry clean. Thick NHS-style spectacles dominated his face. He sported a patchy goatee beard, and was making a real effort to mask his thinning hair through the adoption of a spectacular Bobby Charlton comb-over. However, it was the yamaka and Star of David, hanging from a dainty silver chain around his neck that really confirmed his identity.

'We understand that Benji. We are coming to you because we know that you can apply a judicious degree of discretion. After all, you pointed us in the right direction in the first place.'

'True. Very true. I can certainly promise you that. From what I hear, you've caused quite a stir up there,' he sniggered. The serious dent put into his competition had done his own business a world of good.

'Well, we just want to keep things nice and quiet. I

assume you'll be able to manage that?'

'Oh absolutely. Absolutely. I have no interest in drawing any attention either.' It was a difficult statement to believe given the man's flamboyant habits. However, as they had experienced when it came to selling the drugs, they had very few alternative options.

'All right then. How about we bring the stones to yours for a proper valuation next week? If they're up to scratch, we can finalise a price and make the exchange then. What say you?' Marv held out his hand. Sheftel took it enthusiastically. They identified a suitable date, and arranged the meeting.

In the intervening period, the group took the opportunity to enjoy some downtime. In order to maintain their fitness, Simmo had organised regular fitness sessions, which they conducted in the gym that had been constructed on the premises. Although most of the equipment had been reclaimed or donated, it was all of a decent standard, and more than adequate for their purposes. Some attended enthusiastically, others reluctantly, but when the classes were on offer they all made the effort to participate.

'Keep going everyone. Only two minutes left!' Simmo cried out. He didn't even appear to be breathless.

'Two minutes! How? I'm going to puke.' Frank was doubled over, dripping sweat onto the rubber matting. His weights had remained stationary for some time.

'What's that Frank? You're wrapping?' Simmo ribbed him, whilst continuing to cycle his own barbell. He remained in unbelievable condition despite the fact he was still recovering from his injury.

'No way... Just having a breather,' he managed to retort between gasps.

'How long's this breather going on for? That barbell's gathering moss!'

'Do one... Abu!' Reluctantly, Frank picked up the bar and continued the workout. The counter on the wall clock ticked down, whilst the heavy bassline of a Modestep track reverberated around the room.

'Come on. Thirty seconds!' Simmo shouted encouragingly. The strain was even beginning to show on his face as he dropped from the Rogue rig, having completed a set of pull ups. By now, they were all suffering horrendously. A combination of pride and peer pressure kept every man working until the loud beep of the timing clock finally offered them respite.

'Urrngggh,' Archie groaned, as he lay flat out on the floor, fighting for oxygen. 'Simmo, you're a cruel bastard you know that?'

'We do today what others don't, so that tomorrow we can do things that others can't!' he responded jovially.

'Where... d'ya get... those ridiculous quotes?' Bazza questioned between mouthfuls, as he sat with his eyes closed downing a bottle of water.

'I don't know. Here and there. It's good stuff, no?'

'Na. It's a load of bollocks pal!' Donald was quick to observe.

'Well, I think it was a great sesh today. Cheers mate.' Mike was the only other man who appeared to be as unruffled as the Sierra Leonean. He held out a fist, which Simmo duly bumped back.

'No problem. Same time tomorrow fellas!'

'At least… let me put my lungs… back in… before you start talking like that,' Marv pleaded. He still hated exercise.

'Yes, thank you Simmo. I think. Who fancies heading out for breakfast?' Archie asked. They all agreed, and once adequately recovered, headed to a local café where they had become regulars. As they scoffed their food, laughed, and chatted, Archie looked around.

The strong bond that had developed between them was tangible. That achievement, in itself, felt like a real victory. To witness a group of people recover from their dire situations was a real privilege. In Archie's mind it justified that they were on the right track. As he reflected upon their success, he noticed one of the town's homeless community wander past the window. It was 09:20 and the guy was already wasted. He didn't know the man personally, but in that moment, Archie vowed he would never allow himself to slip into a similar position again.

Soon enough, the day of the meeting with Sheftel rolled around. Archie was slightly nervous that the jeweller may try something on, but Marv reassured him that despite his reservations, Benji could be trusted. Either way, they decided to bring Mike and Bazza as back up just in case. Arriving at his workshop Archie and Marv were treated like returning heroes. Benji had been as courteous and accommodating as he could possibly manage. He even bought pastries from a nearby patisserie. Meanwhile, Mike and Bazza sat in the car outside waiting patiently.

'How much you reckon we'll get for them?'

'Oh, I've no idea mate. Not me area of expertise.'

'Never been to this bit of London before. It's pretty nice.'

'Yeah. Nice and feckin expensive. I hear a wee two bed house round here will set ya back about two million quid.'

'No way man. That's mental. The new site's costing a fraction of that and it's at least ten times the size.'

'Well that's London for ya. I can't stand the place. It's a shitehole, so it is,' the dour Northern Irishman remarked, really emphasising the *shite* part.

'What's it like anyway?'

'What, the new place? Nothing too fancy. Decent location at the edge of the city. It's an old fishing club. It'll need a bit of work to upgrade the accommodation, and there's not much going on in the area. But there's plenty of open space. The setting's dead-on.'

'Sounds decent. Hopefully I'll get a look at some point.'

'I'm sure ya will. It's not going to paint itself.'

Inside, things had become slightly heated. Following extensive research, Marv had assessed that the diamonds they had obtained retailed in the region of £4.25 million. Having reviewed the figure down for a whole range of reasons, not least of which because they were fencing the stones, which were technically illegal contraband in the first place, he had estimated that £3 million would be a fair price. Sheftel was offering £2.5 million.

'Gentlemen, you must understand. These are not ordinary diamonds. So I can't offer ordinary diamond prices.'

'We get that Benji. We really do. However, we've already made a big reduction to their intrinsic value, and let's be honest, a diamond is a diamond at the end of the day. They're not exactly going out of fashion.'

'It's not that simple. I have to rework them to mask their origin. I have to find suitable buyers, and that takes time and money. Most of all, I have to do it without our Polish friends suspecting. I'm inheriting a lot of problems in order to give you peace of mind.' He smiled, but his eyes were all business.

'Okay,' Marv pondered, looking at the floor.

'Okay, so we have a deal.'

'No, let me finish. I was going to say okay, say you have to spend a few thousand advertising, and wining and dining clients. Then spend a couple of weeks doing the work, making sure that you trickle them out to discerning buyers. It still isn't going to cost you anywhere near the amount you're asking as a reduction. No. Three million is a decent price.'

'I simply cannot offer you that amount. You must understand. The diamond market is a small community. Everyone knows everyone else's business. It would be very easy for one of my colleagues to identify the stones and alert someone, who alerts someone else, yadda yadda yadda. If that happens, I'm finished.' The normally buoyant man looked deflated.

'How about this? We can reduce the price slightly. Not to the level you're after, but enough to make the risk more acceptable. In return, we want you to become our sole dealer when it comes to handling any future items. That includes any luxury goods. Jewellery, watches, stones, and such. You take them no questions asked, and assume responsibility for their onward movement. All at a fair price of course.'

'That sounds tempting, but how will I know what the source is, and who might come looking for them?'

'You won't. It's all part of the five star service you'll provide, in return for significant discounts.'
Sheftel took a sip of pungent Turkish coffee. He consumed an alarming volume of the stuff; possibly the source of his frantic demeanour. His eyes flitted around the room, whilst he nodded his head side to side, weighing up the offer. 'What kind of reduction are we talking about? Two point six million?'

'Try two point seven five and we'll have a deal.'

'Two point seven.'

'No. Two point seven five or we're walking.'
Sheftel closed his eyes and sighed. The compromise pained him deeply. 'Sure. Okay. Two point seven five million. You had better bring me some good business.'
As soon as the terms were agreed his mood lightened, and he was back to his old self. Rising from his expensive leather seat, he shook each of their hands in turn, clasping them with both of his for added dramatic effect.

'Mazel tov! This calls for a celebration. Whiskey, champagne, something stronger?'

'No thank you Benji. As tempting as the offer is, we need to get going. We'll take an electronic transfer. Marv will give you the account details.'

'Of course, of course. Let me boot up the computer and call my broker. We'll have it done in no time. In the interim, please, at least have a pastry!'

It took an hour for the transaction to be completed. Archie had opened an account with Banque Heritage in Geneva that could be used as an intermediary for trickling funds into the charity. Masking the source of the money to the trustees was going to be a challenge. However, Archie had persuaded them that the use of this third party account was the best option, because it would provide the most favourable investment opportunities, without incurring too much tax. He had also managed to convince them that a number of wealthy benefactors had donated, but wished to remain anonymous, a service that the Swiss bank was more than happy to provide. Once they had received confirmation that the money had cleared, Marv handed over the case containing the stones to the overjoyed Sheftel.

'Gentlemen, it has been an absolute pleasure. I can assure you these will be well cared for.'

'As long as they remain incognito, so to speak, we don't mind what happens to them. Until next time Benji.'

'So long friends. Safe travels.'

The two men departed Benji's office, content that they had made a good trade. More importantly, they had established a conduit for conducting future business. Their network was growing.

'How'd it go?' Bazza enquired.

'Very well. He played hardball as we expected, but we think we pulled off a good deal. Anyone fancy a bite to eat before we head back?'

'Definitely mate. I'm absolutely starving.' Mike was often hungry, and ate like a horse.

'Spill the beans then. What was the final figure?'

'Two point seven five.'

'That's proper beezer, so it is. In that case, let's go get ourselves some steak!'

'Why the hell not?' Archie was pleased with the outcome. The stones had been shifted, they had established a good line for conducting future business, and so far, no one had come snooping around.

CHAPTER 17

'Well, that was delicious. Thank you so much for the invite.'

'You're welcome Marcus. It was great to catch up. Also, I thought it was about time I provided you with an update. I was in London anyway, so why not kill two birds with one stone?'

'I'm delighted that you called me. It's been fantastic hearing about the progress that's been made. I must say, I'm very impressed you managed to get the second centre up and running so quickly. When will I be able to visit?'

'There's still quite a bit of renovation work to complete, but I reckon it should be done by the end of the month. The first occupants will move in soon after. We've already generated quite a bit of business up north. Probably more than the first centre if I'm being honest.'

'Did you ever follow up the offer from Farouk?'

'I did, but it never amounted to anything. Honestly, I wasn't that surprised.'

'No, I'm not surprised either. The bloke's an absolute Walter Mitty,' Marcus chortled, brushing some barely visible crumbs from the crisp white table cloth. He simply couldn't abide mess.

'On the plus side, we now have people actively employed with several companies. The feedback so far has been very positive. Almost all of them have committed to subsequent bookings. As soon as the next batch is through training, we should have sufficient bodies to sustain all of our commitments.'

'That's brilliant news. I had every faith you could

pull all this together. A bit different from Sarajevo, eh?'

'It sure is. I'd almost forgotten about that tour it was so long ago. Awesome times though. Do you remember when that Bosnian cop pulled us over, and you gave him such a bollocking he started crying?'

'Ha, I do. He probably wasn't expecting to get both barrels the poor chap. We were lucky he didn't call his mum to come and help him out. Those women were bloody ferocious!' The two men laughed out loud. Their bellows drew the attention of the other diners. Several gave them withering looks of disappointment, before muttering complaints under their breath. This wasn't the kind of establishment where people went to enjoy themselves. Marcus stared every one of them down until they politely returned to their meals.

'Fuck them all. I love the food here, but hate the company.'

'You've still got the look I see. Very impressive. Maybe you could come and deliver a couple of lessons at our next training package.'

'I wish. I'd much prefer to be out there rather than stuck behind a desk, and attending endless tedious meetings. I thought retirement was meant to be fun.'

A waitress interrupted their conversation.

'Gentlemen, can I interest you in a coffee or digestif?'

'Double espresso, and a grappa for me please. Archie what are you having?'

'Just a black coffee.'

'No problem, I'll be right back.' She smiled politely, before gliding away.

'Always amazes me when they can remember the

order without writing anything down. She's been excellent, I must say,' Marcus observed, as he continued brushing invisible detritus from the cloth. 'Anyway, I must mention this. Your father's been in touch again.' Archie's automatic defence mechanism was about to kick in, but before he had a chance to speak, Marcus cut him off.

'Before you say anything, he wasn't pestering. Just calling for a catch up. I know you won't be that interested, but he's just landed a pretty nifty gig as ambassador to France. One of the big ones. Maybe you ought to call or email just to congratulate him.'

'I'll think about it,' Archie lied.

'Also, your brothers have been doing rather well for themselves. One's just got squadron command, and is off to Syria next month. The other's been given a diplomatic position somewhere in the Far East. I forget which country.' It wasn't a surprise. Both of them were golden boys. Unlike him, they relished conformity. He had nothing against them per se, but was convinced that the feeling wasn't mutual. As children they had been thick as thieves. Now they barely corresponded.

'Good for them. I probably ought to drop them a line.'

'You should. I'm sure they would love to hear from you. Maybe they could even come and get the tour?' *Not a hope*, Archie thought to himself.

'Perhaps. I suspect they'd probably be too busy.'

'Well, you'll never know unless you ask.' Archie was grateful when the waitress returned with the drinks. It gave him an excuse to move the conversation on.

'Double espresso, and a grappa. Black coffee for

198

you. Enjoy.' She deftly placed the beverages on the table, before once again retreating out of sight.

'When do you think the next board meeting will be? Has Billy been in touch?'

'I'm hoping no later than the end of next month. No he hasn't. Very unlike him actually. Following the last meeting, I'm not sure there was that much to resolve,' he ruminated, taking a brisk sip of his grappa. 'Mainly because you've been all over it, may I add?'

'Okay sounds good to me. Hopefully the little twat's piled in,' Archie responded a little too swiftly.

'Sadly, I fear not.' Marcus's tone was light-hearted, but Archie suspected he felt the same.

'Still, I imagine that he'll be in touch imminently.'

'Well you know where I am. I thought the off-site venue was a success, but we probably ought to host again. If the new gaff's ready, maybe people will be willing to make the trek up there?'

'Sounds like a great idea. From what you've told me, I see no reason why it won't be completed in time. It'll also give us a chance to meet some of the new crew.'

'Smashing. Let's provisionally plan to do that, and we can always adjust if necessary.'

Their evening continued for another ten minutes or so, reminiscing and sharing pleasantries. Marcus was kind enough to pay the bill. Archie vowed he would get the next one. All in all, it had gone perfectly. Better than Archie had anticipated. At no stage had Marcus raised any concerns over finances or any other aspect of *Make Ready*. It seemed that their clandestine activities had remained under the radar. As pleasant as it was spending time with his former boss, the meeting had been wholly orchestrated in order to gauge whether the chairman harboured any suspicions. Archie could never be certain with the wily old fox, but he was pretty confident that there was no reason for concern. Planning for their next operation could proceed.

CHAPTER 18

'Okay lads, let's go again.' The scenario was reset. Everyone took their positions, like a troupe of dancers, practising carefully choreographed movements. Archie was their director.

'Remember, we need to synchronise the entry with knocking out the power. Don't go too soon. We know they've got back up close by. If that arrives, we could be in deep shit if we're not prepared.' Each man checked his equipment. Then, they checked the man next to them. Once each team had given a thumbs up, they initiated the strike.

'Standby, standby.' Pause. Deep breath.

'Go.' Abu simulated disabling the electrical distribution box using a small metal cabinet as an acceptable stand-in. The real thing would need to be forced open in order to gain access to the circuitry inside. As soon as he was content that his task was complete, he clicked his pressel twice. Marv ordered the entry.

'Breach now.' The three teams filtered in through imaginary doorways, each denoted by red electrical tape. For this job, they had been forced to reconfigure yet again. Having gone through the planning process, they had determined that the quantity of teams would be more important than their density. Instead of the usual two teams of three, they formed up as three teams of two, so that they could cover more ground. Simmo had made a full recovery, as had Frank, who stepped back into the QRF. Archie had considered committing the QRF to assist with the entry, due to the labyrinthine nature of the site. However, he had decided that maintaining a reserve was crucial, even if it had to be called in almost immediately. After roughly two minutes, progress reports began to ring out.

'Team One, clear.'

'Team Two, clear.'

'Team Three, clear.'

Accurately replicating the layout of the sprawling farm complex had been a real challenge. Compared to their previous operations, which were conducted in self-contained units, the site included several structures, each of which was notably different in composition. They had also been unable to obtain any decent schematics to work from, less for the main building. It looked like any other typical farmhouse; brick-built and old. Most of the other buildings were much more modern. Their research had revealed that the majority had been constructed without any legitimate planning permission.

In fact, conducting any surveillance at all had been seriously challenging. The complex was very rural, and very isolated, with little in the way of cover for miles around. They couldn't use vehicles, less for the main ingress and egress route. Even then, they had to be used sparingly to avoid arousing suspicion. Not only that, the inhabitants were certainly not amateurs. They had set up CCTV around the perimeter, and conducted regular patrols, under the guise of taking the dogs for a walk.

As a result, the team had been forced to go old-school. Two covert observation posts had been set up in dense foliage overlooking the building at a couple of locations. It had meant infiltrating as three-man teams under the cover of darkness, and spending the entire day in location, before extracting again the following evening. The ambitious endeavour had required the use of some inventive camouflage and concealment techniques. It had also meant enduring long periods of significant discomfort, particularly when the weather had been unfavourable, which being the east coast of the UK, it often was. In total, they had managed to spend six days watching the property from each location, providing what was assessed to be an acceptable pattern of life.

Unfortunately, there were several blind spots towards the centre of the site that they were simply unable to observe. Satellite images, obtained via Google Earth, had provided them with a rough layout of the premises, which was enhanced through the use of a drone. Abu had made the suggestion of purchasing one. It had turned out to be the difference between going ahead with the operation and cancelling it altogether.

'QRF move to position three.' Abu and Frank responded immediately, traversing the dusty concrete floor and making for the predetermined location. Everyone else continued their part of the performance. It smelt mouldy in the huge abandoned space. Every now and then, pigeons flapped overhead causing small particles of debris to tumble downwards. Everything had been reduced in scale to fit within the walls of building. Not perfect, but it sufficed for their requirements. Only the dimensions of the buildings were representative. Or as close as they could estimate.

'QRF in position.' Bazza linked up with them, and directed them where to go. The other notable element they were missing was sufficient protagonists to simulate the inhabitants of the site. For this role, they had been forced to use their imagination. A reasonable compromise, but nowhere near as convincing as a flailing, shouting, lump of flesh to replicate the real thing. It was becoming acutely apparent that they required more personnel. Archie had been considering the dilemma long and hard. Extra manpower would make all their endeavours much more straightforward, but of course, risked exposing the whole enterprise. Ultimately, he had decided it was too soon to involve anyone else in this job. The new recruits would have to wait.

'All teams. Be aware, van approaching along route Stella.' Marv had thrown a curveball into the scenario. The teams knew what to do. Each repositioned ready to ambush the new threat. From the limited intelligence that had been gathered, they believed it to be highly unlikely that their adversaries would possess firearms, and that, afforded the element of surprise, they would be able to subdue them. Donald walked along between the chalk lines representing the main approach route to the farm. He held his arms out in front of him in an effort to simulate holding a steering wheel, but didn't go so far as making *brumming* noises. He *parked up* outside the main building. Before he mimicked stepping out of the vehicle, two of the teams had pounced upon him, wrestling him to the ground. He was secured, and moved to join his fellow, imaginary, captives.

'Items secure. Extract now.' They had decided to minimise the use of vehicles given the lack of approaches, opting for two combi-vans that could just about transport them, their equipment, and any material that they obtained. Marv simulated driving to the collection point in one of the vans, which would also serve as the command vehicle. During the operation, Donald would be driving the other one. Unfortunately, for him, he was currently indisposed with his hands shackled behind his back, a hood over his head, and Bomber taking great pleasure in occasionally nudging him hard enough to topple him over onto the floor.

'Loading complete.' They walked out in unison, splitting into two groups of five, before replicating the procedure for boarding the vans. To any uninformed observer, the sight would have looked quite ridiculous. On reaching the edge of the yawning structure, Archie pulled up his balaclava.

'All right gents. That'll do. Well done. Much better than before. Good response to the van. Let's have a ten minute break, then we'll go again.'

'Surely that was the last time through today?' queried an exasperated Frank. 'We've done it at least ten times already.'

'I know mate. If all goes well, it'll be the last one I promise. We can't take any chances with this one, given how many gaps we've got. Better safe than sorry, eh?' Frank's disdain was evident but he knew the point wasn't worth contesting.

'All right. In that case, none of you had better fuck this up,' he shouted loudly enough to ensure they all received the message.

They ran through the scenario again. Everything went according to plan this time, so Archie called things to a close for the evening. Finding this target had not been easy. And given the complexity of what they faced, it didn't look like the job itself would be any easier. It had been a combination of forensic research, and patient confirmation, which had thrown up the location in the first place.

The laptop recovered from the Poles had contained several pieces of correspondence between their gang, and another group, who had been making consistent trips up north, collecting and delivering cargo. The messages were non-specific, but suggestive enough that they were immediately noticed by Marv. He did some further probing, and discovered documents containing figures and quantities for what he believed to be drug shipments given the terms and scale being used. Subsequently, Archie liaised with Todge to begin narrowing down who the recipients could be.

All they had to go on was a rough area of the country, somewhere in the east of England. Todge tapped up his network. They waited. It didn't take long for him to confirm the likely location that was being referred to. There wasn't much else really going on in rural Norfolk. Even a preliminary scan of the site revealed it to be of interest. The frequent comings and goings at all times of day. The odd mix of luxury vehicles, which looked wholly out of place parked on a muddy farm. The disproportionately high number of young men. It was blatantly evident that they weren't growing turnips there. Archie had spoken to Todge at length about what else he knew about the group.

'Not too much really. I know that they're meant to be mainly local boys, but they've recruited some Ukrainian fellas to provide muscle.' Archie's ears pricked up. 'I've had a couple of dealings with them, buying a bit of Charlie and a few other bits and bobs, but nothing serious. From what I hear, they're trying to expand their operations, and want to open a line through Harwich to Holland direct, rather than having to go via their mates up north. It's going to put a few noses out of joint I reckon.' Todge drew hard on a Dunhill cigarette. Archie knew he had expensive tastes. The silver-tongued drug dealer tilted his head slightly to the side, before releasing a cloud of wispy smoke. His dark slicked back hair, and well-tailored clothes, reinforced a look that screamed *dodgy fucker*.

'That's very interesting. So you reckon they're exclusively distributing from the farm at the moment? Any other locations that you know of?'

'I can't say for sure because I've never been there myself, but it makes sense. If they were set up anywhere else in the area I would know about it. Don't forget, this is my patch.'

'Cool, anything else of interest I should know about?'

'I'm pretty certain that they're not packing. I've not heard about anyone pulling a gat during any deals or anything like that. However, if they're looking to expand, they may have tooled up. Hard to say either way, but I'd look into it if I were you.'

'Don't worry I will. Carefully.' Todge's information had been invaluable. Without it they wouldn't have possessed any real means of developing the target effectively, although of course, he had a vested interest, being the likely recipient of anything valuable discovered there. As much as he was a decent enough bloke, and far more proficient than the vast majority of his colleagues, Archie felt very uncomfortable bringing him so close into the fold. He was not one of them. He didn't share the same values. As far as Archie was concerned, Todge was in it for the wrong reasons. Putting all their eggs into one basket wasn't a great option, but for the time being it was the only one that they had.

Back at the barracks, they stored away the kit in secrecy before getting some rest. The strike would occur the following evening. Every man needed to ensure that they were as fresh as possible. Going in at night time was going to be challenging, given the lack of ambient light available, but it was far preferable to a daylight option, when there would be significantly more activity on the farm. Archie had continuously repeated an oft used military phrase about *owning the night* to reinforce the point. They had invested heavily in achieving the ambition. Not only had they practised extensively in darkness, they had purchased head-mounted night vision devices to complement the monocles already held in their arsenal. Abu had also ensured that the drone they had procured possessed a top-of-the-range thermal camera. It would provide their vital *eyes in the sky* during the operation.

'I'll dish ya gear out at twenty two hundred tomorrow. Be at tha store on time, otherwise y'ull end up running aboot like Stevie Wonder on a bad day.'

'All right, calm down Scrooge McDuck. We're all tired.'

'Shut at ya wee jobbie. I'm skaffin your NVGs now for sure.'

'Go ahead you honking daywalker. Do I look fussed?'

'I'd rather be ginga than a lattle munky boy like you.'

'If you say so. By the way. Your sister's asked for her top back. I said I'll give it to her next time we hook up for sexy time.' Donald looked down at his snug t-shirt that was riding up to reveal his hairy stomach, and reflected that perhaps Abu had a point.

'We'll be there Q Man. Don't worry,' Mike interjected. He just wanted to get into bed.

Slowly, they filtered away to their rooms. Although the most recent insults had been in jest, Archie had begun to notice increased friction within the group. He wasn't surprised. They had been working their arses off without much respite over recent weeks. As soon as this job was complete, he would reassess the apportionment of work, and begin examining candidates for entry into the inner circle. Of those he had witnessed, at least four stood out as strong possibilities. All were committed, disciplined, and industrious. Unfortunately, they were also struggling with inner demons of one form or another. But then again, all of them were, Archie included. It was what made them suitable for their alternative line of work. His next move would be to interview the candidates under the guise of selection for a new position within the charity, where he would be able to assess their motivations and ambitions. Hopefully, some would reveal sufficient details, allowing him to influence them further.

Lying in his bed, he closed his eyes and tried to clear his mind. Thoughts bombarded him relentlessly. As soon as he had managed to push one aside, another popped up in its place, swirling around in a seemingly endless vortex. It had been that way for as long as he could remember. As far as he was concerned, the curse was more of a strength than a weakness. Some of his best ideas were concocted during the quiet hours of the night, but it came at the cost of consistently putting him on edge. A doctor might diagnose it as ADHD. Archie regarded it as a necessary evil for getting his *shit in one sock*. He grabbed his phone, and put in his AirPods, knowing that some music would provide a suitable distraction. Pressing the shuffle icon, a song by an English metal band called Sylosis began playing. It was the kind of music that his father would have described as *noise*, but to Archie it was like therapy. He soon drifted off into a deep sleep.

The following day dragged. Hard. They went about their normal business, doing their best to appear involved, but really, every man was just going through the motions. It was Friday. The new recruits were given an early knock-off to ensure that they were out of the way. Archie had arranged for them to conduct a bonding session in London, putting them up in an upmarket hotel for the weekend, and providing sufficient drinking tokens to ensure that they would be in no hurry to return.

When the time came, the team members appeared one by one, congregating in the briefing room, before dispersing to collect their equipment. It would take them roughly one hour to drive to the target location. Another hour to shake out, and move into position. They had estimated the job would take approximately one hour t to complete, including some fudge factor. All being well, they should be back at base by no later than 03:00.

'All call signs radio check.'

'Team One, okay.'

'Team Two, okay.'

'Team Three, okay.'

'QRF, okay.'

'Q, okay.'

'All, okay.'

'Let's mount up and get going,' commanded Archie, adopting the serious tone he always did prior to an operation. He surveyed the other men, and allowed his lips to curl into the faintest of smirks. Everyone had their game face on. The two vans rolled out of the rear compound. 59 shut the sliding gate behind them, and hopped into the rear vehicle.

'Let's do this thing then, shall we boys?'

CHAPTER 19

All three teams made it to their stepping-off points undetected. It was a particularly dark night. The moon was a slither, casting just enough ambient light for their night optics to work effectively, but insufficient for the naked eye to pick up the shadowy figures dressed in black closing into their target. Abu had launched the drone. He held it off at a distance downwind so that the noise of the whirring blades was barely audible.

'One Bravo outside entry point two of main building. Looks like he's smoking.' He had a black sheet over his head, eliminating the glare from the iPad that was relaying the feed from the drone's camera.

'Team One, ready.' An unnervingly long pause followed.

'Team Three ready.' Team Two had further to travel than the others. They were still crossing a fence line that delineated the site perimeter. 59 cursed as his trousers snagged on a nail that was sticking out from one of the wooden posts.

'Come on mate. Hurry up.'

'I'm trying, I am. This bloody fence is fighting back.' Bomber had already crossed the obstacle, and was waiting in a depression shielding him from direct view from the buildings. Their surveillance had indicated that most of the structures appeared to be in disuse. Only a small handful, located around the main farm house, were likely to be occupied. As a result, the plan was to initially bypass the majority of the buildings, focusing their efforts on the centre of the site, before working their way outwards. That meant getting in very close undetected.

'All right I'm over. Let's get going.' Within sixty seconds, the two men reached their entry position. They could clearly identify the smoking man. His cigarette pulsed luminous green through their night vision goggles.

'Team Two ready.'

'All teams in position,' Marv confirmed, just in case anyone hadn't received the message. He paused for thirty seconds, allowing time for any last minute adjustments.

'Standby, standby.' Just as he was about to give the command to breach, someone opened the doorway next to the smoker. Pale white light arced across the courtyard area. 59 and Bomber were fully illuminated as they emerged from the bushes.

'Oi. Who are you? What the fuck are you doing?' the man who had emerged from the house shouted angrily in their direction. A light turned on in one of the upstairs windows. This was not the start that they had hoped for. The two men knew it was their responsibility to deal with the unexpected situation. Without pausing, Bomber dropped his heavy bag containing the entry equipment, and sprinted towards the smoker, baton drawn. He speared the man to the ground with the force of a bull rhino. 59 followed close behind. The second man, who had opened the door, moved towards the dark mass of Bomber, and attempted to pull him away from his friend. He received a hard whack to the ribs for his trouble, before 59 clattered into him, sending him sprawling.

'Get off me! Get the fuck off me!' the smoker was

shrieking. Any building occupant would definitely have heard him. His cries were quickly followed by another scream.

'Argghhh!' It was an inhuman sound. 59 had pinned the second man, and in his panic to subdue him had applied too much pressure dislocating his shoulder with an audible pop. The anguished man continued whimpering uncontrollably. Change of plan. Instead of making entry into the building, Archie grabbed Simmo and dragged him towards where the tussle had broken out. They had practised for the eventuality, but it took a little time for their brains to adjust to the new situation.

'Team Three, moving to support Team Two.' Arriving at the scene, Archie conducted a quick assessment. Both men had been pinned to the ground. Although they were making a lot of noise, it appeared that 59 and Bomber had them broadly under control. He signalled to Simmo to cuff them both. At the same time, he moved to cover the doorway in case any of their mates showed up.

'Help! There's… Unnghhh!,' the smoker continued crying out. Bomber slammed his head into the ground. Hard. The shouting stopped. Simmo pulled out a plasticuff, and fed it around his wrists. 59 had covered the whimpering man's mouth, whilst locking his other arm in position. As Simmo went to cuff him, he jarred the dislocated limb. It was as if an electrical current had been applied to the man's body. His jolt was forceful enough to throw 59 off.

'Argghhh!' As 59's hand came away from his mouth, another piercing shriek erupted. Fumbling with the plastic loop, Simmo struggled to slip it over the man's wrists. 59 spun round and assisted him. The agonised man had already made enough noise to alert most of the county; there was no point in trying to quieten him down now. Between the two of them they managed to get the cuff applied. Simmo produced a gag and forced it over the man's head, quickly followed by a hood. Archie had occupied the doorway. His frame was silhouetted against the light emerging from within, casting an intimidating shadow across the courtyard.

Scanning the room in front of him, he couldn't identify any other immediate threats. It was the kitchen. Plenty of dangerous implements lying around. He decided to press forward onto the next doorway that led into a corridor. His heart was beating out of his chest. Clenching his baton tight, he approached the entrance, ready to strike anyone who emerged. Suddenly the lights went out. No one had given the order to breach, letting Abu know to disable the electricity. In his stand-off position, he was blissfully unaware of the commotion that was occurring outside the farm house. Fortunately, he could identify that something was awry from the drone feed, and had used his initiative.

The clamouring from outside had died down. The two men had been subdued. Archie could hear footsteps creaking around on the old floorboards above his head. Someone was making their way down the stairs. Bracing himself, he slowly tiptoed down the dark corridor. Now the lights were out he would have a distinct advantage.

'What's going on down there? You all right John? Where's the torch? I can't see a thing,' demanded a panicked voice. From Archie's position, the cramped opening to the stairway was a few metres beyond, on his left. He carefully pushed a little closer, so that he was within striking distance, and waited. Through his NVGs he could see the man reaching out his hand, using the wall as a guide. Stepping down off the final step, his whole body became exposed. As soon as he rounded the corner, the man must have caught the faintest glimpse of Archie's profile because his expression changed to a mixture of surprise and horror. Archie brought the baton down with all his might. It struck the unfortunate individual in the crook between his shoulder and neck. The force dropped him to the floor immediately. From the awkward way he fell, Archie knew that he had been knocked out.

As quickly as he could, Archie manoeuvred the man so that he was lying face down, before applying the detention kit. Bomber and Simmo had joined him in the corridor. 59 had remained outside to watch the two captives. Footsteps continued stomping around above them. Archie indicated the location of the stairway, and then signalled for them to begin clearing the first floor. He would search the remainder of the ground level.

'Team One, Building One clear. Moving to Building Two.' From the report, it sounded like Bazza and Mike were having more success. They had been assigned two of the larger outbuildings where they had identified the bulk of traffic during their surveillance. Archie pressed on into the next room. An estate agent would probably have described it as cosy. The low ceilings made the space feel oppressively small. He could smell the remnants of a log fire, situated in the centre of the far wall. There were no occupants. Sweeping through the living room, dining room, utility room, and a large conservatory, he didn't encounter anyone else. Loud banging rang out from upstairs.

'Ground floor clear.'

'Team Three, move to Team Two. Assistance required.' It was an ominous request, not helped by the raucous clamouring erupting from somewhere on the first floor. As he made his way back to the corridor, Archie could see that 59 had congregated all the detainees in the kitchen, securing them together by their feet. The smoker continued to fight, which was agitating the man with the dislocated shoulder. 59 loomed over them to make sure they didn't get too feisty. When he caught sight of Archie he casually shrugged, before joining him at the bottom of the stairs. They ascended in unison. The old wooden floorboards felt springy underfoot. Archie was slightly concerned they'd give way altogether under their combined weight.

On reaching the top step, they saw Bomber and Simmo stood beside a doorway. Each was taking it in turn, attempting to kick the door through to no avail. Muffled voices came from the other side. Whoever was in the room had barricaded the door with something impenetrable. Brute force might do the trick. The extra manpower joined the effort to break through, but only two at most could fit in the cramped space. Even with their combined efforts, the door would not give way. Archie had a decision to make. Bypass it and move on, or find a way of getting inside. There was no doubt that the occupants would have made a phone call by now. Who knew what reinforcements may be brought to bear? They couldn't take the chance of leaving unrestrained personnel in the house. Archie pointed for 59 to relocate back downstairs to watch the original captives. Meanwhile, he headed outside. The cold night air hit him like a wall. Their main equipment bag had been dropped just the other side of the building. It contained all the tools they would require to break through the sturdy wooden door. As he collected the heavy holdall, Abu piped up on the radio.

'Erm, I assume none of you are climbing out of a window?'

'Damn it,' Archie muttered under his breath. He quickly dropped the load, and raced back around the corner ready to intercept. One man had dropped to the ground in a half-squat. He was wearing only his underwear. Another was scrambling through the tight window frame. The glass panes rattled loudly as he struggled to squeeze through. 59 appeared at the doorway to survey the situation. The first man out didn't wait for his friend. As soon as he had composed himself, he set off running towards the main entry route. Archie sprinted after him, desperately hoping the man wasn't fast. He was. Really fast. As Archie strained to keep up, he could see plumes of condensed breath stringing out behind his quarry, which looked something like an aircraft's vapour trail. Archie's tactical vest made a rhythmic, rattling sound as he charged along. The cold air stung his lungs. He could taste blood. Tears began streaming from his eyes behind the lenses of his NVGs, which he couldn't wipe away.

As they hit the main gravelled track, the man skidded, and stumbled slightly. It was the opening that Archie required. All his energy was directed towards taking his adversary's legs out from under him. Archie had played a lot of rugby in his youth, and knew how to execute an effective tackle. Clamping both his arms round the man's limbs at thigh height, he drove in his shoulder. The man buckled easily under the force, and they collapsed to the ground. Archie could smell his unpleasant aroma. He stank like an ashtray, drenched in sweat and cheap aftershave.

'Please. No. Don't hurt me.' Archie recognised the accent immediately. 'I begging you.' Using an arm bar to hold him in position, the man yelped as Archie applied pressure. It would be difficult to prevent him from escaping, whilst also attempting to apply a restraint. One-handed, he continued locking the man in place. With the free hand, he clumsily reached around his assault rig grasping for a plasticuff. Heavy-duty Oakley combat gloves made it difficult to locate the slender plastic loop, particularly as his victim was attempting to break free.

'Stop man. You hurting me.' After a couple of failed attempts, Archie located the cuff, before wrenching the man over onto his front. Grabbing his other arm violently, he yanked it behind his back, and zipped his wrists together. Then, placing a knee on the back of his victim's legs, Archie removed another plasticuff from his belt and applied it to the man's ankles. As he did, he noticed that the man was covered in numerous crude tattoos, including several Cyrillic words and phrases. Once fully secure, he flipped the now helpless individual onto his back.

'Fuck you man. I kill you asshole.' Archie recoiled as he caught sight of the man's face for the first time, recognising him immediately as one of his assailants from the abandoned furniture store. One of the pricks who had hospitalised him. Unintentionally, his tone instantly assumed a sinister edge.

'Say that again.' An uncontrollable rage descended upon Archie. He lifted a boot and stamped it down hard on the man's torso, completely knocking the wind out of him, and forcing him to cough and splutter uncontrollably. Archie stamped again, this time catching his ribs, causing a muffled crack.

'Naahhh!' his prey squealed, curling into a ball. Another stamp followed. Then another. Archie continued stamping until the man was silent. Then, he stamped some more, indiscriminately striking various body parts. Blood trickled from his victim's head, mixing with the gravel to form a pool of soupy ichor.

'Alpha, are you all right? I say again, are you all right?' Abu had been attempting to raise Archie on comms for some time. During the struggle he had completely blanked out the distraction. His chest was heaving. Every part of his body ached with the exertion. Archie keyed the pressel twice in acknowledgement.

'Cool. Do you need assistance?' Archie pressed twice again.

'Okay. You're not far from our position. We'll close into you.' Taking a knee, Archie took several deep breaths. His vision was beginning to narrow; a sure sign that he was at the edge of his physical limitations. After a few moments, he had composed himself sufficiently to stand up.

'Team One clear. Moving to consolidation point. One Bravo in custody.' Archie wondered if 59 had been able to take down the other escapee. Fortunately, he had. Caught in a no man's land between the window ledge, a prowling Welshman, and the barricaded door, behind which lurked two equally threatening adversaries, he had elected for the window exit. Unfortunately for him, upon landing he had turned over an ankle. The injury was sufficiently painful to prevent him from dashing off, and 59 had jumped on top of him in a heartbeat. Meanwhile, Abu and Frank appeared from a woodblock two hundred metres further down the track from Archie. They jogged in to his location.

'Fucking hell mate. What did you do to him?' Frank's loud squeaky voice carried particularly well in the icy breeze. Archie gesticulated angrily for him to shut up. In response, Frank hooded the man's bloodied skull, picked up the limp body, and flung it over his shoulder in an improvised fireman's carry. The three of them trundled back down the main route towards the farm complex. It was only then that Archie realised what a significant distance he had travelled during the pursuit. Grunting and puffing, they arrived back outside the main building.

They could see the others congregated, with their five captives linked together, in the courtyard. Several were shivering in the cold. In particular, the second man who had attempted to flee from the window. Similar to his more nimble associate, he was also only sporting a pair of boxer shorts. Frank unceremoniously dumped Archie's comatose victim next to the other figures, before attaching him to the chain. As a precaution, he hooded him, not that it looked like the guy was in any state to interfere.

'All teams clear. Beginning secondary sweep.'
There were three remaining outbuildings that required
checking. Abu and Frank took on the responsibility of
watching the prisoners, whilst the other teams dispersed
to conduct the search. Abu took the opportunity to re-
establish the feed from the drone. Nothing unexpected
appeared through the IR camera. It had started to rain.
A steady pattering could be heard on the corrugated
rooftops of the modern barns. Water began trickling
down guttering pipes, making a gentle gurgling sound.
It wasn't good news for the captives. Exposed to the
elements, they would have to endure further discomfort.
Nor was it ideal for the searchers, because the lenses of
their night vision devices had begun misting up.

Archie and Simmo moved swiftly to their target. It
was a large modern structure, partly open-sided,
containing a couple of internal rooms that looked like
static homes. Archie made an effort to wipe his goggles
with a sleeve, but the rain continued obscuring his
vision. As they arrived within twenty metres of the
target, both men were almost startled out of their skin.
They knew that dogs were kept on the premises, but so
far none had made a peep, despite the yelling. One had
finally woken up, and decided it was time to make its
presence known. A large, ferocious, Belgian Shepherd
barked and snarled at them, baring a set of healthy-
looking teeth. Despite its best efforts, the helpless
canine couldn't close the gap to them, because it had
been tethered to one of the posts holding up the
structure's roof. Its chain rattled loudly as it leapt up
and down.

A short distance away, another dog began to bark,

stimulated by the commotion. Simmo hated dogs. As a result, he was somewhat hesitant when Archie indicated that they should press on. He froze in place and shook his head. Archie became more insistent. After a couple of moments, Simmo managed to gather sufficient courage to circumvent the angry, hairy mass. They rushed towards the nearest of the two porta cabins. Peering in through a grimy window, Archie couldn't make out any sign of life, but they needed to be sure. Simmo slipped a crow bar into the flimsy door frame. It popped open without much resistance. Shining a torch inside to help illuminate the dank space, Archie stepped through the doorway. Rows of shelving were covered in dust and cobwebs, and filled by an assortment of farming equipment. No one had been in there for some time. They quickly decided to move onto the next cabin. The dog continued going crazy, but they were now a sufficient distance away that Simmo was able to relax slightly.

The second construction mirrored the first. Someone must have been doing a two for one deal at the mobile home store when the structures were purchased. The same routine followed, Simmo with the crow bar, Archie with the torch. The door pinged open with a noisy metallic twang. The obnoxious smell hit Archie like a punch to the face. Putrid, rotting flesh, mixed with dog faeces, and half eaten bowls of Pedigree Chum. He gagged involuntarily, before quickly reversing into the fresh air. It wasn't entirely clear what had occurred in the room, but it seemed like the gang enjoyed a spot of dog fighting to pass the time. There was no way anyone was hiding in there. If they were, good luck to them.

Content that the building was free of any threats, they returned to the courtyard.

'Team Three clearance complete, nothing found. Returning to collection point now.' As they approached, they could see Frank circulating around the captives. Archie had half a mind to suggest that they should be moved under cover. Left out in these conditions, some would undoubtedly go down with hypothermia. However, he quickly concluded that the wasted time didn't warrant the kind gesture; they weren't running a holiday camp.

'Team Two clearance complete,' was quickly followed by 'Team One clearance complete. We've found something interesting.' Sodden figures emerged from the murk. They returned to the consolidation point, and deposited their equipment.

'All teams, initiating search.' Before Archie could step-off to begin examining his allocated sector, Mike grabbed him forcefully by the arm. Rather than making for the farm house, Mike led him towards the outbuilding that his team had just cleared. Archie wasn't particularly comfortable with the change to the plan. When things weren't conducted methodically was typically when things went wrong. However, he had sufficient trust in Mike to follow. The building they arrived at was ugly. A large grey rectangular box made from concrete. At one time it had probably been used as a storage silo. The main entrance was through a doorway positioned inside a larger sliding metal door, allowing access for vehicles. The poorly oiled hinges groaned as Mike pushed it inwards. There was no heating system inside. The cold air had settled in stagnant pockets. The chill penetrated through to their bones as they entered.

Neatly arranged at regular intervals around the edge of the main space, were further portable homes, identical to the ones in the dog structure. Mike made for the closest one. On reaching the door, Archie noticed that it was padlocked from the outside. Metal grills had been attached to the windows. Mike climbed up the small set of steps that led up to the entrance, and switched on his torch, shining it through the window for Archie to look inside.

Positioning himself next to Mike, Archie craned his head until he was able to peek through the narrow gap. It was difficult to make out the contents of the room. The grill split the beam of light into several smaller shafts that flickered around the interior. Archie lifted his NVGs away from his face. Squinting, he could just about make out a cot bed in the far corner of the room. Then another. Then another. Eight in total. On top of each was a bundle of sheets and blankets. A slender leg dangled from one of the messy bundles. An arm from another. The arm was cradling a head of thick brown hair, which cascaded over the side of the bed. Archie turned to look at Mike, who pointed at the other five cabins in turn. Breaking protocol, he whispered as quietly as he could.

'They're all the same.' *Bollocks*. This was definitely not part of the plan. Archie faced a major dilemma. Rescuing trafficked girls was certainly not on the agenda. What's more, if they decided to free them, it would only provide another line of evidence for anyone wishing to track down the perpetrators of the raid.

However, if they were left locked up, their miserable fates would undoubtedly be sealed, and their situation possibly made even worse. Grappling with his conscience, he decided to postpone the decision.

'Let's crack on with the search.' Mike nodded in acknowledgement. They returned to the farm house, and split up. Archie worked through the first floor, without finding anything of great significance, before returning to the building he and Simmo had cleared earlier. The vicious Belgian Shepherd had calmed down, but went wild again as soon as Archie approached. He determined that he should get the *dog house* out of the way first. Bracing himself, he stepped into the stench. It took about thirty seconds to determine there was absolutely nothing of value inside. Leaving the upsetting sight behind, he returned to the second grubby room. On entering, he quickly worked through each row of shelves one at a time, but found nothing. Hopefully his comrades would have fared better. Once satisfied, he strode back to the congregation point.

Abu was sat at the kitchen table with his head buried in the drone screen. One by one, they all returned to the central point. One by one, they shook their heads, indicating that they had not discovered anything of real value. Archie cursed internally. How had they got it so wrong? His thoughts were suddenly interrupted by Marv's voice on the radio.

'All callsigns, be aware. Two vehicles approaching along Route Heineken heading towards Route Stella.' *Fucking hell. What now?* There was only one reason for someone to be driving down that road. The place wasn't exactly a tourist hotspot. Two vehicles could

226

potentially contain up to ten individuals. Following a very quick appraisal of the situation, Archie determined that the odds were too great to hang around any longer.

'All call signs extract now via ERV.' Without hesitating, they collected all the equipment, and prepared to depart. As they worked, Mike sidled up to Archie getting close enough to speak in his ear without being overheard.

'What about the girls? We can't leave them here.' Archie pulled Mike's ear roughly to his mouth.

'We have no choice. It will take too long to break the locks. Anyway, they're probably off their tits and can't walk. It's too much of a risk. Let's go.'

'Are you serious? We're better than these scum bags. It's inhumane. Please mate. It will only take a minute.'

'Grab your kit and let's go. Now!' Archie's voice had inadvertently soared, and the words emerged louder than he had intended. The others turned to look in his direction. He waved them on. Just as they were ready to make tracks, Frank beckoned him over. Archie reluctantly obliged. They didn't have time for this. Frank pointed at the man that Archie had run down, before sweeping his fingers back and forth across his neck in the universal sign for something not functioning. Archie could tell immediately from Frank's body language. The Ukrainian was dead.

CHAPTER 20

'Well that was a feckin disaster, so it was.'

'I have to agree. It certainly could have gone better,' Marv commented. As ever, he remained more philosophical than the irate Northern Irishman.

'Look, the main thing is that we all returned in one piece. That's an improvement from our previous outing,' Archie chanced.

'That's the kinda crap someone says when they know for sure it's been a complete cluster. The *main* thing is that we returned completely empty handed.'

'Admittedly it could have gone better, but we knew it was sketchy before going in. There's plenty to learn for next time.' It was the best he could think of in reply to Bazza's cynical comment. Archie struggled to sound both upbeat, and sincere. It *had* been a cluster.

'We definitely need to make a regain that's for sure.' Simmo added in an effort to support him. Archie appreciated the sentiment, but it wouldn't be sufficient to satisfy the rest of them.

'I reckon we just get on the smash and forget about it.'

'Wise words as always Bomber. Thanks for your input mate.'

'Well it's better than sitting around ere moaning like a bunch of pussies. You got any better ideas Abu?' He didn't. They sat in awkward silence for a few moments.

'We shad at least review what we did gat. Alls ya empty yar pockets,' Donald suggested, bringing them back to earth. They consolidated all the items they had obtained, just as before. The meagre pile was barely sufficient to occupy a single corner of the trestle table. A handful of notes here. A stack of coins there. Mike produced a small case that contained hypodermic needles, and accompanying bottles of brown fluid. They were unquestionably the drugs that had been used to keep the girls sedated. Five wallets, and a couple of watches, rounded off the haul.

'Hmm. Probably not worth the effort I'd say.'

'Well it's certainly not as good as our first two jobs. You never know, maybe one of these wallets has a winning lottery ticket in it!' As always, Abu tried to make light of the situation, without success on this occasion. 'Let's count it up anyway, and see what we've got.' It was fortunate that their expectations were low. The grand total amounted to less than £1,000.

'Donald, get it locked away with the rest please. We'll convene in the briefing room in fifteen minutes.' The sense of deflation was tangible. Unlike the previous two operations, no one rushed in to review what had occurred, and their part in it. Instead, they dithered and dallied, moping their way to the brightly lit room. They took their seats in silence.

'Right. We all know the drill. Let's start at Phase One. Frank, do you want to kick us off?' It took a full four hours to dissect every aspect of the operation. Most left the briefing more downhearted than they had entered. A lot of soul searching would follow, particularly for Archie. The intricacies of how the target had been identified, how the surveillance was undertaken, how the raid was conducted, and their decisions along the way, were all discussed at great length. At times it had become heated. Confrontations erupted on more than one occasion. All the while, Archie hadn't really engaged.

I killed him.

Even while Mike was berating him for deciding to leave the girls locked up, he could only manage monosyllabic replies. It only made Mike more irate. What was worse, it seemed a couple of others shared Mike's sentiments. Simmo and 59 threw their penny's worth in.

'I think we should have freed them. Imagine what those dickheads are doing to them now.'

'Yeah. I thought we were meant to be the good guys, or am I missing something?'

'Fuck those bitches man. If we'd hung around any longer, who knows what was in those vehicles. For all we know we could have been toast,' Abu dropped the comment in casually, hoping to bring some equilibrium to the conversation. It wasn't well-received. A full blown argument ensued, with accusations and insults being thrown around.

I killed him.

At one stage, Archie could sense them all staring at him. An uncomfortable silence settled in. After an unfeasibly long time, they all suspected it might be an act. Some sort of test to see how they reacted. They were wrong. Somehow, they collectively managed to re-establish an acceptable level of decorum, and worked through the remaining issues.

I killed him.

'Archie mate. You got anything else to add, do ya?' Bazza's dour tones brought him back to the room.

'No. I don't think so. Let's get some kip.'

'Is that it? Are we not going to discuss how you went ape shit on that bloke? Frank said he wasn't breathing. Do you realise what the repercussions could be?' demanded Mike, his inner Mr Hyde erupting in full force.

'Give him a break Mike. We all made mistakes, and things were more chaotic than we had planned for. I'm sure he'll discuss it when he's ready.'

'Whatever Marv. He might have jeopardised all of us because he couldn't control his emotions. What was the deal? Why that guy? You had him restrained; we've all seen the drone footage.' The thermal video was seriously incriminating. It played out in gory detail Archie's savage attack on the man. Its ultra-high-fidelity footage was even clear enough to show the blood pooling around the unfortunate soul's head. It glowed bright white like a puddle of milk. Archie didn't respond. He simply rose from his chair, and walked out the room.

'Oi. Where are you going? We need to close this off. What happened to *Do good, always*? *Better every time*? Or is the whole covenant thing a load of bullshit, just like it sounds?' By now Archie couldn't hear him. He was out of earshot, marching towards his room.

'Well that was all a bit emotional! Anyone fancy a drink?'

'Shut the fuck up Bomber, you moron.' Mike stood

abruptly. His chair toppled over, clattering noisily onto the floor, making the rest of them jump.

'I'm going to bed.' He stormed out of the room, leaving the remaining cohort slightly bewildered. It was not really in Mike's nature to be so confrontational amongst them. The discovery of the trafficked women had really got to him. It took someone with experience to defuse the situation.

'He's fine. Just needs some time to cool off. Whatever happened, Archie was right. The fact we all made it out intact was a real blessing. Things could have gone much worse. I suggest we hit the hay, and reassess in the morning. I'll check on the two of them.' The remaining men were grateful that Marv had volunteered to take on the responsibility. None of them relished the idea of having a deep and meaningful with either of the individuals whilst they remained so volatile.

'All right dudes. See y'all in the A to the M. Peace,' Abu chirped as he held up his customary two fingers, and vacated the room. The remaining men trickled out in a less dramatic fashion.

I fucking killed him.

Archie stared into his reflection whilst brushing his teeth. He had killed people before. Admittedly, the vast majority were at a much greater distance, and often obscured by an enormous dust cloud. Certainly none had been dispatched with a foot. Why was this hitting him so hard? The little prick had assaulted him. Put him in hospital. He had been one of the catalysts for starting *Make Ready* in the first place. As he spat the frothy paste into the sink, the sound of the man's snapping bones flashed into his head. It was a primeval sound. The kind of thing the brain is pre-programmed to recoil from. Archie swallowed, and closed his eyes. His victim's petrified, broken face appeared, and his eyes instantly sprang open again. Why was this happening? If he was honest with himself, deep down, he didn't feel pity or remorse. It wasn't necessarily the most harrowing thing he had witnessed.

Perhaps the adrenaline was still working its way out of his system. Or maybe it was the fear of reprisals. After all, everyone he had killed before had been in the name of queen and country. No one was going to begrudge him ending the lives of bad people in distant lands, particularly if it made them feel a little bit safer. No, this was something very different. An alien emotion that he couldn't get a handle on. One thing he knew for sure was that he was in for the long haul with this one. All the indicators were there. It would be etched into his psyche for weeks, probably months, possibly years. The same thoughts and feelings, replaying over and over again. As long as he could contain them, compress them into a small parcel kept somewhere in a dark recess of his brain, they could be squeezed out of existence given sufficient time and pressure. It was a technique he had employed successfully, numerous times before. There was no reason it shouldn't work this time.

What had occurred during the briefing was disappointing. Unprofessional. He would apologise in the morning. Without his guidance there was a strong chance that the group would fragment. None of them could afford to let that happen. The key would be finding another target as soon as possible. Get back on the horse, and go again.

CHAPTER 21

'I'm telling you, this is it.'

'Are you certain? Seems a bit of a stretch.'

'Just watch.' Marv and Archie sat observing the trawler bob its way into the harbour. It was a pleasant day. Only a smattering of fluffy clouds tarnished the perfectly blue horizon. 'They use a small, privately-leased jetty reserved for yacht club members. From there, the load is taken to a distribution point, before making its way into the city.'

'How regular are the deliveries?'

'From what I can tell, every couple of months or so. Unfortunately, they're not working to a set routine. I'll have to conduct further intercepts to obtain an accurate date.'

'Where do they launch from?'

'Always Londonderry. It seems they have someone on the inside working for the harbour authority there. Probably loyal to the *cause*, so they are,' he said putting on a mock Irish accent. 'At least they think they're being loyal.'

'Who are their customers?'

'Anyone and everyone. I don't get the sense they're too discerning. As long as you have the cash, they'll do business.'

'So from the distribution point, the cargo could be sent anywhere in the country?'

'Yes. Or even abroad. The records show purchases on mainland Europe as well as the UK. It appears to be a very cosmopolitan venture.' As they talked, the boat docked at the jetty. It was met by three men and a woman. They were all dressed similarly. Smart but functional clothing. The type that allowed them to blend into a chic city environment, whilst still being able to perform more dynamic movements if required. The reception party briefly greeted the sailors, before going aboard and disappearing out of sight.

'Does the port authority ever conduct searches?'

'Very infrequently, if ever. They have an arrangement with the club so that their members are not unduly disturbed. Money still goes a long way, if applied correctly.'

'And when they've searched the vessel, I assume nothing has been found.'

'Not that I know of. I'm sure this whole line would have been shut down pretty bloody quickly if they had.' Archie sat back and rested his head. They had been required to wait very patiently for this opportunity to emerge. Yet again, Marv had been pivotal. He had become their key intelligence gatherer, and was constantly developing the role. The older man relished the opportunity of hunting down leads, whilst connecting dots along the way. It was the ledger that they had lifted off the Poles, which had exposed the trail of breadcrumbs, leading to this point. After days of researching different codes, puzzles, and cryptograms, Marv had finally unlocked its secrets in the simplest manner possible. He showed it to Sheftel.

'Oh yes, this is a type of shorthand for bookkeepers. It allows one to record sufficient information to keep the taxman happy, whilst avoiding too much specific detail. It's an old system common in Eastern Europe. It was developed under the Soviets, you know? See here, places. Here dates. Prices. And finally, quantities,' he confirmed as he pointed at each column in turn. 'It's very simple. I can explain it to you in a few minutes if you have time?' Marv lapped it up. Bigrams were used to represent key locations. Each product had a serial number applied. Quantities and prices were decimalised, as a method for reducing the long rows of figures that would otherwise have dominated the page.

'Benji, you are a life saver. I definitely owe you one for this.'

'You do. And I won't forget it my friend!'

Marv spent hours working through the busy pages. It was a treasure trove of information. Unfortunately, the vast majority of it was useless to them. Despite the quantity of entries, there weren't any obvious opportunities upon which they might capitalise. Despondent, Marv was about to give up, and park the ledger back in the safe to gather dust. Then, he had a eureka moment. He considered re-examining the laptop they had recovered. When he matched some of the entries against documents stored on the computer, he was able to piece together specifics about the wide range of activities the gang had been involved in. Of all of them, one stood out as a real opportunity. A boat's name, registration number, and manifest details. It was this kernel of information that had ultimately led to Marv and Archie sitting on a dockside in Liverpool, discussing their next potential operation.

'So what are we talking about in terms of quantities?' Archie enquired.

'According to the records, anywhere between thirty and forty a time. Normally a mixture of hand guns and

237

assault rifles, with the odd shotgun thrown in for good measure.'

'Which would suggest that anyone transporting them is likely to be armed?'

'I think that's a fair assumption.'

'That's a problem. How are they moved inland? Do they provide distribution, or do the customers come and collect?'

'Honestly, I don't know. We'll have to get eyes-on to find out more. So what do you reckon? Could be interesting couldn't it? Of course the next conundrum is identifying a buyer so that we can offload them.'

'It's certainly interesting. I'm just worried that the stakes have gone up yet another notch. Guns would undoubtedly complicate matters, and as you say, we wouldn't be able to offload them for the foreseeable future. Let's head back to the hotel and we can discuss it further.' Archie started the engine, and they headed away from the seafront towards their budget accommodation.

During the previous weeks, Archie's attention had predominantly been focused on opening their new northern branch. It had been the perfect distraction to keep his mind from fixating upon the disastrous events of Norfolk. With the collective efforts of the team, it hadn't taken long to convert the unassuming fishing club into a fully decked out office space, and comfortable accommodation area. *Make Ready* had its third property on the books. To get things kicked off successfully, he had decided to remain on site, along with Simmo and Mike. He and Mike had reconciled their differences after the fractious meeting. Both had conceded that the other had good reason to feel their views were justified, and that they would just have to agree to disagree.

'Look, I can assure you that I would have liked nothing more than to have helped those girls. Fuck knows they didn't deserve what happened to them. I met enough of them on the streets to know what a sad tale theirs is. Perhaps we should have made a quick detour to at least cut open their doors,' Archie offered.

'Possibly. But like you said, they probably wouldn't even have stirred given how drugged up they were. I'm not sure we could have carried them out with us. Still, I wish there was something we could have done for them.'

'Me too. At least we taught their captors a lesson. With any luck, they managed to escape.' The girls hadn't. As it transpired, the cars driving towards the farm weren't reinforcements. They were customers. A group of pissed-up lads on a stag do, who had booked an appointment following their night out. When they discovered the group of men tied together in the courtyard, they quickly changed their plans and drove off. It wasn't until the following afternoon that the men were freed by a colleague bringing in supplies. The business was up and running again that same evening, after his colleagues had disposed of the Ukrainian man's body in a professionally dug grave, somewhere out in the remote woodland bordering the premises. He was simply chalked up as collateral damage.

Now that it was all water under the bridge, Archie and Mike had both thrown themselves headlong into making the expansion a success. Alongside the three original members of the group, who would remain temporarily, six of the ten new recruits had made the new site their permanent home.

The other four recruits, who had been identified as potential candidates for extramural employment, remained in Colchester with the rest of the *originals,* where their performance and motivations could be monitored more closely. Archie was yet to formally raise any job offers.

The group had done a great job of marketing the new centre, even hosting a grand opening event, where a range of businesses were invited to come and see what was on offer. It had already generated a significant amount of business. The trustees had attended too.

'Oh I'm so pleased you've been able to open a second location. I'm sure that the northern community will be grateful.'

'Thank you Sarah. We're delighted too. It's great to be able to reach a whole new demographic. The feedback's been extremely positive.'

'You were very fortunate to have the budget to make the leap so quickly,' Billy declared in an accusatory tone. Did he suspect something? 'Most charities take much longer to establish themselves.'

'I guess we just have a cause that people are keen to support. Perhaps people appreciate their veterans more than you thought?'

'It's probably because most people have never met them!' He delivered the statement as a joke, but there was obvious venom behind the comment. Collectively, they laughed. Archie simply glared at Billy, thinking what a loathsome toad he was. Marcus got them back on track.

'Let's hope they get more of a chance as a result of

the fantastic work being done here, eh?'

'Here, here. I hope that the contacts I provided are bearing fruit.' For once, Farouk had come up trumps. He had facilitated introductions with four reasonably large companies, which had all accepted an invitation to attend the open day. One had already committed itself to utilising their services.

'They most certainly are thank you. It's great that so many businesses have been able to see the set-up first hand.'

'I'm hoping to get a couple more on board if you're able to host them at a later date.'

'We will definitely try to make time for them. The more the merrier!'

'How are the rest of the chaps doing in Colchester?' Helen had remained noticeably quiet for the majority of the day. Something was clearly troubling her.

'Very well thank you. All of them are being kept busy generating new opportunities and, of course, prepping for the next batch of personnel.'

'I notice that you kept some of the new characters back there rather than bringing them up to Leeds.'

'Well spotted. The extra support means that a small group of us can remain more mobile, in order to look for expansion opportunities.'

'That sounds reasonable. Be careful though. The finances aren't looking as healthy as they were now that we're committed to three sites. Of course, the more work you can generate the better. I'm sure today will go a long way towards helping fill the coffers. Either that, or you'll need to befriend some more wealthy benefactors.' Her tone was concerning. The statement was delivered without emotion, when perhaps it could have been intended as a quip. Was she onto them? Had some crucial piece of detail been missed? Archie could only smile sheepishly and respond, 'We'll do our best.'

'Of course you will. Let's go and mingle a bit shall we? A bit of schmoozing should help get them on board.' It was to Archie's great relief that Marcus offered an out. He took it without hesitation, making for the nearest group of suited champagne sippers. By the end of the day, they had managed to persuade seven companies to sign up to their services, the most interesting of which was an outdoors pursuits firm that was looking to increase the number of instructors on its books. It was a fantastic result for the nascent venture, and immediately gave the new group something to focus on.

Much to Archie's relief, the trustees had departed without any further mention of funding or indeed any other concerns. Even Billy had mellowed. Perhaps it was the significant quantity of canapes and booze he had shovelled down his neck. That evening, the Leeds based team enjoyed a small celebratory meal together where Archie was able to get to know the new personnel much better in an informal setting. They all seemed like very decent people, with some interesting stories to tell. The course had certainly proved to be a good selection mechanism thus far. It assured him that the new centre was in safe hands, allowing him to devote his full attention to the Liverpool job.

CHAPTER 22

The following day Archie had departed early in the morning to link up with Marv so that they could begin examining the specifics of the operation. Following their surveillance by the marina, the two men shared supper in their hotel's restaurant. The place was mediocre at best. Something akin to a service station canteen. Food prepared off site, several days earlier, sat stewing under heat lamps.

'So, what do you suggest our next steps should be?' Archie asked, briefly looking up from his barely passable chicken madras. He was keen to hear Marv's opinion. So far the man's advice had always been on point.

'I think, given the number of transit stages involved, we need to start narrowing down our options. To do that, we need to identify when the cargo is least well protected... Most vulnerable... We also need to ensure that our exit routes are kept open,' he suggested, in between large mouthfuls of burger, which he was hungrily shovelling into his mouth.

'Absolutely. What are your initial thoughts?'

'Well, we can rule out Northern Ireland for a start. There's no way the logistics would work. We'd draw too much attention. Also, I suspect that the individuals waving their guns farewell are no joke.'

'Definitely a fair assumption.'

'From what we've seen of the distribution depot, it would be a very tough nut to crack. It's well protected, and in an inaccessible location. They obviously knew what they were doing when they selected it. I guess the bonus may be that they're keeping more stock in there, but at the moment I'm not sure the risk would be worth the reward.' Marv took a big swig of his iced tea, washing down a handful of sweet potato fries. 'That only leaves a couple of realistic options. Either take them whilst in transit, during the sea journey... or, whilst they're en route to the buyers. Given that we're not sure what system they're employing in terms of distribution, it's tough to make a call without further information.'

'A fifth option might be to target the buyers. Possibly less well prepared? More susceptible?'

'Uh uh,' Marv stated, shaking his head vigorously. 'Too many variables. The buyers could be based anywhere. We'd need to be mobile enough to trail them around the country, or god forbid onto the continent. Also, they may only be purchasing a fraction of the consignment. It doesn't make any sense to me.' Archie nodded, whilst scratching his stubbly chin. He stared into the middle distance deep in thought.

'You're absolutely right. In that case we probably ought to focus our efforts on the distribution and sea transit. Let's get a team allocated to each. Purely analytic research for the time being. I don't think we should commit to putting boots on the ground quite yet. Once we have more information we can determine how to progress.'

'Sounds good to me. I can start gathering the initial data we'll require this evening. Shall we get the bill?' The two men paid up and retired to their rooms for the evening. Archie's room was basic but functional. It reminded him of living in the accommodation block when he was in the Army. Outside he could hear the shrill calls of seagulls circling and swooping, scavenging any scraps of food they could lay their greasy claws on.

He had enjoyed what he had seen of Liverpool. This was his first time visiting the city. The interesting blend of industry and culture was very appealing. A change of scene had also been good for his mental wellbeing. Fewer dark thoughts haunted him, and he was sleeping better. By any luck, he was through the worst of it. He had considered sharing his anxieties with Marv, but had decided it would only make him look fragile, weakening his position. Everyone insisted that there would be no judgement, but there always was. He sat down at the desk, opened his MacBook, and booted it up. There were a number of emails requiring his attention. He worked his way through them.

1. Subject: BRANDING REVIEW – Can you have a look at this and let us know what you think?
From: Abu@MakeReady.org

2. Subject: updated course programme
From: Bomber@MakeReady.org

3. Subject: How's it going bro?
From: Theodore.Maine893@mod.gov.uk

How did he get his email address? Archie minimised the page. Rising from his seat, he put his hands up to his face. This was unexpected. He hadn't corresponded with either of his brothers for years. It was an arrangement for which he was almost exclusively responsible, and one that he would be happy to continue. Once upon a time, the three of them had been extremely close. He felt no resentment towards them. It was just that over the years they had drifted apart, having less and less in common. After he began living rough, they simply didn't have a means of staying in touch. Why was Theodore emailing now? Marcus must have provided the contact details. It was the only explanation.

He paced the room, before making himself a cup of coffee. As he sipped, he noticed the screen saver cycle onto a picture he hadn't seen for many years. It was of his Company in Afghanistan. Somewhere near the centre, he was perched on the bonnet of a WMIK. Daz was squatting next to him. For the briefest moment, he was taken back to that tree growing just outside of Sangin District Centre, staring into his friend's lifeless face. He shook his head, refocused, and took another glug of coffee. It had dawned on him some time ago that the episodes didn't stack on top of each other, appearing all at once in some vast, unwieldy, tapestry. They tended to drift in and out of focus. Single moments triggered by some sight, smell or sound. A twisted form of nostalgia. This was just another one of those. It would pass.

He sat back down in front of the computer. Nudging the mouse caused the picture to disappear. He hovered the arrow over the task bar for a while, considering whether to click on the tab that would bring the emails back up. Whilst he thought, he played with the cursor, making it go round and round in little circles, hypnotising him into inaction.

'Fuck it,' he whispered to himself. The emails

popped up. He clicked on the one from Theodore.

Hey bro.
Hope all is well?! I hear you're keeping yourself busy at
the moment with an exciting venture. Great news!!! I'm
really pleased for you mate. It's about time somebody
recognised your talents.

I'm not sure if you've heard, but I've just moved back
to Credenhill, which is awesome. Didn't expect it at all,
but really chuffed they thought I was up to it. Mega busy
as you'd imagine, but I'm sure I could find time to visit if
you're up for it? Just drop me an email and we'll sort
something out.

Don't know if you've heard from Barney? I've not
spoken to him for ages, but dad tells me he's faring well.
He's based somewhere in the Far East at the moment
from what I can tell. The postings are always a gift with
the FO!

Anyway, I hope we're able to hook up; it's been far
too long. Stay safe, and speak soon.

T

Instinctively, Arthur clicked on the reply button. He
paused. What was he going to say?

Hello dearest brother.

Glad to hear you're still Mr Golden Balls. I've
managed to get off the smack, but have started a
criminal enterprise. Oh, and I recently killed a bloke
with my feet.

Have a good life.

Love Archie.

No. He clicked on the little cross in the corner of the page, and closed the lid. It was late. The sky outside was black, but the glow of city lights illuminated the horizon, shrouding it in an orange halo. Urban noises flooded through his window. Honking cars, rattling trains, barking dogs. He could smell the sea on the warm breeze. For a moment, it felt like he was on a holiday in some exotic land. An abrupt knock on the door quickly reminded him that he was in a Travelodge, in Liverpool, planning a heist.

'Hang on a sec,' he called out. A muted voice came from the other side.

'It's just me. I've got some info you might be interested in.'

'Okay, just coming.' *Couldn't this wait until morning?* Marv could often be compulsive, obsessing about details to the point of neurosis. It's what made him such a good investigator. Archie opened the door. Marv was clutching a mass of papers under one arm, and a laptop under the other. He brushed past without invitation. Archie could tell he was deep down a rabbit hole.

'Right. I've managed to pin down some very interesting bits and pieces.'

'Go on. You want a coffee or something?'

'What? No, thanks.' His head was buried in the laptop, and he was tapping away at the keys like a maestro. 'Here's the juiciest nugget.' He spun the computer around so that Archie could see the screen.

'What am I looking at?'

'That, is the forecast for the Port of Londonderry. Normally they don't release the manifest details of smaller vessels on the main site, but legally all ships entering or departing must register their details onto the harbourmaster's schedule. I managed to get into it through a legacy site by registering a false vessel.' Pausing for effect, Marv used a pen to point at one of the rows in the long list. 'As you can see, here's the boat we saw today. A sixty foot trawler, called The Pride of Mersey. Next scheduled departure from Londonderry is in two months' time. Unfortunately, this is only a provisional date, which is subject to change depending on a range of factors such as weather. However, it at least begins to narrow down a window.'

'Great work. Anything else?'

'As a matter of fact, yes. I've also managed to get some details regarding the suppliers from the documents we lifted off the laptop.' He clicked on one of the windows. 'This is a quick summary of all the details I have been able to pull together thus far. Bottom line is that the guns are coming from south of the border via a splinter organisation with historic links to the IRA. It seems they've drifted away from their nationalist roots, and are now more interested in coin. They're obtaining their merchandise from the US, through affiliations with sympathisers, mainly operating on the east coast. They aren't aware that the weapons are being shifted on. As far as they're concerned, they're supporting preparations for the next round of troubles, linked to uncertainty over Brexit.'

'Holy shit. How on earth have you managed to piece all this together sat in your room? There's barely enough Wi-Fi to hook up to YouTube!'

'I have my ways.' The disturbing look on his face made him look even more sly than normal.

'Of course you do. Are you able to consolidate all the key facts into a document and send it to me?'

'Already on it. I'll use the anonymous account. And ensure it's encrypted of course.'

'Sterling work as always my friend. We can invest further tomorrow after some sleep. Fancy a night cap?'

'No thank you. I'm going to go and follow up on a couple of leads, and then get my head down.'

'No probs. In that case, see you in the morning.' Marv collected up his various articles and headed out the door.

The conversation had definitely piqued Archie's interest. Obtaining just a handful of outline details was a big step forward. As challenging as this one might be, it could also be a massive opportunity. It's not like the other operations had been a cakewalk. As always, with adequate investment into planning and preparation, anything was possible. In the distance, Archie could hear the Liverpool Cathedral bells toll. It was midnight.

CHAPTER 23

'Christ. I'm hanging out here.'

'Just keep your eyes on the horizon.'

'I've tried that and it's not working. I need to spew.'

'Well if ya gunna chander, make sure ya do it away from me.' The small craft bobbed rhythmically up and down on the waves. The four men sat, waiting patiently for the command to go.

'Are you sure this was the best option? Couldn't we have stayed on dry land, bruv?'

'I'm afraid not. You're just going to have to suck it up mate.' Abu couldn't hold it any longer. He leant over the side and vomited. Unfortunately, the wind was strong enough to blow half the load back onto the inflatable skirt. It dribbled onto the inside of the boat, carrying with it an unpleasant acidic smell, which made the others gag.

'Urrghh. Just drown me.'

'What's tha matter laddie? Never got issued yer sea legs, eh?' Donald stood facing the wind, with his beard blowing off to one side. In a previous life, he had worked on a fishing trawler for a couple of seasons. He looked completely in his element. Very gingerly, Abu sat back down in his seat. But, the moment he had settled, he immediately sprang back up again, launching himself towards the side. Another torrent of puke projected out of his mouth. This time, most of it managed to escape the confines of the vessel. The portion that did make it out to sea, rested on the surface of the water, floating like a slick of chum.

'Look at the poor little fella. At least it's not me eh

lads? Come on Abu. There, there. Get it all out,' Frank chortled with glee. *At last*, he thought, he could get his own back on the gob shite. Abu didn't even attempt to retort. Archie and Donald joined in, laughing at his expense. Looking off their starboard bow, they could see the other boat. It too contained four people, including one of the two new recruits.

Originally from South Africa, Robbie was an unusual character to say the least. Devoutly religious, vegan, tee total. He was as straight laced as they came. How he had come to be homeless was something of a mystery. It was a conundrum that Archie had never quite gotten to the bottom of, despite extensive questioning. What he did know, was that Robbie was off his trolley. Wired to the moon. Not in the volatile, not knowing what he would do next, kind of way. It was an altogether more consistent lunacy, which could be generously described as eccentricity. It wasn't clear if he had behaved that way prior to joining the Royal Marines, or if it had been a by-product of his experiences. For a man with a university education, he managed to maintain a very simplistic view of the world, and was utterly uninhibited by other peoples' opinions.

After extensive consideration, they had decided to only bring two of the four potentials into the group. The decision was made primarily on the basis that the two not selected clearly had no interest in compromising the excellent charity work they were delivering. Robbie and Tanya, on the other hand, were very obviously seeking something more dynamic. Finally broaching the specifics with them had been tough. Archie had determined it would be best to give it to them straight, but only after ensuring that they were sufficiently wedded to *Make Ready* so that they wouldn't compromise the whole enterprise if they ultimately decided it was not for them. The whole group had attended what might have been loosely termed an initiation ceremony. It gave the occasion a bit of gravitas, which would hopefully assist in compelling the two candidates to say yes. Archie delivered a similar spiel to the one that he had used in Wales, albeit carefully refined now that they had some pedigree. Both understandably had questions. Lots of them. But once adequately satisfied that the cause was worthy, and the risks justified, they had recited the covenant, making their extended responsibilities official. Their addition was extremely timely. This job desperately required the extra manpower.

Running through the planning process had quickly highlighted that ten individuals would simply not suffice, given the requirement to split efforts between sea and land. Following serious deliberation, they had concluded that intercepting the cargo at sea would be the best option based on a number of factors. Firstly, the challenge for the target to reinforce themselves. Secondly, of all the phases of transportation, it was when the guns were least well defended. And thirdly, it offered the widest range of exit options. There were, of course, plenty of serious challenges as well, including the requirement to obtain suitable craft, the short window in which to make the seizure, and the fact that nobody knew how to operate a power boat. The complete list was extensive. However, when weighed against the other choices open to them, it was undoubtedly the most promising avenue for success.

'Target vessel identified crossing phase line Charlie.'

'Buccaneer One acknowledges.'

'Roger that Buccaneer Two.' Based on their calculations, the message indicated that their target should be within range in approximately five minutes. It was five minutes too long as far as Abu was concerned. He continued retching, salty tears streaming down his cheeks.

Of all the challenges they had faced in devising the plan, the addition of waterborne activities was by far the most significant hurdle to overcome. Most of them had very limited experience operating off of dry land. In that respect, Robbie had proven to be an invaluable source of knowledge. His time as a Marine had provided him with a wide range of skills associated with planning, and executing, littoral operations. He was also a keen surfer and sailor, which gave him a superb understanding of tides and currents. Archie also possessed some insights, due to his role in the Commando Brigade, but nowhere near sufficient to deliver an undertaking of this complexity.

The plan broadly revolved around three crucial elements: reconnaissance and surveillance, interception, and extraction. Each had been dissected in detail, and rehearsed extensively with one notable exception. Obtaining the three boats that they required for the job had been a massive headache. Frank quickly discovered that hiring appropriate craft was much more problematic than dealing with their land borne equivalents. Not only were they harder to acquire due to limited availability, once he had identified a suitable fleet, the craft were based in the wrong part of the country and had to be transported to Liverpool overland. What's more, the hiring procedure had required the production of false competency certificates, fabricated licenses, and a range of other paperwork, which had, in itself, been an operation. Nevertheless, he had somehow pieced it all together.

They had opted for highly manoeuvrable inflatable craft, akin to the ones used by the Royal Navy for coastal activity. Fast enough to catch or outrun almost any other vessel they might encounter, whilst being sufficiently robust to endure the unpredictable conditions of the Mersey estuary. Unfortunately, the opportunity to conduct rehearsals had been much more limited than their previous endeavours, for fear of drawing attention. The majority of their practice had therefore been conducted in a simulated environment, blending the use of computer graphics and mock ups of the boats, which they used to practice embarkation and disembarkation. It wasn't as good as the real thing, but served as an adequate substitute.

Yet another major headache they had encountered was establishing a suitable base of operations. Consideration had been given to travelling from the Leeds branch. However, the distances involved were too great. They also wanted to avoid using insecure moorings for the boats. Most significantly, it would have been almost impossible to mask their preparations from their colleagues. At the last moment, Donald had managed to identify an out-of-use ship repair facility where the owner was happy to accept cash payment, and seemed nonplussed about any official documentation.

Its location wasn't ideal, adjacent to active businesses, and a little further along the coast than they would have preferred, but it would do the trick. One huge bonus was the presence of a causeway that would facilitate the fast offload of any merchandise and the boats themselves.

'Target crossing phase line Delta. Stand by, stand by.' The third boat had been assigned as a command and emergency response platform. Following at a suitable distance, Marv and Tanya relayed the position of their target.

'All right chaps, let's get ready to go.' Donald fired up the outboard motor, and allowed it to idle. Unlike their previous jobs, this one was being conducted in broad daylight. The selection of when to strike was out of their hands, being dictated by the scheduled crossing time of their target.

'Abu, come on mate. Get a grip of yourself. It's show time.'

'Coming. Just give me second.' A long string of phlegmy bile linked him to the side of the boat. He wiped his mouth with a filthy sleeve and took his seat. Their research had indicated that there would be no more than four occupants on the target vessel, concluding that a two-to-one ratio should be sufficient to incapacitate them. They had positioned themselves a couple of miles off shore. Far enough away from the busy coastline to avoid detection, whilst remaining reasonably close to their base location, so that they could return within a reasonable timeframe if required. 59 and Simmo waited with the vehicles ready to receive the cargo.

'Go, go, go!' Donald opened the throttle. The boat took off. Salt water cascaded over the bow in a wall of white, foamy, spray. It was pure exhilaration. Gripping on for dear life, the seated men were buffeted about, but somehow managed to maintain their composure. Two hundred metres away, their sister craft paralleled them, skipping over the waves.

'Buccaneer One. Target identified. Sixty seconds out.'

'Buccaneer Two, sixty seconds also.'

'Zero acknowledges.' The messages were shouted, so that they could be heard over the top of the deafening roar. This was by far the most dangerous part of the operation. Conducting any manoeuvres at sea could be hazardous at the best of times. The addition of a moving target, containing a non-compliant crew, who were probably armed, put the level of risk through the roof. Archie would be lying if he said he wasn't nervous.

'Thirty seconds.' The assault teams prepared their grapples.

'Boarding.' Just like the crew of an old pirate ship, they attached their ropes to the unsuspecting vessel, pulling them tight alongside. Approaching from the rear had provided them with the element of surprise. The target hadn't even changed tack. As soon as the two craft were secure, three occupants from each piled onto the target. They had opted for a notably different approach from their previous jobs.

'UK Border Force. Everyone move to the stern now!'

'What's this about? We submitted our papers before departing,' one of the exasperated occupants explained, as he emerged from the pilot's cabin waving a document.

'You've been selected for a random search. We've intercepted a number of craft smuggling immigrants recently. I'm afraid your registration number came up. Now, please move towards my colleagues so that they can assist you.'

'I'll need to see some identification.' Archie pulled out a fake ID card. It would be surprising if they knew what the genuine article looked like. The ruse worked.

'Come on. Let's get this over with.' As suspected, the crew totalled four individuals, all men. They remained surprisingly compliant; worrying behaviour, given the cargo they were supposedly transporting. However, as soon as the plasticuffs were produced, their mood changed.

'Why do you need those mate?'

'Yeah, I've never heard of Border Force cuffing people, like.' Their Scouse accents were unmistakable.

'And why're yous wearing balaclavas?' Mike attempted to placate them.

'Just standard procedure until the search is completed I'm afraid. We've had people pull weapons on us before. We're not allowed to take the chance. Health and safety you know?'

'Bollocks mate. Don't touch me, ye prick.' The bolshie man was large. At least six foot five. Restraining him wasn't going to be easy.

'If you'll just place your hands behind your back for me, it will all go a lot smoother. Please don't make this difficult.'

'Nah. You can go fuck yourselves.' As soon as he began reaching for his pocket, Mike was on him. Despite the man's enormous frame, Mike's expertise enabled him to put his larger adversary into a deep arm hold. Unfortunately, his sheer mass made it difficult to force the man to the ground, where the cuffs could be applied. They began pirouetting around on the spot.

'I need some help here!' Mike cried out. Robbie pounced. Between the two of them, they managed to subdue their oversized adversary. As Mike held his contorted face in the oily brine sloshing around on the deck, Robbie applied the restraints. Concurrently, their colleagues grappled with their counterparts. Only Bazza couldn't take his man down. Unable to get hold of his elusive quarry, and growing increasingly frustrated, Bazza elected to simply barge into him. The unsuspecting man was sent tumbling over the rails of the boat, into the freezing water below.

'Help… Help!' His cries were muffled, as waves splashed over his head. Coughing and spluttering, he attempted to tread water in the choppy sea. Very quickly, it became a losing battle. Due to the freezing temperature, he went into shock almost immediately. The boats were still moving and he wasn't wearing a life vest. Within a couple of seconds, he was already ten metres away. To compound his predicament, the hapless man's head kept disappearing, making it very difficult to track his position.

'Someone grab him. Quick,' one of his mates piped up.

'I can't reach him.'

'Kill the engine.'

'I think it's too late. Where is he?' They scanned the water, but couldn't spot him. The sound of the chugging diesel motors and wind whipping across the surface of the ocean prevented any noise from penetrating. Then, an arm appeared, breaking the surface of the water, followed by the man's half-submerged face. He managed to take a quick series of half breaths, before the icy water washed over him again. Abu grabbed one of the circular lifebuoys hanging from the side of the cabin, and launched it towards the direction that the man had appeared, hoping that he might still possess the wherewithal to grab it. The red and white ring bobbed silently on the surface. Nothing happened.

Suddenly, the man's torso erupted from the water, driven upwards in a desperate attempt to save his life. He thrashed his way towards the preserver, but was so drained of energy that progress was painfully slow, and he began to flounder. With a last ditch effort, the frantic man managed to wrap one arm around the buoy, locking himself firm. Abu took up the slack on the line, before pulling him in towards the boat. Between them, he and Archie managed to drag the insentient man over the railing, and back on board. He was in a bad way. However, they had already wasted too much time with the rescue. Despite his deteriorating condition, they weren't going to take any chances. Abu cuffed and hooded him.

'Let's crack on,' Archie shouted, struggling to make himself heard, whilst the remaining three men, who were obviously shaken by their friend's ordeal, were hooded and frisked by Bazza and Frank. The other boarding team members began scouring the boat. It was not a large vessel, but there were sufficient hiding spaces to make the task challenging. Unfortunately, the Scousers had done a good job. Flinging open cupboards, stowage doors, floor panels, and anything else that looked like it might be sufficiently spacious to contain the weapon crates, they combed through the craft top to bottom, but found nothing. After two minutes of frantic searching, they began to grow desperate. Bedding was removed, kitchen units ripped apart, the engine compartment scrutinised. Still nothing. This couldn't be right. There was no way they would have made the voyage without good reason. Having been unable to witness the boat being loaded with cargo had always been a weak point of their plan; the chances of being spotted were simply too great. But they had done their homework. Archie was entirely confident that the weapons were on board somewhere. The way the men had reacted had been too aggressive to suggest otherwise. Time was ticking.

'We're going to have to get them to tell us where the weapons are,' Archie proposed.

'Leave it to me,' replied Bomber enthusiastically. Archie didn't want to take this step, but it was a necessary evil if they wanted to locate the elusive shipment. The failure of the previous job weighed heavily on his mind. Bomber was the right man for this particular job.

'Right you cunts. One of you is going to tell me where the guns are, or you're joining your mate in there.' He gesticulated towards the roiling grey water, seemingly oblivious that they couldn't see anything.

'Fuck off. We're not telling you nothing ya dickheads,' responded the large man, who was first to speak up. The hood made it difficult to hear him clearly, but they got the gist.

'Oh really. We'll see about that.' Bomber positioned

himself behind the shackled man. 'Someone hand me that jug.' Mike picked up a plastic container hanging off the side of the cabin, and placed it into Bomber's outstretched hand. Carefully, he leant over the side and filled it to the brim with water, before placing it down beside the man's head. Then, he flipped him onto his back. 'Right. You've got one more chance to tell me, before things start getting really bad for ya.'

'Fuck yers.'

'Okay, if that's the way you want it chum.' Bomber picked up the jug, and started pouring the water over the man's hood. The result was an improvised form of water-boarding. The victim began to kick and buck in attempt to break free, but the combined effect of the restraints, and Bomber kneeling on his chest, prevented him from escaping the onslaught.

'Anything to say?'

'Unnggh. Baarrrggh.' The big guy couldn't speak even if he wanted to.

'No. How about some more?' Bomber continued pouring the ice-cold liquid over the man's face. Further guttural noises emanated from beneath the hood.

'Give him a chance to speak.' Mike interrupted.

'NNggh. The. The rope. The rope.'

'What rope?'

'Mnnghh. Tied to the bow.'

'Someone have a look.' Frank and Bazza headed to the front of the boat, to see if they could identify what the man was talking about. After only a cursory search, they noticed a superfluous cord disguised behind one of the buoys. Frank yanked on it. Nothing happened. However, he could feel it disappear underneath the hull.

'There's something there, but we can't get it to come free.' Bomber returned his attention to the now fully compliant man.

'Okay chief. You've got one chance to get this right or I'm keelhauling you. You know what that is don't ya?' The man shook his head. 'Well, I'll tie a piece of rope to ya, launch you off the side, and then pull you underneath the boat, up against all the barnacles. I've always thought it sounded fun. You should have a good view of whatever's down there. If you don't drown that is. Now, how do we get that cargo?'

'Arrggh.' Bomber had placed his knee into the man's groin and applied plenty of pressure.

'There's two clips on the side of the boat, just in front of the pilot's cabin. You need to undo them, then pull on the rope, and hey presto.'

'Did you hear that?' Frank nodded. He and Bazza headed for the location that the man had described. The catches weren't immediately obvious. As with the rope, they had been placed behind buoys to mask their presence. Bazza was the first to locate the one disguised on the port side.

'I've got one. D'ya need me to come and show ya where it is?'

'Yeah. I can't see it anywhere!'

'Look behind the buoy that's in front of the cabin.' Frank pushed the float aside, and cried out.

'Got it!' Both men pulled open the clips. Nothing happened. Bazza rushed to the front of the boat, and seized the rope. This time, it didn't require much effort to begin pulling in. Methodically passing one hand over another, the slimy cord coiled itself on the surface of the bow like a writhing snake. Eventually, something emerged from the water. Frank peered over the side.

'I can see something. Looks like some cases.' Suddenly, the rope went taut. Bazza tried yanking on it in an attempt to free up the jam, but the cargo was stuck firm.

'Shite. I can't pull them up.'

'Here, let me give you a hand.' Frank joined him on the rope. Even with their combined efforts, the cases would not budge.

'Nah, it's not working.' Frank's piercing voice was surprisingly effective in the blustery conditions. Bomber immediately demanded a solution from his victim.

'They're stuck. What's the crack? You'd best hope this isn't a trick.'

'Someone needs to get in the water, and take the stopper off the rail like, otherwise they ain't goin' anywhere.'

'Perfect. Sounds like you're going for a swim then.' Bomber dragged the man to his feet. With Mike's assistance, they led him to the front of the boat, and forced him to his knees.

'You get one chance at this. If you fuck about in any way, and I mean any way at all, I'll stick ya and throw you in for the fish. Play nice and you might make it out of this alive.' They tied a length of rope around his waist, and as Mike locked one of the man's arms, Bomber cut the restraint, before removing his hood, ready to strike if he attempted to put up any resistance. The giant had been sufficiently shocked into conformity.

'Right, get yourself in, and get those crates unlocked!' Bomber commanded. Gingerly, the man hoisted himself over the railing and jumped into the sea. He disappeared briefly, but quickly bobbed back to the surface, gasping for air in short sharp bursts. After a few seconds, they heard a loud metallic clink. The first string of crates floated up, on the port side. The man swam to the other side of the bow, and again fiddled with something underneath the water, resulting in another clink. The other row of plastic crates emerged.

'Get me… back in,' he cried, thrashing about wildly. Any sense of control he may have possessed defeated by the relentless waves.

'Let me think about it,' Bomber's tone provided a clear indication that he was enjoying the spectacle.

'Please… I'm… sinking.'

'Come on mate. Get him back in now.'

'I think he still needs some time to cool off a bit. Shouldn't have gobbed off back there should he?'

'Enough's enough. He did what we asked. Let's just get him tied up again!' Mike shouted more insistently.

'Nah, not yet. I want to hear him beg.'

'Come on… I don't… think… I can… keep swimming.' The man began flagging, as the cold sapped the energy out of him. He was barely audible.

'I'm getting him.'

'Don't even think about touching that rope.'

'Step out the way, now!' Bomber positioned himself so that Mike couldn't access the lifeline. Even with his expertise, shifting Bomber's significant bulk would be extremely challenging, if not impossible, in the conditions. 'Please don't do this mate. We don't need to make him suffer.'

'Yes we fucking do. Serve him right the northern

monkey. I'll pull him in when he's learned some manners.'

'He's barely breathing. Let's just get him on board, sort out the crates, and get the hell out of here!' They remained poised in a Mexican standoff. Neither man wanted to back down. Suddenly the radio crackled in their ears.

'Buccaneer One and Two, Command. Send sitrep.' Archie replied.

'Buccaneer One. We're recovering the cargo now. Extract in approximately figures five.' From the command boat, Marv and Tanya could see that the recovery was taking longer than expected. They were unsure what the strange scene was, unfolding at the front of the vessel, and thought it was best if they checked-in just in case.

'Ack. We'll hold in position.' At this point, the exhausted man was unable to tread water any longer. His head silently dropped away underneath the water. Neither Bomber, nor Mike, was aware, being too embroiled in their own confrontation.

'This is your last chance. Let's just grab the rope and get him in.'

'Who put you in charge? This was my gig. I got the info from him, so I decide when he comes back on board.' Bomber's infantile reasoning wasn't particularly convincing. However, in his mind, he was one hundred percent in the right, and couldn't be persuaded otherwise. Frank and Bazza had made their way up front to see what the delay was.

'Come on lads. What're ye waiting fer?'

'He's left that bloke down there to drown.'

'We don't have time for this. Just get him up and let's go.' The united front was sufficiently formidable to convince Bomber that the man had learnt his lesson. He and Bazza grabbed the rope, and began pulling. It felt like deadweight on the other end. It was. The man was unconscious, hanging limply from the loop tied around his torso.

'We need a hand here. Yer man's got to weigh a hundred and fifty kilos!' Bazza exclaimed. Mike joined them. Their combined strength was sufficient to get him over the railing, and onto the deck.

'Shit. He's not breathing.' The man's face was ghostly pale. A blue tinge had appeared around his lips. When they placed him on the ground, his head lolled backwards, banging onto the metal surface with a thud.

'Let's leave him and grab the crates.'

'Are you crazy? We're not going to let him die in front of us you lunatic.' Mike had placed him on his back and began furiously pumping his chest in an attempt to clear the water.

'Fuck him. Frank mate, you get the ones over there, and I'll grab these ones.' Frank hissed back at him.

'Don't use my name you dopey twat.' As Mike continued working to revive the lifeless mass, the others grabbed a pair of boat hooks. Leaning over the bulwark, both men struggled to latch onto the moving target, but eventually managed to gain a hold, before hoisting the heavy cases up the side of the vessel. Bazza helped drag them on board. There were ten matching containers in total, each made of tough plastic.

'Nice one. Let's transfer them to the boats and get going.'

'This guy needs a medic, or he's done for,' yelled Mike in desperation.

'No time. Let's move,' replied Bazza.

'I'm calling for back up.' Mike keyed his radio.

'Command, Buccaneer Two. We need a medic ASAP.'

'Command acknowledges.' Archie was taken aback by the request. Watching over the prisoners at the stern, he was unaware of what had developed at the front of the boat because it was out of sight beyond the cabin. He hurried to the bow.

'What's going on? Is someone injured?' He looked down to see Mike attempting to resuscitate the man, whilst the others began loading the cargo. 'What happened to him?'

'He drowned because of that idiot,' Mike spat, pointing towards Bomber. 'If he doesn't get attention, he's gone.' The situation was far from ideal. Archie was facing yet another dilemma that placed him in a direct confrontation with Mike. There was no way they had time to wait for back up to arrive. It had been too long already.

'Let me have a look at him.' Archie crouched down beside the man. He took off a glove, and placed two fingers on his neck in an attempt to find a pulse. He could feel something, but only barely. *Shit.* Archie briefly considered his options. They couldn't hang around any longer. He decided to maintain the pretence. Twisting his head to the side, Archie moved his cheek alongside to the man's yawning mouth to see if he could identify any breathing. Not a thing.

'Mate, I think he's gone.' The lie was delivered

sufficiently well to convince Mike. Archie would deal with the repercussions for his own conscience at a later date. For now, they had to get out of there.

'For fuck's sake. I'm going to kill that lunatic.'

'Just cool it. We need to get going. I promise we'll discuss it once the job's over.' Archie had placed a hand on Mike's shoulder. Mike shrugged it off, and rose to his feet.

'Command, Buccaneer One. Hold off. We're extracting.'

'Command acknowledges.' In the meantime, the teams had finished loading the final crates onto the two vessels. Donald had remained on board piloting one of the craft, just in case they needed to make a quick getaway.

'Jesus. Took ya long enough.'

'Not now. Let's just get this over and done with.' No one was in the mood for banter, least of all Archie. Before disembarking the commandeered boat, Abu and Robbie conducted a final sweep to ensure that they hadn't missed anything of great value or importance. Content that everything of interest had been collected, the two men returned to their respective teams. Untying the tethers as they boarded the vessels, they leapt over the railings, before taking their seats. The sea had become even choppier. Each man was encrusted with a thin layer of salt, which looked like a smattering of snow against their dark Border Force uniforms.

'Command, Buccaneer extracting now.'

'Roger, see you at the RV.'

'Highwayman acknowledges. Ready to receive you.' Simmo and 59 had waited patiently at the ship yard with the vehicles. The fleet had grown quite sizable. As well as a Transit van to transport the cargo, they had hooked up three SUVs with trailers for the boats. Despite it being the middle of the day, they couldn't observe any witnesses. The majority of local businesses were either too occupied with their own activities, or had shut down long ago. In any case, they were confident that their cover story of conducting a Border Force training exercise would hold up to scrutiny, it being a regular occurrence in the area.

As the boats pulled away from the target vessel, Archie looked over towards Team Two. Mike was tussling with Bomber. He had grabbed him by the shoulder straps of his life preserver, forcing him back into the seat. The last thing they needed was a full blown punch up out in the middle of the sea.

'Buccaneer Two, Buccaneer One. Get a grip of yourselves. Be professionals. We'll deal with it back at base.' He wasn't hopeful the instruction would work, but he had to at least try. Strapped into his seat he felt helpless. The men remained locked together refusing to budge. Thankfully Bazza intervened, managing to prize them apart. Mike reluctantly took his seat, and the two light craft sped back towards the docks.

CHAPTER 24

They made landfall within ten minutes. Everyone felt absolutely drained, having been pummelled by the powerful inflatable boats. As soon as they arrived, Simmo and 59 sprang into action, helping moor the first boat to the concrete dockside, before hauling the first of the crates ashore. Archie, Abu, and Frank disembarked, and formed a chain. Between them, the van was filled up in no time at all. Simmo released the vessel, allowing Donald to manoeuvre it to the causeway ready for loading onto the trailer. Concurrently, Robbie pulled his craft alongside, and the unloading process was repeated. It was a slick routine. One that they had practised with the discipline of a Formula One pit crew. Positioning the heavy craft so that it could be dragged out of the water, on the other hand, was an ordeal. It took several attempts before the first boat was suitably aligned to attach the winch. Abu took the driver's seat of the SUV, ready to move the vehicle and trailer out of the way once its consignment was secure.

'That's it. Keep it coming. A bat more. Stap!' Donald had dismounted the boat and was shouting instructions to Frank who was operating the winch. Once in position, they attached restraining straps.

'All right. Drive off!' Abu gently applied throttle. The vehicle pulled away slowly up the slope, to a holding area near the yard entrance. The remaining crew returned to the dockside, ready to assist Team Two. Archie remained keen to prevent any further hostility erupting. He was ready to step in if necessary, but sincerely hoped it didn't come to that. Acting as the buffer between an agitated Bomber, and a raging Mike, was not a prospect he relished.

'Last one,' Robbie said, as he handed the final crate to 59, who passed it down the chain, and in through the rear doors of the van. The boat was loaded onto the trailer, this time more efficiently, whilst Tanya orientated the command boat into position for its turn. It transpired that she was a fantastic helmsman. Probably the best of them all. In her youth, her family had regularly holidayed in Malta where her mother originated from. She would often go out adventuring on her uncle's luzzu; a small colourful fisherman's boat. With countless hours of practice, she became extremely adept at handling the craft, even though she was only a young girl at the time.

Despite being a statistical anomaly, Tanya had taken to this alternative life like a fish to water. She had trained as a nurse before joining the Army, subsequently serving as a medic with great success. Her career included the award of a Queen's Gallantry Medal for saving the life of a fellow soldier, who had become trapped in a burning vehicle whilst deployed to Iraq. However, after her parents died in quick succession, as a result of short-term terminal illnesses, the isolation and pressures of military life had gotten to her, and she had made the decision to leave. Unfortunately, without any form of support network following her departure, she had fallen on difficult times. With no abode, and no real money to her name, she had turned to prostitution; the only form of employment she could find that provided a sufficient distraction from the turmoil in her head. The unsavoury environment degraded her to the point of desperation, resulting in an all-consuming drug addiction, which ravaged her body and mind. It had also resulted in several overdoses. Fortuitously, the most recent, although near fatal, had been a sufficiently powerful stimulus to trigger her into taking action. When she had learnt of *Make Ready* from a friend, she had leapt at the opportunity to make a fresh start.

Expertly applying some throttle to the outboard, she brought the rear of the RIB around, and lined it up perfectly with the causeway. Marv waded through the shallow water drenching his boots. He attached the hook of the winch cable to the connection point at the front of the vessel. The thin wire slowly wound its way around the drum. As soon as the connection went taught, Tanya applied a touch of reverse throttle in order to keep the boat straight. It didn't take long to have the final craft secured. She jumped into the passenger seat, and made the call.

'Command boat secure. Good to go.'

'Roger. All call signs extract now.' One after another, the vehicles headed out of the yard, making for the motorway. They had removed all sign of their presence earlier that morning. During the long journey back to the drop off point, there was no jubilation. No whooping and cheering like there had been after their first mission. Everything had suddenly felt more business-like and routine. Archie had taken the precaution of swapping places with Mike so that he wasn't travelling in the same vehicle as Bomber.

'Look, I was just trying to get him to cooperate. He didn't have to be such a knob about it. If he'd just done as he was told he would've been all right.'

'I get that, but you didn't need to leave him in the water for so long.'

'I didn't know he was going to puss out and fucking drown. Should have had some more swimming lessons as a kid!' he chuckled at his own joke. No one else laughed.

'We had agreed to use minimal force to get the job done. That's always been the plan. Pushing it like that could cause serious long-term dramas.'

'What, like kicking a bloke a bloke to death?' Archie could feel himself filling with rage, but managed to remain calm. Externally at least. How dare he bring that up? What grated most was that Bomber had a point. The truth, it transpired, hurt.

'I acknowledge that incident was a mistake, and I've apologised for it. I should have done better. Shown more self-discipline. I was also hoping that we would learn from the episode, so that no one else repeated it. Regrettably, it seems the message didn't get through.'

'Yeah, well, what does it matter anyway? Just one less witness. No one's going to miss him are they?'

'That's not really the point. We need to take the high ground. Not stoop to their level.'

'Why not?' Bomber snapped back. The comment had really agitated him. 'I heard that bullshit so many times in the Army. *We're the good guys. We mustn't behave like them.* Well why the fuck not? Our enemies took the piss whilst we had our hands tied behind our backs. They were laughing at us mate. Just like these wankers are laughing at us now. I say it's time we become the ones doing the laughing. Put the fear of god back into them. I thought that was what this was all about.'

'No, this was about regaining a sense of purpose and pride. Doing the right thing, for the right people. It was never about becoming the bad guys.'

'Well, maybe that's what we are now. And I for one, bloody love it.' The comment really struck a chord with Archie.

He realised instantly that they had collectively crossed a moral Rubicon when he lost control back at the farm, but he didn't realise that it had been interpreted as a green light to descend into chaos. Archie didn't respond. He couldn't. What could he say? The more he reflected, the more he realised that this enterprise was morphing into something beyond his control. It was unreasonable to fire them all up, and then expect them not to behave like savages now and again. Perhaps the outcome was preordained for anyone inhabiting the brutal criminal world. Perhaps it was time to embrace the savagery. His thoughts were interrupted by Bazza.

'Bomber mate. You need to chill out, so ya do. It's about getting the job done efficiently. Leaving the minimum fingerprint. I have no problem with being a bad guy, but I do have a problem getting caught. A couple of bodies floating about in the Irish Sea is a pretty big feckin fingerprint.'

'Yeah. Spose.' It seemed Bomber wasn't in the mood for intellectual debate after all. He tipped his head to one side, rested it against the window, and shut his eyes. Within moments he began snoring. The cogs whirred far too slowly for anything to faze him. Bazza followed suit soon after. The constant motion of the boats, turmoil of the seizure, and fresh air, had been

tremendously fatiguing. Archie watched them with
envy. There was no way he was going to sleep with all
the thoughts flying around in his head. He needed a
distraction.

'Good job today Robbie. Those boarding drills
worked a treat.'

'No problem, eh. We used to do them all the time,
back when I was in the Fleet Protection Group.'

'Well, without your expertise we would have
struggled.'

'I just hope we got what we came for. The lads have
said we can move onto the next level once we're tooled
up.'

'Did they? Well, I'm not sure about that. Let's see if
we can find a suitable buyer first. The plan was never to
take the weapons out on jobs with us.'

'You're the boss. I'm just the new boy. I'll do what
I'm told.' Robbie was concentrating on driving. He
didn't once look up at Archie. He was a very difficult
man to read.

'It doesn't work like that. Everyone needs to
contribute if this is going to be a success. We're all here
because we bring something different to the party.'

'I get it. But there needs to be a hierarchy. A
structure. You know that's what these boys wanted.
What they needed, eh. And that's what they've got,
because you gave it to them.'

'Of course there's some structure. We've got to
maintain a few roles and responsibilities, otherwise it'll
be anarchy. But I like to think everyone's more or less
empowered to make their own decisions. We all have a
voice.'

'Maybe you can't see it mate, but not everyone wants a voice. Plenty of people in the world are just happy to go along for the ride. Me included.'

'Hopefully you'll change your mind. You've obviously got a brain on your shoulders. We need people like you in the organisation if we're going to succeed.' It was at that moment, Archie realised that he was delivering exactly the same speech that he had been on the receiving end of, so many times over the years. The one about fulfilling potential. Now he was faced with the challenge of growing an effective team, he was beginning to appreciate why people had been so insistent. It wasn't for his benefit. It was for theirs.

'Brains. Pfftt. I don't know about that, brah. If I had any brains I'm not sure I'd be sitting here! I guess god just had some strange plans for me, eh?' Archie involuntarily let out a short burst of laughter.

'Fair one. I'm not sure it was god who put me here, but someone definitely has a sick sense of humour.' They spent the majority of the remaining journey in silence. Archie turned on the radio, which was set to BBC Radio Four. It was the comedy hour. Hearing the programmes brought back memories of his childhood. Growing up, his father constantly had the radio on in the background, no matter where they were in the world, somehow always tuned to that same channel. At the time he found it extremely dull, but now he was older, it provided a welcome, and strangely comforting, distraction.

Briefly stopping for fuel, he disembarked from the vehicle and stretched his legs, whilst Robbie filled the tank. The other two were still out for the count. They had ditched their Border Force uniforms shortly after departing the docks, burning them in a skip. The smell of scorched fabric stilled lingered on his clothes. He decided to buy a coffee, and headed into the brightly lit store. Marv and Tanya were already inside.

'All right. How's it going?' he asked.

'All good. Glad that's over with. I wasn't sure what to expect,' Tanya replied in a hushed voice. She was sipping on an orange juice.

'Same here. Never been too keen on the oggin.'

'Me neither. How's everyone doing?'

'Okay, as far as I can tell. Mike's still super pissed with Bomber, which I can't blame him for. We'll cover it all in the debrief once we get back.'

'I'm just glad that my expertise weren't required. Hopefully it was all worth it.'

'I'm confident that it was. As soon as we've dropped off the boats we'll head for Colchester. Shouldn't be more than a few hours from here. Is Marv looking after you?'

'He is, in his own way. The pervy old bastard keeps flirting with me.'

'Yep, he'll do that. He'll get bored eventually if you don't indulge him.'

'Oh I won't. He couldn't afford me anyway.' She smiled, before heading to the till to pay for her drink. Despite appearances, she was a strong woman. Archie knew she wouldn't take any shit from them. Her compact frame was deceptively powerful. During sparring practice she had even managed to incapacitate Frank, who must have weighed at least twice as much as her. He had been concerned that her presence would change the group dynamic. He had seen it all too often in the military. Everyone was worried about the woman's wellbeing, when they should have been more concerned with how the men would alter their behaviour. Women were more than capable of doing the job. It was the blokes that would soften themselves, assuming incorrectly that they needed to become protectors. Fortunately, Tanya had made it abundantly clear from the outset that she didn't need anyone looking after her. Archie wasn't surprised that Marv had taken to her. He had always liked a challenge. The feisty blonde woman was the perfect balance for him; attractive, but a bit rough around the edges.

Having paid for their snacks and beverages, the three of them returned to the vehicles. It had taken a while to refuel, because they had needed to use the lorry lane in order to accommodate the wide trailers. Only one vehicle at a time could utilise the pump. They arrived in Southampton an hour later, returning the RIBs to the hire company. In an ideal world, they would have waited a few days to allow some of the heat to die down. However, because there was nowhere to store the boats in Colchester, and because they were confident there would be nothing on the books that could be traced having paid in cash, whilst ensuring that their identities had been masked, they had determined it would be best to offload them as soon as possible.

For the homeward leg they swapped drivers. Archie took the opportunity to jump back into his original vehicle so that he could talk to Mike, and assess the mood. He knew only too well what it was like to be on the receiving end of his wrath. He could sense the mood was gloomy, but thought it would be best to defuse the situation prior to the debrief.

'How's it going mate?' Archie asked sincerely.

'Honestly? I've been better.'

'I know. That whole episode was far from ideal. I would have tried to intervene if I knew what was going on.'

'It's not your fault. It's that simple twat. I don't know why we put up with him. He's a fucking liability.'

'That's a bit harsh. Granted, he doesn't always think before he acts, but he's always been a solid part of the crew.'

'He *never* thinks before he acts. I don't care if he's part of the foundations. He has to go.'

'Let's not start talking like that. Don't forget, I've fucked up as well. More than once. He'll need some readjustment for sure, but he'll learn from this, and make the necessary improvements.'

'No he won't. Unlike you, he's too thick to realise when he's in the wrong. It simply won't penetrate that dense skull. For him, it's all one big sick joke.'

'Come on bruv. He's pretty flippin odd, but he's not that bad,' Abu chipped in.

'Look, I know he's one of the *originals* and everything, but I think it's time for a change. I guaran-fucking-tee you he's going to do something nuts one day, and it will end up with one of us getting hurt. We've got some new bods who are much more promising. One could easily take his space.'

'Mike. I know you're upset, and I understand why. But please try to keep things in perspective. I asked him to get the information out of the guy, and he did. If he hadn't, we wouldn't have the guns, and the whole operation would have been jeopardised. In the heat of the moment he lost his head. That's all.'

'He didn't lose his head. I saw it in his eyes. He loved torturing that guy. He was getting off on it. Watching him drown was the cherry on top.'

'I think you're being harsh. We've always known he's got his foibles, but he's not a psychopath. Sometimes if you're a hammer, all you see are nails.'

'Well he's got the IQ of a hammer that's for sure!'

'Not my point Abu, but fair one.' His wisecrack helped break the tension, but only slightly.

'Can I just ask you to try and rise above it for the time being? We need to keep the after action review constructive. Fighting Bomber will make it anything but. If you can avoid him, I'll have a word, and we can work something out between us.'

'Absolutely I'll avoid him. I don't want to be anywhere near the moron. But I won't change my mind. As far as I'm concerned, if he's not finished, then I am.'

CHAPTER 25

'Archie. Archie. Wake up.' Abu had placed a hand on his shoulder. They had arrived back at base. One of the blindingly bright external security lights was shining directly in Archie's face, and he felt completely disorientated. Reaching up to his ears, he removed his AirPods. Moments before, he had been immersed in a vivid dream. More precisely, a vivid memory. One from long ago that he thought he had shaken off.

'What time is it?' he queried with a croaky voice.

'Twenty two thirty.'

'Okay. Let's go to the briefing room, and get this over with.' Abu walked away, leaving Archie to unpeel himself from the comfort of the seat. Closing his eyes, he rubbed them with the back of his hands. The abrupt return to reality had been unnerving. Reaching into the door well, he grabbed a bottle of water, and swigged half the contents. His body was tense. Deep within his ears he could hear the blood pumping around his head. Somehow, a taste of burnt dust clung to his palette.

'Come on. Get a grip of yourself,' he muttered, so quietly that the comment was barely audible. Having taken a brief moment to transition back to reality, Archie clambered out of the car, and made directly for the briefing room. The atmosphere felt oppressive. Everyone sat in silence. Mike and Bomber had occupied different sides of the room, which was something of a relief. He had half expected them to have engaged in a full-blown fist fight. Some of the low mood could probably be attributed to fatigue. The remainder, simply tension between team mates who had been through a stressful experience.

'Sorry I'm late in. I'd completely conked out. Thank you for gathering so promptly. I know everyone's tired. However, as I'm sure you all appreciate by now, this is a very important element of the operation, and one that we must capture in the moment. For Tanya and Robbie, the format is very simple. We run through each phase in detail, dissecting what went well, and what we need to improve upon for next time. Nothing you won't already be familiar with.' Their two eager faces reminded him of the first time they had gone through this process. The other faces in the crowd didn't look quite so perky.

'Before we kick off, let me just address a couple of things. We all know that there was an incident between Bomber and Mike.' He thought just tackling the elephant in the room head on would be the best approach. He eyeballed each of them as he spoke.

'Please don't allow that to become the entire focus of this process. If we do, we'll miss other important details. We will discuss it, but separately, in a more appropriate forum. Bomber. Mike. Agreed?' They each nodded reluctantly without looking at each other.

'The next point of business is that today was a success. We pulled off a complex operation, involving many intricate moving parts, and retrieved the cargo. Let's be clear, that's a win. We need to keep things in perspective. What we need to examine now, is the way we got there, and if there was a better way of doing it.' He could feel his words weren't really landing. They just wanted to scatter, and get some rest. Perhaps it could wait. Maybe this would be more productive in the morning. Much to his relief Marv spoke up.

'I can start if you want.'

'Sure. Please go ahead.' Archie gratefully replied, before the discussions got into full-swing.

They were done and dusted in an hour and a half. It was the fastest review that had been conducted to date. And it wasn't as if they had skipped anything. Everyone had contributed, building upon what they had learnt during previous jobs. Archie reflected that he may have misread the situation, projecting his lethargy onto the rest of the team. Even once they had concluded, the consensus was that they should push on through the night, to inspect their haul, and reset the equipment. There was no sense in risking one of their colleagues walking in and asking difficult questions. Before leaving the room, Archie pulled Bomber and Mike to one side. Despite the strong urge to leave them to it, he considered that tackling the issue early would be the preferable option.

'Look chaps. I know this is awkward, and that you really don't feel like reconciling your differences right now. However, we can't afford to have the friction hanging over us. I know exactly what it's like from our previous gig. I can tell you from experience that it's not healthy. Mistakes were made, and in a tense situation it became understandably heated.' They couldn't even look at each other. 'May I suggest that we meet up tomorrow and chat things through properly? No judgement, just resolution.'

'I don't know what the problem is to be honest. I was just doing what I needed to, to achieve the mission. You get it, don't you Archie?' Mike snapped.

'Are you crazy? You acted like a fucking animal. I

can't work with idiots like you. Tomorrow morning I'm gone.'

'Come on mate. Please try and calm down. Let's not try to solve this now. Why don't both of you go and get some kip, and we'll reconvene in the morning?'

'I'd rather see what we got.' Bomber couldn't resist the urge to see what was hidden in the crates. Despite the circumstances, he maintained the innocent enthusiasm of a child at Christmas.

'Fine. You do what you want. I'm going to get my head down.'

'Okay. How about we meet at nine o'clock to go and grab some breakfast? If you still feel the same way, we'll work something out.' Mike rolled his eyes, gave a slight nod, and stormed out the door.

'Christ. I don't know what his problem is. He needs to chill the fuck out.'

'He's just wound up. I'm sure he'll have calmed down by the morning. In the meantime, I would appreciate it if you would consider apologising to him. We can't afford to lose anybody. Certainly not as good an operator as Mike. Even if you think you're in the right, I need you to swallow your pride. Can you do that for me?' Archie pleaded, adopting the most sincere tone he could manage.

'Let me think about it. He spoke to me like I'm some sort of mug. You know I don't stand for that.'

'I understand. Let's go and help the others.' Archie desperately wanted the situation resolved. The truth was, it would be almost impossible to replace Mike. His expertise was invaluable. He had proved, time and time again, that he was a lynchpin for the whole operation.

Everyone respected him. Honestly, given the choice between Mike and Bomber, it was a no-brainer. And yet Bomber had his merits too. More importantly, Archie wasn't certain that he would be able to trust his discretion should he be ejected from the group. In an ideal situation, he would be able to persuade both to remain. Stuck between a rock and a hard place, Archie could see no easy way out.

When he arrived, the store room was a hive of activity. All ten crates had been laid out on the tables. Frank was in the process of breaking the seals, whilst others worked on reconditioning their gear. In order to ensure a water tight seal, the smugglers had used an ingenious method of vacuum packing, which sealed the boxes tight, and prevented water from entering. It also made the containers devilishly hard to break into. After several attempts to prize open the lids, Marv suggested that brute force might not be the answer. A more scientific approach could be a better option. Abu fetched his safe cracking set, and used the electric drill to create a vent for air to enter the crate, breaking the seal. After all receiving the same treatment, each crate proved much easier to open. Their contents were laid out for the group to survey.

'Will ya look at that?' Donald exclaimed, as he stood back and admired the sight.

'They sure is purtty' Abu added, in a faux American accent.

'Happy days, ladies and gents. Let's see what we've got, eh?' Robbie began picking up each gun in turn, and carefully inspecting them. His weapon recognition skills were by far the best out of all of them; a by-product of his South African heritage.

'All right. First up,' he announced, as he turned the pistol over in his hands, pulling the top slide to the rear, and locking it in place. 'It's a classic. Glock 17. There's an aftermarket sight fitted, but other than that, all original. Serial number's been filed off. Three spare mags.' He carefully placed the gun at the end of the table, and moved onto the next one.

'Another Glock 17. Same treatment with the sights.' In total, the first four crates contained sixteen of the popular Austrian pistols. All of them had been expertly prepared for criminal use. There was no way of tracing their origin.

'Onto some bigger boys now.' He pulled a sub-machine gun out of the next case. Like the handguns, it was finished in matt black.

'Nice. Very nice. This, my friends, is an H&K UMP. Iron sights, folding stock, factory fore grip.' He pressed a button, which unfolded the stock increasing its length by about a third. Then, cocking the weapon and holding the bolt to the rear, he used a torch to peer inside.

'It's the nine millimetre version. Looks like military spec. Still fully auto. We've got six mags, and it looks like a spare Holosight in this case. This must be worth a bit of money, eh?' Robbie positioned the SMG on the next table, categorising the weapons as he worked his way through. A further seven UMPs emerged, all in the same configuration. Again, all had been sanitised of markings. Six crates down, four to go.

'Last up. It looks like a mix of shotguns, and ARs.' The larger weapons occupied significantly more space.

Robbie held aloft a hefty looking shotgun, and pumped the mechanism to the rear.

'A SPAS 12 with folding stock. This is one beautiful piece of machinery, eh. Looks like the twelve point five inch barrel. It's the most common variant. Holds eight shells.' The shipment contained only two of the meaty weapons, which were stored in a single case.

'Next. Another classic. Colt M4. I think it's an A1, judging by the gas piston system. Must be a slightly older model before Remington started producing them. Clean set up without any attachments. Six mags. My weapon of choice!' The M4s were placed onto the assault rifle table. A total of six of the famous American firearms were contained in two crates. An ACOG optic accompanied each weapon, which were highly desirable in their own right.

'Finally, for you Soviet fans.'

'All right. AK-47. Now you're talking,' Bomber interrupted.

'Actually, an AK-74. Chambered in five four five. Not as much punch as the seven six two, but higher velocity, and more accurate. This is a pretty modern variant. Yep, it's got the updated safety so it's an M version. Rails, fore grip, this can't be more than a couple of years old. Serious bit of kit, eh?' The final crate contained three of them. Robbie placed the AKs next to the M4s. With all their accessories lying alongside, they barely fit on the table. He stood back and admired the collection.

'Iechyd da. We hit the jackpot boyos!' 59 pumped his fist in celebration.

'Hell's yeah. A grand day's work, so it was.' Bazza

joined in with the self-congratulation.

'What d'ya think they're worth?'

'Honestly I've got no idea, bruh.' Robbie used the term of endearment for everyone, even Tanya who had asked the question. He considered it to be gender agnostic.

'They've all been prepped for off the books use, which makes them much more desirable. The Glocks must be about two grand each, the UMPs at least five. Couldn't say for the shotties. Maybe another five thousand, eh. I would guess that the M4s and AKs are a bit more, say seven. I suspect it will really depend on the market.' He paused, attempting to do the calculation in his head. 'Someone help me out. Maths isn't my strong point.'

Tanya pulled out her phone and tapped in the figures, before announcing, 'One hundred and forty five thousand. Not too bad at all fellas!' Many of the *originals* looked perplexed. It wasn't the response she was expecting. Frank was the first to query the figure.

'That can't be right. Try doing it again.'

'Yeah, seems a bit on the low side,' Simmo added. Tanya re-typed the figures.

'No, it's correct. Robbie's estimates might be off, like he said. Why, is that low? Seems like a lot of money to me!'

'Well, compared to our first couple of jobs it's less. Way less. Don't forget, our overhead costs were much greater, what with the boat hire, trailers, and everything else,' Simmo responded, making no attempt to mask the alarm in his voice.

'You mean to say I sat in that fucking boat for Christ

knows how many hours, throwing my guts up for one hundred and fifty K?' Abu directed the question at Archie, although the exclamation was intended more for general effect. Archie wasn't sure how to respond. They had conducted their research, albeit not in as much detail as he had desired. The reward in no way matched the risk. In all honesty, they were expecting more. Where was the error? The estimate of value? The quantity? The type of weapons? Even accounting for these variables, they were way off the mark.

'Let's not be too hasty with the pity party. We don't know what their true value is yet. We won't know for sure until we find a suitable buyer. It's nothing new. We had the same issue with the previous jobs.'

'Yes, but with the previous jobs at least we had someone to offload them to straightway,' Simmo observed, reverting to his usual calm tone. 'Or at least an idea of where to begin. These are a very different prospect.'

'Very true. However, we knew that going in. It was always a weak point in the plan. I'm sure we'll be able to source someone in no time, given the connections we've built. Let's focus on finding solutions not problems.'

'Here's one solution.' Everyone turned to look at Bazza. 'Let's keep them.' No one spoke so he continued. 'Think about it. Every time we do a job, it's getting more and more risky, so it is. If we want to continue taking down bigger and better targets, we're going to have to begin integrating more protection at some point. People are already getting hurt. Maybe this is a way of ensuring compliance, without putting ourselves in harm's way.'

'No way José,' Marv retorted immediately. 'As we've discussed, many times before, this puts us into a very different ball game. A bunch of people running about with guns attracts a lot of attention.'

Donald added to the dissent. 'Aye, I'm not sure we wanna go all Lock Stock laddie. It'll end in trouble.' A clear division developed almost immediately. Generally, it was the elder members of the group, and Archie, who were opposed to the idea. The remainder wished to keep hold of the arsenal, with a view to employing the weapons during future operations. After a heated debate, they were no closer to a resolution. This job had created too many unexpected rifts for Archie's liking.

'We've been talking about this for a long time now. I don't think we're going to agree any time soon. Perhaps we ought to get them stored away safely for the time being.' The prospect of someone walking in, and discovering something resembling a scene from the Matrix, was weighing on his mind. Light had begun to seep in through the window blinds.

'Leave it to ma.' Donald began repacking the weapons into their cases. He had already made an inventory, whilst they were in discussion. Conscious of the time, everyone assisted. Whilst they did, most couldn't resist trying the guns on for size. Various weapons were shouldered, pointed towards imaginary targets, their mechanisms toyed with. Curiosity even got the better of Marv, as he held aloft one of the fearsome shotguns. Once safely packed away in their cases, the group ferried the guns into the safe, before Donald locked them away.

'Last few bits to do, then we can get some well-deserved rest. Frank, you okay with the vehicles?' Archie asked.

'I could do with a couple of bods to help shift them around, but other than that they're okay.'

'Cool. Marv, what about the radios?'

'All sorted mate. Everyone's returned their batteries for charging, and I've packed all the handsets away.'

'Okay. Anything else anyone requires assistance with?' Silence followed. 'In that case, finish off what you need to. Once you're done, check in here, before we all bomb burst.' It only took a further thirty minutes to get everything in order. Gratefully, they departed for their accommodation after Archie called proceedings to a close.

Yet again, he struggled to sleep. No matter what he tried, all he could do was toss and turn under his duvet, which became increasingly entangled with his legs. The sheets felt greasy. There were just too many issues racing through his mind. It felt like every time they conducted an operation the bar shifted a little higher. Things just kept becoming more and more complicated. What's more he just couldn't shake the memory that had been unearthed, whilst snoozing in the car. It took him to a dark place. He recognised it as clear sign that he must be under significant stress. Certain memories, the ones that he had worked very hard to lock away, only seemed to return when he was feeling particularly anxious.

As exhausted as he unquestionably was, there was no point in simply lying in bed and suffering. He had experienced it too many times before to think there would be any chance of success. A shower might wash away some of the tension. He peeled himself out of bed and traipsed into the bathroom. Turning on the shower he allowed it to heat up before stepping in. The feeling of the fresh water washing away the salty brine was wonderful. On reflection, he should have showered before getting into bed in the first place, but at the time he was just too shattered. The smell of the shampoo was invigorating, just what he needed. He stepped out. As he was towelling himself off, someone unexpectedly knocked at his door.

'Hang on,' he called out. The knocking persisted, becoming increasingly urgent.

'Archie, it's Five Nine. You need to hurry mucker. There's been a drama.'

'Okay. Just a second.' *What now?* This day just needed to end. He hurriedly pulled on a set of jogging bottoms and a t-shirt, and opened the door. He could tell immediately from 59's expression that whatever was wrong, it was serious.

'It's Mike. He's done something stupid.' The Welshman didn't need to say anything else. They hurried down the corridor towards Mike's room. Rounding the corner, a small group had gathered outside his door, including some of the uninitiated members of *Make Ready* who had been attracted by the commotion. The situation was far from ideal. They needed to be kept at bay at all costs, just in case something untoward was divulged.

'Okay everyone. Let's make some space. It would be really appreciated if you could return to your rooms.' No one reacted. 'It wasn't really a request. Move it.

Now!'

They looked taken aback, but dutifully dispersed, murmuring as they went. Archie leant over, and whispered to 59.

'Make sure no one hangs around here.' 59 nodded gruffly. Adopting the stance of a bouncer, he positioned himself where he could block any curious bystanders. Meanwhile, Archie entered the room. It was distinctly Spartan. There were no pictures on the walls. Everything was neatly arranged. Archie realised that he had never ventured in there before. Tanya and Simmo were kneeling by the bed, on which Mike was sprawled out. He wasn't moving. Tanya looked up.

'He tried to hang himself,' she relayed. Archie had half-expected it, but couldn't believe he was hearing the words. *Shit*. What was he thinking? Why?

'Please tell me he's still alive!' he gasped.

'He is. But he's in a bad way.'

'Who found him?'

'I did.' Simmo replied. 'I came to check on him, after everything that occurred today. I thought that he could use some company.' His eyes were as wide as saucers. The discovery had really distressed him. He and Mike were tight, after spending so much time conducting surveillance together.

'What happened?'

'I tried knocking but there was no response. After a while, I got concerned and tried calling him in case he had gone out, but I could hear his phone ringing in the room. In the end, I decided to force my way in. The door wouldn't budge though,' Simmo described, before inhaling deeply. 'I felt something on the other side.

Pushing hard, I was able to make enough of a gap to squeeze through. He was hanging off the back of the door. He'd attached a belt to the closing mechanism.'

'Holy shit,' was all Archie could muster.

'I cut him down, moved him to the bed, and checked him over. He had a faint pulse, but wasn't breathing. I conducted CPR, and he began to breathe again, but he hasn't woken up.'

'It's lucky Simmo got here when he did. Another minute or so, and there's no way he was coming back.' Tanya was holding her fingers against Mike's neck, monitoring his pulse.

'Well done mate. Good work. How's he doing?'

'His pulse is strong, but he's struggling to get enough oxygen in. I suspect he's suffering from pulmonary oedema. His trachea is badly bruised with ligature marks. He really needs to be intubated to assist with his breathing.' She was matter of fact. Her years of medical experience had resurfaced.

'Five Nine, can you come in here?' Archie called out.

'What is it?'

'Tanya needs some kit. Can you help her out?'

'Sure thing. What do you need?' He took out his phone, and opened the notes page.

'Have you got an endotracheal tube and pump?'

'Yes. Anything else?'

'I'll also need succinylcholine, and a decent painkiller. Something like sodium thiopental would be perfect.'

'Decent pain killer I can do. Not sure what the first thing is. I know I don't have any of it.' 59's medical knowledge was nowhere near as comprehensive as Tanya's.

'It's a relaxant to help with the tracheal intubation. Without it, I risk damaging his airway.'

'Is there anything else we can use?' Archie asked.

'Not really. I can force the tube in, but it might cause subsequent issues. The alternative is we get him to a hospital.'

'Hospital should only be a last resort. We don't know what he'll say if he's drugged up. Perhaps if we lubricate the tube it will help?'

'It will assist, but it's more to do with the space available. Without expanding the airway it's going to be a tight squeeze. I'll give it a go, but if I think it's going to cause him further harm, I'll insist on getting him some proper attention.'

'Fair enough. It'll be your call.' 59 rushed off to gather the items. Archie couldn't comprehend how this could have happened. Mike could be highly strung, and the incident earlier in the day had irritated him. But to do something like this was extreme. Of the entire group, he seemed the least likely to snap. Evidently, he was carrying a heavier load than Archie had realised.

'Is there anything I can do to help?' Archie enquired, feeling like a spare wheel.

'Not really. I'd love a glass of water if you could grab me one please.'

'Of course.' As he turned towards the sink, Archie noticed the belt Mike had used lying by the door. It was amazing how something so innocuous and mundane could create so much drama. He picked up the glass that Mike used for his toothbrush, and washed it out. He was sure that Tanya wouldn't mind. It was then he noticed the envelope taped to the mirror. There was no way Mike would want anyone reading it now. Archie folded it in half, and stuffed it into a pocket before returning to the room.

'Here you go.'

'Thanks.' She saw it off in one go.

'Simmo mate, you all right?'

'Yeah fine. Just a bit shaken up, you know?'

'I'm not surprised. Just relax. We'll make sure he's looked after.' Simmo was slumped in an armchair in the corner. He looked spent. A combination of shock, the long day he had already endured, and the exertions of performing CPR, had totally drained him. 59 returned, carrying a bag of medical items. Beads of perspiration clung to his forehead.

'Here you go me darlin. I brought everything I thought would be useful.'

'Thanks. Give me the painkiller first, and whilst I administer it, prepare the IT.' He obliged, passing Tanya the syringe kit, and small vial of clear liquid. Within a few seconds, she had assembled everything required, and administered the injection into Mike's forearm. His body noticeably relaxed, as the tension in his muscles released.

'Okay. Hand me the tube and the pump. I need you to put your hand underneath his neck, and tilt his head backwards to open up the trachea. Hold it there until I say you can let go.' 59 had lathered the clear plastic tube in KY Jelly to help it slip down Mike's throat. Tanya briefly examined the assembly, familiarising herself with the design. Once content, she indicated to

59 that he should proceed. Carefully placing one hand under the back of Mike's neck, he used his other hand to slowly tilt his head backwards. When he released Mike's chin, his lower-jaw naturally fell open.

'Okay, here goes.' Tanya slid the end of the tube into Mike's mouth, and began feeding the remainder in. Twisting it slightly this way and that, the whole length disappeared without any obvious resistance. 'That was easier than I thought it was going to be. Right, Five Nine sit yourself here, and begin pumping the ventilation bag once every five seconds. You're going to get tired, so you two,' she ordered looking up at Simmo and Archie, 'Be prepared to take over. In the meantime, I'm going to examine his chest to see what we can do to reduce any buildup of fluid.' They collectively breathed a sigh of relief, pleased that Mike had been stabilised for the time being.

'I should have said. I'm going to need a stethoscope. Any chance you brought one up?'

'Fraid not. There's a couple in the medical supplies downstairs.' Archie thought he'd be of more use fetching and carrying, rather than as an idle observer.

'I'll go. Anything else?'

'Not that I can see. Looks like Five Nine brought pretty much everything I'll need.'

'I'll be as quick as I can.' Archie hurried downstairs, heading straight for the store room. Rooting through the conveniently labelled plastic boxes, neatly arranged on the shelves, he identified the one that contained the stethoscopes, and grabbed a set. Whilst returning to the room, he reflected upon how fortuitous it was that Tanya had joined their ranks. Without her knowledge, there was no way Mike would have survived. They sustained the pumping for a further hour, working in ten minute shifts. Tanya carried out a series of tests with the equipment available to her, and concluded that although there were signs of fluid on Mike's lungs, the damage wasn't too serious. As a precaution, they left the tube in place to assist his breathing whilst sedated.

'I think we're through the worst of it. To assist recovery, he'll require a diuretic to reduce the oedema, and plenty of rest. I highly recommend he sees a doctor at the first opportunity. He may have sustained more damage than immediately apparent, including possible brain damage. And clearly, he'll need to talk to someone about what caused him to do this in the first place.' She looked at the three men for acknowledgement. Archie instinctively toyed with the letter in his pocket.

'Of course. As soon as we're sure he's compos mentis, and isn't going to say anything compromising, we'll get him professional attention.'

'I mean it. What I've done is just a sticking plaster. Without a thorough examination, he could easily deteriorate.'

'You have my word. Amazing work by the way. I don't know what we would have done without you.'

'No problem. Glad that I could be useful. I'll stay here to monitor his recovery. It would be appreciated if someone could assist. The other two might as well get some rest.'

'We're all staying, no question,' Simmo blurted out, vocalising what the others were thinking. 'Pumping that bag is fucking hard work. He's going to owe us big time when he wakes up!'

CHAPTER 26

Mike's recovery was astonishingly quick; a combination of his incredible physical condition, and pure bloody mindedness. Despite the risks involved, he received a thorough consultation at a private clinic, which confirmed that he had suffered no lasting damage. The attempt to take his own life had though, taken a significant toll in other ways. Already an understated individual, Mike pretty much became a recluse. He would spend days, locked away in his room unwilling, or unable, to have interaction with another soul. Simmo, Tanya, and a few others, would occasionally check in to ensure that he was at least eating, but they were all met with monosyllabic responses, or more often than not, silence. The incident with Bomber was quickly forgotten about. No one wished to raise its spectre, for fear of reigniting whatever it was that had triggered Mike's extreme response in the first instance. For the majority of them, the best approach had been to focus upon their own routine, and move on.

Despite extensive efforts to identify a suitable buyer for the weapons, one had not been found. They came close with a Dutch outfit, who allegedly required the weaponry to provide close protection for a prominent biotechnology firm involved in animal testing. It later transpired that they were, in fact, interested in up-arming in order to conduct a heist against a rival gang. Sheftel had brought the opportunity to their attention through his connections on the continent. Archie had cancelled the arrangement as soon as he learnt of their ulterior motive. Partly, because of the risk of someone putting two and two together and tracing the weapons back to them. But mainly because it seemed counterintuitive to remove the guns from circulation and deprive one set of scum bags of them, only to put them into the hands of another group of scum bags.

Make Ready continued to thrive. Business was good, and consistently improving. A sure sign of success was that three of the new recruits had been offered full time employment by firms that had utilised their services. It looked like further job offers could be in the pipeline. Their catastrophic success was actually creating something of a dilemma. The entity's raison d'être was to rehabilitate and reinvigorate homeless ex-service personnel so that they could get on with their lives, but they also required people to run the charity. Denying recruits the opportunity to take advantage of new job opportunities would mean undermining the core principle upon which the organisation was developed in the first place.

Another training course was successfully delivered, and a further ten individuals joined the cohort. It wasn't a struggle keeping them busy, with plenty to occupy them. In total, almost thirty people were now on the books. Although they had the capacity for a dozen or so more, beyond that it was difficult to see how they would be able to expand any further in the short-term. Following the relative failure of their most recent operations, the coffers weren't exactly overflowing. Archie met with the board of trustees. They agreed that perhaps a tweak in approach was required. Instead of keeping people on the books for the long-term, the charity would become a pathway for suitable individuals to find employment, once they had been given the opportunity to redevelop themselves in a protected environment. This would improve through-flow, whilst freeing up space, and still achieving the desired end state; fewer people on the streets and more reinvigorating their lives.

In the meantime, they put out the feelers in search of their next operation. For the first time, the group was confronted with a choice. Both Todge and Sheftel had something on offer. It was a very welcome development. The opportunities that they had uncovered of their own volition had not been particularly successful.

The latter's was a very similar proposition to the job that they had executed in Newcastle, this time based in London. A new competitor had established themselves in the Docklands. They were undercutting the market with cheap stones being imported directly from Sierra Leone. The diamonds were being processed on site, before being distributed into the city and beyond, to overseas markets. Although a tempting prospect, the complexity of the environment would make it extremely challenging. For the time being, they decided to put the opportunity on hold.

During their conversations with Sheftel, he had also divulged another more concerning piece of information. Lukas Symanski, the head of the Polish gang they had ripped off, was actively seeking out the people responsible. According to Sheftel's cousin, the man was absolutely incensed that someone had had the audacity to strike his repository. He had directed several of his men to begin tracking down leads. So far, they hadn't discovered any specifics linking the job to the *Make Ready* crew, but word was getting around, which provided a detailed description of the perpetrators and their modus operandi. It was a development that they would need to keep a close eye on.

Todge's opportunity was a more appealing proposition for a number of reasons. He had been moving up in the drug dealing world, thanks to their previous business. In fact, he had been busy establishing himself as one of the biggest players in the east of the UK. In order to grow the business, Todge had established connections with a French group, operating out of Marseilles, who were looking for a slice of the British market. They had come to an arrangement, whereby the French would transport heroin, originating from East Africa, as far as the south coast, at which point he would take over distribution within the UK. Unfortunately for him, the gang controlling smuggling operations for the majority of southern harbours wasn't so keen for him to set up shop. He had explored other avenues, but the only feasible route, which he could reliably sustain, would be through Portsmouth. What he had proposed was the delivery of a sufficient blow to put them out of operation for a short period, which would create a window of opportunity for him to establish a foothold. For this, he required muscle. Muscle that he didn't have. This is where Archie and the team would step in.

Todge had become aware of a large shipment that his competitors were transporting from Folkestone to one of their warehouses on the outskirts of London. He even had the date and route, thanks to a careless driver inadvertently disclosing the information to one of his associates. If they could intercept the shipment, Todge would purchase it at a favourable rate, whilst benefitting from the interruption in supply. As far as Archie was concerned, it appeared to be a win-win situation. Even a cursory glance at the problem drew their attention towards the possibility of conducting an ambush on one of the quieter roads along the route. Comparatively, it should be a simple affair; at least this time they would be on dry land. However, there was one major concern. Reportedly, the shipment was always accompanied by some form of protection, the composition and nature of which was unclear. It was, therefore, this aspect of the operation on which they focused the majority of their intelligence-gathering efforts. Abu, Simmo, Bazza, and Robbie had been tasked with scoping the parameters of the operation. They had deployed to the south coast in order to become more familiar with the terrain. Meanwhile, Marv, Donald, and Frank had begun working on the logistics plan.

'Shouldn't be too tricky. I reckon we just kip in the vehicles, and remain as mobile as possible for this one. No need for accommodation or storage space.'

'Aye, I agree. It leaves less of a footprint.'

'What about transporting the goods? Do you reckon we hijack the vehicle, or transfer to one of ours?'

'Definitely transfer. We don't wanna risk a tracker.'

'It would be quicker though. Shifting the load would take a bit of time. We'll be out in public for all to see with our balls blowing in the breeze.'

'I still thank that using unfamiliar vehicles is a recipe for disaster. Also, wa'll probably have ta disable it ta get aboard. What d'ya thank Archie?' He had been loosely following the conversation, but had been finding it hard to concentrate lately with so many distractions clouding his mind.

'What's that Donald?'

'Ah was asking whether ya thank it would be better ta transfer the drugs into one of our vehacles?'

'I think so. There're too many variables using a hijacked one I would say. Let's not count it out until we've heard back from the recce guys, but I believe that using one of ours would be a safer option.' Donald gave the others a smug look, before they returned to their discussions. Marv raised the next point on the schedule.

'Now, what about storage? Are we bringing everything back here, or would it be better to offload them directly to Todge?'

'Let's definitely get it back in here. We'll need to make an inventory so we can estimate the value. I wouldn't trust that crafty drug dealer with it until we've had a look ourselves. He'll definitely try to rip us off.'

'Frank's right. We need ta retain some leverage over ham. I know he's come up trumps in tha past but ya never know.' They continued exploring the various options for some time.

Archie drifted off into his own thoughts again, only speaking to provide curt answers to questions specifically directed at him. It had been this way since the night that they had discovered Mike. The disappointing series of events had led him to fundamentally question the merits of the whole endeavour. It felt like everything was spiralling out of control. That they were drifting down an unintended route far away from the original intentions of the project. And whether he liked it or not, the train had already left the station. After all, this was as much about his own ego and fulfilment, as it was about providing others with an opportunity. As much as he tried to justify it to himself, something just wasn't sitting right. He couldn't shake the feeling of guilt.

After days of soul-searching, he finally decided that the best option would be to talk to Mike. He wasn't certain that his suicide attempt was the source of his distress, but it was as good a place as any to start. What he did know for sure, was that Mike would not be a willing participant. Sheepishly, Archie approached Mike's door, having plucked up the courage to confront him. The short walk from his room seemed to take forever. He knocked. No answer. He knocked again. Nothing.

'Mike mate. It's Archie. Have you got a minute? I need to chat to you.' *Have you got a minute?* What a ludicrous question. Of course he did. It's not like he was exactly rushed off his feet in there. It was just a polite way of saying *this is important, so pay attention*. To his surprise Mike replied.

'Not now. I just want to rest.'

'I know, but it's rather urgent. I'd really appreciate it if we could talk. I'll be as quick as I can. I promise.'

'I'm not really in the mood.'

'Of course not, I understand. But I really must insist. There won't be a better time. I'll just keep coming back.' Archie was sure he could feel the look of despair developing on Mike's face on the other side of the partition. After what seemed like an eternity, he heard the lock turn. Mike opened the door ajar. Inside it was dark. Really dark. The only light source came from a small TV. Piles of empty plates and cups, sat in places they really shouldn't be. The normally barren space had transformed into a chaotic wasteland. Mike looked frail. His hair and stubble had sprouted in irregular tufts, which he had made no effort to control. His ordinarily alert eyes were now dull and listless. Archie knew his condition had deteriorated, but it was a shocking sight nevertheless.

'How are you doing?'

'Fine. Just trying to rest.'

'That's good to hear. Hopefully you'll be back to one hundred percent soon.'

'Yeah. Maybe.'

'Look, I'm going to cut to the chase.' Mike sat on his bed. Archie pulled up a chair, maintaining sufficient distance to ensure the atmosphere didn't become uncomfortable.

'I need to talk to you about the night you hanged yourself.' Archie could tell immediately from his reaction that Mike was not keen to relive it.

'Mate, I'd really rather not. Can't we just forget about the whole thing, and move on? I'll be fine.'

'I wish we could. But I'm going to be honest with you. It's as much for my sake as it is yours,' Archie said earnestly. The comment surprised Mike. So far everyone had simply indulged him, not knowing how to handle the situation.

'What do you mean?'

'Well, and I've not spoken to anyone about this, I'm beginning to have flashbacks and anxiety attacks. I thought I'd purged all those memories and moved on, but the events of that day seem to have triggered something that I just can't shake. I can't concentrate. I can't communicate. Honestly, I feel like I'm losing my grip on reality.'

'Holy shit. That's not good. I've always thought you were so driven. So together. I knew you'd had issues like the rest of us, but you seemed to have overcome them. There weren't any signs you were suffering.'

'Like I say, I wasn't. It took years to get over it, but I was definitely back on track. It feels like everything I pieced together is falling apart again, and it's beyond my control.'

'You should have said something. It's not like there aren't enough people around who can empathise,' Mike commented. Archie knew he had him.

'I know, but it's so difficult to talk about all this bullshit, as you know only too well. Would you indulge me for a while? I know it's a strange thing to ask, given what you've been through, but I trust your counsel more than anyone else around here.'

'Of course mate. Not sure why you think I'd be of any use though. I mean, look at the state of me.' He gesticulated towards his filthy, stained tracksuit. The sight of it reinforced the slightly off-putting smell, circulating the dingy room.

'Do you mind if I open the curtains a bit? It's really dark in here. I might open the window a crack as well if that's okay?'

'Go for it. This place probably needs a bit of fresh air.' Mike sniffed a couple of times before needlessly observing, 'My socks are honking.'

Archie pulled open the thick curtains, allowing some natural light to flood in, which unfortunately revealed the full carnage of mess. He undid the lock on the window, and opened it slightly. The fresh cool air had an immediately positive effect on the stagnant atmosphere.

'That's better.' He returned to the chair and composed himself.

'What's bothering you then?' Mike enquired. He looked genuinely intrigued. It was a positive sign. If Archie was honest with him, perhaps he would open up as well.

'It's hard to pin down exactly. More of a general feeling than a specific issue. However, there is a particular episode that keeps recurring in my head.'

'Go on.' Archie sighed hard, and then began.

'Back in two thousand and six I was deployed to Afghanistan. As you know, it was like the Wild West back then. We got into loads of scraps, pretty much every day. It felt like what war should be, you know?' Mike gave a knowing nod of approval.

'For a while, my Company was posted down to Garmsir. It was properly basic. Living off the wagons, getting air resupplies, bouncing from PB to PB. Most of the time, we had to split into smaller groups because of the vast area of ground we were covering. Sorry, do you mind if I grab a water?'

'Sure. See if you can find a clean glass.' There was no chance. Archie found a dirty one, and gave it a cursory wash under the tap.

'Anyway. One day we got into a massive contact somewhere down in the green zone. I knew it was fruity, because as I was calling in a danger close strafe from an A-Ten, the coax cable got shot out from my radio. I'd already started sending through the target coordinates, but I didn't have a back-up handset, so we lost our air support until I managed to swap it out with one from one of the other lad's radios.' Mike had leant forward slightly. 'As the comms came back up I finished sending the nine-liner, and popped a smoke to mark our position. I warned everyone that the strike was inbound so they needed to keep their heads down. What I wasn't aware of, is that the pilot had already committed to his run, based on the information I had sent before we lost comms. As a result, he used the smoke as a marker for the target, and not friendly forces.'

'Jesus mate, that's not good.'

'No it wasn't. I could hear from the sound of the jet approaching that something wasn't right. Its trajectory was just a bit too close for comfort. I heard him call *tipping in hot.* Then the world erupted. 30mm exploded all around us. The tree line next to me got torn to shreds. As he pulled away, I could just about hear the *baaarrrrppp* of the cannon, through the ringing in my ears. I checked myself over, and couldn't see any immediate damage. But when the dust cleared it was mayhem.' Archie paused, looking anywhere just to avoid making eye contact with Mike.

'The guy I had just swapped the handset with was lying face down in the dirt not moving. Another bloke was slumped on his side, leaning against a wall that he had just been blown headfirst into. I froze. I was too panicked to react. For the first time in my life I felt completely paralysed. Totally numb to what was happening around me. I remember picking up my rifle, and aimlessly pointing it at things for no reason. Suddenly, one of the Senior NCOs grabbed me by the shoulder, and shook me. He asked if I was all right, before dragging me into some cover. I just sat there. I didn't say a thing. The fighting went on, whilst I cowered in the shade like a frightened little boy.' Tears began filling Archie's eyes.

'After what felt like a lifetime, we were ordered to extract. We headed back out towards the desert. I don't really remember the journey. I was in some sort of trance that just about allowed me to put on foot in front of the other, but not much more. Once we got back to the patrol base, I was made aware of the full implications of the airstrike. Two KIA and four WIA. I simply shut down. The guilt was too much to bear. As fast as I could, I found the most remote corner of the compound, and physically curled up into a ball. I felt pathetic. Ashamed. How could I live with myself after that? Momentarily, I thought about putting the rifle in my mouth and pulling the trigger, but didn't have the courage to commit. So instead, I simply mentally checked out. I managed to get through the rest of the tour without really contributing anything. Once I got back to the UK I asked for a transfer, which I was granted immediately, and pretty much ran away from the issue. It's chased me ever since.' Archie sniffed his nose, and looked up. Mike was hunched forward, resting his forearms on his thighs. He looked Archie directly in the eye.

'Look mate. Stuff like that sometimes just happens. It's not your fault. It was the circumstances you were in.

The combination of a whole load of stuff going wrong, at just the wrong time. No one intended for anyone else to get hurt.'

'Perhaps, it still doesn't excuse why I didn't double check, why I didn't follow the process. That's what I was trained to do, but I decided to cut corners. It resulted in others paying the price. It was unforgivable.'

'Of course it wasn't. You were in an extraordinary place, doing extraordinary things. It just all became too complex for a brief moment. That part was out of your hands.'

'I'll never see it like that, but thanks. At the moment, the whole thing is just haunting me. It's a phantom that I can't make disappear. I'm pretty sure that deep down, it's because I've been having that same feeling of being overwhelmed with everything that's been going on. I have to say, the thought of you hurting yourself because of me certainly didn't help.'

'What are you talking about? I didn't do it because of you.'

'Yes, you did. If I hadn't gotten us all into this position in the first place, there's no way you would have done what you did.'

'Are you joking? If I hadn't been here, I would've done it a long time ago. And I would have made sure it worked,' he stated seriously. '*Make Ready* was the only thing keeping me on track. I needed it in my life. It's been an amazing opportunity, and I wouldn't change a thing.' He paused briefly. 'Okay. Well maybe Bomber would be less of a twat if I could choose, but other than that it's all been gravy.'

'Then why did you respond the way you did that

night?' Archie questioned.

'Truthfully? I don't know. In the moment it just seemed the right thing to do. Like you, I hadn't told anyone about what was going on in my head. I wish I had. So many people have told me it's important to open up and be truthful, but as you know, it's not that simple. Why should they be a part of it?'

'I hear you brother. Who's to say that they've earnt the right?'

'Exactly. I guess the events that day on the boat had more of an impact than I realised. The needless suffering just sort of tipped me over the edge.'

'Well, we needed to get the information out of them somehow. Admittedly, Bomber went too far, but we achieved what we wanted.'

'Did we though? At what cost? I've got no problem with hurting other human beings, but there needs to be a justifiable purpose. Watching that man drown just brought back too many unpleasant memories.' Archie smiled internally. They were definitely getting somewhere.

'Tell me. Now's as good an opportunity as any other. At least now you know I'm a fuck-up as well!'

'I already knew that,' Mike smirked. 'Again, it's hard to tie it to one single thing. Christ knows there have been enough. However, if I'm honest, there is one episode that stands out.'

'Go for it.'

'Well, I was in Iraq on a patrol around Basra. It must have been about the same time you were in Helmand. Honestly, it was mostly pretty quiet at that time. Nothing compared to what was going on in Afghanistan.

Shaibah was like a holiday camp, and although we would get mortared pretty frequently, there weren't too many firefights or anything like that.' He reclined onto his side, placing a hand onto his forehead.

'We were getting towards the end of a mission, and in the process of heading back into camp. Then it all kicked off. I was on foot, but we had a small vehicle convoy of Snatches with us, which I guess telegraphed our position. Suddenly, the lead vehicle was hit by a roadside bomb. It went up like a Christmas tree. Ammo started cooking off, and pinging all over the place. Then, to our genuine surprise, a handful of AKs opened up on us.' Swallowing hard, he continued.

'It wasn't the first time I'd been in a contact, but it was definitely the most intense. It felt like they were actually shooting at *me*, you know? At the time I was just a private, so I took cover, and waited for someone to give some orders. No one said anything. Nothing came through on the radio. I thought they were too busy, just trying to stay out of the firing line, so I took up a fire position, and tried to spot where the rounds were coming from.'

'It's not easy spotting them, is it?' Archie offered.

'No, it definitely wasn't. After a couple of minutes, I realised something didn't feel right. Suddenly, it occurred to me. Like an absolute amateur, I hadn't changed the batteries on my radio. No wonder I couldn't hear anything. Pretty stupid, eh?'

'Easily done, but yeah, you crowed it hard,' Archie replied, using a slang term for an inexperienced soldier.

'So, I found a decent spot where I could take off my daysack to swap the battery out. Just as I removed the

315

dead one, an insurgent appeared around the corner carrying an assault rifle. He held it by his waist like they do. You know, some Rambo wannabe shit. I looked directly into his eyes. I mean deep into them. Like when you're crossing the road, and you catch a driver's eyes whose car is approaching too fast and is about to hit you. It was an intense connection. He pulled the trigger and, click.' Mike imitated the action. 'His drills were so bad he obviously hadn't cocked the weapon properly. A round had jammed.'

'Bloody hell. You must have bricked it.'

'Nope. I didn't even hesitate. There were only about four metres between me and him. I launched myself forward with all the energy I could generate. He wasn't a big bloke. I easily knocked him to the floor. The gun went skidding off across the road, whilst he held his scrawny arms up trying to protect himself. Without thinking, I started laying into him with the only thing I had to hand; the radio battery. It wasn't that weighty, so it took a lot of blows to knock him out. I mean, a lot.' By now, a thin layer of perspiration had developed on Mike's brow.

'Even when his neck had gone floppy, I kept pounding away. I can remember the flesh on his face tearing away in strips, leaving long bloody gouges behind them. I'm not sure why, but he started convulsing. I could feel his body bucking underneath me, and strange gargling noises started coming out of his mouth. They weren't sounds that I'd ever heard a human make before. Or ever since. By that stage, I was exhausted. Still, I kept beating that face, until all that remained was a bloody pulp. Even his eyes became dislodged. By the time I'd finished, they were staring in completely different directions.' Mike looked frantic. Reliving the incident in such gory detail was clearly traumatising. Archie instinctively reached out, and placed a hand on his shoulder.

'After I was sure he was dead, I simply stood up, and finished the battery change. Habit meant I even put the old one, which was caked in gore, back into my daysack so that I didn't lose it and get billed. As soon as I put the headset back on, I heard my section commander telling us to regroup at the rear of the vehicles. So I grabbed my kit, and hurried off to join them. They asked me what had happened. I had blood all over me. I simply told them that I had killed a bad guy. That was it. I didn't need to mention anything else. No details were required. It stayed our little secret. Mine and the insurgent's. I jumped in the back of a wagon, and we headed back to base. Throughout the whole journey, the others were telling tales about the contact. I didn't say a word. And I never have. I've carried it with me ever since.' Archie was stunned. He was intimately familiar with the sketchy moments people had experienced on operations. But he had never heard of anything quite so visceral, so brutal, occurring. Even plunging a bayonet into someone would have been a less disturbing episode than that horror show.

'I don't know what to say. Thank you for choosing to share it with me. I know it's not easy opening up. It's good to get it out in the open I suppose?'

'I'm not sure. The strange thing is, I'd never really felt guilty or affected by it, until the moment I was standing on that boat. I saw the same look in that

Scouser's eyes that I saw in the Iraqi's, and it triggered something.' Looking pensive, he paused briefly and then continued.

'Actually, there's no doubt that something's been building for years. Maybe it was about time I talked about it. This obviously isn't healthy,' Mike sighed, holding out his hands, and gesturing towards the ramshackle room.

'No. I think it probably isn't,' Archie responded. They both sat in silence for a moment, before Mike spoke up.

'So where do we go from here now? Now that we've had a good sesh, wallowing in mutual self-pity, that is.'

'No idea. It's new territory for both of us. I guess first I give you back this letter, which I sincerely hope you won't ever need again. Then maybe get you out of that stinking tracksuit, get the hell out of this shitpit, and grab something decent to eat.'

'Sounds like a plan,' Mike grinned back.

CHAPTER 27

Planning for the ambush progressed apace, once Archie
and Mike were back on board. Following their
discussions, they had both made a commitment to
refocus, and to talk more openly if they felt themselves
slipping away. Thus far, they had been able to sustain
their promise. It had been invaluable having such a
detailed itinerary available for the operation. A suitable
location had been identified to make the stop. Not only
did it provide good ingress and egress routes, but there
were also well-concealed locations for the cut-offs, and a
natural embankment that would prevent their quarry
from escaping. Best of all, the traffic flow there was
normally limited, particularly at the time of day that the
convoy was planned to transit through.

They had spent hours driving the route. Meticulously
examining every aspect of the mission. Minimising the
unknowns, and ensuring that they narrowed down the
options to only those that they assessed had the best
chance of success. Rehearsals had featured heavily. It
was as if their appetites had been renewed following the
challenges of the previous jobs. This time, they were
determined to get it right. By far the most difficult
decision had been one that Archie had hoped to avoid
altogether. The intelligence and surveillance efforts that
they had conducted revealed an uncomfortable truth. It
was Robbie and Bazza who brought the information to
their attention.

'I'm one hundred percent sure. No question. The
escorts are carrying, brah.'

'How can you be sure though?'

'We fucking saw them, eh. Those muppets were brandishing weapons in broad daylight.'

'What if they're replicas?'

'No way man. I saw them loading up spare mags. No one would bother going to the effort if they weren't the real thing.'

'How many did you see then?' 59 joined Archie in the line of questioning. Bazza answered.

'There were four that we saw who definitely had guns. Could be more, but given the composition of the escort, I'd say it can't be more than six, total.'

'What are we talking about? Longs, shorts, both?'

'Well, from what we witnessed, none were carrying rifles, if that's what yer askin.'

'At least that's something. Doesn't mean they don't have them though, does it?'

'We can't rule it out, that's fer sure.' Bazza sounded typically morose, whilst recanting the information.

'If it is as you say it is I'm not sure this one's going to be a goer.' Archie surprised them all with his candidness. 'We've taken the chance with jobs before, when guns were only a possibility. Now that we know for sure they will be present, I think it's a game changer. What happens if one of us gets shot? How on earth do we explain a gunshot wound, or worse still, the death of a supposed charity worker, somewhere in deepest darkest Kent?' He looked around the room for consensus. Mike was the first to speak.

'Archie, we've always known this is dangerous stuff we're doing. That's why we've developed appropriate responses to deal with it. We all know the risks, and we've all bought into the cover story. If one of us goes down, then we simply disappeared in the night never to be seen again. No one will look too hard for a formerly homeless vet. We're all troubled individuals after all, remember? Guns don't change a thing as far as I'm concerned.'

'Mike's right,' Abu chipped in. 'Those putas probably don't even know which end to use. We've got the advantage. As long as we do it right, it's all good bruv.' Archie looked around the room. From the expressions on their faces he could tell they were well committed to this one. In his heart, he knew that they needed a win. This opportunity had been handed to them on a silver platter.

'Okay. Let's assume that they're armed. What does that mean from our perspective? We can't exactly disarm them with colourful language, so that means we need to tool up as well. If at any point, and I mean *any* point, we get spotted with a weapon, we are monumentally fucked. That's not even mentioning the repercussions if, god forbid, someone fires off a round. Our whole approach has been stealthy. Under the radar. And it's worked because we haven't drawn attention. Someone reports gun shots, and we'll have an armed police unit on the scene within minutes.'

'That's why we've been selective about the location,' Simmo offered. He had visited the site several times. 'It's isolated, man. Well out of the way of any civvies. The embankments would mask any noise. Same for the cut-offs.'

'If we do it right, no one's going to be shooting anyway,' Robbie added.

'What about ammo? We have the guns but only a

couple of boxes of nine mil. There's no point in going out there without it.' To everyone's surprise, Tanya spoke up.

'I can sort it out.' Everyone turned to look at her. 'What? This isn't my first rodeo you know lads.'

'Are ya joking? How on earth can ya do tha?' Donald enquired, sounding slightly hurt that she would be stepping on his quartermaster's toes.

'One of my regulars was a right dodgy bastard from the US. Back in the states, he's an arms dealer. A very successful one.' She had their attention. 'It just so happens, he also regularly travels to the UK for business, including the black-market kind. Once upon a time, when we were together, he told me a bit about some of the deals he was orchestrating, including supplying a shit load of ammunition to an outfit based in London. He wasn't bullshitting either.'

'How d'ya know?' Donald enquired.

'He showed me.'

'What. Why would he do tha?'

'Because he loved to show off. And he didn't think that showing a hooker was at all risky. For whatever reason, he told me that if I ever needed anything from him, to give him a call. Bless him, I think he was in love, the dirty bastard.'

'Well blow me. Well done lass.' The large, bearded jock clapped his hands with glee.

'Are you sure he's trustworthy though? Or if he's even still in the business?'

'Mike. Trust me. I know he'd do anything for me. And yes, we can trust him. He still sends me messages now and again. He would love to get the business. Even if he didn't want to cooperate, I've got enough to blackmail him with a dozen times over. He's a married man, after all.' The wry grin on her face confirmed to everyone how confident she was of her position. 'Oh, and he's definitely still dealing. He sent me a present just before I joined you guys. It's in my room. A chrome 1911, with beautiful filigree engraving. Told me it's for my protection. Probably the best gift I ever received.'

'What are you waiting for? Send him a message,' Bomber urged. He could hardly contain his excitement.

'Whoa, whoa, whoa. Hold up everyone.' Archie torpedoed the atmosphere of enthusiasm. 'We haven't even agreed on a course of action yet, and you're already thinking about bombing-up mags. This guy sounds like a liability. Another part of this endeavour that could go horribly wrong if not managed correctly.'

'Archie. I hate to say this mate, but I think you're horribly outnumbered on this one.' Of all people it was the ordinarily cautious Marv who put the nail into the coffin of Archie's dissent. 'We need a win, and like we've discussed, this could be a big one. There's no point in bringing an extendable baton to a gun fight. If we're going to do it, we need to go big. Make them think that even breathing in our direction is a bad idea. We can only achieve that through the use of overwhelming force. Ironically, it's the safest option.'

'He makes a good point bruv. Despite being an old twat.'

'Surely someone else agrees with me here? Can't you see this is a huge turning point?' He carefully scanned the room hoping that someone, anyone, would speak up. No one made a peep. All he could manage saying was, 'I see.'

'To reassure you, this is not the first time we've thought about this option. Believe it or not, but all of us have chatted about the merits of using firearms for every job we've done. So far, the answer's been a no. But this time it makes sense. Honestly, it's the only way,' Marv revealed. 'So, should Tanya make that call?' Archie could feel their eyes boring into him. He let out a long sigh, before reluctantly agreeing.

After the discussion, things moved rapidly. The Yank turned out to be even more outrageous than Tanya had suggested. He couldn't wait to see his bit on the side again, booking a flight almost immediately. The fact that she was after his business was just the icing on the cake. He was, of course, disappointed to learn that she was no longer on the game, but the promise of cold, hard cash more than made up for it. After a couple of one-on-one meetings between him and Tanya, they arranged to bring Archie and Donald into the mix, to tie down the finer details.

'Well, it sure is good to meet you fellas. Tanya's told me all about y'all. Please, have a seat amigos.' His strong Texan drawl was unmistakeable.

'Archie, Donald, this is Jed. Jed, Archie and Donald,' Tanya introduced them.

'Delighted to make your acquaintance. Always good to meet fellow veterans. I've always liked you Brit boys. You sure do know how to fight. And drink. Speaking of which, what can I get ya?' Archie and Donald gave each other a knowing look, and tried not to laugh. He was a walking, talking caricature. Although technically a geriatric, Jed Peterson III was sturdily built, and quite tall. He sported a moustache that would make a walrus wince, and from what they could tell, wore the finest pair of cowboy boots this side of the Mississippi. They were even adorned with gold toe caps, shaped like little skulls. His Stetson was placed on the low table in front of them. *Unbelievable* Archie thought to himself.

'Ya served did ya? Where was tha Jed?'

'I'm sorry young man. I haven't the faintest clue what you just said. What is that accent?'

'Glaswegian mate. Don't tell ma ya never met a Jock befar.'

'Tanya my dear, what *is* he sayin?' Jed asked. He looked genuinely perplexed.

'He's Scottish. They're a bit strange up there. Don't worry, no one understands what he's saying.'

'Oh, I see. Can't say I've ever had the pleasure of visiting the place, but I hear it's wonderful. If it's good enough for Trump, it's good enough for me.'

'It's all right. There's some good bits and some shit bits, just like anywhere.' Jed loved the way that Tanya was so direct with everything. 'He was asking where you served.'

'I see. Well, Nam was my main excursion. Two tours, sixty seven and seventy. I was on an ODA with MACV-SOG. You know what that is?'

'Green Berets, if I'm not mistaken.' Archie knew all about the infamous Special Forces unit. He'd worked alongside them in Afghanistan on more than a couple of occasions.

'That's right. Good for you son. God I miss those days. How about you fine gentlemen? What exotic countries have you had the pleasure of visitin'?'

'Both of us have been around a bit, as you can probably tell by the look of us. Bosnia, Iraq, Afghanistan, a couple of other places.'

'Well hats off to y'all. Them's some nasty ass countries. Always been good customers though.' He let out a laugh that was altogether too loud, and too heartfelt for the joke.

'Aye, good one Jed.' Donald joined in with the mirth in an attempt to create some sort of bond. It worked. They chortled away together, until Jed decided it was time to talk business.

'Good to see we agree on something. Now, shall we get down to brass tacks? Tanya tells me you're on the hunt for some ordnance. Well you've come to the right man. I can get you whatever you need, for the right price of course.' He took a large swig of bourbon from a cut crystal glass. The venue was lavish. It was his favourite bar in London, just on the outskirts of Kensington. It wasn't the type of place that Donald would ever have visited growing up. As a result, he drained his pint of strong lager far too quickly. The waiter almost choked when he waved him over to order a second.

'Thirsty I see. I heard you Scots enjoy your liquor. You're doin' your country proud son! So, what are you after?'

'It really depends on cost, but as a minimum, we'll need nine mil, and five five six.'

'Those I can do, no problem at all friend. How much we talking?'

'I would estimate three thousand of the nine mil, and

fifteen hundred of the five five six.'

'Shit, I thought you were going to ask for something difficult. When do you need them?'

'No later than two weeks.'

'Piece of cake. I'll handle the delivery and everything. All you need to do is tell me a venue, and be there to pick it up.'

'That won't be a problem. Tanya can give you all the relevant details.' For a man about to commit such a serious crime, Jed was impressively nonchalant. He'd obviously done this a few times before.

'I guess we ought to get onto the vulgarities of talking about cost. What were you thinking Jed?'

'Well, that all depends on a number of factors.' This was his favourite part. He knew he had them over a barrel.

'Okay, and what are those?'

'First of all, I'm going to give y'all a discount you understand. Why? First, because you're fellow vets. Second, because I'm so damned fond of Tanya here. And third, well dammit, because I just like the way y'all roll.'

'That's very decent of you.'

'Now, as you'll appreciate, ammunition ain't exactly growin' on trees in these here parts, so I'm not givin' it away. But here's what I'll do. If this is a one-off deal, I'll sell y'all the nine for five bucks a piece, and the AR rounds for eight bucks. By mah calculations that's twenty seven thousand dollars. Including delivery, let's round it up to thirty.'

'And what if we ask fer more?' Donald enquired.

'Well that depends now, don't it? Let's say we can

open up a regular line of business, I'd be willing to do y'all a thirty percent discount on your first order. A nice even twenty would do.' Archie didn't even need to consider the offer.

'We'll stick to this order for now, thanks Jed. Where's the ammo sourced from?'

'That's fine by me. Just know it's a one-time offer. You'll be payin' full price for any subsequent orders. I get all my European merchandise from Serbia. They ain't too careful when it comes to official registration documents, if y'all catch my drift?'

'We understand. And you're certain that no one would be able to trace it back to us. Or you for that matter?'

'That's a god damned, cast iron, guarantee son. Trust me, I know for sure. My bullets have found their way onto more than one crime scene, and I ain't had so much as a cop stop me for a bust tail light.' He appeared to be telling the truth. Archie assessed that he had no reason to lie.

'In that case, you have a deal at thirty. I assume you'll be able to make the time line.

'I'll do even better than that. How does next Tuesday sound? I believe that's four days from now.'

'Perfect. We'll work out a suitable RV and let you know. I assume cash would be preferable?'

'Cash'll do nicely. Waiter!' he shouted unexpectedly across to the young man polishing glasses behind the bar. 'A round of bourbon for me and my friends here!' They spent another hour or so drinking with the crazy Texan, before they managed to make their excuses and escape. Archie was actually very fond of him. His stories from Vietnam were incredible. He was, very simply, a man who loved to have fun. As they departed, Jed grabbed Tanya and gave her an enthusiastic kiss on the lips, taking her somewhat by surprise. She handled it like a pro, told him to stop misbehaving, and disappeared out the door as quickly as she could.

'Thank fuck that's over with. Let's get the hell back home.' She almost sprinted to the tube station.

Jed was a man of his word. His delivery driver met them at a remote layby, close to the Essex coastline, in the dead of night. Frank and Donald arrived two hours early, to make sure that nothing unexpected was waiting for them. They also brought a backup team in a second vehicle, just in case of any issues. As it transpired, there was no need for the theatrics. At exactly the agreed time and place, a white van arrived. The middle-aged man driving it, very calmly handed over the crates of ammunition, and received the cash in the return. There was no fanfare. No *show me yours and I'll show you mine* nonsense. It was pretty much the same process as receiving an Amazon delivery, except with the added bonus that they didn't even need to pay up front.

After the bullets were safely locked away, they focused on assembling the remainder of the equipment that would be required for the multifaceted operation. The planning process had consistently reinforced the necessity to disable the target vehicle carrying the drugs. From what they had gleaned, it was a reinforced van that would require some time to break into. As long as it remained mobile, there would be the threat that it could either escape, or worse still, badly injure one of them. Abu had researched the best methods for achieving a rapid entry. He had settled on a thermal lance. The cumbersome piece of equipment would not be the easiest item to transport, but would be able to cut through any armour that they came up against. He managed to source one second-hand from a local junkyard, which wouldn't show up on any records of sale. Their other key concern was separating the van from its support vehicles. Whatever approach they took, it was going to be extremely challenging. The fewer people they had interfering with the scene, the more efficient they could be, and the less likely it was that they would draw attention.

It was Bomber of all people who came up with the potential solution. They agreed that pulling the same trick as they had on the boat might well be a good option. By wearing police uniforms, they should be able to gain the initiative, creating at least a short window of opportunity. Whilst their opponents were still feeling the effects of the shock of capture, they would use CS gas to incapacitate the occupants of the cars, before detaining them. It would hopefully provide a non-lethal method of neutralising the threat, whilst creating the time and space for the heist to occur.

Fortunately, they were able to source the gas grenades from Jed. He proved to be just as reliable as he had been with the bullets. The merchandise arrived only forty eight hours after they had submitted the order. They also procured respirators for all members of the cut-off groups, and body armour for everyone. The brash Texan was already proving to be a valuable resource. Surveillance efforts were predominantly focused upon gaining a forensic understanding of the route and ambush location that had been selected. Marv created a three dimensional computer graphic that they could use to simulate different options, whilst a replica of the site was established in some isolated woodland for conducting rehearsals.

Once they had committed to a course of action, further use of the route was minimised in order to avoid any unwanted attention. The final piece of the puzzle was selecting a suitable method for tracking the convoy. This was possibly the most exigent aspect of the entire operation. Even with the plethora of technology available, it would undoubtedly be a difficult task to achieve if they wished to remain undetected. From the intelligence that had been pieced together, it was clear that their adversaries were no amateurs. Any hint of a tail or lookouts would alert them to the danger, most likely committing them to an alternative route, or cancelling altogether.

Several options were discussed at length: plant a tracking device; follow the convoy using motorbikes; position observation posts along the route; bribe a crew member to provide updates. All of them had their merits and drawbacks, but nothing stood out as a clear winner. In the end, they determined that a low-risk, albeit somewhat unreliable, approach would be best. After all, the fact that they possessed the details of the route, and the likely departure time, was in itself a rare luxury. They would maintain eyes-on the point of departure, and a couple of key junctions along the way, with the final approach covered by the use of a tail vehicle, and Abu's drone. It was by no means failsafe, but they assessed it would significantly minimise the likelihood of being spotted. The fact that the transportation was scheduled during the hours of darkness would also help their cause. Once content with their preparations, they gathered in the briefing room for a final discussion.

'Let's quickly talk through some actions-on. Bazza, what's the plan if cut-off group one is compromised?'

'Depending on the nature of the compromise we either deflect the attention and crack on, or collapse to the alternative position. The main thing is to maintain the stand-off distance between the target vehicle, and any support.'

'Happy days. Tanya, briefly talk us through the med plan please.'

'It's pretty straightforward. First response is self-help. All of you need to be carrying a personal med kit. Next will be buddy-buddy, once any threat is dealt with. As soon as you call it in, I'll make my way to the point of injury to provide support. We'll then extract the casualty to our support vehicle located at control point one.' She confirmed the location on the screen. 'We'll maintain position there until the order to extract. A decision will be made on whether to return directly to this location or head to the clinic, depending upon the severity of the injury. In the case of multiple casualties, I'll triage and attempt to treat in situ, before we use the same extraction plan. The support vehicle can comfortably hold up to three casualties, so please no more of you than that try to get yourselves hurt!'

'Cool. We'll of course conduct a final equipment check before stepping off. Abu, what happens if we lose track of the convoy?'

'Depending on where we lose it will determine what

we do, innit? If we don't see it departing for whatever reason, we'll pretty much be screwed from the start, but everything will remain in position to try and pick it up until we get ordered off. If it's lost en route, we'll use the motorbike to try and locate it. If it can't, we'll stay put, until the call to pull off. If it's lost beyond the final OP, we'll assume it's inbound, and prepare for the ambush. That's our last safe moment, after which we'll be committed.'

'Spot on. There's also the option that it's lost between the first two OPs, in which case we'll remain patient to see if we can pick it up again before committing the tail if necessary.'

'Roger that boss man.' Archie had never really become comfortable with the idea that he was at the top of the tree, but he understood that someone needed to provide direction, and help pull them all together. For a man who had made a point of avoiding responsibility throughout his life, he had somehow wandered into a position where he now had more of the stuff than he knew what to do with. Despite his natural inclinations, he actually quite enjoyed it. Perhaps he was finally growing up.

They continued discussing the various eventualities that could befall them for a little while longer. Everyone was fully engaged. It felt like the first time that they had gone through the process. The introduction of firearms had made the stakes feel that much greater, resulting in a renewed sense of focus. Once their discussions had been completed, they went their separate ways to conduct final preparations, and get some rest before the big event. Most immersed themselves in checking, and re-checking equipment. Some found other distractions to take their mind off what was about to come. A couple of fortunate souls managed to sleep. Archie spent the majority of the intervening period running through the sequence of activities in his head, trying to ensure that they hadn't missed something important during the planning process. As far as he could tell, they hadn't. There were always unknowns. It was part of the game. Still, something felt uncomfortable. Whatever he tried, he couldn't shake it. He briefly considered discussing his concerns with someone, but was acutely aware that they would tell him to stop worrying, and to believe in the process. In the end, the desire to focus on something else, anything else, drove him to open up his laptop and read through his emails. There at the top, was another from his brother.

Subject: Re: How's it going bro?
From: Theodore.Maine893@mod.gov.uk

Hi there,

Still not heard from you bro! I hope I've got the right address and everything is okay. I'm emailing from a US TOC so haven't got much time, but was hoping to chat if you get a chance. The offer's still there for a visit as well if you're up for it. I should be back in the UK in about a month or so.

I heard from Barney. He's out in the Philippines the lucky bugger. Maybe we'll get an invite to visit him at some point!!!

Please do reply if you get a chance. It would be great to know how you're doing and have a catch up. Dad sends his best as well. I'm sure he'd be thrilled to hear from you...

Yours

T

He was persistent. Archie had to give him that. His finger hovered over the mouse, dangerously close to clicking the reply button. The moment just didn't feel right though. It would have to wait until after this job. Archie mentally vouched to commit to sending his brother some correspondence then, but for now he had other things to concentrate on.

CHAPTER 28

Robbie and Mike sat waiting in the first cut-off vehicle. It had been parked well-back from the road, concealed behind a hedgerow. Their neatly arranged equipment was laid out in the spacious boot of the SUV. Their weapons were placed by their sides, tucked out of sight. At this juncture, they were committed. The convoy had passed through the final check point. Tanya had confirmed that their target was on its final approach into the ambush site. She had been tailing it on the motorbike for the final portion of the journey. Further up the road, they knew that the Stop Group would be poised for action, just as they were.

Timing would be everything. If the trap was sprung too early, the entire convoy would be bunched together, potentially creating a dangerous bottleneck. Too late, and they would miss the opportunity to stop the target vehicle altogether. Their orders were clear. Keep any reinforcements from supporting the transport vehicle. Masquerading as police officers would hopefully allow them to maintain control of the situation for long enough to achieve this aim. But, there was also a good chance that the disguises may incentivise their adversaries to take extreme measures in order to avoid capture. There was no way of knowing until the moment arrived.

'You ready bud?' Robbie asked his colleague.

'Yes.' All of Mike's focus was dedicated to watching the winding road for any sign of approaching headlights.

'All right. Maybe let's grab the kit, eh?'

'Not yet.'

'Okay. I hate this waiting you know?'

'Yes,' was Mike's curt response, intended to inform the talkative South African that he was trying to concentrate. Robbie didn't receive the message.

'Cool brah. I guess it's part of the job. I just wish we could be doing something useful.'

'We are. We're waiting.'

In the Stop Group, similar nervous conversations were occurring. Abu had the drone up, tracking the convoy. He sent regular succinct updates over the radio.

'Target through Blue Two, to Blue One.' It would be less than two minutes before the lead vehicle reached the first cut-off group.

'Not long now boys. Let's get ready to rock and roll!' Bomber exclaimed. He grasped his M4 like some beloved childhood toy.

'Everyone make sure you stick to your arcs. We don't want to be tripping over one another. Simmo, you got the stinger ready?' Archie asked.

'I'm good to go mate.'

'Make sure you let the lead vehicle pass before deploying it. We don't want to create a road block.'

'Relax. We've been through this enough times. I've got the markers. I know what I'm doing.'

'Of course you do. Sorry, just nerves.' Abu had his head buried in the screen.

'All call signs. Lead vehicle passing Blue One.' Marv popped up on the net.

'Standby, standby.' He was situated on a parallel road in the command vehicle, well out of view. A dirt track provided quick access to the site, just in case it was required. Tanya had peeled off from tailing the convoy,

co-locating with him just in case back up or medical
assistance was required. He had the bank of scanners set
up on the dash board, monitoring the emergency service
channels. If something kicked off, he would become
their key link, coordinating an appropriate response.
They all desperately hoped it wouldn't come to that. A
further hundred metres further up the road the second
cut-off group was also conducting final preparations. 59
and Bazza's primary function was preventing any of the
convoy escaping. They were also charged with
segregating the lead escort vehicle from the van carrying
the drugs. Achieving the secondary task would be
challenging, but achievable, if everyone else managed to
get their timings right.

'You all set boyo?'

'Yeah, I'm good to go mucker.'

'These NVGs are a right pain in the arse.'

'Tell me about it. I'm pretty sure the ambient light's
good enough to go without them, so it is.'

'I guess we had better stick to the plan. Wouldn't
want to get into trouble now, would we?'

'Dead on mate. I think I can see some headlights
now.' The lead car of the three vehicle convoy cruised
past the first cut-off position. They were sticking to the
speed limit of forty miles an hour. Inside Mike could
make out three passengers.

'Lead vehicle passing Cut-Off One. Three up.' This
was it. As soon as the vehicle was beyond the marker,
the Stop Group would deploy their traps, boxing the van
in place. The cut-off positions would do likewise,
preventing the supporting vehicles from reinforcing.
They had a window of fewer than five seconds for

success. The first car transited through the ambush site, heading towards the second cut-off group. Simmo prepared to deploy the stinger strip, which would disable the van by blowing out its tyres. He kept his eyes locked onto the marker post. As soon as the van passed, he would throw out the device. Next to him, Archie was poised to do the same in order to prevent the vehicle from attempting to reverse out of the ambush. Simmo could see the van approaching. It was riding low on its suspension; a positive indication that it contained the cargo they were after.

At the precise moment its front bumper reached the marker, Simmo launched the stinger across the tarmac. The device made a satisfying rattling noise as it extended towards the steep far bank. As soon as the front tyres connected with the metal spikes, they burst with a loud pop. The momentum of the vehicle carried the rear wheels over the top of the strip, which also disintegrated on impact, before the driver could react. Archie threw out his stinger to the rear of the van, firmly securing it in their trap.

'Stop Group. Target disabled. Approaching vehicle now.'

Concurrently, Cut-Off Two had managed to block off the lead vehicle, using the combination of another stinger strip and their own SUV, which they had pulled out across the road.

'Cut-Off Two. Support Vehicle Two disabled.' Unfortunately, things did not go as smoothly for the first cut-off group. Before Robbie was able to spring his trap, the vehicle had sped up, probably reacting to the commotion in front. Thankfully, it was an eventuality that they had anticipated, and prepared for. He announced the alteration over the radio.

'Cut-Off One, be aware Support Vehicle One approaching Stop Group at speed.' Abu immediately grabbed a spare stinger, and ran down the lane towards the oncoming vehicle. As late as he dared, he deployed it. The extra speed carried the car further than they would have liked, but a reasonable distance remained between the support vehicle and the van. A handful of metres beyond, Abu could see Robbie and Mike sprinting up behind the vehicle.

'Armed Police. Show me your hands! Show me your fucking hands!' Even muffled by the respirator, there was no mistaking the command. The stunned passengers inside the vehicle complied. Mike and Robbie had their UMPs trained on the car. The flashlight attachments fitted to their weapons were dazzlingly powerful. Inside, they could see the three men instinctively turn their heads away. Before any of the occupants had time to react, Robbie smashed through the driver's window using the butt of his submachine gun. The safety glass shattered into thousands of tiny pieces, which fell inwards onto the startled man's lap. Mike already had a CS canister prepped in his hand. He tossed it into the vehicle. The choking white smoke, instantly billowed inside the car, quickly followed by a cacophony of coughing and spluttering. One passenger made to open his door, but Robbie kicked it shut, forcing the unfortunate man to continue inhaling the unpleasant fumes.

'Stay in the fucking vehicle! Don't move.' They knew it would be impossible for the occupants to endure the toxic environment for any length of time. The longer they were incapacitated inside the vehicle, the longer they weren't interfering with the main event occurring just up the road. Both men knew what the effects of the debilitating gas felt like. Their victims would be suffering horrendously. They left them trapped. Only after a full two minutes, did they fling open the doors of the vehicle, before dragging the helpless men out onto the road, where they cuffed and hooded them.

Meanwhile, Frank and Donald had set up temporary road blocks beyond each of the cut-off locations. They were designed to ensure that no one would interfere with the scene of the ambush. They had installed flashing blue lights onto their saloons and placed out hazard signs, creating the illusion that there had been an accident and making the overall deception more credible. When combined with the uniforms, they hoped that the sight would be sufficiently convincing to persuade any unwary motorists to turn around. It was a key element of the plan. If anyone witnessed what was occurring further up the road, it would result in a major dilemma that none of them wished to confront.

59 and Bazza neutralised their target vehicle successfully, the only hiccup being that one of the occupants appeared to be impervious to the effects of the CS gas. A rare genetic condition granted him immunity. So while his colleagues were desperately enduring the burning pain in their eyes and throats, he was struggling to pull his weapon from its holster in an attempt to engage his assailants. Fortunately, 59 had noticed that his movements were far too composed for the situation. Keeping his UMP trained on the man's head, he used his

free hand to open the door and drag the man out of the car before he could fully release his pistol. As he tumbled from the car, the weapon fell to the ground. 59 kicked it away out of reach.

'Stay on the ground! Don't move! Now put your hands behind your head. Do it!' he barked. Too dazed to react, the man capitulated. 59 restrained him, before moving to assist Bazza with the other two occupants. They were far easier prospects. Unlike their friend, the potent gas had worked its magic on them. Their eyes were puffy and red. Tears streamed down their faces. Their persistent coughs simply wouldn't go away no matter how much they tried to clear their lungs. As a result, they made no attempt to resist.

'Cut-Off Two, all Bravos secure.' This was the message that the Stop Group had been waiting for. Up to this point, they had allowed the two occupants of the van to remain seated with their hands on the dashboard, whilst Abu and Bomber kept their M4s trained on them. It was easier to manage each piece of the puzzle one at a time; divide and conquer. It meant that each group could provide some level of mutual support to another, if required. As long the men remained in the van, they would be easy to control. The vehicle wasn't going anywhere. During planning, the group had been concerned that the up-armoured vehicle might have bullet proof glass fitted. However, they had concluded that it was unlikely that their adversaries would have employed such a drastic, and expensive, option. Just to be on the safe side though, they had ensured that the ammunition Jed supplied would be capable of penetrating pretty much any protection that had been installed.

The Stop Group sprang into action. Unlike the support vehicles, they opted not to use any gas. The extraction of the cargo would be much simpler without the requirement for respirators. Simmo got them moving.

'Step out of the van! Keep your hands up! Move slowly! Do it now!' he commanded. Hesitantly, the two men opened their doors and exited the vehicle. 'Move away from the van! Get on your knees! Place your hands behind your head! Now!' Without uttering a word, the men did as they were instructed. Archie and Simmo approached them cautiously, before applying restraints.

'Transport Vehicle secure. Making entry now.' Simmo manhandled the two men so that they were sat next to each other. He then cuffed them together. Once content that they no longer posed a threat, Abu got to work. The thermal lance was a cumbersome piece of equipment, but fortunately the large oxygen gas canister and battery could be manoeuvred on a trolley. As Abu prepared the cutting tool, Bomber wheeled the canister over to the rear of the van. With a loud click and a roar, the lance sprang into life, and Abu set about removing the hefty lock from the rear doors. It didn't take long at all for the heavy-duty cutter to vaporise the surrounding metalwork. The lock fell inwards with a loud bang as it hit the interior floor. Caustic fumes drifted on the air, filling their nostrils with the sharp smell of molten steel.

'Okay, I'm in. Just give it a second to cool, and let the smoke clear,' he relayed, with none of the normal mirth in his voice. Everyone waited nervously. Their

captives remained alarmingly compliant. It was a sure
sign that they were professionals. They knew that they
were in a compromised position. Rather than needlessly
expending energy, they conserved it for the right
opportunity to arise. Their captors would need to remain
vigilant.

'All right. Let's do it.' Abu grabbed one of the rear
doors and pulled on it hard. It sprang open with a clang,
providing access to the dark interior. Bomber was right
on his shoulder. Shining his torch inside they could see
khaki holdalls neatly stacked on top of one another.
They filled almost half the space. There were roughly
thirty of them in total. Without hesitation, Abu began
carefully inspecting one of the bags, to ensure that it had
not been fitted with an anti-tamper device.

'Hold the light here will you mate?' Bomber obliged,
pointing the barrel of his weapon towards the zipper.
There was nothing that Abu could identify on the
exterior. He carefully pried apart the zips very slightly,
and checked inside as best he could. Once content that
there were no surprises, he created a large enough
opening to inspect the contents. Fishing inside, he
pulled out a well-packed brick wrapped in a plastic
coating, before using a knife to make a slight incision.
Pulling the blade free, the brown stain on the blade and
distinctive vinegary scent told him all he needed to
know.

'Got it boys. Let's begin offloading.'

'All call signs. Cargo secure. Beginning offload
now,' Archie transmitted, ensuring everyone remained
informed.

'All call signs. Checkpoint Two. Be aware, vehicle

approachin ma position,' Donald's voice abruptly reported over the net. The timing of their unwanted guest could not have been worse. They were at a crucial point of the operation, when they were at their most vulnerable, distracted by the transferal of the drugs.

'Car. Single male occupant. Confrontin now.' As Donald relayed the information, the Stop Group began hurriedly removing the weighty bags from the van, ferrying them to their own vehicle. It was not parked too far away, but removing the entire load would require several shuttles. From their position, 59 and Bazza could observe the rogue vehicle's headlights moving in their direction, before coming to a halt. One of the brakes was squeaky. The shrill noise carried well in the still night air.

It was enormously frustrating not being privy to what was occurring at the checkpoint, but they trusted that Donald would play his role in convincing the driver to turn around. Behind them, they could hear the bustle being made by the Stop Group as they flung the bags of heroin into the rear compartment of their combi-van. The flashing blue lights of the checkpoint vehicle became unavoidably mesmerising through the lenses of their NVGs.

'Offload complete. Awaiting confirmation from Checkpoint Two.' They knew they couldn't leave before the potential witness had departed. And so, they waited. Holding their positions. Abu and Bomber had mounted the combi-van, leaving Archie and Simmo to watch over their two captives. Mike and Robbie did likewise at the first cut-off position.

Suddenly, a deafening bang erupted from Cut-Off

Two's location. It caught everyone completely by surprise. No one more so than 59, who instinctively swivelled towards the source of the noise. As he did so, a bright flash appeared in his NVGs, accompanied by another percussive crack. He felt the impact in his groin, let out an ear-splitting yelp of pain, and dropped to the floor holding the wound as best he could manage.

Bazza, who was on the other side of the stricken vehicle, rushed round to provide support. He could see a hooded figure on his knees pointing a pistol in 59's direction. Another round went off, narrowly missing the prone Welshman. Bazza shouldered his SMG and fired two rounds. One hit the man in the chest. The second in the side of his head. A single jet of blood spurted from the entry wound, before his body dropped to the floor, as if someone had flicked off a switch. His torso made a dull thud as it impacted with the dark tarmac.

'Cut-Off Two, Command. Send sitrep,'Marv demanded. Bazza's heart was racing. Fumbling, he struggled to locate his PTT switch.

'Cut-Off Two. One Bravo down. One friendly injured. Require medical assistance. Now!' Despite his best efforts, he couldn't mask the alarm in his voice.

'Moving to your location.' Tanya had reacted as soon as she heard the gun fire, and was already making her way to the location. As soon as he was content there was no further threat, Bazza closed into 59.

'Shit... It hurts… so it does. I need… some help here mate.'

'It's all right. I've got ya buddy. Don't worry. Medic's on her way.' Bazza checked 59 over to ensure he didn't have any other wounds. Once content that there was only the one to his groin requiring treatment, he pulled out his first aid kit. Blood was escaping at an alarming rate. It looked like the bullet had severed the femoral artery. They both knew what the repercussions could be if not treated fast.

'All call signs, Check Point Two. I think our man's heard the shots. I'm tryin ta get him away from the site.'

'Check Point Two, Command. Ack. We need to clear the route ASAP.'

'I'll do ma best.' Tanya arrived, as Bazza was attempting to apply a tourniquet to the top of 59's leg.

'How's he doing?'

'Not great. I've applied a tourniquet, and was about to dress the wound.'

'Let's have a look.' She used an LED head torch to illuminate the area.

'I'm... not feeling... too...' 59's weak voice tailed off, before he passed out.

'Shit. He's lost a lot of blood. Five Nine. Five Nine can you hear me?' He didn't respond. She pinched his earlobe to see if there was a reaction. There wasn't. The pallor of his face provided a clear indication of his deteriorating condition.

'Take your hand off the wound.' Bazza obliged. Lifting 59's tactical rig out of the way, she could immediately see that a piece of webbing had become lodged underneath the black strap of the tourniquet, resulting in a poor seal. Blood continued escaping.

'We need to reapply the tourniquet. Put pressure back on, whilst I loosen it.' With some difficulty, she unwound the small piece of plastic that provided the final compression, before undoing the Velcro strap.

Pulling the wayward webbing aside, she reapplied the strap as tightly as she could manage, before re-twisting the plastic windlass rod, and securing it in its housing. The effort required was industrial; more like plumbing than medicine. Once content that the seal was as tight as it could be, she refocused her attentions upon dressing the wound.

'All call signs, Checkpoint Two. I've managed te convince the bloke ta leave. He definitely heard the gunfire. Ready te extract,' Donald transmitted.

'Command, roger that. Cut-Off Two, send sitrep.' Bazza replied immediately. 'Treating the casualty. Should be ready to move in figures two.'

'Command acknowledges.' Tanya had ripped open a sterilised dressing, securing it in place with a compression bandage. 59 would require fluid and plasma, but not there by the side of the road. She would administer a drip from the back of the command vehicle. As soon as she was content that he was patched up as well she could manage with the tools to hand, she informed the others.

'Casualty ready to move. I need someone to collect the bike when we extract.'

'Command acknowledges. Stop Group, send one person to extract the bike from my location now.' As Tanya and Bazza laid out the lightweight stretcher, Archie signalled for Abu to go and collect the stranded vehicle. He was the only one of them who had the relevant license. He left his M4 with Bomber, to secure it out of sight in the combi-van. 59 was shifted onto the canvas frame, and they lugged it off towards the command vehicle, but not before carefully spraying down the area with ammonia in order to contaminate any blood that may have been left behind as evidence. Bazza also ensured that he collected the two spent shell casings from his weapon. As soon as they had placed 59 in the back of Marv's vehicle, he gave the signal to move.

'All call signs, Command. Begin extraction now.' Individually, they collected in their equipment, and conducted their own final checks to ensure that nothing incriminating had been left behind, before mounting their vehicles. One by one, they reported over the radio.

'Checkpoint One, ready to move.'

'Cut-Off One, ready to move.'

'Stop Group, ready to move.'

'Cut-Off Two, ready to move.'

'Checkpoint Two, ready to move.'

'Command. All calls signs, move to extract point now.' In unison, the vehicles filtered onto the road, and headed for the pre-arranged destination. It was a tight squeeze making it past the stricken cars and van, but with some gentle nudging they forced a path through. Their captives remained strung together at the side of the road, staring into the blackness of their hoods. Not a single one had said a word throughout their ordeal. Less for the misguided soul that had shot 59, now a stiffening cadaver lying in the middle of the road, none of them had even attempted to resist. Their inaction was testament to a well-executed plan.

In the back of the command vehicle, Tanya struggled to insert the IV needle as the SUV bumped along the country lane. She had connected 59 to a small heart rate monitor, which indicated his pulse was weak and dropping fast. Eventually, she managed to get the fluid bag attached, hanging it from one of the grab handles.

'What the fuck happened back there?' Marv had been holding off from asking the question until he could see she was not so occupied.

'No idea. All I saw was a body by the side of the road, and Bazza kneeling next to Five Nine. I've got no idea how that guy shot him. He even had his hood still on.'

'Bloody hell. How's he doing?'

'Bad, and getting worse. If he's not operated on very soon he's not going to make it.' Marv couldn't believe what he was hearing.

'So we need to commit to the clinic now?'

'Yes.' He transmitted the message immediately.

'Archie, it's Marv. Five Nine's deteriorating fast. We need to go with the clinic option. Can you warn them off?'

'Yep, no dramas. I'll call you to confirm.' The news was as surprising as it was concerning. None of them knew how the attack had come to pass. As far as Archie was concerned, everything was running on rails. He unlocked his mobile, and found the number of the private clinic. It began ringing. A woman soon answered the call.

'Good morning. Grange Clinic, how may I help you?'

'Hello, I'm afraid my friend had been involved in a shooting accident and requires medical assistance. We're driving to your location now. My name is Christopher Bailey. My colleagues and I have an arrangement with Doctor Talbot. He should be aware.'

'Of course. Let me just check with him now. Can

you please hold?' Before he could answer, soft lounge music filled his ear. He informed Marv using the radio.

'Call made. I'm just awaiting confirmation. You head straight there. We'll return to base using the route as planned.'

'Roger that. We're on our way. Let me know if there are any issues.'

'Will do. Out.' The music continued. Archie's mind was racing. They knew that something like this could occur, but actually confronting it was challenging. It was all the more frustrating because everything else had gone so well. The injury created a number of loose ends that would need tying up, but nothing insurmountable, and nothing that they hadn't already considered.

'Hello Mr Bailey. This is Doctor Talbot. I hear you've had an accident. Can you tell me what's happened?'

'My friend has been shot.' It suddenly occurred to Archie that he had no idea what the nature of the injury was.

'I see. Can you provide any further details?'

'Hang on a second.' He pushed the mute button on the phone, and got on the radio again. In the other vehicle Tanya was fighting a losing battle to save 59's life. His vitals had steadily dropped despite her efforts.

'Marv, I'm on the phone with the doctor now. Where's the wound? Is there any other relevant info I can pass on?' Behind him, Marv could hear the monitor emitting a steady solid tone. He knew what it meant.

'Pull over now! I need some help!' Tanya called out. Marv pulled to the side of the road with a screech. The combi-van almost ran into the back of them. It parked up as well. Archie watched as Marv jumped out. With the doors open, the interior lights had turned on. He could see Tanya hunched in the rear, steadily pumping up and down with extended arms. Marv clambered in next to her, disappearing out of sight, presumably administering mouth to mouth resuscitation. The whole vehicle rocked rhythmically from side to side. In any other circumstances it would have looked distinctly suspect. As he stared at the scene playing out in front of him, he could hear Doctor Talbot's muffled voice emanating from the phone's speaker.

'Hello. Mr Bailey are you still there?' After a minute or so, the rocking stopped. Tanya sat up. She was holding her face in her hands. Marv slowly exited the vehicle, his shoulders slumped in a very telling way. He looked up at Archie and shook his head.

'Mr Bailey, can you hear me?' Archie unmuted the phone and dejectedly held it to his ear.

'Hello doctor. We no longer require your assistance. Thank you.'

CHAPTER 29

'How though? I don't understand. The bloke was cuffed and hooded. I saw Five Nine kick the weapon away! I should have been coverin him, so I should.' Bazza was inconsolable. He held himself responsible for the calamity. Abu uncharacteristically made an attempt to console him.

'Listen bruv. We all had our jobs to do. Yours was to concentrate on your blokes, not his. It was just one of those things. No one could have seen it coming.' The mood was sombre in the quiet, empty, space of the briefing room. It felt like the waiting room of a funeral parlour. They sat facing each other in a circle. Some clutched cups of tea and coffee, others simply lowered their heads, staring vacantly at the floor. A group of lost souls, desperately searching for answers, and attempting to understand how things could have gone so horribly wrong.

'All we know is that somehow the guy broke free of his cuffs, and had the balls to go for his weapon. Fuck knows how he managed to locate it, but he did. The fact he managed to hit Five Nine was pure chance. On a different day, things could have gone another way. You all know that. It's always a matter of small margins in our game,' Marv advised. As the eldest member of the group, he felt it was his responsibility to try and keep them grounded. They'd all experienced loss before. They knew that the best response wasn't to wail and moan. To try and make sense of every little detail. But it was really hard not to. In truth, the series of events leading up to the shooting, like with so many similar tragedies, had been an accumulation of tiny misfortunes that ultimately led to catastrophe.

The man that 59 thought he had secured had managed to maintain his composure, largely due to his ability to withstand the effects of the CS. This had allowed him to position his arms in such a way as to avoid the cuffs from being secured as tightly as they may have been; ironically it was a technique that the man had learnt whilst once serving in the Army. In the rush to detain him, the hood hadn't been pulled quite all the way down one side of his face, allowing a slight gap through which he was able to survey his surroundings. The distraction caused by a vehicle arriving at the checkpoint had created a sufficient window for the man to slowly creep his way in the direction that the pistol had scattered. The headlights of the approaching car had fully illuminated the weapon, which was tucked up against the grassy verge of the road. Without the light source, it would have been unlikely that he could have located it. 59 had remained watching the scene at the checkpoint for a second too long. It allowed the man to cock his weapon and fire off the first shot. The desperate man only fired because he was out on parole, and facing a lengthy jail sentence if re-arrested. Without such a motive, there was no way he would have engaged what he thought was an armed police officer. When the bullet struck 59 in the leg, it had hit the fatal point, because at that precise moment he was swivelling around to see where the first round had come from.

What was done was done. Nothing could change it. In their hearts they all knew it. But taking the time to acknowledge the occasion felt like the right thing to do.

Like something they were compelled to do. Despite the magnitude of what had befallen them, the most challenging issues were still yet to be tackled. Reluctantly, Archie attempted to get them back on track.

'Okay. I hate to do this. I really do.' He scanned the room. Their sullen faces didn't alter one iota. 'We need to talk about the game plan for confronting Five Nine's death. Once we've done that, I can assure you we will make time to grieve.' Rubbing an eye, he struggled to compose himself. 'As we've always agreed, and all committed to, there can only be one option. It's not a comfortable choice, but for the sake of this entire endeavour, and all of us sat in this room, it's the only feasible approach. And it's exactly why all that time ago I attempted to explain the importance of the covenant to you. For moments like this. Each of the tenets means more now than they ever have before.' He vocalised each one deliberately, allowing time for them to sink in.

'My brother before me. No outsider knows. Once in never out. Do good, always. Better every time,' he paused, before continuing. 'Like all of us, Five Nine signed up to this creed. And, like us all, he tried to live by its tenets. In death, he must make one last sacrifice. He must disappear without a trace.' It was a bitter truth. One that they all knew may one day come to pass, but never for a moment thought actually would. The plan was simple. Two of them would take the body and dissolve it using concentrated hydrochloric acid. Meanwhile, the others would ensure that there was no trace of the operation having ever occurred; a precaution that they had employed following every job. This time, its importance was all the more acute. The barrel would be transported to an industrial waste site, where it would be integrated into thousands of tons of various other chemicals, and then disposed of for a small fee. When inquiries were inevitably made regarding his whereabouts by colleagues, and regrettably in 59's case possibly his family as well, they would simply say he packed his belongings and left. Someone would attend to that as well. After all, he was a troubled individual suffering from serious mental health issues, and had been acting erratically during the days prior to his disappearance. The police may ask a few questions, and make a cursory attempt to locate him, but the sad truth was that he was just another homeless veteran who simply couldn't cope with the pressures of life anymore. It was a sad reminder to them all just how disposable they really were. Archie continued.

'There are a couple of other pressing matters that we need to deal with. Firstly, a decision needs to be made regarding the witness. We're not certain how much he saw or heard. Fortunately, Donald managed to get a look at his number plate, which gives us options. Secondly, we need to assume that the police are going to get involved. It's something we've desperately tried to avoid, but with a dead body in the middle of a public road, I don't think there's any doubt they'll take an interest. We need to know what they know.'

'What d'ya mean options?'

'I'm sorry?'

'Ya said options. What options are ye talkin bout?'

'Well, for starters, we need to find out who the chap is, where he lives, what he does for a living. Then we can make an assessment of how much of a liability he might be. After we have that information, we can determine how to proceed.'

'Proceed, as in off him, proceed? Mate, there's no way we can do tha! It's pure madness.' The bulky Scotsman had furrowed his brow, and began shifting uncomfortably in his seat.

'I'm not saying that. But we need to keep all options on the table. For all we know, he made you. Or he saw something. Or heard something over the radio. There's no way he's going to keep a shooting to himself, is there?'

'I dunno, but either way we're not in the game of takin out witnesses. I thought we were meant ta be tha good guys here.'

'We are. But no one's going to be doing any good if we're all stuck behind bars. I'm not saying that we simply go and kill the guy. Of course not. But we do need to know what the implications for us could be if he decides to talk to the wrong people.'

'Archie's right. We can't take the chance. At least let's do some investigating just to be sure.' Simmo offered some support.

'Look man, I was the one that spoke to him. I looked him right in tha eyes. And I'm tellin ya, he's not gonna speak ta nobody.'

'We simply can't know that for sure. Is it really worth the risk for the sake of some further research? What does everyone else think?' Only Frank had the courage to speak up.

'I think we all know what needs to be done. As uncomfortable as it is, we need to track this fella down, and see what he knows. I'm happy to take it on if someone'll join me.' A long pause followed.

'Go on then. I'll be your wing man.'

'Really. No other volunteers? All right then Abu. You'll have to do I suppose,' Frank moaned. He was quietly pleased that his feisty little antagonist would be joining him. At least it offered the hope of some light relief, during what could become an ugly task.

'For tha record. I'm still not best pleased with this course of action. But if tha consensus is that it needs done, I won't stand in your way.'

'Thank you Donald. Like I've said, at the moment let's just get a feel for what we're dealing with before we commit to anything. Now, about the police involvement.' They continued discussing the possible loose ends that had been left open during the operation. Any chinks in their armour. Of course, there was the possibility that physical evidence had inadvertently been left behind. Stray hairs, blood, skin. The bullets fired by 59 would inevitably be recovered, and although Jed seemed confident they couldn't be traced, there were no guarantees. The captives they had left behind would be arrested and questioned. It was unlikely that they would be willing participants. The beauty of targeting criminals was that their disdain for their rivals was only outmatched by their hatred for the police. Still, it was possible that one of the two of them could be leveraged, and might provide some vital evidence. It took several hours of discussion, attempting to explore all eventualities. Even then, they weren't confident that every base had been covered.

'I can certainly find out where they're being held. I'd imagine with the weapons found at the scene there's no way they'll be released on bail. Beyond that, it's going to be almost impossible to get to them.'

'That would be a great start Marv. We'll have to think about how to obtain the inside track on what they've divulged. I'd imagine that our two best options would either be through the legal system, perhaps some mercenary barrister, or somebody in the prison system. Neither's going to be easy to crack without any connections.'

'Let me have a look into it Archie. I still have a few connections from my time inside. Depending on where they're being held, it might throw up some options,' Mike suggested. It was easy to forget that several of them had spent time at Her Majesty's pleasure.

'Yeah. I'll do the same. You never know. Worth a try, so it is,' Bazza added; another former-inmate.

'Okay, see what you can do. I'll start investigating the legal route. I think that will do us for now. There's plenty to be getting on with. Before anything else, let's at least see what we managed to accomplish. Donald, will you do the honours?'

'Aye, gladly.' They all gathered around the trestle tables. Thirty sizeable canvass bags sat aligned on top of them. Each bag contained approximately twenty kilos of high quality heroin. Each kilo of heroin was worth roughly £30,000. In total, they estimated the heist had netted them £18 million. Of course, Todge wouldn't pay street value for the merchandise. After deductions, the figure that they could expect to receive would be closer to £12 million. All of a sudden, the significant sacrifices that had been made became ever so slightly more palatable. Arrangements were made to conduct the exchange the following week.

Todge was good to his word. In the end, he had unexpectedly paid £14 million. He explained that the extra money was a bonus for taking his competitors out of the game, enabling the expansion of his own operation. Such a large sum of money would take some time to filter through the charity, but at least it meant they could sustain their activities for the foreseeable future. It might even facilitate the opening of a new branch; space was, yet again, becoming a scarce commodity. In the interim, everyone had leaned in to resolve the plethora of issues highlighted during the after action review. First and foremost, they had to deal with 59's body. It was a painful but necessary task.

Bazza volunteered to submerge him in the barrel of acid. His feeling of guilt endured, and he simply couldn't be persuaded otherwise. Archie was adamant that he should assist him. The two of them transported the corpse, which had been secreted in the boot of one of the saloons, to a secluded site that they had previously used for rehearsals. It was a location where they were confident that they wouldn't be disturbed. Neither was entirely sure what the process should be. After several attempts to manoeuvre the cumbersome load, they managed to contort 59 into a position where he would fit into the plastic container. They had expected a fizz, some sort of smell, anything. His body just sat there. Suspended in the liquid, like a creature preserved in a specimen jar. Eventually, the tissue began to break down. The clear fluid took on a pink hue. In the end it took a full day for everything to disintegrate.

Once content that nothing incriminating remained,

they disposed of the barrel at a specialist site. They paid cash. No one even batted an eyelid. Just like that, 59 had been reduced to molecules and erased from existence. Although his physical form had gone, Archie and Bazza were determined that his memory must remain. As soon as they returned to base, the entire group gathered to commemorate their fallen brother.

The whole terrible affair had been a sobering reminder of the perils that they all faced. Internally, Archie began questioning whether he should shut it all down. Had *Make Ready* become a poisoned chalice that simply needed to be put down? He had never intended for things to become so extreme. Far from helping people, the enterprise was harming them. How could it be justified? After long, careful consideration, and extensive discussions with the rest of the team, he resolved that 59 would have wished them to continue, in spite of the tragedy. Eventually, he had convinced himself that they were still doing good work supporting the veterans' community, and that the benefit quite simply outweighed the cost.

Soon after, Frank and Abu managed to locate the witness with relative ease. A quick search of his number plate threw up a smorgasbord of useful information. Peter Jenkins lived with his fiancée in Ashford. A manager at a small software firm, he kept a predictable routine from which he rarely strayed. Unfortunately for him, he was also extremely talkative. It became immediately obvious that he had informed several of his friends, family and colleagues, about his encounter that evening. What wasn't as clear was what he had divulged, and whether he had formally spoken to the police. They maintained surveillance, awaiting any sign that he might compromise them.

Uncovering any details regarding police knowledge of their activities, proved nigh on impossible. Mike and Bazza did as they had promised, using their old contacts to see if there was any buzz in the prison system. However, no one was able, or willing, to provide any information. Archie encountered similar barriers whilst trying to identify a legal professional who might be able to assist them. For the time being, they would have to endure the shadow of uncertainty lingering over them. It wasn't something that they were used to. Previously, they had always been so careful to avoid detection. This was a new challenge that would need to be managed appropriately.

Despite all the unknowns and the high-drama, life went back to normal. The charity continued going about its business. Another batch of recruits was welcomed through the door, and deployed, contributing to the ever-growing success of the legitimate side of the business. 59's absence wasn't really questioned once it had been highlighted. He had always been a reasonably solitary person. Aside from a few comments about how he was even more invisible than usual, no one took an interest. It was heart breaking really.

The respite gave them all a chance to reflect and recover, after what had felt like an extremely uncomfortable ride. In an instant though, the calm was shattered.

'Archie, he's talking to the police.'

'How can you be sure?'

'Because we saw him in the police station bruv,' Abu

added quickly, backing up his colleague.

'Okay, fair enough. But he could have been talking about anything. A stolen wallet, a speeding ticket, a missing cat!'

'Nah mate, he's providing them with information about the operation. Trust us. We checked.'

'How much did he know?'

'We've got no idea, but he's made at least two visits, which suggests there's something they're interested in.'

'Okay, thanks for the update. Let me think about how to proceed.'

'There's no time to think mate. We need to act, and fast,' Frank's snapped.

'Let's not be too hasty. There are too many unknowns to commit to a single course of action. Let's do our research, and make a plan like we always do.'

'I hate to agree with Uncle Fester here, but I don't think we've got time. Before we know it, he's told them everything he knows, and is up on a witness stand testifying. We need to nip it in the bud as soon as, chief.' This was a decision that Archie simply didn't want to confront. Taking action against an innocent bystander was a completely different ball game from the one they had been playing. Unfortunately, there was no way of knowing exactly what young Peter had told the police. If there was any doubt, there was no doubt. He knew what needed to be done, but couldn't bring himself to entertain the thought. Instead, he opted to push the burden back on the two men who had been monitoring him.

'What do you suggest then? You know the situation best.' They looked at each other surprised by the response. Both had already discussed their options at length.

'Look, we know there's plenty of different ways to play this, but only one way to be sure. He has to go, doesn't he?' The question was genuine. They just wanted reassurance that they had Archie's support.

'Isn't there another way? Couldn't we just confront him? Tell him he needs to stop.'

'Yep, we could do that, but we don't have the resources to back it up. How long would we need to follow him? A year? Two years? We'd have absolutely no guarantees. There's only one way to be certain.'

'Sure, but this is different. Everyone else we've hurt have been crooks. Scumbags that deserved it. This guy is a civilian.'

'You've changed your tune since the debrief. You knew what was required then. What's changed? We know for *sure* that he's a threat now.' Archie paused. He was slightly taken aback by Frank's insistence. In that moment, the emotions of everything that had occurred had made it very easy to hypothecate. To see things with clarity. Now, with the evidence staring him in the face, it was a completely different experience. Reluctantly, he conceded.

'All right. We need to talk to the others though. They get a vote too.'

'Of course. I'll gather everyone now.' It didn't take long for them to come to a collective decision. Even those who were originally dissenters had recognised the requirement to take decisive action. Archie hoped that it would be impossible to find a volunteer, but two of them stepped up almost immediately. Bomber was no surprise, but Abu's consent was unexpected.

'Are you sure about this chaps? We still have other options.'

'No. We don't. I'm happy to clip the bloke. Just give me an opportunity to do it. Better than us all ending up in jail innit? We've come too far to back out now mate,' Bomber cautioned. His words hit Archie like a wrecking ball. The man was right. He'd dragged them all along on this journey with him. Now they had gained a momentum all of their own. Even if he wanted to, he wouldn't be able to stop them. They had gained exactly what he had promised. Purpose.

Archie maintained a distance from their preparations. All he knew was that the optimum time to strike would be whilst the target was out on his regular evening run along the canal, and that they intended to move as soon as possible. All of them were acutely aware that the addition of another dead body to the tally could result in further loose ends. However, at least this approach would put them back in control, with the knowledge that if done right, there would be one less string attaching them to the heist.

The duo departed the following night, having made all the requisite arrangements. All Archie could do was wait. It proved an agonising ordeal. He attempted focusing on charitable business to take his mind off the matter, but to no avail. The more he looked for distractions, the more his mind focused upon the terrible choice they had made. He even considered responding to his brother's emails, or at his lowest ebb, contacting his father, but couldn't quite bring himself to commit. When Bomber and Abu returned, having successfully fulfilled their duty, Archie felt an unnerving mixture of relief and regret. It wasn't long before the details of the missing man were being plastered across the media. From what was reported, there was no indication at all that they had any further information regarding his whereabouts. The pair had executed the task perfectly. Peter Jenkins's body would never be found. Neither wished to discuss the details of the hit. Even Bomber was notably reserved, electing simply not to mention anything at all. They had done what was required. End of story.

However, within a couple of days it was very clear that everyone's mood was becoming increasingly low. Archie wasn't sure if it was the dawning realisation of the gravity of what they had done setting in, or if they were on a come-down from all the excitement. Either way it wasn't sustainable. They desperately needed a distraction. Fortunately, it arrived almost immediately. Archie's phone rang in his pocket.

'Howdy pardner. How's it hangin my man?'

'Jed. Is that you?'

'Sure is. I hear y'all made good use of my merchandise. I told you it was clean now, didn't I?'

'It seems so for now. I sincerely hope it stays that way.'

'Of course it will. Have some faith brother.'

'Anyway, how can I help you?' Archie queried, genuinely intrigued.

'Well, it's more like how can I help you?' Jed declared in his usual upbeat manner. It was an unexpected development. They had only met once. What on earth could he have to offer?

'Okay. I'll bite. Tell me what you're thinking.'

'How'd you boys and girls like a trip State side?'

'I'm not sure. What are you proposing?'

'Well after our meetin, I got to thinkin. What ya'll are doin for our comrades is simply magnificent.'

'What do you mean?'

'Oh, don't play coy with me Archie. I ain't the sharpest tool on the ranch, not by a long shot. But Tanya told me just enough for me to put two and two together, and come up with five. The charity. It's genius son.' Archie was shocked. How on earth could he possibly have linked them to *Make Ready*? He was certain Tanya wouldn't have mentioned anything directly. She was far too switched on for that. Perhaps he had investigated them. 'Don't worry. Your secret's safe with me. I give you ma word.'

'How did you find out?'

'Well I ain't gonna divulge my methods, but let's just say I'm careful about who I do business with. I wasn't born yesterday. Anywho, hows about it?'

'How about what?'

'Why, coming to visit me. I have a very interesting proposition for you. Did you know there are estimated to be sixty thousand homeless vets in the US? Almost a million veterans are living in poverty. That can't be right now, can it? I've seen what you're tryin to do for your brothers in arms over there in Great Britain. I'm sold.'

'What exactly are you suggesting?'

'It's very simple. Expansion son, expansion. There's a prime market here just waitin for someone to utilise the opportunity. Same model, different country, bigger rewards. What's not to like?'

'I'm not sure it's quite as simple as that. There are so many implications. I'd need to talk to the trustees, find a suitable window of opportunity. I wouldn't even know where to begin.'

'Sure you would. That's why I want you to come and see for yourself. I've had enough of watching our brothers and sisters sufferin, same as you. Someone needs to take action, and that someone is us. I want us to do it together, using your model. I'll help you set up everythin, give you the right connections. Grease the wheels, so to speak. All y'all have to do is say yes.' His southern twang was captivating. He had a way of somehow making everything sound wholesome.

'When are you thinking?'

'Hell, as soon as possible. I'll host y'all right here on my ranch. There's plenty of room. Bring as many as you want. All expenses paid for by me of course. No obligations, I just want to show you the possibilities. So whadya say?' Given the circumstances, it didn't take Archie long to make up his mind.

'Okay. Let's do it.'

'Well now, that's the spirit! I'll ask my assistant to get in touch and arrange the details. Archie my man, I promise you this will be the start of great things. Just y'all wait and see.'

ABOUT THE AUTHOR

Jonathan Oates served for over sixteen years as an
Officer in the British Army. The majority of his career
was spent with airborne forces, and included combat
tours of Afghanistan. He read history at the University
of Leeds, and has subsequently completed an MBA with
the University of Northampton. Despite
having possessed the ability to write since circa 1985,
Make Ready is his first novel. He currently lives in
Switzerland with his wife and two children, and is
passionate about fitness, heavy metal, and travel.

Find out more at:

 @archibaldmaine

 @archibaldmaine

archibaldranulphmaine@gmail.com

Printed in Great Britain
by Amazon

44935366R00222